"I'VE A GOOD MIND TO PULL OUT ALL THOSE DAMNED PINS," HE THREATENED.

"Such beautiful hair should be free, like the wild-flowers, like the meadow larks, like the . . ."

"Don't you dare! If I didn't know better I'd think you were drunk!"

He grinned down at her. But suddenly his expression grew sober, the black eyes hardening to marble. "Maybe I am . . . but not on liquor," he muttered. Damn. What was she doing to him? "I'm drunk on something else even more potent. More dangerous," he continued, his gaze suddenly fiercely intent on her wide eyes, and parted lips, then shifting down to the ivory mounds of her breasts above the décolleté of her gown.

"Annabel," he demanded tautly, "why do you have to be so damned beautiful?"

She stopped struggling to free herself and stared back at him, dumbfounded. "You . . . think I'm beautiful?"

"Too damned beautiful." Suddenly, he caught her mouth in a kiss that was so rough, it was almost savage. Her lips trembled beneath the heat and violence of that kiss and she released him reluctantly as he pulled away . . .

"Annabel, if only you knew . . ."

JILL GREGORY

WHEN THE HEART BECKONS

A DELL BOOK

Published by
Dell Publishing
a division of
Bantam Doubleday Dell Publishing Group, Inc.
1540 Broadway
New York, New York 10036

ISBN: 0-440-21857-8

Printed in the United States of America

Published simultaneously in Canada

April 1995

10 9 8 7 6 5 4 3 2

RAD

To my beautiful daughter, Rachel,
who enriches my life
with her wonderful spirit,
her wit and intelligence,
her dreams, and her laughter.
Honey, this one's for you!
With love forever and always.

Prologue

Something strange quivered in the sultry southern air.

The stoop-shouldered peddler felt it prickle his skin as he drove his horse and cart along the rolling, violet-laced hills outside of Richmond. The peddler's name was Jonah E. Banks and he had traveled this particular shaded and lovely road many times before, but there was something in the air today, something clinging to the hemlock leaves, whispering among the lush grass and blue lobelia, something which made him swallow hard and peer over his shoulder with an uneasy grimace. It was a sadness, a sense of *loss*. A heartrending melancholy which made the skin on his burly forearms prickle. Jonah coughed nervously and glanced sideways through baggy, faded blue eyes, peering through the trees at the abandoned, white-columned house nestled well back from the road.

Something moved across the crumbling stone porch and his heart skipped a beat. A shadow—no, a woman —he thought in astonishment. A slim woman with flowing crystal hair, a woman whose pale gown of indeterminate color floated about her in shimmery splendor. No, no, it was only a shadow after all, a trick of the sunlight,

Jonah realized. He blinked and stared again. But the lovely vision of shining femininity was gone, and only the dazzling flicker of sunbeams remained.

Your imagination is playing tricks on you, the peddler told himself. Briskly, he snapped the reins. He had business to conduct in the city, and beyond. There was no time to waste imagining ghosts flitting through the woods or skulking about old deserted houses. He had wares to sell and miles yet to travel. First he would traverse the South and then the grand untamed West. Work to do and supper to eat and riches to seek.

The peddler disappeared around a bend in the road. The moment the clip-clop of his horse's hooves ceased, the warm honey-scented air on the hillside began to hum with echoes of old tunes and voices.

Savannah Brannigan tapped her toe and stared at the path that Jonah E. Banks had traveled.

Then she moved slowly forward down the porch steps and around to the back of the house, drifting across the weed-strewn lawn, toward the stand of red cedars which clustered like brave sentries beside the tiny meandering brook. This was the place she had loved, the place where in years past she had come to think and wonder and pray.

Where was the brooch? Savannah glanced around helplessly, searching for guidance. She hadn't lost it in Richmond at all, but in St. Louis, the day of the fire. But still . . . something told her it was nearby.

Her movements were graceful flickers among the green-gold leaves, as light and quick as fairy wings. Her spying days were long over, her days on earth as a human woman a remnant of the past. She was only spirit now, spirit and soul, yet there was about her such a strength of purpose that her airy passing actually rustled the leaves upon the spring-clad trees.

It had been exactly one year since her passing. Her daughter was now ten years old. She stared at the house where Annabel had been born, where she, Savannah, had lived throughout the war and had planned each of her spying missions for the Union, and as her spirit floated around it, she remembered everything she had done and had been forced to do, the good and the bad.

She bent her head. When she gazed upward she was no longer in Richmond, but in another place, miles and miles away.

St. Louis, the place Annabel now called home.

Gertie, Gertie is my daughter happy? she silently beseeched her aunt, who opened the kitchen door at the moment and emerged from the three-story brick mansion with a shopping basket tucked beneath her plump arm.

Gertie glanced up, her kind, dimpled face wearing an expression of odd sharpness as she glanced about, then she shrugged her rounded shoulders and proceeded down the walk.

Savannah swept through the house, drifting among the fine large rooms with their grand furnishings, gliding past gold-framed paintings which hung upon mahogany-paneled walls. She passed beneath intricately corniced ceilings and magnificent crystal chandeliers. She saw the beauty and the splendor. But she sensed tragedy and sadness beneath the magnificence. Fear smote her as she wondered what effect the dark history of this house would have upon her daugher.

Annabel. Where was Annabel?

She heard laughter, and in the garden she saw her girl, with hair the color of cinnamon, playing tag among the flowers and fountains with a boy only a little older, perhaps twelve or thirteen. They darted through the garden, laughing, shrieking, and then Annabel, glancing over her shoulder, distracted perhaps by the odd sensation of gentle fingers brushing her cheek when no one was there, tripped suddenly upon a loose stone in the pathway and fell headlong into a large marble cat. It toppled over, and the cat's head broke with a crack and shattered onto the stone.

Savannah drifted beneath an elm to watch as at that moment a man emerged from French doors and glared at the two children standing guiltily among the flowers.

"If you have nothing better to do with your time than make noise and break valuable statuary, Brett, I can certainly find something of more usefulness for you to turn your attention to. Haven't you any studies to complete?"

"I've finished everything for the day, sir."

"Then come inside and sit in the library until I've time to go over your studies with you. I won't have you romping about like a heathen."

"But, sir," Annabel chirped up, her little face flushed as bright as the poppies growing in their neat beds, and her hands clenched nervously together as she stepped forward. "It was my fault—"

The boy shoved her neatly aside, stepping quickly between her and the massive, frowning, gray-haired man in the doorway. "I apologize for breaking the statue, Father," Brett declared. "Annabel didn't want to play in the garden at all—she wanted to walk to the park, but I insisted on the game."

"Next time you'd best use a little sense and an ounce of care," the man barked. He waved his hand impatiently. "Quickly, boy, I don't have all day to stand here in the hot sun. There's work to do, and until you learn to behave yourself like a serious and proper young gentleman you can sit in the library and think about the kind of conduct that becomes a young man of your station and your name. If you want to make something of yourself in this world, Brett McCallum—and to keep ahold of this empire I've built for you—you'll need to make proper use of your time, and not squander it on stupid games and reckless behavior."

Savannah watched as her little girl cast the boy a worried look, no less anxious for the adoration in her eyes.

"But the game was *my* idea, Brett," she whispered furiously. "You shouldn't be the one who is punished."

"Quiet." He softened the order with a light tug on her braid, then grinned at her, and with a quick jaunty wave, strode forward to where his father stood glaring.

Together they disappeared into the great, silent house and Annabel was left alone in the sunshine.

She stooped to gather up the pieces of marble in her skirt, then suddenly straightened, and all the pieces tumbled out again.

"Who's there?" The little girl glanced around uncertainly. Her face grew still and alert. "I know someone is out here."

Savannah wanted to reach out to her. "My precious daughter!" she cried silently with all of her heart and soul, but as Annabel watched and listened, still as a statue herself, Savannah felt herself being pulled inexorably toward the stables west of the garden, drawn farther and farther from the baffled little girl she'd left behind.

The stables. Savannah felt a creeping horror descend upon her as she found herself before the long building. She stared at it, as dreadful images writhed all around her. Time spun, blended, whirred together like grains of sand shaken in a bottle. In the past . . . or perhaps the future . . . an evil deed had happened here . . . to an evil man . . . begetting an even greater evil. . . .

It will touch Annabel.

The ice-cold knowledge came to her on a gust of

late afternoon wind, and suddenly the sun vanished and the trees shook and gray rain plummeted from the sky.

Then she was drifting, floating, flying, her spirit caught in the wind which blew away the spring sunshine, and she was on a high mountain ledge in wild beautiful country where horses roamed free, looking down at an oval valley where a boy—no, a strapping young man— labored near a meadow stream. He was building a cabin, heedless of the light rain falling all about him.

The brooch . . .

Savannah searched the tall mountains, north, south, east, and west, as sagebrush tumbled down the slopes of the valley and distant thunder echoed through the gray and purple mountains. She had come in search of the brooch, the brooch that Ned had given to her as a wedding present, the brooch that should have passed on to Annabel. She could not rest until it was restored to her daughter. But her wanderings had only led her to this high rocky place and to the young man below building the cabin.

She looked down at him and shivered.

He wore a black shirt, pants, and boots, with a gray leather vest and a belt adorned with hammered silver. *And two guns in a leather holster.*

A blue scarf was knotted loosely around his neck. He was tall, handsome, and strong, Savannah noted, with dark hair that reached to the edge of his collar, hawklike features, and long-lashed black eyes set in a lean quiet face. But a bleak emptiness echoed out from his heart. And she knew all at once that he was a lost soul. His spirit was as hard and relentless as the surrounding mountains and she did not understand why her search had brought her to him and to this wild, pine-scented place.

Savannah. It is time. Come back to me now.

Ned's spirit called to her and as always she returned

to him. Yet as she left the rain and the thunder and the timeless mountains behind, soaring through the thin white air above the aged pines and spruce trees, the restlessness still tormented her soul and she knew one thing.

Annabel was not safe from the evil and would not be safe until the brooch had been returned . . . returned to Annabel, to its rightful owner and its rightful place . . .

And the handsome young man would somehow play a part . . .

The dark-haired cowboy in the valley paused with the ax raised above his head. He lowered the blade and turned. Was that a woman sobbing? He wiped the rain from his eyes with the back of his hand and scanned the high gray peaks from where the sound had seemed to come.

No, how would a woman come to be here in the fierce treacherous brakes of the Mogollons? It was only the wind and the rain playing tricks on him.

He shrugged and turned back to his work, ignoring the rain and the eerie moaning wind, which sounded so desolate, so pitifully lost and sad. He was alone, which was exactly as he wanted it—alone with his thoughts and his memories and his bitterness—and with his father's ugly secret.

There was no woman, no sobbing—only the rough, lonesome Arizona wind sweeping down from the pine-scented rim.

A woman. He smiled sardonically to himself. It was not his destiny to share this valley, this cabin, or this life with a woman, any woman, he told himself as he hefted the ax again. He was too ornery, too mean and cursed with stubbornness and pride ever to bring a woman anything but long-term misery. Yes, he'd felt a longing to belong to someone. To come home to someone. But that was not to be. His fate was that of a wanderer, a hired gun, a man unattached to anyone or anything but his own instincts for survival.

This cabin was the only place he would ever remotely consider anything like a home. He had left his real home behind for good. But when he occasionally tired of riding and tracking and killing, when he yearned for escape from his name and his reputation and his enemies, even for a short spell, it would be here for him. Hidden. Quiet. Peaceful.

He stopped and listened. Gone. The sobbing sounds he'd thought he heard were no more.

A woman. Here, in the brakes. The idea of it was loco.

The rain ceased, and across the meadow his horse whickered. He pushed the jagged edges of loneliness away and concentrated his energies on constructing a good, solid cabin. He was content, he told himself. Perfectly content. There was peace in solitude, in the raw wild beauty of this secluded valley, and in the knowledge that he was the only one there.

Chapter 1

"Go ahead—*do it*," Annabel Brannigan urged herself silently as pale gray fingers of dusk brushed the city streets beyond the window. "Don't think about it anymore—just march in there and ask him."

Yet still she hesitated, lingering beside her spotless cherrywood desk in the outer office of the Stevenson Detective Agency, the amber glow from the kerosene lamp casting golden shadows across her face. The fear of failure clamped around Annabel's heart like a vise, and her pert, usually lively, countenance, which men had been known to think uncommonly beautiful, was masked now in doubt. Annabel's long fingers unconsciously smoothed the folds of her brown serge skirt as she fixed her gaze on her employer's closed door. While the city noises hummed outside the third-story window and a dog barked importantly somewhere down the street, the brass clock on the mantel of the neat but shabby office ticked off the seconds, and Annabel waged a battle within herself.

Coward. Just do it. Annabel's gray-green eyes darkened as she steeled herself for the moment to come. It was unlike her to hesitate over any task, whether pleasant or unpleasant, but so much weighed upon the result of what she was about to do that she couldn't quite bring herself to begin. She was going to ask Mr. Everett Stevenson the most important question of her life. And if she failed to persuade him to say "yes" . . .

You won't fail.

She straightened her shoulders, tightened her spine, and strode briskly across the floral-carpeted outer office toward his private sanctum.

Before she'd moved four steps, the door opened and Mr. Stevenson himself glared out at her. He looked like a tough, barrel-chested pirate with his thick neck and jowls, shaggy black hair sprinkled with gray, and stony dark eyes which glowered out ferociously from beneath furry brows. A rapier intelligence gleamed in that fierce, seamed face of fifty-odd years, an intelligence as intimidating as his quick and blunt temper, yet unlike most of his other employees, Annabel had never been alarmed by his curt speech or blistering bursts of temper. She had grown up in the household of a man far more demanding and austere: compared to Ross McCallum, Everett Stevenson was as patient and mild-mannered as a Sunday-school teacher. But tonight she felt a quiver of anxiety as he fixed her with his familiar scowling stare and his voice boomed across the tiny room.

"What's this—you still here?"

"Yes, Mr. Stevenson, I—"

"I see the other one is gone," he barked.

"Maggie, sir . . . yes, she left a few moments ago . . ."

"Well, then," Everett Stevenson demanded, "why are you still hanging about? Late finishing up, eh?"

"I'm not, sir. I—"

"That letter to Mr. Doyle of the M and R Railroad!" he bellowed.

"It's finished, sir." Annabel responded promptly.

"The contracts for the Adler factories investigation!"

"Finished, sir."

"The response to Bakersville on that theft inquiry . . ."

"Posted this morning, sir."

"The summaries of the Rockson case!"

"Filed, sir."

"And the memo to all our operatives regarding the new payment schedules and bonuses?"

"Finished, sir."

Stevenson threw her an incredulous glance and raked a hand through his shaggy hair. "Well, then, why in blazes are you still here, Miss Brannigan?" he roared. "Go home!"

Everett Stevenson II shook his head, stomped back into his cramped and paper-littered office, and slammed the door.

Annabel squared her slim shoulders. She gave her head a shake, loosening not a wisp of her businesslike, tightly coiled chignon. *Now or never,* she told herself furiously. *Don't be such a yellow belly.*

But what if he won't agree?

Consternation caught at her with the thought, but she pushed it away. *Think about Brett and Mr. McCallum,* she instructed herself, and took a deep breath. Brett! Her heartbeat quickened as an image of Brett McCallum's heartbreakingly handsome face flashed in her mind. Even after all these years, her feelings for him were as strong as ever. The thought that he was in pain, in trouble, that he was alone and on the run in a strange land filled her with anguish.

And Annabel knew one thing. She had to help him. And that meant she had to persuade Everett Stevenson to her point of view.

This morning she had found the McCallum file on

the worktable beside the filing drawers. It had been a shock seeing that all-too-familiar name here in this office. And when she'd learned that Ross McCallum had hired the Stevenson Agency—and why—she'd had to sit down and choke back the anxiety that coursed through her.

Now she narrowed her eyes, swept across the carpet, and pushed her employer's door wide.

"I'm still here, Mr. Stevenson, because I would like to speak to you," she blurted out before she could lose her nerve.

Stevenson, already enthroned again behind his desk, stared at the cinnamon-haired, slender young woman as though she had lost her mind. Then his heavy brows swooped together suspiciously and he lifted a firm, hairy hand.

"No raises, Miss Brannigan," he declared sternly. "I can't afford it. Not that your work isn't excellent, young lady—it is—but ask me again next year when things have picked up a bit and—"

"This isn't about a raise, sir—at least, not exactly," Annabel interrupted and glided farther into the room before he could order her out. "Mr. Stevenson, I've been working for your detective agency for six months now and I believe that I'm ready for a promotion."

"A promotion?" Stevenson watched her slip without invitation into the chair opposite his desk—the good wing chair usually reserved for clients. He regarded her with the same look of wonder he might have worn if she'd told him she'd swallowed her typewriter. "Miss Brannigan," he said slowly, distinctly, as if speaking to a dim-witted child. "You are a clerk. A first-rate clerk, I'll grant you that, but a clerk nonetheless. There is no room here for promotion. The only other position available in this firm is that of an operative and you certainly can't mean—"

"Oh, yes, sir, I certainly can." She nodded with as much coolness as she could muster. "*I do.* I wish to become the Stevenson Detective Agency's first female investigator."

Everett Stevenson regarded her in amazement for a good twenty seconds. He then ran a hand through his hair. "Go home, Miss Brannigan. Go home to your embroidery and your beaus and your comfortable rocker by the fire. You don't know what you're saying."

"But I do." Annabel leaned forward earnestly, her sensitive face taut with determination. "And I won't leave until you've seriously considered my request—sir."

"Your request," he said between clenched teeth, "is impossible. We don't hire women as investigators. I told you that when you started working here."

"But—"

"The matter is settled." He glanced down at the mountains of papers piled across his desk, and then returned his gaze to the delicate young woman across from him. Neat as a pin she was in her crisp white shirtwaist and brown serge skirt, her hair smoothed perfectly back from her fine-boned face, wound tightly in a faultlessly businesslike chignon, even at the very end of the working day. She was disciplined, this Annabel Brannigan. And sensible. And sweet, beneath all that crisp competence. Damnation, why hadn't some whippersnapper married her already and ensconced her in a kitchen with a parcel of bawling babies, leaving no space in her life for such a ridiculous notion? A female investigator, indeed!

He waved a weary hand in dismissal. "Go home, Miss Brannigan," he repeated. "Stop wasting my time."

Annabel moved not a muscle. She stayed glued to her chair, her sensibly booted feet planted on the floor, and stared him down.

Then she began to speak slowly, clearly, distinctly, matching his clipped, businesslike tone syllable for syllable.

"Mr. Stevenson, you are a brilliant man, and a shrewd businessman—and that is why you are going to hear me out. Because you know deep down inside of you that I would make an excellent investigator for the Stevenson Agency, and you know that I would be an asset to this company. You know that I'm efficient, clever, and I learn very quickly. And," she added, a sharper note entering her soft, musical voice, "I know something about you. Your goal is to surpass the Pinkerton agency in name and reputation. But you will never do so if you don't consider what I'm about to say."

Despite himself, Everett Stevenson found himself riveted by his clerk's firm words. From the moment she had started working for him, Annabel Brannigan had shown herself to possess an intriguing combination of charming femininity and quicksilver intelligence. Despite all his bluster, he liked her. There was no question that she was the most competent clerk he'd ever employed: she was industrious and serious in her work, she kept the office running smoothly, and she got along well with both his clients and his other employees. She was invaluable. In fact, she had become so much a fixture in the office that he'd almost forgotten her initial goal six months ago of coming to work for him as a private investigator. But obviously she had not forgotten it at all.

Too bad, Stevenson thought. *If only she were a man, I would certainly give her a chance. It would be interesting to see what she could accomplish . . .*

"Go on," he heard himself saying, to his own surprise.

Annabel's face brightened. A flicker of hope licked through her. *He's listening. Stay calm and professional, don't let on what is really at stake . . .* She rose and moved closer. "People who move ahead take chances, Mr. Stevenson," she said, marveling at the calmness of her voice. "They rely upon their instincts, they make use of every opportunity afforded them. I am giving you an opportunity, sir. An opportunity to employ an operative with as keen an investigative mind as your own, someone with unfailing instincts and a genius for solving puzzles, someone who wants to succeed in this field every bit as much as you do."

Annabel placed her hands on his desk, leaned forward, and spoke with firm authority.

"Consider this: My mother was a Union spy during the War Between the States. She received her orders from Pinkerton himself and earned a certificate of honor from President Grant. So you see that a talent for handling danger and intrigue and for retaining composure under pressure comes naturally to me. It's in my blood." She rushed on before he could interrupt. "Not to mention the fact that after working in this office for six months I've learned a great deal—from you and from the agents assigned to your cases. I've watched and I've listened. Mr. Stevenson, there's no doubt in my mind that I'm ready. All I'm asking for is a chance."

"I'll admit that you're bright, Miss Brannigan," he exclaimed, "the brightest woman I've ever met, matter of fact, but—"

"There is another reason you should hire me at this time, sir," she interrupted, locking her eyes on his the way she'd seen him do with others a thousand times.

"That being?"

She tossed her *pièce de résistance* at him the way Andrew Carnegie might fling his groom a coin of gold. "The McCallum case. Mr. Stevenson," she said in a tone of smooth self-assurance, "I can find Brett McCallum."

Chapter 2

There. She'd said it.

Annabel fought back a surge of excitement. Even the incredulity on Everett Stevenson's face didn't discourage her now, for she had spoken those all-important words, and deep down she knew them to be true.

"Now you're being ridiculous," he barked and waved his hand dismissively in the air. But she had sounded so positive, and looked so confident, that he eyed her with a particle of doubt, and a fraction of interest. "The McCallum case is one of the most important and most challenging to come along in a month of Sundays. Even if I were inclined to give you a chance to prove yourself—which I'm not—I would never start you off with a case like this one—"

"I know Brett McCallum."

Now she had his full attention. Her words seemed to echo in the silence of the office.

Stay calm, Annabel told herself, as a creaking wagon clattered noisily along the street three stories below. *Don't start chattering like a monkey, the way you do when you're nervous. Don't let him see how important this is to you.* She forced herself to nod coolly, and waited a moment, letting her words sink in, watching the shock and then the interest settle over his face.

"I know Brett McCallum as well as or better than his own father," she continued silkily. "I can find him. Quicker, quieter, and cleaner than anyone else in the country."

Annabel held her breath.

"Tell me more," Stevenson said slowly. "Exactly how does my efficient little office clerk happen to know a wealthy young gadabout like Mr. Brett McCallum?"

She draped herself back into the wing chair. "I'll be happy to explain."

It was an uncomplicated story, though an intensely personal one. Annabel took care to keep her emotions out of it, and to hide from him her feelings toward Brett. Mr. Stevenson would never entrust her with this assignment if he knew how much Brett meant to her. He would say that her emotions would get in the way of clear thinking, and he would use the fact that she was a woman to deny her the chance to search for Brett. So she kept all those feelings locked inside of her heart, and concentrated on telling him only the facts: about how she had gone as a child to live with Aunt Gertie when her mother had died, how Aunt Gertie had been the McCallum family cook, how she had grown up in the same household with Brett, who was two years older than she.

"We were tutored together by old Mr. Rappaport, we rode horses together, climbed trees in the park, played soldiers, ate our meals together—except for the times his father summoned him to formal family dinners with guests," she explained. "Brett always hated that, he said he felt like a piece of bric-a-brac set out on a mantel for display. . . . At any rate," Annabel went on, hurriedly redirecting her thoughts as Everett Stevenson rolled his eyes, "Brett and I were very close. We were best friends. I know how he thinks, how he feels, what he likes to do. Once when he was twelve he had a terrible argument with his father, about whether or not Brett could ride a certain horse, something silly like that—and Brett ran away. He disappeared. The whole household was in an uproar because his older brother had run away from home years before and never come back and . . . well, never mind. The point is, no one could find him. *No one*. But I did. I went to the swimming hole and I found him lying under a walnut tree and we talked and after a little while I convinced him to go back home and face his father."

"He isn't twelve years old anymore," Stevenson remarked, frowning. "You won't find him at a swimming hole."

"No, but I will find him." Annabel's eyes flashed with determination. "I suggest you follow your instincts, Mr. Stevenson. You know that I'm right. You know I'm familiar with every case that's come through this office in the past six months, you know I study them and can discuss every single one at length, and you know I'd make an excellent investigator. Give me a chance."

There was a long silence. Everett Stevenson II studied her, examining her from the top of her delicately slim eyebrows to the bottom of her black kid lace-up boots.

Annabel hardly dared to breathe. It took all of her self-control to keep from quivering with excitement. Watching her employer, she guessed she had won. She could tell by the way Stevenson's eyes were lighting up with a dawning hopefulness, by the tension in his jowls, by the way he leaned back decisively in his chair and let out his breath in a long whoosh.

"Very well, Miss Brannigan, I can't deny that you make sense, as always, and I am nothing if not a sensible man. I'm going to take a chance on you, and you'd best not disappoint me."

"No, sir, never!"

He gritted his teeth at the breathless happiness suffusing her face. This girl was green as spring buds. Damn, he hoped he was making the right decision. But the McCallum case was the biggest one to come his way in some time, and Annabel Brannigan's personal knowledge of Brett McCallum could prove the key to finding him. "I'll give you a month," he said, fingering the late-day stubble on his jaw. "But if I don't see some real progress by then I'll assign Hix to the case."

"That won't be necessary, Mr. Stevenson. I'll find Brett before then."

"Hmmm. We'll see. Take the McCallum file with you tonight, review it, and get started at once. I expect you to set out for the Arizona territory tomorrow—young McCallum sent his father a letter from some little town called Justice, so that's where you start. The letter is in the file along with every other scrap of information Ross McCallum was able to provide me during our interview last night. But remember, Mr. McCallum expects regular reports, so you keep me informed."

"Of course, sir, and may I say you've made a brilliant decision." Her eager smile lit every shadowy corner of the room. She jumped up before he could change his mind. "I promise I won't disappoint you. And don't worry about the office—Maggie will do a splendid job for you, I've trained her quite thoroughly, and . . . oh, by the way, may I assume that my pay and bonuses will be the same as the other operatives?"

"You may not assume any such thing. You are a beginner, Miss Brannigan. And a woman. You can hardly expect—"

"Very well. I'll accept the same wages as Lester Hodding when he began working for you—a three-month trial period and then full pay like all the other agents . . ."

"Done, done," Stevenson growled. He waved her off. As she turned away wearing a wide triumphant smile, and nearly skipped toward the door, he spoke again.

"Miss Brannigan."

"Yes?"

"Have you ever been to the Arizona territory . . . or anywhere farther west than Jefferson City?"

"No, sir."

His brows drew together. "Then what in blazes makes you think you can handle the hardships and dangers of an untamed wilderness? Conditions are primitive, why, they're downright perilous as a matter of fact—"

"No need to talk me into it, Mr. Stevenson," she called out cheerily, and put a hand on the doorknob. "I've already committed myself to this assignment, and I wouldn't dream of disappointing you now."

She was gone with a rustle of skirts.

But by the time she had made her way down the narrow steps and out of the building, with the McCallum file clutched tightly in her hands, a knot of doubt was beginning to unravel inside of her. She wasn't concerned about traveling out West or about the rugged, possibly dangerous conditions she might find there— Annabel had reconciled herself to that earlier this morning, when she'd made the decision to go after Brett. No, she was worried about what would happen when she found him—if she found him at all.

You will. You must.

And what then? Would he see her in a new light, not merely as the childhood friend whose braids he had pulled, whose knees had been skinned along with his own when they'd fallen together out of the maple tree?

Would he at last see her as a woman—a desirable woman, one he could love?

Annabel knew that none of the other boarders at Mrs. Stoller's boardinghouse could understand why she had turned down three heartfelt proposals of marriage. Everyone at Mrs. Stoller's knew everything about everyone else, and the three young men who had made offers for Annabel Brannigan were no exception. But the one thing everyone didn't know was that since childhood her heart had belonged to a man she thought she would never have.

Maybe Brett and I won't work out everything between us just as I wish—maybe we'll remain only friends, but either way, I have to find him. He's in trouble. He needs me. She walked briskly along the six long blocks toward the boardinghouse, pondering the strangeness of the situation. *Brett needs me. Me! Not those airy, beautifully frilly society creatures he's been squiring about for the past few years, but me, because I can find him and discover why he ran away. I can help him solve the trouble, whatever it is, and help him set things right . . . and maybe, at last, I can make him fall in love with me. . . .*

Annabel stopped short and took a deep breath. No, this wouldn't do. She was getting ahead of herself, as usual. That would serve no purpose. The important thing was to find Brett, to help him—and Mr. McCallum. And in the process, to prove herself to Everett Stevenson.

One thing at a time, she warned herself as her footsteps echoed softly along the dusky deserted street. *You haven't even seen Brett in two years—unless you count spotting him in the park with that heiress Elizabeth Rainsford that time he never even knew you were there.*

Brett had always liked her just fine—he'd liked pulling her braids, and throwing snowballs at her in the winter, and trying to beat her at chess (succeeding only on rare occasions)—but he had never fallen in love with her and during her growing up years Annabel would rather have swallowed a live frog than let him see her true feelings.

But now maybe it's time, she thought, hurrying past the neat rows of houses, all the while thinking, planning. She was impatient to study the file clutched in her hands, to glean from it whatever clues would aid her in her search. And as the early spring breeze fluttered past her light as daisies and the lavender dusk deepened toward amethyst, Annabel was quietly aware of the hope glowing deep within her heart.

Was she a fool to feel this way? Was there really a chance for her with Brett? Why, he had never even kissed her. Not even once.

But he will, before this is all over, she vowed to herself. She grinned sheepishly as she turned onto Grove Street, where the boardinghouse loomed at the corner. She didn't care about pay or bonuses or anything of that sort—one kiss, one touch, one loving word from Brett would more than compensate her for whatever lay ahead.

She could only be glad that Mr. Stevenson didn't know that beneath the cold, professional demeanor of his newest investigative agent beat a hopelessly romantic heart.

A heart which had given itself over years ago to a dark-haired young man with laughing eyes and a gentle soul.

You'll be seeing him soon, she whispered to herself, running lightly up the steps toward the brightness of the boardinghouse. *And you'd best make the most of this opportunity to find and win him. Because as far as love and happiness go, Annabel Brannigan, this could be your last chance.*

* * *

"This could be your last chance, Mr. McCallum."

The words hung heavily in the tobacco-thick air of Ross McCallum's oak-paneled study.

Ross McCallum leaned back in his green leather chair and glowered at the somber-suited young man standing opposite him, a foot away from the massive mahogany desk. "Are you threatening me, son?"

"No! No, sir, of course not. I just mean . . ." Charles Derrickson mopped his brow. He took a deep breath and studied the gray-haired giant behind the desk in trepidation. His employer was scrutinizing him as if he were a slab of bacon about to be thoroughly chewed and swallowed. Not a pleasant sensation. His fingers tightened around the ledger books as he continued. "It's only that I've gone over and over the figures—all of them—and the situation is growing serious. Very serious indeed. Your setbacks in the past six months have been significant. Selling the Ruby Palace might be your last chance to shore up all the other enterprises."

Ross McCallum puffed on his cigar and studied his earnest young man of business with a slight curl of the lip. Well-intentioned, yellow-livered young pup, he decided scornfully. Derrickson had done an admirable job these past four years, but he lacked backbone and temerity. McCallum's dark prune-colored eyes squinted above the plume of his cigar smoke as he noted Charles Derrickson's spindly wrists, his thinning hairline, his soft white hands clutching the heavy ledger books with the reverence of a preacher holding his Bible. "I like you, Derrickson," he growled, and stabbed the air with his fragrant cigar. "You do fine work, and I think you're sharp as a tack. And you know nearly as much about business as I do. But, boy, I'm not planning to sell the Ruby Palace Hotel to Lucas Johnson—or to anyone else for that matter. I'm not planning to sell anything. Got that? Not the flour mills, not the bank in Kansas City, not the railroad stocks, not the boot factories, and not my shares in the McCallum and Ervin Steel Company. Not now, not ever. Have I made myself clear?"

"Perfectly, sir." Derrickson swallowed. "Believe me, I know how upset you are about your son and how determined you are to maintain business as usual. I understand that you don't want to hear this right now—but, sir, I would be remiss in my duties if I didn't emphasize to you that this is a golden opportunity to bring in some much-needed cash—"

"I said *no!*" McCallum surged to his feet like a general confronted by an errant sergeant. "Get out now and put your energies into getting the machinery repaired at the mills, and posting a reward for the scoundrels who robbed the bank. Don't sell anything. Don't let out a hint that we're in trouble. We'll ride this out and prosper yet. The McCallums always do. We don't quit, Derrickson, you got that? McCallums stay, fight, and win."

"Yes, sir. I'll do just as you say, sir. Of course you know best, sir."

The door closed softly behind him as he slithered out. Ross scowled, stuck the cigar between his lips, and stalked to the windows overlooking the expansive emerald gardens of McCallum House. Dusk draped the hedges and the silver pond, shaded the stone-bordered flower beds, and the gleaming statuary Livinia, as a young bride, had selected to grace the garden so many years ago. But Ross McCallum saw neither the amethyst splendor of the sky, nor the spreading loveliness of the twilit gardens, nor even the noisy little squirrel perched on the lowest branch of the sycamore tree outside the window. He saw a young man with dark brown hair and blazing eyes who stood in the garden and shouted at him.

"Tell me the truth, damn it! The truth, for once in your stinking life! Tell me!"

Ross McCallum closed his eyes against that blinding, painful memory, against the anguish in his son's face. *First Cade, and now Brett,* he thought. *Like Livinia, they've both left me. I'm alone.*

But he refused to feel sorry for himself. He was a McCallum. No sniveling or whining allowed. He would get Brett back, damned if he wouldn't. Cade he knew he would never see again, not after thirteen years, but Brett . . .

Ross's chest began to hurt. Like a huge fist tightening, knuckling, squeezing . . . He closed his eyes and clenched the cigar between his fingers until the spasm of pain passed. Then he staggered slowly from the window, past his desk and the side table set out with brandy decanters and glasses, and sank into the green and gold tapestry wing chair beside the fireplace. *I have to keep going—no slowing down, no giving in to this damned weakness of the heart,* he thought, despising his own debility, wishing he could conquer it with the same bold ruthlessness he'd used to conquer every other enemy in his life. At any cost, he had to keep his business empire running smoothly until Brett returned. All these accursed problems were mounting up alarmingly and if he wasn't careful there wouldn't be any McCallum empire to hand over to his son.

But I'll be damned if I'll sell anything, especially the Ruby Palace Hotel. That had been his first big business success, opening the door to all the rest.

I just have to concentrate on business, Ross decided, his glance coming to rest on Livinia's portrait, which hung over the green leather sofa against the wall. *Sort everything out. End this streak of bad luck.*

Bad luck, was that all it was? He was not a superstitious man, but he had an eerie feeling that there was more going on here than met the eye, much more than he had hinted at to that private investigator, Everett Stevenson. Who had come to Brett with the truth and shattered all the illusions Ross had taken such pains to create during all these years? Why were so many of his businesses experiencing losses and troubles within the past six months?

If I didn't know better I'd think I was cursed. Cursed with a punishment for what I did so many years ago. Or I'd think that Boxer himself had come back to exact vengeance on me. But Boxer is dead. Buried at the bottom of the sea. With no one ever the wiser.

And I don't regret it, Ross McCallum thought, sitting up straighter as the pain in his chest eased to the merest flicker. That piece of scum deserved exactly what he got.

Ross took several deep breaths and glanced around the large, well-lit comfortable study, as if looking for comfort in its handsome leather and brass appointments.

Soon the Stevenson Agency will find Brett and return him to me. We'll sit right here and share a bottle of port and talk everything over. I'll explain. And he'll forgive me. And together we'll bring the McCallum empire back up to snuff. Together we'll show the world what the McCallums are made of.

The house was very quiet. And for just a moment he thought he heard Livinia's frail footfalls above, and he could picture her pacing from her dressing table to her silk-curtained bed, back and forth, back and forth, with tears flowing down her pale cheeks.

Sorrow gripped him, but he fought it off. The past was dead. Livinia, Boxer, even Cade. Dead—and gone. But Brett was very much alive and he *would* come back.

Ross McCallum squashed his cigar in the cuspidor beside his chair and stood up, his powerful hands balling into fists. He had to focus on the businesses. On everything he had built for his son. Because that toad-eating Derrickson was right about one thing—the losses he'd suffered in the past six months had been significant. And if he wasn't careful, he could lose everything he'd spent his life and his sweat and his blood in building.

His gaze lifted yet again to the hauntingly beautiful portrait of Livinia, sad and elegant in her blue satin ball gown, clutching the lilies he'd given her that morning before she posed. A tremor shook his powerful shoulders. He stilled it at once. The tremor was not from pain, but from sudden, overwhelming grief as he again thought of that horrible day when Brett had confronted him and demanded to know the truth.

Oh, God, he prayed, and Ross McCallum's lips moved stiffly over the unfamiliar words of humble appeal. *Let me have the chance to explain. Keep Brett safe from Red Cobb; don't let my son's death be added to my account as well. I know I have much to answer for, but please, let me have another chance with my son . . .*

Just one. One more chance.

"There will be other chances," Charles Derrickson said confidently as he sank into into a gilded chair in the Royal Suite of the Empire Hotel and reached for a glass of Madeira.

"Oh, yes, there certainly will be." Lucas Johnson strolled back and forth across the Aubusson carpet, his expensive shiny black boots making a soft thud with each step. "You keep at him, Derrickson," Johnson instructed him slowly. "Subtly, with finesse, but don't let up. You hear me? Wait a few days, and then try again."

"Yes, sir, I will."

"It's only a matter of time," Johnson reiterated, pausing before the white marble fireplace to down his own goblet of Madeira before continuing his deliberate circuit around the spacious parlor. "Everything will fall into place."

He stroked his fierce brown mustache as he prowled the room with the coiled, dangerous energy that characterized him. He was a handsome man and he knew it. Tall, lean, with fire-blue eyes and proud, aristocratic features, he looked every inch the gentleman of means in his broadcloth suit and starched white cravat, with his gold watch and fob tucked neatly inside the satin pocket of his vest.

Johnson smiled with sly anticipation. Divide and conquer—an amazingly effective strategy. With Brett gone, Ross McCallum was alone, bereft and distracted. That made him weak. As weak as an old lead mule cut off from the pack, Johnson concluded. The son of a bitch had no one to turn to for support, few friends in the business community who would lift a finger—his own ruthlessness had earned him too many enemies to count—in short, Johnson decided, McCallum was ripe for the kill.

"Have you heard from Bartholomew?" Derrickson inquired.

"Oh, yes." He broke into a wide grin, the same sensually charming, confident grin that had set countless female hearts aflutter over his forty-odd years. "A telegraph message came this morning. It's good news. Cobb will be closing in on Brett McCallum very soon."

"Really."

"There is no doubt that he is in the Arizona territory," Johnson said coolly, halting before the velvet-curtained window overlooking the street. His smooth melodic voice was filled with satisfaction. "Young Master Brett may well be dead before that private investigator Ross hired even reaches the Arizona border." He turned from the window, the cruel smile that always frightened Derrickson twisting his lips. "With any luck, that is."

"Yes, sir. With any luck." But Derrickson suddenly set the wine glass down, unable to take another sip. Deceiving and outfoxing a ruthless financial giant was one thing, but killing a young man in the prime of his life was quite another. Derrickson was queasy about this aspect of the job. He was only glad it had nothing to do with his own end of things. He would take care of Ross McCallum, and Bartholomew and Cobb would handle the dirt.

Derrickson watched Johnson through uneasy eyes. Johnson seemed to vibrate with exultation. *The man is pure evil,* Derrickson realized suddenly. A shudder ran between his shoulder blades. *He loves this little plot of his,* Derrickson thought. *He savors every twist and turn of it.*

"What if Cobb doesn't get to young McCallum before the private investigator starts poking around?" Derrickson ventured, afraid Johnson would notice his nervousness if he didn't say something soon. "What if the investigator gets in the way?"

Lucas Johnson crossed to the side table and poured himself another glass of wine. The gold and ruby ring on his finger glittered in the suite's golden lamplight as he lifted the goblet to his lips and drank.

It was a stupid question, he thought in contempt. The answer was obvious to anyone but the most jelly-spined little worm. Derrickson was good at sneaking around between the pages of his ledger books, but he was worthless in the larger arena of this private little war where any tactic was acceptable. Any tactic at all.

"If the investigator gets in the way," Lucas Johnson murmured, his eyes electrifyingly blue above his starched white linen cravat, "then that will be too damned bad for the investigator, won't it? Cobb has his orders. He won't let anything get in his way."

Evil, Derrickson thought again, quelling the instinct to rise and flee the room. *Pure evil.*

But he had to stay now and dance with the devil. There was no turning back. Not for him, or Johnson, or Cobb, or McCallum. Not for any of them.

It was going to be a fight to the death.

Chapter 3

Arizona Territory

"Watch your step, miss," the curly-bearded stagecoach driver warned Annabel as he helped her to descend the rusty steps and then gave the coach door a slam. Annabel gripped her floral carpetbag and stepped down into the dust. "Welcome to Justice," the driver muttered drily, and as she glanced swiftly around at her surroundings, she had to stifle an involuntary groan of dismay.

She found herself in a small, dirty hovel of a town lined with a dozen crudely constructed buildings: false-fronted stores, saloons, a livery stable, a lodging house, and two hotels. It was a beaten-up-looking town, dreary and dilapidated, a place of grit and tumbleweed, groveling beneath the flower-splashed foothills and mountains to the north.

Well, what did you expect, she chided herself, as her fingers closed more tightly around the strap of her carpetbag. *You knew you weren't heading for Paris or New Orleans or New York City.* But if Brett wanted to lose himself out here in this great big towering Arizona territory, and more specifically, within this tiny little flea-bitten town, it surely would be a good place for him to do it.

She had been the only passenger on the stagecoach to alight at the mournful little town called Justice, and she couldn't blame the others for wanting to travel on. Not a soul was visible in the street in either direction, unless one counted the grizzled ancient rocking and humming to himself on the broken-down porch outside the mercantile. Tumbleweed blew like torn brown lace across the road, the sky glowed a sickly rose and greenish gray hue as the May sun melted toward the horizon, and everywhere were heat, dust, unpainted wooden shacks, and horse dung.

Justice.

Despite the dismal aspect of the town, and her weariness and hunger after days of jolting stagecoach travel, a tingle of anticipation raced through her. Brett had been here in this town only a few weeks ago—he had sent his father a letter from here. And because of that, thank God, she had a place to start.

A fresh urgency had overtaken her need to find him after she had studied the file. According to Everett Stevenson's report, Ross McCallum had told him that his son was in danger—he believed a gunfighter named Red Cobb was tracking Brett to kill him. A business acquaintance passing through Kansas City had heard local gossip that the West's newest, youngest, deadliest gunfighter was hunting down an easterner named Brett McCallum—but no one knew why.

Those words had filled Annabel with icy dread. Why would this gunman be after Brett? He was the most affable, easygoing of men. The file had contained no further answers to that question, so Annabel had been left to worry and to wonder. As she had traveled by train and by stagecoach across the country, she'd speculated about whether Red Cobb might have some connection to whatever trouble had caused Brett's running away from home.

Annabel dimly remembered that Brett's older brother had run away from home when he was seventeen, only months before she had come to live with Aunt Gertie at the McCallum house. She'd never met him, never even seen a photograph of him, for Ross McCallum had forbidden even so much as the mention of his name. But Brett used to talk about him sometimes when he and Annabel played together, always wishing his brother would come home.

Now Brett, too, had run away. Annabel knew many would say that Ross McCallum's demanding, iron-fisted tyranny had no doubt driven him to it, as it had driven his oldest son away years before. But Annabel remained mystified, for unlike those who worked for Ross McCallum or courted him in business or social circles, Brett had never been intimidated by his father. He and Ross McCallum had had a formal but harmonious relationship. Brett was too easygoing and understanding to rebel against his father the way his belligerent older brother had done. Annabel had never heard him speak a single cross word to the man who had ruled the McCallum business empire with the strength of Zeus. What could have happened to cause Brett to leave as he had, without a word or a letter or a warning?

There had been an argument—Ross McCallum had admitted that much to Mr. Stevenson during their interview. But he had given no clue what it was about or even how serious it had been.

Annabel had been able to think of little besides the danger Brett was in throughout each stage of her journey. Terrified that this gunfighter, Red Cobb, would find Brett before she did, she had tossed and turned in tormented anxiety each night in her Pullman car, and when she had left the train for the stagecoach leg of the trip, she had stared out the window for long tense hours, willing the moments to pass more quickly so that she could reach Brett in time.

There was another reason for urgency, she knew, something contained at the very end of Mr. Stevenson's report. But as her reflections turned to this additional troubling aspect of the case, the stagecoach driver interrupted her thoughts.

"You'll want to stay at the Copper Nugget Hotel right over there beside the mercantile." He spat a runny tobacco wad into the street. "The other hotel ain't fit for a lady. You sure about stopping here, miss, 'stead of going on to Winslow with the others? Justice is a rough little town."

"Oh, yes, I'll be fine, Mr. Perkins. Why, Justice looks perfectly charming to me," Annabel murmured as two men crashed through the glass windows of the Thunderbolt Saloon and fought in the street, rolling atop one another, arms and legs flailing.

"I have business here, you see." Annabel shrugged her slender shoulders and flashed him a reassuring smile. "So right now Justice is the only place I want to be."

He tipped his hat to her respectfully. If he had any questions regarding what business a pretty and proper-speaking young woman in a serviceable gray twill traveling suit and matching bonnet had in a bleak little town like Justice, he kept them to himself. But he gave his head a shake as he clambered back up onto the box. He'd long ago given up trying to figure out most easterners and all women.

The air shimmered with late afternoon heat as Annabel approached the hotel. She felt hot and sticky with perspiration beneath her dark gown, and longed for a bath. Though her hair was still pinned firmly in its tight chignon, she felt the faint sheen of travel dust filming her cheeks and neck. How good it would be to soak in lavender-scented water, to scrub her hair with fragrant suds, to rinse away the grime of travel. Perhaps after she had checked into the hotel and asked a few questions about Brett, she would have a bath, a hot meal, and a good night's sleep.

She struggled to subdue the weariness that tugged at her as she trudged up the steps. Fortunately, the only baggage she had to carry was her carpetbag. It contained everything she expected to need on her travels— everything except the small, pearl-handled derringer she had purchased in Denver and which she kept tucked discreetly inside her reticule.

But in her opinion, the most important possessions stuffed inside the carpetbag were the small photograph of Brett which Mr. McCallum had provided Mr. Stevenson, and the thick file about the case, the entire contents of which Annabel had by now nearly committed to memory. There was also an amber necklet that had belonged to her mother, along with matching teardrop earbobs, and her aunt Gertie's worn old diary. Annabel had never read the diary, but she treasured it, for along with a fine old lace handkerchief, it was all she had left of that stout, warm-hearted lady since she had passed on three years ago. Aunt Gertie had been her only family since she was nine, and sometimes at night in her bed at the boardinghouse Annabel's eyes would fill with lonely tears for the aunt who had taken her in when she was orphaned and given her a safe and loving home. And she would swear that now and then when the wind whirled in through the shutters of her window she could still hear Gertie O'Flannery's crackling voice crooning the old Irish ballads she'd loved so well.

But as Annabel entered the lobby of the Copper Nugget, she was not thinking of the past, of her happy childhood in the great house on Maplegrove Street, but of the future, of finding Brett and extricating him from whatever difficulty he was in. A small bell tinkled overhead as she crossed the threshold, and both the bespectacled clerk and the dark, broad-shouldered man standing before him at the hotel desk glanced around briefly to see who had entered.

The clerk noted her with benign interest, blinking and pushing his spectacles farther up the bridge of his nose. But it was the tall, dark-haired man's reaction that gave Annabel pause.

There was something swift and dangerous about the way he turned to look at her the instant that bell sounded, reacting like a man trained to expect and deal with sudden trouble. She actually felt a stab of fear as his penetrating black eyes flicked over her like a whip. She'd never seen such ruthless eyes. He wore black, all black—except for a pale blue silk bandana knotted loosely at his throat. Snug-fitting black trousers, gleaming black boots, black silk shirt, black Stetson—and a black gun belt slung low at his hips, where two black pistols rested against powerful thighs. Even his eyes were the same deep onyx, she noted with something of a shock. They glinted like coals, and their calculating ruthlessness, added to the fact that they were set within a hard-jawed, arrogantly handsome face, disconcerted her so much that the carpetbag slipped from her aching fingers and clumped loudly to the floor.

But after that first glimpse when he ascertained that she was only a harmless woman, the man turned away, dismissing her. He hunched his massive shoulders forward and shifted his attention back to the clerk, who began once again poring over his registration book.

"Ye-es, here it is. He was here for three nights. Nice young man." The clerk's voice quavered a little. "At least, he *seemed* quite nice . . . one never can tell, you know . . ."

"Who was he friendly with in town?"

"Friendly, sir?"

The dark-haired man placed one large fist on the desk top. "Did he bring a saloon girl up to his room?" he inquired, his deceptively soft voice taut with impatience. "Did he gamble with anyone local? Did you see him in the dining room with anyone?"

The clerk licked his lips. He peered at his questioner with something more than obsequiousness: from Annabel's angle he looked positively frightened.

She edged closer, curious, wanting to hear.

"Well?" the big man demanded harshly.

The clerk swallowed several times before speaking again. "No, sir, I didn't see him with anyone—leastways, not that I can recall," he squeaked. Then his eyes lit with sudden relief. "Oh, yes, there was one fellow. The blacksmith—Will Chatham. That young fellow bought Will dinner one night—they sat right over there, yessir, they did. Will's livery is down at the end of Main Street, if you . . ."

But the big man had already muttered a low "Thanks," and turned quickly away, wheeling right into Annabel with such force that she was knocked backward. With lightninglike reflexes his arms shot out and gripped her, preventing her from falling.

"Where in hell did you come from?" he demanded, scowling in irritation.

Caught off guard and distracted by the overwhelming strength of those massive corded arms, Annabel blurted out the first words that sprang to mind. "From St. Louis," she blathered, and immediately felt absurd.

A vivid blush heated her cheeks. To cover her error, she added with an acid tang, "A city where gentlemen take care to avoid crashing into ladies with whom they are not acquainted."

But the handsome giant was not crushed by her setdown in the least. He had the audacity to grin, a mocking, distinctly unpleasant grin that set Annabel's teeth on edge. "Do they crash into ladies with whom they *are* acquainted, ma'am?" he asked with the soft menacing purr of a tiger, and as he spoke, Annabel felt his fingers tighten like rawhide bonds around her flesh.

She opened her mouth to reply indignantly, but for a moment no words came out for it was dawning upon her that she was caught in the grip of the most intimidating-looking man she had ever seen, a man as strapping as Hercules, and as rude as a bear, a man clearly not about to release her until he was good and ready.

Fear and fascination tingled through her. Some of the investigators at the Stevenson Agency were hard-looking characters, men with toughness and experience who knew how to track down and apprehend dangerous criminals, but in terms of danger, none of them could compare to the aura of deadly menace that emanated from the man before her.

Hercules would be a fitting name for him, she decided. Yet for all his brawny muscularity, she had noted a litheness as well as strength in his movements. He was undeniably, magnetically attractive, if one liked dangerous men, which Annabel assured herself thankfully that she did not. Those unrelenting black eyes of his made her shiver. And it was *not* a comfortable feeling, not in the least.

He must be a gunslinger or a bounty hunter, she thought, staring up at him in dazed silence. Beneath his hat, his features were rugged and stern. A hard mouth, an aggressively jutting jaw that suggested both tenaciousness and strength, a straight, no-nonsense nose. Perhaps most significantly, there was the keen, glinting intelligence in his eyes, an intelligence which would make him a formidable adversary. All the harsh planes and angles on his face somehow combined into a compellingly handsome countenance, but his was a rough, deadly beauty, formidable as a boulder carved of granite.

Handsome or not, dangerous or not, she could hardly stand here like a ninny and allow him to imprison her like this. Since it didn't appear that the intimidated clerk was going to come to her aid, she had better extricate herself.

"Kindly let me go," she requested in the coolest, haughtiest tone she could muster. "I am certain you have much better things to do with your time than to engage in nonsensical conversation, and so, sir, do I."

His mouth twisted into a cold smile so derisive it could only be interpreted as a sneer. "Damned right about that, lady." He released her, gave one mocking doff of his hat, and strode past. The next moment he was gone through the door without a backward glance, letting it slam insultingly behind him.

"Who was that man?"

The clerk's Adam's apple bobbed in his scrawny throat as he leaned toward her, his narrow string tie dangling against his limp white shirt and jacket. "That was Roy Steele, ma'am. The gunfighter. You don't want to get in his way. He's on someone's trail."

"Obviously. Why?"

The young man, thin and prissy in his dusty dark suit, shook his head warningly. "Don't know, and don't care. You shouldn't either, ma'am. He's dangerous—there's no one deadlier with a gun, not even Red Cobb or Wyatt Earp. And Steele has a real mean temper. I sure wouldn't want to be in Mr. Brett McCallum's shoes right now for all the silver in Nevada. That nice young greenhorn is as good as dead."

"Did you say *Brett McCallum*?" Dread tore through her. "Is *that* who Steele was asking about?"

"Yes, ma'am, but . . ."

"I'll be back shortly. Watch my bag, if you please."

She darted outside just in time to see the gunslinger striding up Main Street, no doubt toward the livery. She followed, moving nimbly behind him at a discreet distance, her skirts and reticule gathered in one hand. *Dear Lord,* she thought, watching the smooth purposeful grace of his stride. *It looks like Brett has two gunfighters after him: first someone named Red Cobb, and now this horrible Mr. Steele.* She couldn't help the apprehension tightening her lungs. From all she had seen and heard, this Roy Steele was not a man to take lightly . . .

At one point he paused and glanced back and Annabel had the uneasy feeling that he sensed he was being followed, but she quickly stopped and peered into the window of the feed store, behaving as if the sacks and barrels inside contained the most fascinating goods she could ever hope to see. After a moment, she casually glanced over her shoulder and noticed that Steele had disappeared.

Dodging past a dandified gambler in a richly ornamented silver vest, who looked far too prosperous for this grim godforsaken little town, she headed for the blacksmith's stable and crept around to the back. Sure enough, there was a door. And it was open.

Annabel slipped inside, moving as quietly as a mouse beneath snow. It was dark inside and smelled strongly of horses, manure, and saddle leather, but after a moment her eyes adjusted to the dimness and she saw the horse stalls with a few animals feeding inside, and saddles, tacks, and various tools hanging above the benches that lined the walls.

Up front she could hear voices. She inched forward as her eyes slowly adapted to the dimness, taking care not to let the floor squeak beneath her feet.

"What in tarnation do you want with him?" a young man's voice demanded angrily, but Annabel could hear the uneasiness beneath his outward belligerence. She edged closer to the door.

"Reckon that's my business, Chatham," Roy Steele replied in a hard tone. "Answer my question."

"Well, I reckon anything Mr. McCallum said to me that night we had dinner was my business," the blacksmith shot back. "Now get out of my place."

"How do you know Brett McCallum?"

The blacksmith was silent for a moment before answering. "My pa used to be foreman in his father's flour mill in St. Louis years ago. We met once or twice when we were kids—and he recognized me when he was passing through town. I sold him a horse. He bought me dinner. That's all I know."

"Where'd he head when he left Justice?"

"Can't tell you that. Don't believe he mentioned it."

Annabel heard a sudden sharp hiss of breath. "Maybe this will trigger a memory," Steele said softly.

And peering around the corner of the horse stalls, Annabel saw that Steele was now pointing his gun at the blacksmith's head. "I'm going to count to three."

"You're bluffing!"

"One . . ."

"What . . . what do you want with him?"

"Two . . ."

"Steele, damn you, no!"

"Three . . ."

"He headed for Eagle Gulch!"

Steele nodded. "What kind of horse did he buy?"

"What? Oh." In the pale orange glow of the twin kerosene lanterns hanging on the wall, Annabel saw the young blacksmith grimace. Sweat glistened on his round, fleshy face. "A sorrel gelding," he muttered in frustration. "Good stock."

Steele holstered the gun in one swift, fluid movement. "Much obliged. But there's one more thing. Don't tell anyone else where McCallum has gone."

Chatham shook his head in bewilderment. "You mean someone else is tracking him besides you?"

"Could be. So if anyone asks—*anyone*—give a false answer, my friend, or I'll come back and kill you myself before you even know I'm there."

"I won't . . . say a word," the blacksmith croaked. Steele, after regarding him intently for a moment, turned on his heel and stalked from the stable.

Annabel waited, pressing back against the stall. She heard the blacksmith return to work, swearing under his breath, and then she eased her way to the rear door and out once more into the quickly falling dusk.

But as she rounded the corner of the building, heading back toward the hotel, she suddenly collided with a rock-hard wall of sheer male muscle looming directly before her.

"Ma'am." The harshness of Roy Steele's voice raised gooseflesh on her arms. She tried to answer in kind.

"Mr. Steele."

"You know my name."

For the second time since she'd met him, Annabel felt the hot blush warming her cheeks, but she recovered smoothly. "Why, yes, the clerk at the hotel mentioned it. May I pass, please?"

"Uh-uh."

"Mr. Steele . . ."

"You're not going anywhere until you answer a question. Why are you following me?"

"Following you? Mr. Steele, you obviously have an exaggerated sense of your power over women. I assure you I am not . . ."

"You are."

She shook her head and let a light laugh trill from

her lips. "Well. If you aren't the vainest man I've ever met. Merely because I happen to find myself in the same vicinity as you twice in one day—to my own regret, I assure you . . ."

Icy fury clamped down over his implacable features. "Stop prattling. Answer my question or I'll . . ."

"You'll what? Shoot me? Oh, heavens, I am quite shaking in my boots!"

Annabel was amazed at her own audacity. Truth be told, she was shaking in her boots; her knees rattled quite humiliatingly beneath her serviceable traveling skirt. But she kept her face schooled into an expression of outraged scorn. If there was one thing she hated, it was a bully, and Roy Steele was nothing but a bully, she assured herself.

A bully who looked as if he would like to wring her neck. He reached out one hand and for an agonizing second Annabel thought he was really going to choke her, but he only gripped her by the shoulder. "If you weren't following me, lady, what the hell are you doing in this alley? A little while ago, I saw you behind me on Main Street, pretending to look in a shop window."

"You're quite mad, Mr. Steele. *Quite* mad. And if you don't let me go this very instant . . ."

"Steele! Freeze!"

A voice like hell's own thunder roared through the alley. Annabel and Steele both spun toward it.

Annabel's eyes widened at the sight before her. Good God, not one, but two vicious-looking gunmen glared at them from less than twenty feet away.

They must be outlaws—or gunfighters, Annabel guessed, fighting back a rush of faintness. Her heart was banging against the wall of her chest like an Indian war drum. She'd never seen such dirty, unkempt, savage-looking men.

Unshaven, their faces pockmarked and tough as

buffalo hide beneath their stringy brown hair, they looked like the type of men who would as soon wring a cat's neck as pet it. They both wore long greasy yellow dusters over dirt-stained pants and cracked boots that were torn and splattered with mud. One man was taller than the other, with even tinier, beadier eyes. Annabel noted in alarm that his gun was drawn and pointed straight at Roy Steele. The other man had a long mustache and a scar looping from his cheek down across his pointed chin. They bore a startling resemblance to each other: the same long gangly build, the same flat, squashed noses, the same aura of evil radiating from them, right down to the expression of leering hatred on their faces.

"Who are they?" she whispered to Steele, swallowing past the lump of fear in her throat.

"The Hart brothers. Outlaws. Reckon they mean to kill me."

"In that case, I think I'll be going," she murmured, but as she took one tentative step away from him, the taller gunman fired off a shot that scattered pebbles near her feet.

"Don't neither of you move none!" he ordered.

His brother spat into the dirt and grinned at Steele.

"Steele, you son of a bitch, I'm gonna blow your damned head off."

"Or else I will!" his brother vowed.

The gunfighter answered with a cool laugh. "You reckon so, Les?"

Annabel could scarcely believe her ears. There was no mistaking the icy nonchalance in Steele's voice. Peeking over at him, she saw that there was no fear on his face. Not a trace of it. Only a sneer of contempt. She drew in a deep breath though her lungs were tight with fear. Glancing at the other two men, her heart sank.

The hatred on their faces had hardened with his cool words and arrogant demeanor. *Steele,* she thought and it was almost a prayer breathed in the late afternoon stillness, *you'd better be good. Damned good.*

Chapter 4

"**Y**ou kin wipe that smug look off your face, Steele, 'cause we got you now, and you know it," Mustache crowed with glee. "You knew we'd get you for killing Jesse. Wal, your time has come. You're going to hell where you belong."

Steele kept his gaze riveted on the men, but spoke to Annabel in a calm, offhand tone. "I'd get out of here if I were you."

"H-how do you suggest I do that?"

"Run."

Run. Run away and leave him there to face these cutthroats alone. Well, why not? He certainly seemed able to take care of himself, and he was hardly her concern. Yet Annabel hated the idea of dashing away like a scared rabbit before these two ugly lumps of vermin. "I never run, Mr. Steele," she murmured, her gaze fixed warily on the Hart brothers all the while. "It's so undignified . . ."

"You little fool. This isn't a parlor game. Run."

Les waved his gun. "What're you talkin' to your lady friend fer? Pay attention, you low-down bastard— you're about to die!"

Steele let out another low, cold laugh. The sound of

it chilled Annabel's blood. "Does this female look like any lady friend of mine, Les? Hell, I don't even know this woman. And I don't want to. Get her out of here so the three of us can settle this."

"Mebbe she'd like to watch. How 'bout it, little lady? You want to watch this hombre die?"

"I'd much rather have a cup of tea at the hotel," she confessed, trying to smile though her lips felt like cardboard. "And I'd like to ask your permission to go there right now and do just that—but first I feel I must point out to you that two against one is hardly fair odds, gentlemen. And you might not realize this, Mr., er, Les, but you already have your gun drawn! That's not a typical gun duel, not at all, from everything I've seen and read. Why, you'll go to jail."

Mustache shoved his hat back on his head. "Not if there ain't no witnesses."

The implication of this remark made Annabel swallow hard. "I admire you for thinking ahead," she managed faintly, "but perhaps you gentlemen could just discuss this first . . ."

"No more talk." Les Hart suddenly went tense with readiness, his eyes razoring in on Steele once more. "Steele, you never shoulda killed our brother."

"We've been waiting a long time to git you, and we're not goin' to wait a minute more," Mustache growled. "I jest wanted to see the look on your face and now . . ."

"Watch out! Behind you!" Annabel shouted, her arm lifting to point and instinctively the two men jerked around.

At the same moment Roy Steele knocked her to the ground.

Then the street exploded in a thunderous, violent blur.

Gunshots rent the air, dust and smoke billowed,

blood erupted. Annabel, face down in the dust, heard herself screaming.

She stopped at last, jamming a dirty fist into her mouth and lifting her head to stare in disbelief at the bloody tableau.

The Hart brothers sprawled dead in the alley. At least *one* was dead, she amended, gulping down the sick nausea that rose in her throat. The other still twitched in a grotesquely horrible little dance. After what seemed like endless seconds, his elbows and knees went still and the gurgling in his throat stopped.

Roy Steele stood calmly, feet planted apart, surveying the scene. He looked as cool and remote as a glacier. His gaze flickered to her, his black eyes gleaming above the wisp of blue smoke that curled upward from his Colt .45.

"I *told* you to run."

Dear God. Annabel shuddered and felt a dizzying weakness shoot through her. She fought it off with an effort and struggled to her knees. But as she gazed in horror at Steele's harsh face and saw the utter coldness there, a coldness that was bleaker than death, dread pierced her.

This man, this cold-blooded gunslinger who had killed two men with blinding efficiency and now stood calmly looking over their bodies without a trace of emotion, this man was after Brett.

He would kill Brett as surely as he had killed the Hart brothers. Unless she stopped him.

A crowd appeared out of nowhere. Men ran toward them, one of them wearing a badge that glinted out beneath his vest. And then the crowd surrounded all three men and Roy Steele was swallowed up in their midst.

"It's the Hart brothers!" someone gasped. "I saw

them, Joe, they were going to shoot this fellow and the woman in cold blood!"

Annabel felt strong arms helping her to her feet. "You all right, ma'am?" the light-haired man with the badge asked.

She nodded, mumbled something, and he turned his attention away from her. "Seems like a clear-cut case of self-defense, Mr. Steele, according to what Seth just said," she heard the sheriff intone as he let her go and strode toward the bodies. He hunkered down and studied first Mustache and then Les. Steele waited impassively, his black eyes flickering without interest over the whispering crowd.

Annabel didn't wait for more. She turned and staggered away, escaping around the corner of the building. There she paused, clutching the rough wood wall with both hands to stay upright. Thankfully, no one had noticed her leave amidst the hubbub in the alley.

At the hotel, she tried to appear more tranquil than she felt as she asked for a room. Once upstairs, with the door locked and her carpetbag resting on the white-and-green quilted bed, she paced back and forth reliving in her mind all that had happened.

An image of the Hart brothers—filthy and cruel—swam before her mind's eye. She pushed it away. She couldn't bear to think about them, or about the gunfight, or the blood in the street . . .

When she was younger and would scamper unnoticed about the McCallum house, Annabel would now and again hear Ross McCallum bellow that he needed a drink when he was particularly upset or angry about something, and at the time she hadn't understood why, but now as she paced around her room she felt the urge for the first time in her life to consume strong spirits. Turmoil roiled through her. She'd nearly been killed. If not for Roy Steele, she *would* have been killed.

Don't think about it anymore, she instructed herself as the memories churned through her like flashes of nightmare. *Think about Brett. Think about your assignment. Think about what you're going to do next.*

She wished she could calm down, that her feet could stop this endless pacing over the creaking floorboards of the dingy little room, that her heart would stop racing.

Think about Brett.

Her performance so far had been dismal, she decided, her fingers knotted together before her as she walked back and forth. Roy Steele had spotted her straightaway. He'd known he was being followed, and if the Hart brothers hadn't interrupted, heaven knows what he would have done to her to find out why.

But on the other hand, Annabel conceded fairly, she had managed to gain some very valuable information by eavesdropping at the blacksmith's shop. *One,* she reviewed mentally, soothing herself by listing her thoughts in an orderly fashion, *you now know that Brett was headed toward Eagle Gulch—that's a lead, an important one. Two, you know that Roy Steele is pursuing him.*

But was Steele in cahoots with Red Cobb, or was he after Brett for his own nefarious reasons?

She chewed her lip as she wheeled about and started across the floor once again. Either way, she would have to be smarter and quicker than Mr. Roy Steele. Somehow she would have to find Brett first.

Annabel stopped pacing and stared unseeingly at the faded watercolor on the peeling, yellow painted wall. Brett was a strong and healthy young man, and as she remembered, a good shot with a pistol—he had been the one who secretly taught *her* how to shoot, matter of fact—but he would be no match for Roy Steele, Annabel knew. None at all.

She bit her lip in anxiety as she remembered the

lightning speed with which Steele had killed those two scoundrels in the street, and the single-minded ruthlessness that was so much a part of him.

Maybe he'll come after me once he's finished talking to the sheriff. The thought made her sink down on the edge of the bed. *At the very least he'll have more questions about why I was following him.* Then another possibility suggested itself to her and she drew in her breath. If Steele were as eager to track down Brett as his conversation with the blacksmith indicated, he just might ride right out of Justice and head for Eagle Gulch without wasting any more time.

Annabel put aside her nervousness as best she could. She went to the window, pushing aside the dusty green burlap curtains to peer out into the street. She stood there a long time, watching. Waiting. Darkness settled over the town. Through the gray shadows of encroaching night, she saw the shop windows go black one by one, and saw the street grow still. Only the tinny piano music from the saloons broke the quiet.

Then, just as she was growing too weary to stand there another moment, she saw him.

He walked up the street, his steps smooth and deliberate. The low-sailing moon illuminated his big, darkclad form, and caught the stern, roughly handsome features of his face. Annabel felt a shiver chase up her spine. Something dangerous and foreboding and frightening about him made her want to shrink back from the window, lest he glance up and see her there. And yet at the same time, something about him drew her, fascinated her. He stirred something unknown deep inside her.

She couldn't move, couldn't tear her gaze away. Paralyzed, she remained like a frozen marble statue, unable to resist the mesmerizing pull of that tall, muscular form.

But he wouldn't see her, she realized thankfully at last, because she had the lamp turned down and the room was in darkness behind her. Yet as she watched him stride along that narrow, dark, and lonely street, moving with such easy grace, he suddenly glanced up at the hotel windows. She caught her breath and ducked back, but not before she had the unnerving sensation that he had seen her.

No, no, that was impossible. She'd been standing in darkness. Yet she held her breath for long dreadful moments after that, wondering if he would come pounding up the stairs to find her and question her again. At any moment she expected to hear the sound of his boots upon the stairway, to hear the doorknob rattle and turn.

But silence reigned in the dingy little hotel and Annabel realized in relief that she was letting her imagination run away with her again, something both Aunt Gertie and Brett had often teased her about. Down the hall, the quiet was interrupted only now and then by some cowboy's whoop of excitement, followed by a woman's laughing shriek. Then nothing. From downstairs wafted the aroma of beef stew—Annabel's stomach grumbled from hunger, but she hesitated over leaving her room because she might run into Roy Steele again.

And if she did? And he questioned her? What could she possibly say to him, what excuse could she offer for following him to the blacksmith's?

Think, for goodness' sake, think. She closed her eyes, and took a deep steadying breath and then it came to her.

Of course. When in doubt, invent a story. She was certain her mother must have had to think quickly many times when she was in a tight spot during the war. So . . .

Steele was a gunslinger, wasn't he? That meant his gun was for hire. She could simply tell him that she needed protection and wanted to hire him. That she'd heard from the hotel clerk about his profession and she'd planned to approach him about taking on the job —but she'd lost her nerve when he'd attacked her in the alley—yes, *attacked,* Annabel decided. That was a good word; it would put him on the defensive.

Now. From whom am I running? Annabel mused swiftly—and then her fertile imagination hatched the answer. A former beau was after her, that was it—a ruthless man who wanted revenge because she had turned him in to the law after discovering that he had swindled her out of her inheritance. . . .

But even as she spun her tale and committed it to memory, she heard a sudden thud of hoofbeats. Annabel lifted the curtain once more and peered down into the darkened street.

In the pale pearly glow of moonlight, she could just make out the face and physique of the man who was riding out of town.

It was Roy Steele.

No need to spin him a tale, no need to face down those cold black eyes. Steele was gone.

To her surprise, a sharp pang of disappointment lanced through her.

Ridiculous. She shook her head, immediately realizing how foolish that was. She was going to see Roy Steele again. In Eagle Gulch. If there wasn't a stagecoach going there tomorrow, she'd have to hire herself a horse or a buggy and ride there herself. He already had a good head start, but that couldn't be helped. She couldn't exactly start out now in the dark for an unknown town—she had no idea how far away it was or in which direction. Steele had an advantage over her there.

But come daylight . . .

I'm coming, Brett, she promised fervently, staring out into the Arizona darkness as if she could somehow conjure up his charmingly handsome and beloved face in the shadows of the moon. An ironclad determination swept over her.

I won't let Roy Steele find you first. I'll help you out of whatever trouble you're in and bring you safely home. And soon.

Soon.

The urgency grew in her, a quiet insistent clamor that would not be denied. For in addition to the threat to Brett from Steele and Red Cobb, there was the part of Mr. Stevenson's report she hadn't wanted to think about, but which haunted the further recesses of her mind. It flitted into the center of her thoughts as she turned back to her room and fiddled with the lamp, sending a pale amber glow into the four dusty corners.

The plain truth was that Ross McCallum was ill. And in trouble. It was difficult to imagine the powerful broad-shouldered Mr. McCallum with his fierce aristocratic countenance and roaring voice suffering any kind of weakness or setback, but Mr. Stevenson had written down a conclusion at the end of his report, and Annabel had read it in shock. No details had been given, but Mr. Stevenson noted that he had reason to believe that Ross McCallum's heart was weak and that he was under a doctor's care. Moreover, the McCallum business empire was in trouble. Stevenson had heard rumors from movers and shakers in the city for months, and though Ross McCallum had merely hinted at some problems and setbacks, Everett Stevenson suspected the situation was far more serious than Ross would admit.

Reading his notes, Annabel had realized in horror that if Brett did not return home soon, he might have nothing to go home to. No fortune, no business interests —no father.

She turned from the window and began to plan. There was not a moment to lose.

Chapter 5

Early the next morning Annabel purchased a frisky white-legged mare called Sunrise from Will Chatham at the livery stable, tied her carpetbag and a canteen to the saddle, and set out for Eagle Gulch. According to the hotel clerk's directions, the town was no more than twenty-two miles due south of Justice.

"If you hit the river, you've gone too far west. Keep the foothills to your left and you'll be all right. Eagle Gulch is a right nice town. A little bigger than Justice. But . . ."

He had peered curiously at her from behind his spectacles. "Wouldn't you rather just wait until next week when the stage comes through? Ma'am, it's not safe for a woman to travel alone such a distance."

"You needn't be concerned. I can take care of myself."

"It's pretty rough country out there . . ."

"I'll be careful." Annabel gave him a wave and a smile before hurrying out the door.

The possibility that she would find Brett today in Eagle Gulch buoyed her as she rode along the high plateau bordering the outskirts of Justice. She had the derringer tucked inside her boot, she wore a comfortable white shirtwaist and dark blue riding skirt, and on her head was a sombrero she'd purchased in Denver to protect her from the sun, its chin straps dangling as she rode. As far as journeying alone across the desert was concerned, she wasn't much worried. She had a good horse, an excellent sense of direction, and an immutable purpose.

Eagle Gulch by late afternoon—or bust.

It was a brilliant spring day, crowned by a clear azure sky, soft breezes, and wildflowers blooming on the mesas and all across the rolling prairie. Gazing out at the awesome beauty of the Arizona wilderness as she nudged Sunrise into a trot and left drab Justice behind, she thought, *Maybe I'll find Brett today. Maybe he's in Eagle Gulch, and when I ride into town, there he'll be, walking right toward me. He'll shake his head in amazement to see what a becoming young woman I've turned into, and he'll hold out his arms to me . . .*

And maybe, the greatest miracle of all, he would finally gaze at her with love in his eyes—love and wonder and delight, and realize that all along he had felt for her what she had always felt for him . . .

The red mountains shimmered in the distance. She rode past groves of cottonwoods, followed the trail through winding ravines and high-walled canyons, and guided the mare past boulders and across narrow, gushing creeks. The hours rolled by, and Annabel continued to be awestruck by the splendor of the canyons, by the majesty of the distant mountains and gray-green prairies, and by the lovely sea of golden poppies and purplish pink owl's clover flowing across the mesas. But as the afternoon wore on, the refreshing spring breezes wavered and died. The air grew still, hot, heavy as lead. A molten sun burned high above, its relentless rays piercing like daggers through the heat-glazed air.

Annabel found herself forced to pause for frequent

sips from her canteen and to rest now and then in the shade. And still the trail stretched endlessly ahead. She began to wonder if she had turned the wrong way and would ride on and on endlessly without ever reaching civilization again.

But as the afternoon waned into the early stages of twilight, she reached the edge of a town almost as rough as Justice, but larger and slightly more prosperous looking. Annabel had never been so glad to see any place, except for the time she had first arrived at the McCallum house after traveling all day and Aunt Gertie had led her into the kitchen and given her good fresh bread and a chunk of cheese and a large wedge of strawberry pie. Now she surveyed Eagle Gulch from a rise at the edge of town, her hand resting lightly on the pommel of her saddle, and she smiled to herself.

It might be only a raw frontier settlement, but it was civilization: people, shelter, food, hotels, and stores. She hadn't encountered a single soul in the wilderness all day long.

After seeing that Sunrise was watered, rubbed down, and fed in the stables, Annabel turned her attention to securing a room at the Kincaid Hotel. The faded rose-papered lobby was empty except for the stout young clerk poring over some kind of ledger books with a grim air. So far she'd glimpsed no sign of Brett, but there had been no sign of Roy Steele, either. That was good news.

The clerk proved to be a friendly sort, so after arranging for her room and receiving a key, Annabel decided to begin her questioning with him.

"Perhaps you can help me." She smiled hopefully at him and was encouraged when he gave her a gap-toothed grin.

"Be glad to try."

"I'm searching for a friend of mine who passed

through Eagle Gulch recently. A young man—his name
is Brett McCallum. Do you happen to remem . . ."

The clerk, who had been listening attentively, suddenly stiffened. He paled beneath his ruddy tan and
dropped the pencil he'd been fiddling with.

"Never heard of him."

She raised her brows in open skepticism and then
leaned forward. "Are you sure? I know for certain that
he headed this way."

"Well, he must have changed his mind, then, and
gone somewhere else instead. Maybe to Winchester,
maybe to Tucson. All I can tell you is that I don't know
nothin' about Mr. Brett McCallum and no one named
Brett McCallum has set foot in this hotel."

She regarded him shrewdly. "Did a man named Roy
Steele tell you to say that?"

"How did you . . ." The clerk flushed. "I got no
idea what you're talking about, miss."

Annabel sighed. It was no use. She remembered
how Steele had threatened the blacksmith if he revealed
any information about Brett. He'd obviously done the
same thing to this poor man. And to how many other
people in Eagle Gulch?

Dismay washed over her. How would she find Brett
if no one would tell her what they knew about him? The
head start Roy Steele had stolen on her last night could
prove disastrous if it caused her to reach a dead end.

*Then you simply have to press on—work more quickly
and urgently than ever. Find someone in Eagle Gulch
whom Steele hasn't spoken to yet, or someone courageous
enough to risk his wrath and give you some answers.
Hurry!* a voice inside of her urged. *You have to find Brett
first. If Steele gets to him before you do . . .*

She gripped the edge of the registration desk. She
couldn't let that happen.

"Is Mr. Steele still in town?" she demanded, and the clerk's gaze swung away.

"I don't recall mentioning Mr. Steele . . ."

"Please." Annabel touched his large, freckled hand and gazed at him with imploring eyes. "This is terribly important. Just tell me if he's still in Eagle Gulch. I swear to you he'll never know you said a word."

The clerk gave one quick nod. "But you'd best steer clear of that hombre," he whispered. Then as if alarmed by his own foolhardiness, he busied himself once more with his ledger book, ignoring Annabel as if she had suddenly become invisible.

She turned slowly away and carried her bag up to her room. At least she knew one thing. Steele was here in this town. She'd have to watch her step and try to avoid him. The last thing she wanted was to have to explain herself to that cold-eyed gunfighter, especially when she was this close to finding Brett.

Her green-painted room was every bit as spartan as the one in Justice, except for the rather pretty floral-patterned coverlet on the high narrow bed. Annabel sank down upon it and tugged off her boots. As she lay back wearily on the bed and closed her eyes, she began compiling a mental list of people likely to be aware of Brett's presence in town. Hotel clerks, chambermaids, merchants, saloon keepers, and yes—saloon women, for Brett adored females and Annabel knew that he would certainly flirt congenially with any or all women he encountered while slaking his thirst in a saloon.

Well, she'd better get started. Steele already had a jump on her.

She performed a quick toilette, washing her face and hands, brushing and repinning her hair into its flawless chignon, and stuffing her aching feet back into her boots. She took care to secure the derringer in its hiding place once more before slipping downstairs and out into the street just as the sun glided along the western sky in a splash of gilded lavender and rose.

Annabel headed immediately for the Hot Pepper Saloon, no more than three doors down from her hotel. There were four saloons in this town and if she had to enter all of them to find what she needed to know she would do it, but she couldn't help hoping as she dodged into the alley behind the saloon that such a step wouldn't be necessary. She knew that the last thing she should do was draw attention to herself by entering the saloon openly, so she pushed open the back door and eased inside a small corridor, hoping she would be lucky enough to obtain the information she needed here at the Hot Pepper, without having to visit all of the others.

It was noisy and crowded in the enormous main room of the saloon. Smoke drifted above the green felt gaming tables and curled against the red-flocked wallpaper. Brass chandeliers gave out bright, garish light to illuminate the costumes of the saloon girls, who hurried here and there among the men, pouring drinks, lighting cigars. But it was dim and relatively quiet in the back corridor in which Annabel found herself. There was a short stairway on her left and she studied it speculatively, while out in the saloon, laughter roared and glasses clinked and someone banged out a popular ballad on the piano.

She set a foot on the bottom step, but at that moment a woman burst through the doorway off the saloon, her head turning as she called out to someone at the bar. Annabel ducked back against the wall, out of sight, and held her breath.

A cloud of musky perfume assailed her nostrils as the woman sauntered into the corridor and started up the stairs.

Annabel craned her neck ever so slightly to get a glimpse of her. The woman was tall and statuesque, her buxom figure resplendent in a gown of dark violet satin trimmed in black. Her face was not what Annabel had expected. Though painted, it was nevertheless an attractive, pleasant face. She wore an expression of keen anticipation.

Annabel made a decision. She would follow the woman upstairs. It was exactly the kind of opportunity she'd been looking for, a chance to ask questions about Brett in private, without having to venture into the main part of the saloon, where she might attract attention.

She followed the woman up the short flight of stairs and reached the landing in time to see the violet skirts disappear through a door on the left.

No one else was in sight.

The floor creaked beneath her as Annabel tiptoed down the dim hallway, lit only by a single bronze torchère. She knocked softly on the door through which the woman had passed.

"Who the hell is there?" an irritated female voice called out at once.

"Someone who needs to speak with you. Please open the door."

There was silence. Annabel's heart skidded suddenly as wild laughter erupted abruptly from a room down the hall, followed at once by a man's grunting, and the violent creak of bedsprings. From inside this room, however, there was no sound at all. Or was someone whispering?

She put her ear to the door and nearly fell in as the door was suddenly yanked wide. A brawny arm seized her and tugged her inside before she had time to do more than gasp.

Roy Steele kicked the door shut behind her and pinned her against it so hard she could scarcely breathe.

"You," he said in cold disgust.

Chapter 6

Annabel's heart hammered against her rib cage. For a moment she could do nothing but stare helplessly into the icy depths of those black eyes. Then panic kicked in and she began to wriggle.

"Hold still," Steele commanded.

"L-let me go."

"When I'm good and ready."

"Who is she, Roy?" the woman asked. She stood beside a small table, pouring whiskey from a crystal decanter into a tall glass. As Annabel peered past Steele's grim face in the hopes that the woman would help her, she was dismayed to see that far from looking troubled by Annabel's predicament, the woman looked merely amused.

"That's what I'm going to find out." The unyielding determination in his voice chilled Annabel even more than the hard expression on his face. Her heart sank farther at the gunslinger's next words.

"You'd better get out of here, Lily. It won't be a pretty sight."

"Just don't shoot her in my bedroom, Steele, that's all I ask," the woman sighed, strolling past the velvet-canopied brass bed, drink in hand.

"The last time you shot someone in here, it took me half a day to scrub the blood out of the carpet."

Steele swung Annabel away from the door as the tall woman approached. "Honey," Lily said, her tone not entirely unsympathetic as she studied the young woman held helplessly in the gunslinger's unbreakable grip, "whoever you are, you got on the wrong side of the wrong man. Let it be a lesson to you."

Then she was gone, the door clicking ominously shut behind her.

Annabel stared into Steele's glacial eyes and managed to blurt out three words.

"I can explain."

He backed her against the wall beside the gold-curtained window. "Then do it."

"Let go of me first."

"You're not in a position to negotiate anything, lady."

"T-true. But you're scaring me half to death and I can explain things much better if you let me go."

His eyes narrowed, but he released her. He moved back one step, and folded his arms across his chest. Annabel moistened her lips. Even with this slight distance between them, she felt trapped, overwhelmed. There was no way to escape. Roy Steele was too big, too strong. He could grab her again anytime he chose and they both knew it.

She peered past his broad shoulder at the door, wishing she could somehow dash out, flee down the hall, and disappear. Let Roy Steele comb every hotel in Eagle Gulch in search of her. She'd have a chance to outwit him then, and in a pinch Annabel would stake her wits and brains against those of any man, even this one, with his shrewdly intelligent eyes and knowing sneer . . .

"Don't try it," he warned, and she realized he had seen her glance and guessed her thoughts.

"Actually, Mr. Steele, I'm glad to have this opportunity to talk to you," Annabel countered, looking up at him as steadily as she could.

"I'll just bet you are."

"A gentleman doesn't question a lady's word." She licked her lips.

"I never claimed to be a gentleman, and I sure as hell wonder if you're much of a lady."

Indignation rocked her, but she controlled herself with an effort. This was hardly the time to defend her dignity. She had to extricate herself from this, and fast. "May I sit down?" she asked coolly.

"No. *Talk.*"

The sharp impatience with which he bit out these words made Annabel decide she'd better plunge ahead without irritating him any further.

"I've been wishing to engage your services," she said, trying to sound crisp and professional. "You *are* a gunfighter, are you not?"

"You've been following me all over the place for the past two days, lady, so you tell me."

"Yes, well . . . I wish to engage your services."

"To do what?"

"To protect me. There's a man who wants to kill me."

"Doesn't surprise me."

Annabel's eyes flashed with the raw heat of summer lightning. "I am willing to pay good money for protection. That is, I *was*. But since your attitude is so rude and so very insufferable, Mr. Steele, as to hardly inspire confidence, I believe I will take my business elsewhere. I won't be troubling you anymore . . ."

He blocked her path as she started to sweep toward the door.

"Not so fast."

He gripped her wrist and held it, not hard, but hard enough so that she couldn't wrest free. Annabel bit her lip, her hopes plummeting.

He doesn't believe me, she thought, and wondered with a wild tug of fear what he would do to get the truth from her. Lily's casual words rang in her ears. *Honey, whoever you are, you got on the wrong side of the wrong man.*

Searching Steele's face, a face that was at once magnetically handsome and terrifying in its coldness, she yearned to find some hint of mercy, of sympathy, even of plain decent interest stamped upon his features, but there was none. There was only hard skepticism in his eyes, and callous disbelief in his expression.

She had never seen anyone so chillingly dangerous. A shiver of dread ran through her as she pondered what he would do if he suspected she was pursuing the same man he was after—that her goal was to save Brett, putting her at direct cross-purposes with him. No matter what happened, he couldn't find out. He must learn nothing about her connection with Brett, nothing that would endanger Brett further or aid Steele in whatever dark purpose he was engaged in.

"Suppose you tell me a little more about this man who wants to kill you," he drawled, and she felt her pulse racing beneath his thumb.

So he's testing me, trying to check out my story. There was still hope then of convincing him. Annabel tried to think what her mother might have done when presented with a similar sticky situation during the war. *Keep going,* she decided. *Stick to your story and don't give an inch. Don't let him see your panic.*

"Well, his name is Walter . . . Walter Stevenson," she improvised rapidly, blurting out the first surname that popped into her head. "I thought he was a friend, a very close friend, a suitor, actually, but he swindled me out of my inheritance—five thousand dollars, Mr. Steele! Why, I was never more hornswoggled by anyone in my life! I threatened to report him to the authorities and he said he would *kill* me if I did. Well, naturally, I didn't believe him at first, but then . . . oh, dear, this is the most unnerving part. The next day I was very nearly run down by a carriage in the street—and I recognized the driver, it was Walter's groom! I was so frightened I didn't know what to do, so I left town—started for New Mexico to visit my . . . my brother, who lives there, you see, but someone has been following me and . . ." Annabel took a deep breath and lifted wide helpless eyes to his face. "I have money, Mr. Steele, I can pay for your protection. If you'll only escort me as far as New Mexico until I reach the safety of my brother's ranch . . ."

What on earth will I do if he agrees? she suddenly wondered in stark horror, somewhat awed by her own newfound ability to spin tales on short notice. But the next moment she realized she didn't need to worry about that, for Roy Steele displayed no signs of giving a damn about her supposed predicament. The expression on his face was as menacing as ever.

"Why is it that I think you're lying?" he growled.

"Really, Mr. Steele. Why would I lie?"

There was silence in the room as their gazes locked. Steele examined those astonishingly clear and intense eyes of hers and against his will caught himself drowning in their pure gray-green depths. She wasn't being straight with him, he sensed that, but he couldn't put his finger on what was wrong with her story. Instinct, that was all he had to go on, but it was the same raw gut instinct that had kept him alive all across New Mexico, Arizona, and Nevada over the past ten years. This beautiful young woman with the delicate waif's face and the long, velvet lashes was lying to him. He was sure of it.

Roy Steele suppressed the urge to yank her close and shake the truth out of her. The warmth and vibrance of her seemed to reach out and grab him by the throat even from here, even touching only her slender wrist between his fingers. If he were to put his hands on her again, he might not be able to answer for the consequences.

He didn't seize her, but he was rawly aware of her pulse fluttering beneath his thumb. That delicate throbbing seemed to exemplify her vulnerability, and as he felt it, and stared into her innocently upturned face, something hot and seething twisted inside his gut.

Let it go, he told himself. *What does it matter, if she's lying or not? You're leaving here in the morning and going somewhere she'd never be able to follow. Whatever underhanded scheme this beautiful little bitch might have, it won't matter anymore by tomorrow. You'll never see her again. Let it go. Let her go.*

For a moment he thought she could actually read his thoughts, for she suddenly tugged her wrist free. To his own surprise, he let her. He watched motionless as she began to inch her way toward the door. In the sunset light that bathed Lily's lush room, her hair was the color of burnished pennies. What would it look like if it wasn't wound up so tight, he wondered, and then coldly stopped himself from this line of thinking. He must be going loco.

"It's obvious this arrangement isn't going to work out," she was murmuring. "So I won't disturb you further. Please forget about my proposition, Mr. Steele. I'm sure I'll find some other protector who will respect the seriousness of my situation . . ."

She really was something, he thought, his eyes fixed intently on her as she edged ever closer to the door, talking all the while. Lovely as a prairie flower, and she sure looked innocent, but if there was one thing he had learned over the years it was that few people, especially women, were quite what they seemed.

He let her get all the way to the door and begin to open it before he moved. Then he lunged swiftly, shoving the door shut and holding it there with one powerful shoulder.

"Your name."

"I . . . beg your pardon?"

"I want to know your name."

"It's . . . Annabel . . . Annabel Brannigan."

"Well, Miss Annabel Brannigan, I don't buy your story. Not for one damned minute. But I'm going to let you walk out of here in one piece under a certain condition."

"Mr. Steele, I feel I must tell you that you are hands down the most rude and vile man it has ever been my misfortune to meet . . ."

"More rude and vile than that scoundrel who supposedly swindled you and tried to kill you?" he demanded swiftly.

Annabel caught her breath. "Second only to him," she flung out.

"Do you want to hear the condition or not?"

"Do I have a choice?"

"None at all."

"Well, then?" She stifled the impulse to snipe at him further. Her only goal now was to escape Roy Steele's relentless questions and the confines of this room—and then to somehow come up with a way she could continue tracking Brett's movements without attracting Steele's notice.

"Stay out of my way." Steele's eyes bored into her. "I don't want to see you sniffing around again like a little dog looking for its master. Don't trail me, don't watch for me, don't ask about me—don't even glance at me if I happen to run into you again before I leave this two-bit town. Is that clear?"

She forced the words out from between tightly clenched lips.

"Perfectly."

He nodded, and opened the door for her. She started toward it, but froze at his next words. "And one more thing."

"What is it?"

"If some hombre is really after you, go find yourself a sheriff and get some help from the law. Men like me, we're not cut out to play nursemaid to little girls still wet behind the ears. Next time, you could land in worse trouble than the kind you found yourself in tonight." His eyes raked her from head to toe and he finished in a low, cool drawl. "I'd hate to see that happen."

"Oh, I'll just bet you would, Mr. Steele," Annabel retorted. She flushed as his eyes met hers with a mocking glint.

"May I go now?"

"Yep."

She spun away from him and stamped out of the room. To her fury, she heard him chuckle as the door clicked shut behind her.

Oh, so I've amused you, have I? she fumed as she stalked down the stairs and across the little corridor toward the back door. Uproarious laughter rushed out from the main room of the saloon. She glanced over and saw Lily sitting on a tall stool at the bar, pouring whiskey for two young cowpokes. They were ogling her like a pair of moonstruck calves.

Annabel scowled. She doubted much more time would pass before the woman returned upstairs to Roy Steele and they continued with whatever they'd been about to do before Annabel had interrupted them. And

Annabel had a very good idea what that might be. Thinking about it brought scarlet color to her already flushed cheeks. She slammed the door of the Hot Pepper Saloon on her way out and marched back to her hotel.

Well, while Mr. Roy Steele was otherwise engaged, she would be free to do some more sleuthing—unhampered and uninterrupted.

"I want a bath," she informed the clerk as she stormed into the lobby. "Kindly send a chambermaid to my room with hot water immediately, if you please."

And so, less than a quarter of an hour later, a stocky, dimpled young woman named Polly Groves was pouring steaming buckets of water into a bathtub behind a screen in Annabel's room. And Annabel stuck a photograph of Brett under the girl's nose and asked her if she'd ever seen this young man before.

"Yes, ma'am, he stayed here a whole week."

Annabel nearly dropped the photograph into the tub. *"He did?"*

The girl bobbed her head and set the bucket down on the floor.

"Sure as snakes crawl. Who could forget a handsome feller like that? And he was a real gentleman, too. So polite and refined-like. Even when he was drunk."

"Drunk?" Annabel stared at her. "Brett was *drunk*?"

"Most every afternoon and evening." Polly shrugged. "But he was nice as can be. Now most men when they get drunk, they get kinda mean, or low-down rude at least. You know what I mean. They say things that'd make you blush." The girl handed Annabel a thick white towel. "But Mr. McCallum wasn't that way atall."

Drunk. Annabel frowned. She'd never once known Brett to overindulge in liquor. He was naturally good-natured and high-spirited, and had the most moderate habits of anyone she'd ever known. She couldn't even imagine him in an intoxicated state. Something must be very wrong, she decided, her eyes clouding with fresh concern.

"Did he say where he was going after he left Eagle Gulch?"

"Why? Is he a friend of yours?"

"Yes, a very good friend, and I must find him. Polly, this is very important."

The girl nodded and pushed a few straggles of raisin-brown hair back from her perspiring brow. "Well, matter of fact, he did say something to me," she conceded. "Like I told that other fellow who asked, Mr. McCallum passed me in the hall the day he left Eagle Gulch. I was sweeping the stairs and I remember moving aside for him to go down—and he said, 'Polly, I hope the girls in the rest of the territory are as pretty and sweet as the ones here in Eagle Gulch.'"

The chambermaid dimpled with pleasure at the memory. "It stuck in my mind because I kept thinkin' how nice it was that he remembered my name. A lot of the customers here—even the ones who stay for weeks at a time—don't even bother to find out my name, much less remember it . . ."

"What did you mean when you said you told this to 'that other fellow who asked'?" Annabel interrupted. "Who? Who else asked you about Brett McCallum?"

She found herself clenching the folds of her riding skirt between her fingers as she waited for Polly's answer.

The girl watched her uncertainly, obviously noting Annabel's tension. "There was this man," she said, "he came here to the hotel, oh, about a week ago. And *he* asked me some questions about Mr. McCallum, too. But he didn't have a photograph or anything," she added, "he just said he owed Mr. McCallum some money, and he wanted to pay it to him and . . ."

"What did he look like? What was his name? Do you know anything at all about him?"

Polly pursed her lips, thinking. "He was an easterner," she offered. "A thin fellow, with spectacles on his nose—and he wore one of them fancy bowler hats. Mr. Bartholomew—that was his name! He didn't seem like the type who'd be pards with a gunfighter like Red Cobb, but . . ."

Annabel felt her heart freeze. She grasped the girl's arm, her fingers taut. "What's this about Red Cobb?"

"Well, he passes through Eagle Gulch now and again, and so I know what he looks like—he's young and right handsome, matter of fact—doesn't look like a killer at all but . . . to get to the point, the fellow who asked me about Mr. McCallum had supper downstairs two or three times with Red Cobb. What's the matter?"

"N-nothing. I'm just trying to sort this out." Annabel paced across the room, stared out the window, then whirled back to the girl. "Did Mr. McCallum say anything else to you—mention any town, or any person —did he mention someone he might be meeting or visiting?"

Polly shook her head and picked up the empty buckets from the floor. "No, ma'am, all he said was what I told you. Is he all right? You seem awful worried about him."

"I-I have news for him—and his family isn't exactly sure where to find him."

"Now that's a powerful shame. I wish I could be more help. But . . ." She stared at Annabel doubtfully. "How are *you* going to find him? Excuse me, ma'am, but you don't exactly look like someone who knows the Arizona territory too well. Ever been here before?"

"No, but don't worry about that, Polly. I'll find him. And before anyone else does either."

"Are you in love with him?" Polly blurted, then flushed, shifting in embarrassment from one foot to the other. " 'Scuse, me, I shouldn't ought to have said that, but I can see from the way you're so upset that you care for him—can't blame you none either, him bein' so handsome and so nice." She gave a short, wistful little laugh. "I could've fallen in love with him real easy myself, given half a chance."

"Yes, Brett is wonderful," Annabel said softly. Her heart swelled suddenly with emotions, and she gazed down at the photograph in her hands. "I do love him, it's true," she admitted. "And that's why I'm going to find him."

"Good luck to you." Polly took one last glance at the photograph before turning away with her buckets.

"Thank you, Polly."

When the girl was gone, Annabel stripped off her dusty clothes and sank into the steaming tub, but her mind could not stop racing. Despite the soothing warmth of the water or the perfume of her favorite lavender-scented soap which she'd brought with her from St. Louis, she couldn't slow the whirling turmoil inside her.

At first when Polly had told her about the thin bespectacled easterner inquiring after Brett, she'd thought that perhaps it was an investigator from another agency, that Ross McCallum had hired two companies to search for his son, deducing that whoever found Brett first would be entitled to the fee. That would be just like him. But how did Red Cobb fit in?

She was stumped. And worse, she had an uneasy feeling about this. She couldn't put her finger on it, but she sensed that this Bartholomew was not employed by Ross McCallum, that he and Red Cobb were working together to find Brett—and for some sinister purpose of their own.

And they had a good head start on her—at least a week. By now they might have found him. By now he might be . . . dead.

No. Don't think like that. Brett is alive. He has to be. His father needs him and I need him—and he will be found, she told herself. *He'll be found alive and well.*

But where?

Unfortunately, she was fresh out of leads. His trail ended here.

Unless . . .

Unless Roy Steele knew more than she did. Unless the clerk downstairs or someone who worked at one of the other hotels had given Steele the information he wanted before he ordered them not to tell anyone else, as he had done with the blacksmith in Justice.

I'd bet Mama's amber necklet he knows exactly where to look next, Annabel thought, sitting up in the tub with a whoosh of soapy water that cascaded over the sides.

She shivered all over despite the steaming water as she realized what she might have to do. Steele had warned her not to follow him again, warned her to stay out of his way. But she might have no choice.

If she couldn't get answers from anyone else in Eagle Gulch, if he had effectively silenced everyone who might shed light on Brett's trail, then there was only one thing left to do. When Steele left Eagle Gulch to go after Brett, she would have to be right behind him.

And this time, Annabel thought, crossing her arms across her cool, shivering skin, if she wanted to save her neck, she'd have to make sure she did not get caught.

Chapter 7

Merciless sunshine poured down from a hot cobalt sky, baking Annabel's perspiring skin until she felt like a limp, glazed, and oft-basted turkey. Her throat was so parched she could barely swallow, yet she dared not stop to drink from her canteen or rest her horse. If she did, Steele might get too far ahead of her and then she would be hopelessly lost out here in the pine-scented ridges and gullies along the Mogollon Rim.

She had never felt so alone, so small and utterly vulnerable. Admit it, she told herself with a gulp as she ducked beneath the low-hanging branch of a pine. *So frightened.*

This had been a harebrained idea right from the start. Following Steele. It was madness. If she lost him, she would be as good as dead. And if she ventured too close and he realized that she was following him . . .

Annabel didn't want to think about what he would do to her then.

What had Lily said? *Don't shoot her in my bedroom.*

Well, out here in the Mogollons he might have no compunctions. No one would be obliged to scrub up the blood.

She decided she'd rather take her chances getting

lost in the wilderness than risking the wrath of Roy Steele, so she hung back as far as she dared. The trail was leading down now, away from the forested edge of the Rim, winding lower into the treacherous canyons and ravines below. The going was slow and difficult, and as the sun continued to blaze overhead, Sunrise picked her way along the narrow rocky pathway flanked by white grass and ferns.

Annabel took comfort in knowing she had provisions, at least. There were jerky and biscuits in her carpetbag, along with two canteens of water—and her derringer hidden inside her riding boot. But she prayed she wouldn't have any use for it. It wouldn't help her against an Indian attack, and she wasn't quite sure which wild animals inhabited this rugged section of the Arizona territory, but if they hadn't reached a town by dark, she knew she'd have to build a fire and stay awake all night to make sure that no one and nothing sneaked up on her . . .

Does this man never get tired? she muttered through dry, cracked lips as she followed the tracks Steele's horse had stamped in the earth. There was no sign of him below, only the drooping petals of wildflowers among the rocks, an occasional lizard sunning itself on a ledge, and the looping flight of eagles high overhead. The sun crawled toward the western horizon, its rays seeming to grow more piercing as the hours passed and the mare trudged along beneath the cloudless, windless sky. Annabel concentrated on following the trail, all the while assuring herself that soon . . . very soon . . . they would come upon a town, and Steele would stop for the night to drink and bed some whore like that Lily, and she would quietly check into a hotel and ask about Brett and discover that he was right there in town and . . .

Annabel reined in, gasping in horror. *No. Oh, no, it*

couldn't be. She rubbed her bleary eyes and stared down once more at the trail before her.

Trail? What trail? There was none—not a single mark in the dirt.

Steele's tracks were gone.

This can't be, she thought in desperation, and turned Sunrise back a little ways to check the path she'd been following. But now as she leaned down, she realized that it was impossible to tell if the blurred hoofprints on the trail were those of her own horse, or Steele's, or a combination of both. The wind had picked up and was blowing the dust about this way and that and Annabel quickly turned her mare around and urged her forward again, fighting off panic.

He couldn't be far ahead. *Keep going and you'll pick up his tracks soon enough,* she told herself, and nudged the mare to a trot.

All about her were sheer tall rocks and ruddy canyon walls. Above, the craggy ledges of the rim shimmered gray and purple in the blazing sun. It looked like the exact same spot she had passed over an hour ago.

But it couldn't be. She pressed on, staring hard at the ground, willing herself to see the trail that had been there before, that she'd followed without any problem at all . . .

There was no trail. Only earth and grass and rock and the high plaintive wail of the wind which rose around her in a swirl of dust as if to mock her.

"Keep going," Annabel whispered to herself in despair. Her hands shook as she lifted the reins and blinked against the sun's glare and the biting sting of the wind.

Steele smiled coldly to himself.

He'd lost her in Willow Canyon, not far below the

craggy northeast corner of the rim. So long, Miss Brannigan. Adios, and good luck.

It had been child's play, as easy as breathing. Poor Miss Brannigan, he reflected, as his big bay descended a gorge lined with oaks. This was rugged country. Intimidating to someone who didn't know the ins and outs of it. But Steele knew it as intimately as he knew Lily Pardee's boudoir. And he also knew that Annabel Brannigan—a greenhorn if ever he'd seen one—would never be able to follow him.

She was probably scared—and mad as hell—Steele reflected as he spurred Dickens on toward the next grassy ravine, moving at an easy pace. Satisfaction flickered through him. Served her right. Little Miss Liar would simply have to give up, turn back, and follow her own tracks back to Eagle Gulch. If she didn't dawdle, she could reach the border of the town before dark.

But as the wind picked up and the branches of the low oaks and pines shook all about him, Steele swore under his breath. The tracks would be hard to follow now. What if the damn fool woman didn't recognize her surroundings enough to retrace her steps? She'd be lost, stranded in the godforsaken Mogollons.

And it would be his fault.

Hell no, it wouldn't be, Steele argued with himself as he guided Dickens down a narrow rutted trail that twisted like a snake. It was her own damn fault. He'd warned her not to follow him. Whatever happened now, it was only what she deserved.

That morning, when he'd sensed someone trailing him, he'd immediately circled up onto the ledge overlooking the trail outside of Eagle Gulch for a look. And he hadn't been too surprised to see Annabel Brannigan riding hell for leather below. What did she think she was doing, when he'd warned her plain and simple to stay away?

He'd thought about heading her off and confronting her right there, scaring her away and being done with it, but he'd been so furious that he'd decided to lead her on and let her suffer the consequences of getting lost in forbidding, isolated country and having to eventually give up and turn back.

But there was something that bothered him about this whole thing, and Steele couldn't stop thinking about it. He couldn't understand why she persisted in following him, particularly when he'd made it so clear he wouldn't look too kindly on her if it happened again. That half-baked story she'd given him yesterday about someone wanting to kill her hadn't quite rung true. She was a pretty good liar, he reflected, remembering the wide-eyed appeal in her eyes, but not good enough.

Yet he couldn't figure what the real story could be.

It doesn't matter, he told himself as the trail wound past a thicket of pines and some twigs crackled underfoot. *You'll never see her again.*

Because she'd probably die, stranded, out in the brakes, a caustic inner voice pointed out to him.

Steele scowled at the looming canyon walls and the towering rim high above. He couldn't afford to waste time thinking about Annabel Brannigan. "Let's go, boy," he urged the bay, his fingers tightening on the reins. He focused his concentration on his quarry. "We're going to catch him soon," he reflected silently. "And at this point, I'll be damned if I'm stopping for anyone—particularly some pesky woman who's got no business following me in the first place."

A glow of purple and gold radiated across the sky as the sun dipped lower and the air beneath the rim turned cool. Annabel halted her mare in a clearing beneath a ledge and gazed around her with hopeless eyes.

I can't go forward and I can't go back, she thought in

despair. Her eyes ached with strain, and her shoulders burned with exhaustion. For the past two hours she'd been trying to retrace her steps back to Eagle Gulch, but the wind had wiped out her trail, and all the canyons and hilltops looked alike. She couldn't get back to the top of the rim. Twice she'd found herself going in circles.

The land was beautiful, but also cruel, she realized on a gulp of fear. It would not aid her, would not reveal its secrets to her. She was its prisoner now, a wanderer without map or knowledge with which to free herself from this vast, wild, and all-engulfing prison.

She'd have to make camp . . . somehow.

The main thing was not to panic, she reminded herself, but she couldn't help the tiny flutters of fear quivering through her nerve endings. Then, as she swung out of the saddle and her feet scraped against the dirt, there was a clatter of hoofbeats and she glanced up in alarm. But before she could do more than gasp, a trio of dark-garbed riders surrounded her.

Oh, God. Annabel's mouth went dry. They were long-haired, foul-looking men. Desperadoes, Annabel guessed in one blazing instant of fear, and then she lunged downward for her gun. But before she could pull it free of her boot, one of the men leapt from his horse and grabbed her. He seized her arms and spun her about to face him, his hiss of laughter emitting a cloud of foul-smelling breath that nearly made her gag.

"Lookee, here, Moss—what'd I say about our luck changin'? When was the last time you saw a purty little female out here in the brakes?"

"Sure she ain't a mirage, Curtis?" Moss called out, grinning behind his sandy handlebar mustache.

"Better pinch her, Curtis, and make sure." The third man, younger than the others, a stocky, cheruby blond with golden stubble on his chin, leaned forward eagerly in his saddle.

The scrawny, beak-nosed man holding Annabel pinched her bottom and she jumped, twisting futilely in his arms.

"She's real, all right," Curtis crowed, and dragged her chin up so that she was forced to meet his shining little blueberry eyes. "Honey, I don't know what you're doing out here all by yerself and I don't care. It's no place for a lone woman, and that's for sure. But me and Moss and Willy are goin' to take real good care of you. Don't you worry about nothin'."

"You'd better let go of me and get out of here while you still can breathe, mister." Annabel spoke through pain-clenched teeth, fighting to keep her voice steady despite the terror firing through her. "My husband and the others will be returning soon and they won't take kindly to you laying your hands on me."

"Husband?" The boy with the golden stubble, Willy, threw a worried glance around the clearing. "Hey, maybe we should hightail it out of here before . . ."

"She's lying." The man called Moss dismounted and started across the clearing toward Annabel and Curtis, his gait slow and deliberate. His face was as flat and cold as a wedge of stone, his shoulders brawny beneath his grease-stained vest. "I saw her ride up through the canyon myself. She was alone. She's lost, Willy, I told you that."

"No," Annabel said quickly. "I got separated from my party . . . but they're looking for me and they'll be here soon. If you don't want any trouble . . ."

Moss reached her, drew back his arm, and slapped her backhanded across the face. The blow was hard, well aimed, and quick as a jolt of lightning. The three ominous figures blurred as pain crashed through Annabel's jaw and spiraled across her tongue and teeth.

"Now you shut up," Moss said almost pleasantly. He stroked on his handlebar mustache. "There's only one thing a woman is good for and talkin' ain't it." He studied her a moment, his wolfish eyes squinting appreciatively as they swept over her slender, femininely curved figure, noting the gentle swell of her breasts beneath her lace-edged, close-fitting shirtwaist, and the striking loveliness of her neatly coiled hair and delicate features. He smiled at the shock, pain, and fear on her face, felt cruel pleasure when he noticed her full, pretty lips were trembling. Hell and damnation, she was sure a find.

"Yep, lady, you'll do just grand," he approved. Then he jerked his thumb toward a long, flat rock at the edge of the clearing. "Set her down over there, Curtis, and keep an eye on her. We don't want our little darlin' here runnin' off and gettin' lost in the woods."

Her breath seemed locked inside Annabel's lungs. As Curtis dragged her to the rock and pushed her down to sit on it, she glanced desperately about for a way of escape. But behind her was only the trail leading back into that seemingly endless ravine. And ahead of her, the tiny clearing which seemed suddenly full of men, horses, and guns.

Instinct told her that Curtis, Moss, and Willy were wanted men, fugitives. The furtive way they glanced around, studying the layout of the land, their unkempt appearance, and Willy's alarm when she'd mentioned her mythical husband all pointed to the fact that they were on the run and lying low. But not low enough to pass up the chance to grab themselves a lone woman, a woman foolish enough to think she could cross the Arizona wilderness on her own . . .

Well, I might be foolish, but I'm not spineless enough to let them have me without a fight, she told herself grimly, forcing back the terror which would immobilize her if she'd let it. She watched Moss and Willy tend the horses and make camp. Curtis stood beside her, grinning. It would be dark soon. And she'd be alone here in the mountains with these criminals, with no one to hear her screams, or her sobs . . .

And at that moment, she remembered she still had her gun.

"Curtis . . . may I call you Curtis?" she asked softly, keeping her voice low enough so that the others wouldn't hear.

He grinned at her. His teeth were small and yellow and chipped. They made his blueberry eyes gleam even brighter. "Sure can, sweet thing. What do you want?"

"Water." She fluttered a hand to her throat, trying to look weak and helpless. "I'm so thirsty. I've been riding for hours, lost, just wandering around . . . there's water in my canteen. Would it be all right with you if I get some?"

"Nope. Can't let you off this rock or Moss'll get mad. But jest maybe I'll get it for you. What'll you give me if I do?"

A bullet between the eyes, you repulsive little worm. But aloud she murmured only, "My endless gratitude," and tried her best to look suitably cowed.

Curtis gave a shout of laughter. "Hey, Willy, this here woman's going to give me her endless gratitude in exchange for some water from her canteen. How 'bout that? Think I should do it?"

"I'll do it." Willy dropped a load of firewood into the dirt, and trotted over with his own canteen, holding it out to her. "Help yourself, honey. But I'm gonna expect all the gratitude you've got." He chortled at his own humor, and Curtis joined in, but as Annabel reached reluctantly for the canteen, Moss's voice rang out harshly.

"If she gets to be too much of a distraction, I'll have

to kill her. Now that can be *after* we've all had our fun with her, or before. It's up to you, boys."

Willy grabbed the canteen back before Annabel had a chance to take a sip. "Aw, Moss, we wasn't meanin' no harm." He scowled and trudged back to the pile of firewood. "What's the big hurry? That posse was two days behind us . . ."

"Shut up, you damned fool," Curtis barked, and threw Annabel a worried frown.

So she'd been right. They were wanted men. And with this fact confirmed, Annabel suddenly knew that they would certainly kill her. They would not hesitate once she became inconvenient to them, once they'd had their fill of "fun."

She sat perfectly still. Curtis, still frowning, spoke in a low tone. "You want water? Well, stay there and keep quiet and I'll get you some. But don't you try nothin'." He gave her one keen, warning glance, and then loped toward Sunrise and her own canteens.

Wait, Annabel told herself, as her heart thumped like a trip-hammer. *Not yet.* She forced herself to sit motionless on the rock, her fingers gripping the warm stone. *Two more steps, three . . . wait until he's not looking. . . .*

Go.

She sprang up like a jackrabbit with paws on fire and ran toward the trail. There were hoarse shouts behind her as she ducked under a low-hanging cottonwood branch, and then she heard the pounding crunch of booted feet in pursuit. Yells, oaths, and the furious scuffle of heavy, running feet exploded through the late afternoon stillness.

Run! Faster! Her skirt caught on the edge of a jagged rock, but she tore it free and fled on across the winding path, searching frantically for someplace to hide . . .

The path fell away sharply, dipping and winding downward toward the bottom of the ravine, where a stream murmured among white boulders. She stumbled over rocks and brush, skittering as fast as she could down the path. There was no place to conceal herself, nothing to hide behind—she would have to keep going and try to outrun them. And somehow try to use the gun . . . Annabel told herself, gasping for air as she ran. If they came close enough and she could get off a shot or two before they shot her, maybe she could even the odds . . .

Then she saw exactly what she'd been praying for. A big red boulder, nestled on a rocky outcropping off the main path, directly beneath a sheer cliff. She glanced back swiftly up the track and saw that there was no sign of either Curtis, Moss, or Willy, though she could hear them coming. But they wouldn't see where she went . . .

Swiftly she dashed off the path and toward the rock and ducked down behind it. Her hands were slippery with sweat but she managed to yank the derringer from her boot. She held it in her shaking fingers, trying not to drop the damned thing. *Calm down, think. There's no room here for mistakes,* she told herself, and drew several quick deep breaths. Then she braced herself behind the rock, rested the barrel of the gun on top of it, and aimed straight at the path.

Her heart was pounding so hard she thought her chest would explode, and her lips were dry, but she stared frantically at the trail and waited . . .

"We'll get you for this, you sneaking little bitch!" Curtis's voice bellowed from around the bend, and the pounding of heavy footfalls stormed closer.

"You're goin' to be real sorry, lady, that you caused us all this trouble!"

That was Moss. She winced, remembering the slam

of his hand against her jaw. She ignored the throbbing in her cheek and clutched the gun tighter.

She almost didn't hear the other, softer sound until it was right behind her, and then it was almost too late.

Boots scraped against rock. Someone jumped down behind her. She gave a small, horrified gasp, and whirled about, firing the derringer instinctively. The bullet bored straight through the hat of the man before her, leaving a gaping hole. He swore, twisted the little derringer from her hand, and seized her in a powerful grip.

But it wasn't Curtis, Moss, or Willy who pushed her down against the boulder, holding her still. It was Roy Steele.

"I just bought this hat two weeks ago, Miss Brannigan," he grated through clenched teeth. "Didn't have a mark on it. Reckon you owe me fifteen dollars."

Chapter 8

Annabel clutched desperately at his shoulders, her fingers digging into iron muscle. "It's *you*!"

"Last time I looked."

"My God . . . I almost killed you."

"Can't argue with that." Steele's eyes narrowed on the bruise across her jaw. "What happened to your face?"

"Oh . . ." She let go of him long enough to touch a fingertip to the raw, tender spot. "They . . . he . . . those men . . . !" she blurted in a frantic whisper. Then she dug her fingers once more into the solid muscle of his arm as if clinging to a life raft. It didn't seem strange at all to feel the shock of relief that was flooding through her at the splendid, awe-inspiring sight of him. Gazing into his face and reading the deadly gleam in his eyes, she nearly wept for joy. "Thank God you're here," she continued on a ragged gasp. "Mr. Steele, you must help me. Those men . . . they're going to kill me!"

"Don't count on it. I reserve that pleasure for myself." Steele thrust her down behind the rock as Curtis, Moss, and Willy bolted into view and charged down the track like a small herd of stampeding cows. He was aware that his flesh still tingled strangely where her delicate fingers had gripped it. Crouching beside him, Annabel Brannigan looked shaken, desperate, yet utterly breathtaking. The eagerness of her vivid eyes, fixed on his with such total appeal and confidence in his ability to save her, made him flinch.

"Stay down—and take this," Steele ordered tersely, giving her back her gun just as the other men's voices exploded from the trail.

"Where the hell did she go?"

"Damn it, Curtis, this is all your fault. Falling for those big innocent eyes of hers . . ."

"I'm gonna skin you alive, girl," cheruby Willy shouted, his voice echoing through the walls of the ravine, bouncing down toward the stream below. "I'll beat you 'til there's nothin' left but broken bone, I'll make you sorry you ever tried to—"

"You boys got some sort of problem?" Steele asked coolly, rising as the three men came even with the ledge. They spun toward him in amazement, but refrained from grabbing for their guns when they saw he was already pointing his black-handled Colt at them.

Curtis's mouth fell open. "Who the hell are you?"

Annabel could control herself not a minute longer.

"He's Roy Steele, that's who," she announced with infinite satisfaction, popping up beside him. Her eyes sparkled with deep joy. She felt almost drunk with relief as she wagged a finger at the three desperadoes. "You're in a lot of trouble now—all of you."

"Steele? Roy Steele? Right. Sure, he is." Moss gave out a horselaugh. "And I'm Wyatt Earp."

Willy giggled and scratched his thigh. But Curtis was staring. "I . . . saw Roy Steele once, Moss. In Tombstone. He knocked a man through a window for beating a whore . . . I saw the whole fight . . . and . . ."

His voice trailed off. He swallowed convulsively, and his swarthy skin turned the color of chalk.

"And what?" Moss snapped.

"And . . . that's him."

"Very good, Curtis," Annabel said, nodding. "Mr. Steele is unforgettable once you've seen him in action, isn't he? I personally saw him kill three men in Justice and I never saw such fast shooting in my life . . ."

"Will you be quiet?" Steele burst out beside her. "Stop talking and let me handle this."

"But these men are after me," Annabel pointed out, peering up at him with a determined set to her lips. "Last time, the men were after you, and so of course, it was your problem. This time they're after me, and so I insist on playing a part in—"

"You want to kill one? Fine, which one? Just take aim and get it over with."

Annabel saw Moss and Willy grow as still as Curtis. My, my they didn't look nearly so dangerous now. They looked as if they were ready to pee in their pants.

"Well," she said slowly, regarding each of them consideringly. "Moss is the one who hit me."

"Then go ahead." Steele nodded his head. "At this range your derringer will do the job. But I get the other two."

"Deal." Annabel agreed, and raised the derringer coolly.

"You're loco!" Moss shouted, purple color flooding his face. He wasn't pulling on his mustache now, Annabel noted with grim satisfaction, he was shifting nervously from one foot to the other. "You can't shoot me in cold blood! You're a woman. Women don't just go around shooting people in cold blood—"

"Her being a woman didn't stop you from hitting her," Steele interrupted, and Annabel couldn't help the

electric quiver that ran through her at the ice-cold menace in his tone.

"That's right, so say your prayers, Moss," she said,
"because this is one woman who doesn't take kindly to
being treated the way you and your friends treated me."

"But I didn't touch you . . . I was gonna give you
water!" Curtis yelled, his head bobbing up and down.
"Tell him—tell Steele I was getting the canteen for
you . . ."

"I think we've had about enough of this," the gunfighter sighed in disgust. "Time for you liver-bellied
snakes to throw down your guns."

Annabel watched as one by one they obeyed this
command. Sweat poured down the faces of the three
men, and she marveled at how much less dangerous
they looked now that they were unarmed and she had a
weapon in her hand—and Roy Steele's tall, dark form
beside her.

"I'll just pick up those pistols," she offered and
started forward around the rock, but suddenly Steele
yelled behind her.

"Get out of the way!"

Too late she realized she was blocking his bead on
the three men. Too late she saw Curtis and Willy grabbing at hideaway guns tucked inside their belts, and too
late she realized Steele couldn't shoot because she was
in his line of fire. She tried to duck as gunfire erupted
behind her, and Moss flung his hefty form forward in a
hurtling leap straight at her.

The ledge rang with shots as Moss hit her full on
and knocked her to the ground. Pain thudded through
every fiber of her being as he fell on top of her and
seized the derringer. Dimly, she heard more shots, then
grunts and hideous groans. Sunlight nearly blinded her.
Through a white haze she saw Moss crouched over her,
saw him lift his arm and point the derringer. She tried to

raise her hand to knock the gun aside, but burning pain looped through her shoulder, and faintness blurred his looming image.

She waited for the shot, but it never came. Instead a bullet ripped through his chest and he toppled over, blood spurting everywhere.

A strange tingling sensation washed over her. Her shoulder throbbed, and as if from a long way off, Annabel heard a moan, and realized it was her own voice.

Then a tall form blocked the sun and she closed her eyes, little pinpricks of red light dotting the blackness in her mind. She felt herself slipping, fading. Hands groped at her, lifted her, and she heard a man's sharp intake of breath.

"Brett?" she whispered, a huge lump of happiness bubbling inside her as the blackness grew thicker and the red lights disappeared one by one. "I was going to find . . . you," she breathed, clutching at his hand as he gripped hers in a relentless grip. "But you found me . . . oh, Brett . . . I have so much to tell you."

And then the darkness hugged her tighter, and Brett lifted her up and she let herself be carried into the soft sweet cottony thick blackness.

Chapter 9

"Easy."

Annabel opened her eyes and through a sheen of moonlight saw Roy Steele hunkered down beside her. He was watching her, his expression unreadable in the dimness.

"What . . . happened?" she whispered, confused, trying to remember the chain of events leading up to this moment. And then a shudder ran through her as she suddenly recalled the fight on the ledge, the gunshots, Moss pointing the derringer at her . . .

"They're dead. It's all over. Take it easy."

Steele's calm cool voice pierced through the ugly memories and she focused on his face. "You shot Moss . . . before he could . . ."

"Yep."

"What happened to them . . ."

"Dead and buried," he said curtly. "No need for you to think about those hombres again."

She tried to sit up, but sharp pain twinged through her shoulder and she gasped at the intensity of it. "I've been shot," she exclaimed in surprise.

"Yep. That son of a bitch nailed you right before I plugged him."

Steele ruthlessly eased her back to the ground. She was lying on a bedroll in the clearing, a wool blanket tucked across her shoulders, protecting her from the evening chill. Thoughtful, Annabel decided, closing her eyes. As the mountain breeze fanned her cheek, she was grateful for the blanket's fuzzy warmth.

"Is it serious?" she asked suddenly, forcing her eyes open despite her weariness.

"Only a scratch. The bullet just nicked you. You'll live."

He didn't sound as if he cared particularly one way or another, but he had obviously bandaged it for her and brought her back here to the clearing. He'd covered her with his blanket, and let her sleep in his bedroll. Hmmm. Mr. Steele, she thought, I think I'm beginning to see right through you.

Annabel regarded his grim countenance for a moment in silence. "How can I thank you? You've saved my life today several times over . . ."

"Don't thank me too quickly. I'm not finished with you, yet, Miss Brannigan. Not by a long shot."

The clearing was dark, but for the fragile amber glow of a small campfire. They were alone here in the shadow of the Mogollons, camped on a tiny clearing beneath the towering pine-forested rim, yet she was not afraid—either of the treacherous black canyons and ravines all around, of the animals rustling through the darkness beyond the fire—or of him.

"I suppose you're going to shout at me," she sighed.

"Shout at you?" he growled. "Is that all you think I'm going to do?" He leaned closer, his eyes flaring with anger. The menacing twist had returned to his lips. "After I warned you not to follow me? I told you I'd make you sorry if I ever caught you trailing me again . . . and now . . . what's wrong?"

Annabel closed her eyes quickly then opened then,

giving her head a tiny shake. "Nothing. It hurts, that's all."

He swore under his breath, then his lips tightened. "Serves you right. If you'd stayed in Eagle Gulch you'd be safe and sound and—"

"I am safe and sound, Mr. Steele," Annabel interrupted him, speaking quietly. Her eyes met his in the firelight. "I'm with you."

He made an incoherent sound, stood up, and wheeled away from her. Annabel watched his broad, rigid back as he paused beside the rock where Curtis had kept her under guard.

"Mr. Steele," she whispered after a moment.

He turned back and stared at her, lying in his bedroll, only a blanket and her camisole covering the smooth naked skin, with tiny wisps of bright coppery hair curling rebelliously about her cheeks and forehead, finally coming undone from those relentless pins of hers. He wondered what she would look like with her hair all loose and flowing, and why she always wore it so tightly bound.

"Mr. Steele," she repeated, her voice so soft it made something ache deep inside him.

"*What*?" he demanded, covering the effect she was having on him with the curtness of his tone.

"Is there anything to eat?" Annabel gave him a bemused smile. "It seems that I'm starving. And thirsty. Maybe it's strange to be hungry after being shot, but I haven't eaten much all day. I was too busy trying to keep up with you . . . er, maybe we'd best not talk about that."

"We are going to talk about it. Right now."

Annabel watched him stride back toward her. His face was shadowed by firelight, yet she could see the tension in it. And the anger. But she wasn't afraid of him any longer. At least, not in the way she had been.

Though a little apprehensive quiver did go through her as he crouched beside her again and peered down at her, she wasn't afraid he would hurt her. It was a different kind of fear, something to do with the spreading warmth inside her, the odd rapid beating of her heart—but she didn't allow herself to explore the strangeness of this any further . . .

"Tell me the truth, Miss Brannigan."

"Annabel."

"Miss Brannigan," he repeated deliberately. His voice was even and controlled. "You were following me."

He was so close she could see the long black lashes of his glinting eyes, see the rhythmic rise and fall of his broad chest beneath his black silk shirt. She found herself staring at his hard, sensual mouth. "Admit it, Miss Brannigan. Now."

Well, there was no point in denying the obvious. She nodded.

"Yes, Mr. Steele, I was following you."

"Against my direct orders."

"Yes."

"Because you're looking for Brett McCallum."

Her mouth fell open. "How . . . how did you . . ."

He captured her chin in his hand and held her head still, forcing her to stare directly into his eyes. He was studying her face carefully. "Just answer the question."

"Ye-es." Annabel was flabbergasted. And stunned by the heat of his touch. She couldn't escape those brutally appraising eyes, couldn't seem to move a single muscle. All she could do was wait for him to go on, wondering all the while how much he knew and how he'd learned it. But he didn't speak—he only stared at her piercingly, as if trying to read the very depths of her mind. She had time to study him in turn, to note the weariness that stamped his rough, handsome face, something she hadn't noted earlier. She was beginning to understand something important about Roy Steele. Whatever he might be, he was no cold-blooded killer. But why he was after Brett remained a mystery to her.

Ask him. Just ask him.

She swallowed. "Mr. Steele, why are *you* searching for Brett McCallum?"

"I'm asking the questions, Miss Brannigan."

"So am I," she pointed out.

For the first time since she'd met him, he actually smiled at her. A real smile, not that coldly mocking grimace she'd seen before. He let go of her and rocked back on his heels.

"You are the damnest woman," he muttered, half to himself.

It wasn't exactly flattery. She'd heard many more flowery comments than that from the three suitors who'd asked for her hand in marriage, but coming from Roy Steele, it almost sounded like poetry.

Suddenly, he reached down beneath her shoulders and lifted her so that she was gathered close against him. He was so strong, she realized, he could probably snap her in two, but his arms merely glided around her back, supporting her. She winced when the movement, careful as he did it, gave a slight jolt to her shoulder, but then she was swiftly settled in the hardness of his arms, still wrapped in the blanket, a strangely safe, comfortable feeling enveloping her. He smelled nicely of pine and sage. She was unable to ignore either the sheer male warmth or the solid muscular strength of him. She felt like a cradled doll. It was a dizzying, totally new sensation. His face was only inches from hers, and in the moonlight she could discern the rough stubble of a day's growth of beard along his jaw and chin, and the taut lines around his eyes, which only seemed to add to his rugged handsomeness.

Had she ever seen a more compellingly attractive man? She doubted it. Even Brett, kind, sweet, laughing Brett with his straight brown hair and boyishly appealing features, his effortless charm and air of dashing gaiety, had never had quite such a powerful effect on her. She wondered what it would feel like to stroke Roy Steele's thick coal-black hair or to trace a fingertip along the harsh planes and angles of his face. She found herself gazing in fascination once more at his sarcastically curled, sensual mouth, then her glance flitted upward to meet the keen blackness of those hawklike eyes. She'd never before looked into such mesmerizing, glinting eyes.

A shiver coursed through her, but not from the cold.

She felt warm—no. Hot. Almost as strangely hot and tingly as she'd felt when she'd been shot.

"Miss Brannigan," he said very low, his voice growling over the hiss of twigs in the campfire, "if you want to eat supper tonight—or any night in the future—you'll answer my questions. All of them. Because I'm giving you nothing—no food, no coffee, no answers, until you've explained yourself to me. Got that?"

"It's rather more than clear," she murmured back, peeping up at him without resentment.

"So start talking. I want to hear exactly why you're looking for Brett McCallum—the truth. And I want to hear it now."

There was really nothing to do but comply. Annabel's brain raced to concoct exactly what she would say, but it was difficult to think when he was close to her like this, when the warm male scent of him enveloped her and tantalized her senses, when they were so alone here in this rock-walled clearing that she could almost imagine there was no one else alive in the whole world —only the two of them stranded in these vast, dark, dangerous Mogollons, locked together at the crown of the most ruggedly beautiful and awesome spot on earth.

But she did her best.

She reached the swift conclusion that she would tell him the truth—or at least, the *almost truth*.

"I'm Brett's fiancée," she said quickly, aware of how still he had gone, how his eyes watched her with a deep black intensity made all the more menacing because his muscles all tightened reflexively at the same moment.

"I'm very worried about him . . . and that's why I'm trying to find him. He ran away, and we heard . . . his father and I . . . that a man named Red Cobb is out to kill him and I must find him first and bring him safely home." She moistened her lips. "Your turn."

Her words had had no visible effect on him except one. His eyes became hard glinting obsidians, devoid of all warmth and feeling. Annabel felt a rush of fear at the utter coldness of them. Maybe she'd been wrong in thinking this man was not as harsh as he appeared, maybe he would strangle her right now without another word . . .

"Ross McCallum sent *you* to find his son?"

There was so much cold fury in his words that she felt her heart start to hammer. "Not . . . exactly. He . . . doesn't know . . . he's ill and I . . . came on my own."

He released her and rocked back on his heels, that cool deadliness seemingly stamped in stone upon his granite features.

"Ill?"

"His heart is not strong."

If possible, his expression turned even icier. "Go on."

"Brett means more to me than anyone else in the world. I've known him nearly all my life—we grew up together. The only family I've ever had is gone—my mother died when I was a child and my aunt passed on three years ago . . . and now I'm afraid of losing Brett too." The words rushed out of her all on their own, caught in the floodtide of her suddenly unlocked emotions. "I've nothing to lose, Mr. Steele, in hunting for him. He's all I want . . . all I've ever wanted, really, and I must find him and see if he . . ."

She broke off in consternation. She'd been about to say "see if he could ever love me," but she swallowed the words back and said instead: "and see if he can explain what has made him run off like this. We were planning to be married, but something terrible must have happened to make him leave . . ."

Steele shook his head in amazement and pulled her close once again. "What in hell ever made you think you could find him?"

Annabel bristled. "Let me remind you that I'm very close to finding him, Mr. Steele." Her eyes flashed. "As close as you are."

"You're lucky, lady. Damn lucky."

"Luck had nothing to do with it."

"You might have died out here in these canyons. Hell, you *would* have died—and worse—before those varmints I shot got through with you. If I hadn't come back . . ."

"But you did, Mr. Steele." Annabel's voice was soft over the hissing fire. She shifted slightly in his arms, inadvertently brushing her breasts against his chest. She felt the quick inhale of his breath. *So, Mr. Gunfighter No-Feelings Steele, you're not as immune to human emotion as you pretend to be.* The knowledge gave her confidence and made her smile at him as she lay within the circle of his arms. "Now it's my turn to ask a question," she said firmly. "I've already figured out that your showing up here was no accident—you lost me on purpose in the Mogollons, and then you came back for me just as purposefully. Why?"

"Why do you think?"

"You thought I wouldn't get out from under the rim alive, and you didn't want my death on your conscience."

"I'm a gunfighter, Miss Brannigan," he told her dryly, his mouth twisting into a sneer. "I don't have a conscience."

But Annabel was no longer fooled. "You're lying, Mr. Steele. I think there is much more to you than you care to let on to the world. I think you have a conscience and a soul and a sense of honor. And . . ."

He released her and set her back on the bedroll with one swift motion that sent a tiny shock of pain throbbing through her shoulder. He gave no sign of noticing her sudden wince. "You're loco, lady." In one fluid movement, he was standing, pushing his hat back on his head. "Completely loco. Now stay put and I'll fix you some grub."

He stalked away and grabbed up a coffeepot and tin cup. Annabel closed her eyes, trying not to think about the ache in her shoulder. She concentrated instead on pondering how she'd handled Steele's questions.

All in all, not bad, she decided. She couldn't help but feel satisfied with the story she'd told. It was close enough to the truth to be entirely believable. And, she thought, far better that he should think she was Brett's fiancée than an inept private investigator. And he would think she was inept if he knew the truth—because up until now she hadn't managed to be discreet—not discreet enough, anyway. But she was going to get better at this, she promised herself—it just might take a little time and practice.

What disturbed her was that Steele still hadn't told her anything about why _he_ was searching for Brett. But he would, Annabel vowed to herself. Before this night was over, she would know exactly what kind of a problem she was dealing with.

Moments later, Steele presented her with a ration of beef jerky, some hardtack biscuits, and a cup of steaming black coffee.

"I'm sure it's not what you're used to back in good old St. Louis but it'll have to do," he told her as he helped her to sit up. But this time, as he did so, the blanket slipped down, leaving her all but naked from the waist up, her creamy breasts nearly exposed except for the wispy lace of her camisole.

Steele's gaze slid automatically and intently to the lush ivory mounds peeking over the thin lace even as Annabel yanked the blanket up and over her shoulder with her good hand. But she had not missed the disconcertingly intense gleam in Steele's eyes. Flushing, she began to realize for the first time how he must have had to tear her blouse in order to bandage the wound.

I do hope Brett appreciates everything I've gone through to find him, she thought suddenly. Gritting her teeth, she reminded herself that sacrificing her dignity was a small price to pay to save Brett from Red Cobb— and possibly from Roy Steele, too.

"There's another shirtwaist in my carpetbag," she managed to say in a calm tone, as she awkwardly used her good hand to hold the blanket in place. "Would you please get it for me?"

He grunted something she couldn't quite make out. All of the sudden he was incoherent, she thought in exasperation. But he did walk toward Sunrise, who was grazing along with his horse and those belonging to Curtis, Moss, and Willy. When Steele returned she saw thankfully that he had the bulging carpetbag in tow.

Rummaging through the bag, he accidentally pulled out a pair of silk drawers instead of the shirtwaist. Annabel gasped in chagrin as the firelight illuminated them. "You . . . you . . . put those back!" she sputtered.

Steele grinned. It transformed his face, lightening all the taut lines that gave him such a harsh aspect, making him look suddenly like a mischievous little boy.

"Take it easy, Miss Brannigan. Reckon I've seen a pair of ladies drawers before," he commented drily.

"Well, you haven't seen mine—and . . . and you won't ever see them again, so . . . so . . . you just put them back!"

To Annabel's relief he did stuff the drawers back inside, but the infuriating grin stayed on his face. A moment later, he yanked out the fresh white shirtwaist, and along with it tumbled Aunt Gertie's diary.

"What's this?"

"Never you mind. May I have the shirtwaist please?"

But a mood of devilment seemed to have come upon him now and he withheld both items from her grasp, holding them just beyond her reach, studying the bound leather book and the lace-collared shirtwaist with equal interest.

"Sure. After I see what this is . . . a diary? Yours?"

"No. Now give me that!" Reaching forward to grab it from him, Annabel's felt a fresh wave of pain from her wound as the bandage tore loose. She grabbed it instinctively just as blood oozed out between her fingers.

"What are you doing?" Steele demanded furiously. He instantly dropped the shirtwaist and the diary down beside the plate of food and grabbed Annabel before she could sink back in pain. "Why can't you just sit still?" he fumed. "Now I'm going to have to bandage it again, and it might hurt, but you deserve it."

"Your . . . fault," she gasped. "You wouldn't give me the shirtwaist or the diary . . ."

"Don't talk. Sit still and take this like a man . . . er, like a woman . . . whatever. Go ahead," he said roughly, as he drew a roll of bandages from inside his own saddle pack a few feet away, "Cry if you want, I don't give a damn."

"Mr. Steele, one thing you'll learn about me is that I never cry," Annabel flung out, but she had to bite back tears as he worked at rebandaging the wound. It had begun to throb again and she concentrated on taking deep breaths and keeping the tears from rolling down her cheeks until Steele was finished.

He glanced at her pale face, at her lips that were quivering with the effort of suppressing tears. "Here. Drink this. Don't argue, just drink it," he ordered, handing her a flask from his pack.

"Is it whiskey?" she asked doubtfully, eyeing the flask with a mixture of both doubt and curious anticipation.

"No, it's arsenic." Impatience flicked through his voice. "Of course it's whiskey. Drink up."

He held the flask for her as she drank, coughed, sputtered, and at last swallowed.

"Drink some more." Steele ruthlessly put the flask to her lips again. "It'll dull the pain."

The fiery liquor burned through her throat and insides quickly. She felt only a faint flush of embarrassment when he helped her slip on the shirtwaist and his fingers began to move deftly over the buttons.

He's certainly done this before—worked at a lady's delicate little buttons, Annabel thought as his hands slid expertly past her breasts down toward her belly. *Only he's probably much more accomplished at unfastening buttons than the other way around.* A faint pink blush stole up her neck. It was difficult to breathe. She told herself this must be the liquor. The liquor was also making her very warm, despite the evening chill. And deliciously relaxed.

"Thank you," she heard herself whispering when Steele had finished. He refrained from attempting to tuck the long blouse into her skirt.

"You're welcome."

He moved away from her, tossing a few more twigs into the glowing embers of the fire. Annabel ate in silence, watching the sparks and flames. Occasionally, she glanced at Roy Steele, who had busied himself with the horses, not only his own and Sunrise, but the horses belonging to Moss, Curtis, and Willy. By the time he'd returned she had finished the jerky and biscuits and taken a few sips of the coffee. The whiskey was making her sleepy.

"There's just one thing I need to know," she murmured, fingering the spine of Aunt Gertie's diary, which was lying beside her.

Steele came around the campfire and stood over her, staring down expectantly.

Above, the sky glittered with a million diamond bright stars. They bathed the rocks and mountaintops in a faint eerie glow that glimmered like quicksilver.

"I'm listening."

"Why are *you* looking for Brett McCallum, Mr. Steele?"

Silence. A rabbit or some other creature darted through the brush beyond the rocks. Then Steele answered her, his voice dry and hard. "That's my business."

"But I told *you* . . . that's not fair!"

"Don't expect life to be fair, Miss Brannigan. You'll be doomed for disappointment."

"You can't . . . want to kill him . . . like Red Cobb," she blurted out, suddenly wondering if she'd been wrong about him all along, if she'd made a terrible mistake. Roy Steele seemed to read her mind.

"And if I do?" he asked coolly.

"I'll . . . have to kill you first."

He knelt beside her. He was staring at her hair. "I believe you would. At least you'd try." As he spoke, he reached out and gently tugged a hairpin from her chignon. "Even after all I've done for you," he mused sardonically.

"Well, I wouldn't *want* to kill you," she said defensively. "I'm very grateful to you—but I won't let you hurt Brett. I won't . . . what are you doing?"

"Removing these damned pins. Surely you don't sleep with them all stuck in your head like that."

"No, of course not, but I'm perfectly capable of taking care of my own hair, Mr. Steele."

Yet the feel of his large hands gently removing the pins and freeing her luxuriantly springing curls made her insides quiver with an achingly sweet longing.

"Are they all out?" she asked faintly.

"Yes."

"Are you satisfied now?"

"Yes."

But he wasn't. God help him, he wasn't. He felt about as unsatisfied as a man could get. She was even lovelier now than before, if that was possible. A tall, slender angel with hair the color of fire splashing down around those adorably fine-cut features. Her eyes glimmered like mysterious oriental jewels, and there was a promising softness about her full mouth that was driving him wild.

She was too delicate, too fine and beautiful for this rough land. He leaned forward. He didn't know what he was doing.

Walk away, a voice inside of him commanded. *Before it's too late.* Getting involved with this woman would be the worst move he could possibly make. A fatal move. *Damn it, think about who she is. Walk away.*

But she drew him like a powerful magnet stronger than the pull of gravity. He leaned in closer, intoxicated by the soft, wildflower scent of her. He was about to kiss her.

"Why are you really looking for Brett?" she breathed, and set one slender restraining hand upon his chest, as if that would hold him back if he really chose to plunge forward.

He caught her hand in his, his fingers tight around it. "You never give up, do you, Miss Brannigan? In that respect, if no other, the two of us are alike."

He snaked his arms around her so suddenly she could do no more than blink before he brought his lips down on hers. His hand still imprisoned hers tightly, his strong fingers enclosing her long, slender ones like an iron glove.

Against all of his instincts, all of his intentions, all of his cool common sense, he kissed her. A long, hard, ravaging kiss that was nothing if not thorough.

Annabel's senses soared as his mouth came down fiercely upon hers. She had never ever been kissed like this before. She knew she should be outraged, but instead she felt . . . awestruck. Dizzy. Excited with a sweet, spiraling joy that swept through her entire body.

Her suitors back home had each become amorous on the day they made their proposals to her, obviously hoping to woo her with passion, but nothing had prepared her for the onslaught of dizzying sensations Roy Steele rained down on her with his hard demanding mouth and bruising kisses. For he didn't just kiss her once and let her go, no, that would have been bad enough . . . he kissed her many times, at first hungrily, fiercely, and then he paused for only a fraction of an instant, giving her time to catch her breath, but not much—no time to speak, or think, or protest, before he kissed her again, more deeply, exploringly, possessively, his tongue forcing her lips apart and thrusting inside her mouth with arrogant demand, like a general taking command of the battlefield.

The stars swam above, insects hummed below, the campfire hissed and crackled in the tiny starlit clearing, but Annabel found herself so firmly held and kissed and mesmerized by the gunfighter who had wrapped his arms around her that she was aware of nothing but the rough feel of his body against hers and the scorching sweetness of kisses that robbed her of all reason. Steele gave her no chance, no time, no breath to protest.

Not that she wanted to.

After that first startling moment, Annabel found herself caught up in a rush of deliciously indecent feeling. Her heart was pounding so hard she was sure he must feel it against his own implacable chest. Her mouth burned beneath his, and the flames seemed to spark a wildfire deep inside her soul. She never even realized when she began kissing him back, but she was suddenly leaning against him, parting her lips beneath the onslaught of his, fervently returning those sumptuous kisses which made her knees feel like butterscotch pudding and her brain reel as if she'd just fallen headfirst off a cliff.

And then a loud popping noise exploded in the clearing and Steele dropped her like a sack of coal, spun around, and in one fluid movement went for his gun.

But there was no one there. It was only a long twig falling suddenly into the fire, popping as the flames consumed it in one great orange burst.

"Hell and damnation," Steele swore. He holstered his gun, closed his eyes a moment, and then glanced back at the woman sitting shaken by the fire.

What in hell had he been thinking—worse, what in

hell had he been *doing?* Of all the women on earth, she was the last woman he could get involved with—the very last one. Not that he was involved, he told himself hastily, taking a deep steadying breath. It had just been a passing inclination, a weakness of the flesh. Instinct—a primal physical attraction to this vulnerable and damnably appealing woman—had temporarily won out over reason and good sense. That's all.

But you can't afford for that to happen, he reminded himself, and with smooth habit, assumed the old familiar mantle of cold ruthlessness again. He slipped it back on as easily as most men slipped on a pair of comfortable overalls. So that when he turned back to Annabel Brannigan, he looked every inch of who and what he was, of who and what he had made himself into during all these rugged, solitary years roaming the West.

Roy Steele, merciless gunfighter. Dangerous loner. Killer of all who crossed him or got in his way.

Annabel stared at him in horror, confusion, and dismay. Chagrin at how shamelessly she had kissed him poured through her. Her disloyalty to Brett was shameful. She felt herself choking on the humiliation of it. And there was something else. Disbelief at the transformation in him. That noise in the clearing had summoned forth the real Roy Steele. The cold-eyed man who moved with the speed and danger of a panther, who held his gun with such frightening steadiness, who sneered at the world through eyes that lacked all human warmth and pity. The man who had so frightened her in Justice and Eagle Gulch, the cruel emotionless gunman who had threatened her in Lily Pardee's boudoir and who killed men with the same dispassionate ease some men killed mosquitoes.

Oh, God. Why had she let him kiss her? Why had she kissed him back?

She was in love with Brett!

She had to say something, anything to bridge this horrid embarrassing moment. She couldn't bear him looking at her so coldly, as if she was a stone or a twig or leaf, something inanimate in his path.

"I am *shocked,* Mr. Steele!"

"That so?"

"Yes. You . . . took advantage of me by . . . by taking such liberties. How dare you."

He advanced to stand over her again. Annabel felt naked—wholly exposed beneath those relentless eyes, as if he could read the truth inside her poor flimsy soul. So she made her voice as icy and crisp as she could. "I can only assume that you forgot that I am very much in love with Brett McCallum and that we are engaged to be married."

"I reckon you forgot, too," he returned with a smile that mocked her, a smile that never reached his eyes.

Tears burned suddenly behind Annabel's eyelashes. Her shoulder ached, her head spun with confusion, she was cold, and she was ashamed. Not to mention furious. She pushed a strand of hair from her eyes and spoke with quiet vehemence.

"In the future, I demand that you keep your distance from me. My gratitude for your saving my life does not extend to granting you . . . personal favors."

"Future?" Steele gave a cool laugh. "Lady, there's no future to talk about. Tomorrow, I take you to the nearest town and leave you there. And this time you'd better stay put."

"I can't do that. I have to find Brett before you do. Because I don't know what you're going to do to him when you find him so I have to warn him, and protect him."

"Not from me you don't."

"I don't?"

Steele tugged open the saddle blanket rolled up beside his pack. He threw it down on the ground ten feet away from the bedroll where Annabel Brannigan was huddled.

"Nope, you don't. You've got my word."

"Your word."

The doubt in her tone had no effect whatsoever on his grimly set features. He continued steadily, in a voice that suggested he couldn't care less if she believed him or not. "Brett McCallum did me a good turn once and that's why I'm looking for him. I heard Cobb was gunning for him, and I aim to see that nothing happens to him."

"You're going to stop Red Cobb from killing Brett?"

"That's right, and I'm able to do a hell of a better job of it than you, so you can just hitch yourself a ride on a stage headed back East and sit there nice and pretty until Brett comes back to marry you. And that's that."

I don't think so, Mr. Steele.

"How do I know you're telling me the truth?" Annabel tried to keep her voice as cold and even as his. But it wasn't easy because her heart was still racing, and her lips were bruised from his kisses.

"You don't. But you have no choice, Miss Brannigan." He doffed his hat to her tauntingly, then tossed it down on a rock and settled his long frame onto the saddle blanket.

"We'll reach Silver Junction tomorrow and you can wait there for the next stage. Sweet dreams."

Annabel lay down, trembling. The ground was cold and hard, even with the bedroll. The air was alive with the hum of crickets and other insects, and with strange animal rustlings in the brush. An owl or a hawk swooped overhead, streaking gracefully across the scudding clouds which now obscured the moon. She felt tiny and alone up here on this godforsaken clearing, with this grim, cold-eyed man.

At least she hadn't let Roy Steele reduce her to tears. Not when he had bandaged her wound, and not when he had kissed her and made her forget . . . everything, even Brett.

She hadn't cried. That was something.

But her conscience stung worse than her injured shoulder as she shifted her legs and gazed upward at the vast midnight sky. Annabel hated disloyalty, and she hated weakness. She had been guilty of both by forgetting about her love for Brett for even an instant.

It was the situation, nothing more, she told herself. *Roy Steele saved your life. He took care of you. He took you by surprise, pretending for a little while to be a gentleman. You allowed yourself to be fooled.*

She wondered if somewhere along the way, her mother had been fooled by someone she was dealing with, someone from whom she had to get information, or follow, or decide whether to trust. *I'm a beginner,* she reminded herself. *I'm allowed to make some mistakes.*

But not this one, not again. She would keep her distance from Roy Steele from now on.

And if he thought he was getting rid of her in Silver Junction, he had another guess coming. Everett Stevenson would skin her alive if she returned without Brett—not that she would—because she could never trust Steele enough to take him at his word. No, she would stick to the gunfighter until they'd found Brett together and she'd spoken with him and convinced him to go home.

And just let Mr. Roy Steele try to stop her.

I'll never fall asleep tonight, she thought miserably, tossing uncomfortably on the bedroll. A chill rose up from the ground, seeping into her bones. Her shoulder hurt. *I won't get a single wink, and I need all my rest and*

*my wits to deal with Roy Steele. Somehow, I have to figure
out if he's telling the truth or if he really poses a danger to
Brett. I have to find a way to make him take me along with
him. I have to remember to telegraph Mr. Stevenson from
Silver Junction and tell him of my progress. Progress? Dear
Lord, what progress? I've gotten lost, I've been shot, I've
kissed a man who might well be my enemy. . . .*

Her thoughts swirled together in an uneasy tangle.
The next thing she knew, morning sun bathed the clearing in pale luminous light.

Morning? How, Annabel wondered foggily, *did it get
to be morning?*

But it was. Steele towered over her. Behind him
glowed a milky white daybreak sun, a dazzling violet sky.

"The horses are already saddled. Breakfast is ready.
If you're traveling with me, even as far as Silver Junction, you'll have to keep up," he said, glaring down at
her with all the warmth of a cobra. "Red Cobb won't let
up on his hunt for Brett, and neither can I. Get moving
or get left behind."

Annabel gritted her teeth as she struggled to sit up.
Her wound throbbed. She felt the bandage pull apart,
and knew without looking that it had started to bleed
again. But she'd be damned if she'd say a word to Roy
Steele.

"Pleasant morning to you, too," she muttered,
scowling as she tossed her tangled curls back from her
eyes. She darted a quick glance up at Steele and cursed
inwardly. The man was inhuman. He looked rested, fit,
shaved, clean, and mean as a wolf.

It was going to be a long day.

Chapter 10

They rode for hours in silence along the rocky ravines leading down into the brakes of the Mogollons. A cooling breeze fanned Annabel's sweating face as Sunrise followed Steele's big bay along the precipitous pathways which the gunfighter seemed to know so well and traverse so effortlessly. The extra horses plodded behind. The going was rough, but even a gentler trail would have been torture. Annabel's shoulder throbbed with each step of her mount. But she sat the mare with concentrated effort, refusing to make the slightest noise or complaint, biting back a gasp or wince each time the pain reverberated through her shoulder. Their pace was sedate, leaving Annabel to suspect that Steele was going slowly on her account, out of consideration for her wound and her inexperience at riding these harrowing trails, yet even so, the grueling ride took its toll on her.

But she said nothing of her anguish as the sun broke through the clouds and the day grew warmer and the hours slipped by. I'd rather die right here in the saddle than let on to Roy Steele that this is killing me—much less ask him to stop on my account, she vowed silently, but her upper lip was damp with perspiration, and her hands shook as she gripped the reins. There had been no time that morning even to pin up her hair in its usual chignon—she'd scarcely had time to smooth out the tangles before they'd broken camp—so now it curled limply around her cheeks and neck, and Annabel longed to toss off her hat, scoop up her long heavy mane, and let the air cool the overheated skin at the nape of her neck. Hot, tired, and aching, she'd have traded her two best Sunday dresses with their silk ribbons and lace (both rolled up neatly inside her carpet-bag) for the opportunity to stop and rest, but there was no way she would beg Roy Steele for one ounce of mercy. So she kept her misery to herself.

Shortly past noon Steele took a curving path leading into a forested area and they soon reached the shallow bank of a meandering stream. He followed the path of the stream, dipping through leafy pine glades and stands of spruce until at last the brook veered down a thicketed rise into a rolling, lovely oval valley.

Annabel gasped in delight. The valley was walled on two sides by rocky ledges of gray and purple mountains. Between these two walls, the splendor of broken canyons and mesas and distant prairies extended as far as the eye could see. It was a heavenly spot, wild and unspoiled. The valley was carpeted with deep grass and consisted of gently undulating meadows scattered with tiny blue and white and purple wildflowers. And, in the midst of it all, stood a log cabin, poised on a long bench of land. The cabin, not far from the stream, was enchantingly nestled amidst the sparkle of golden aspens ringed by tall pines.

Annabel gazed at it in awe, taking in the brilliance of the sun, the vivid turquoise sky, the endless luxuriant grass, the mountains, the sweep and panorama of the most spectacular scenery she'd ever envisioned cupped about the small wood cabin. Never had she seen a more wild, unspoiled, gorgeous sight.

"Let's go," Steele said beside her.

"We're stopping here?"

When he nodded, Annabel tried to conceal her relief, hoping he hadn't noticed the catch in her voice. She was so thankful she could have shouted, but she kept her elation to herself.

There was still one little problem, though, she conceded as the horses halted before the cabin. She still had to find the strength to dismount without falling down at Steele's feet.

It seemed she needn't have worried about that. Before she knew it, he had jumped from the saddle and stalked toward Sunrise. He reached up for her and lifted her down.

But to Annabel's surprise, instead of setting her down, he carried her toward the cabin door.

"What are you doing?"

"You're done in."

"I'm *what*? Who says? I'm perfectly—"

"Lady, you look like you've had about all you can take for one day. I don't need you fainting on me and injuring that shoulder anymore. It's been bleeding this past hour."

"You . . . knew?"

He kicked open the cabin door and strode across the threshold. "Hard to miss all that blood," he said drily, and glancing down, Annabel realized that the trickle of blood she had seen staining through the bandage had now begun to gush. The sleeve of her shirtwaist was soaked.

"Stay here and don't move," he said curtly, setting her down on a lumpy old horsehair sofa set against the cabin wall. "I'll get the salve and bandages."

It was not much of a cabin, only four log walls, a floor of packed earth, a stove and fireplace in the corner. But it appeared to be snugly built, with no cracks or chinks in the log walls or ceiling which would let in rain, sleet, or snow. There was a wooden bench pulled up before a rickety pine table near the south window, and a three-legged stool next to the old sofa. A kerosene lamp sat in the center of the table. No rug or curtains or pictures or knickknacks alleviated the stark barrenness of the crude little structure.

Yet the place had a safe, friendly feel to it. Annabel eased herself down on the sofa in relief, hoping they could stay and rest for at least a little while. Steele was determined to reach Silver Junction before dark, and she had no idea how much farther it was, but she would take any respite she could from the ordeal of riding with a wounded shoulder.

"Do you want to take the blouse off, or should I cut off the sleeve?" Steele's voice broke into her dazed reverie as she gave in to the pain and weariness.

She opened her eyes and stared at him. "It's ruined anyway," she whispered. "I'll take it off. But . . . don't watch."

"Suit yourself."

He busied himself riffling through his pack while she struggled out of her shirtwaist and positioned the blanket he had left with her across her breasts.

Steele glanced over at her and his eyes narrowed. Her attempts to retain all proper modesty might have amused him, except that she was so serious and painstaking about it. That suggested one thing. She was as innocent as she was lovely. He suppressed a groan. Just what he needed, an innocent beauty in tow, one who was every bit as stubborn as she was enticing. This situation was growing more complicated and less to his liking by the minute. Added to that, when he returned to her side, set on tending the wound, she looked even paler and more ill than she had before.

For a moment, fear chilled him as he wondered if

the wound was infected, but when he inspected it, it looked clean enough, and it was healing.

"So far, so good," he muttered with a scowl. "But if it gets infected you'll have real trouble. Better keep it still for a while and don't move." Steele stepped back and returned the salve and extra bandages to his pack.

"But we have to go on. I thought you wanted to reach Silver Junction by tonight."

He shrugged. "It can wait. You've had enough riding for one day. Maybe two. We'll stay put for the time being until the wound has had more time to heal."

Annabel stared at him as if she couldn't believe her ears. "But you were in such a hurry! And so am I. We must find Brett before Red Cobb does," she added firmly. "That means going on today. I thought you said you wanted to help him . . ."

"I do. But I don't reckon he'd look too kindly on my dragging in a half-dead fiancée and dropping her at his feet."

She gripped the blanket excitedly, holding it up to her shoulders. "Does this mean you're going to take me along with you all the way—until we find Brett?"

"I didn't say that."

"Yes, you did. You said—"

"I said we wait until you're well enough before we ride on to town, and then you stay put while I go find Brett."

"But I *am* well enough. Mr. Steele, we must go on —if anything happens to Brett I'll never forgive myself!"

He gave her a long look. The memory of the way she'd kissed him last night still burned in his brain. Who'd have guessed that so much sweet passion flowed beneath all that irritating stubbornness? He had to force himself to focus on the here and now. She was going to marry her beloved Brett McCallum, and that was that. What happened last night could never happen again.

"If you love your fiancée so much, you won't underestimate him," he said coolly. "From what I understand, Brett McCallum comes from some pretty tough stock. He can probably take care of himself just fine, without your help or mine."

"Under ordinary circumstances, perhaps. But Red Cobb is a dangerous man. I've heard that he . . . and you . . . are probably the deadliest guns in the territory."

"Only in the territory?" Steele scoffed. "Hell, I'm crushed, Miss Brannigan. I thought my reputation was wider than that—extending throughout all of the West."

"This is hardly a joke!"

"And neither is your wound."

He stomped outside and Annabel watched him as he began tending to the horses. He worked with an easy confident strength and great efficiency—much the way he kissed, she reflected woefully, all too aware of the electric little tingles shooting through her at the memory. She mustn't think about last night, not about one single moment of it—not about the wondrous fire that had spread through her when his mouth captured hers, not about the way she felt when he held her, or touched her hair, or pulled her so intimately against him.

It must never happen again! she warned herself, furious at the breathless longing that swept over her for just a moment as she relived those riveting moments. Then she banished the memories and the emotions with a frustrated groan. Stop it! Just stop thinking about it and those ridiculous feelings will go away.

She sank back down against the dark lumpy cushions of the sofa, but her brain couldn't seem to swerve from its forbidden path. Did he kiss his precious Lily that way, she wondered darkly, glaring unseeingly at the open sky outside the window, and digging her nails into the sofa cushions with vicious force. Did he look at her with that same searing intensity, and hold her as tightly, and . . .

No more. Annabel closed her eyes and used all of her willpower to shift her thoughts away from Roy Steele.

Rest, she told herself. *You need to regain your strength if you're going to be of any use to Brett—and to poor Mr. McCallum back in St. Louis.*

She was worried sick about both of them, and with good reason. She was still no closer to knowing what had caused Brett to run away than when she began. She was hot on his trail, true, and now she was close to getting Steele to agree to let her travel with him until they found Brett, but there were still too many unanswered questions. She was supposed to be an investigator, but so far she had learned very little of value—except that Brett had been drinking since he'd left home . . . drinking heavily, and he was headed . . . where? It suddenly dawned on her that Roy Steele had not even told her where he was riding, where he thought Brett had gone.

Well, now you have a goal for tonight, she told herself, settling her spine more comfortably against the sofa. *Tonight you must prod Steele for information, find out if he really wants to help Brett and just what he knows about Brett's whereabouts.*

She thought back to some of the stories her mother and later Aunt Gertie had told her about her mother's exploits during the war. Savannah Brannigan had used her intelligence and daring to learn valuable secrets for her Union contacts. Her beauty had been an advantage, but only because she had combined it with strategy and resourcefulness to pump her southern acquaintances for information so subtly that they never realized they were being split open and inspected like fruit about to be speared and eaten. For a moment she wondered if her mother had ever suffered qualms of conscience about deceiving and spying upon people who considered her a friend. She must have—but at the same time, Annabel mused, she must have believed with all her heart that she was acting on behalf of a higher cause, trying to help the Union, and her own husband, perhaps saving his life by shortening the war or giving the North an advantage in a battle where otherwise Ned Brannigan might be among the fallen.

And I must think of a higher cause, too—and that is saving Brett's life and helping him and Mr. McCallum, Annabel told herself as the afternoon sun slanted in amber beams through the window and warmed her face and bare shoulders. *If it means using every wile I possess on Roy Steele to ascertain if he is truly friend or foe, then I will. If it means trickery or downright lying to discover what he knows about Brett's whereabouts then I will. But if he ever catches on to me, I'll be in dire trouble.*

Then he'd best not catch on, she decided briskly, and suddenly glanced about. She was alone in the cabin, and there was no longer any sign of Roy Steele outside. *He must be watering the horses by the stream,* she reasoned, and sat up straighter. Steele's saddle pack was on the floor near the stove. All thoughts of a nap forgotten, she dropped the blanket and was off the sofa in an instant, scurrying across the floor clad only in her camisole and skirt, intent on the open saddle pack.

She knelt down and carefully, using both hands, began rummaging through it. Flinging out several shirts and bandanas, and a pouch containing dried jerky and hardtack, she dug around inside the roomy leather bag. Cartridges and ammunition, a bowie knife, some socks and woolen drawers which she shoved aside, a wooden shaving brush and razor, some soap and toiletries and . . . nothing.

Nothing. Not one personal item, photograph, letter,

piece of jewelry, or keepsake to suggest a family, children, wife, lady friend. Nothing.

She sat back, stunned. She didn't know whether to feel pity or fear. It was disconcerting to discover that Steele traveled about with nothing personal whatsoever among his possessions—nothing of the past or of the future, nothing signifying any ties ever to anyone or anything . . .

"What the hell do you think you're doing?"

Annabel jerked around. Roy Steele glared at her from the doorway of the cabin.

"I'm . . ."

"Go on."

". . . looking for the whiskey. My arm hurts and I thought a few sips would help dull the pain."

The coldness in his expression left no doubt of his disbelief. "It's there," he said, jabbing a finger downward. "Right beside you."

"Oh, is it?" Annabel feigned surprise. "I guess I overlooked it in the jumble."

"Ahuh."

"I'm . . . sorry if you minded my searching for it myself, but I didn't know exactly where you'd gone or when you'd be back."

"Well, go ahead. Take a sip. What are you waiting for?"

She opened the flask, and at that moment became aware that she was wearing only her camisole. She felt her skin growing hot. "I think I'd better dress first."

"But you're hurting. Go ahead, Miss Brannigan, drink your fill."

To her consternation, he came forward into the cabin and blocked her path as she sought to return to the sofa, where her carpetbag sat on the floor. Annabel's cheeks flamed as he allowed his glance to linger speculatively on the swell of her breasts above the lace-edged camisole. His expression was unreadable, but there was arrogance in the set of his shoulders beneath his dark blue shirt, and in the way his eyes gazed mockingly at her beneath his shock of hair.

He was deliberately seeking to humiliate her—to punish her for searching through his pack. He knew as well as she that she'd been lying—but he couldn't prove it. So Roy Steele had found his own way of getting her back.

It was working. She felt awkward and helpless as a captured sparrow beneath his intent gaze. She lifted the flask to her lips, took a quick sip, and then sidestepped him nimbly. "There, that's better. Now if you don't mind turning the other way . . ."

"And if I do?"

"Well, do as you please." She had reached the carpetbag. He had *let* her reach the carpetbag, she acknowledged. Awkwardly, she set down the flask and riffled through her belongings until she found yet another shirtwaist, this one pale yellow. But as she lifted it out of the bag, he suddenly took it from her and held it behind him.

"Not yet."

"What are you doing?"

"First, you're going to be honest with me. What were you really looking for in my pack? No lies. I can always tell when you're lying."

"You cannot." She gaped at him. "C-can you?"

A light mocking smile answered her, one that never reached his eyes. "Your lips part just a little, Miss Brannigan. Like they're doing right now." He reached up slowly and rubbed his finger along her bottom lip with a light caress. "And your eyes darken almost to jade."

Annabel went very still. His finger was still tracing the lush outline of her lower lip, rubbing back and forth with a feather-light motion that was sending goose bumps down her spine.

"Those are both dead giveaways, Miss Brannigan," he said softly. "You haven't fooled me yet."

"Oh . . . well . . . I . . ." Annabel struggled to think clearly despite the dizzying warmth surging through her. Her mouth felt on fire everywhere his finger was touching. And she couldn't seem to tear her gaze from the glinting depths of his eyes. She fought to concentrate on what he was saying, for the implications of his statement filled her with distress.

If she couldn't even lie convincingly, how would she make a decent private investigator? Surely her mother never had such a problem or she wouldn't have been able to survive throughout all the war years without getting caught.

But somehow she couldn't think clearly about this at the moment. Her limbs were melting like long, slender candles that had been tossed into a roaring hearth.

And he was still touching her mouth.

"I'll . . . have to work on . . . controlling that," she heard herself murmuring, and suddenly Steele's fingers moved to her hair and twisted a handful of her wildly cascading curls.

"Only problem is, some things just can't be controlled," he said slowly. There was an intentness in his gaze that sent waves of panic spiraling through her chest. She wanted to close her eyes and escape the intensity of his gaze, but she couldn't. She couldn't look away, couldn't move away, couldn't even think beyond the giddy sensations reeling through her.

Don't. Steele checked himself as for a fraction of a second he swayed dangerously close to the enchanting minx before him. *Don't get involved with her any more than you already are. For God's sake, she's Brett's fiancée.*

This last thought more than any other shook him to

his senses. With a shock, he realized how close he was to gathering her in his arms and kissing the adorable astonishment right off her lips. Instead, he tightened his resolve with the iron self-control that had become as natural as breathing to him over the years, and let go of her velvety hair.

"What were you looking for?" he asked, taking a step back, counting on distance to quell the fire racing through him. It didn't, so he reminded himself again who she was, and why he couldn't even think about touching her.

"I wanted to see if there was any clue where we were headed . . . where you expect to find Brett."

"Why didn't you just ask me?"

"You're not always forthcoming with answers, Mr. Steele."

He'd been trying hard not to look at the creamy enticement of her breasts swelling above that damned lace thing she was wearing. But it was getting more difficult by the moment. Silently cursing himself for not being immune to her allure, he decided he'd better act quickly or risk losing what was left of his sanity.

He thrust the shirtwaist into her hands and wheeled away. "Here. Put this thing on and then we'll talk."

Annabel felt a moment's surprise. Something in the tautness around his mouth just before he turned away, in the rigidity of that quick, rough movement, told her something she hadn't fully realized before: Roy Steele was attracted to her. He was distracted *by* her. He was not nearly as cold and remote as he would like everyone —including her—to believe.

She felt a delicious pleasure sweep through her. It was always flattering to engage a man's admiration, but to attract the interest of a man like Roy Steele gave a special glow. He was so dangerous, so outwardly unreachable. But she had reached him, touched him.

Then her brain clicked in on another thought and all her silly pleasure fled. Brett!

Annabel flushed the color of a sunset sky.

If Roy Steele were to see her blush, she realized, he would most likely think she was embarrassed by him or by her state of near undress, but it was not so. Remorse at having forgotten her love for Brett once again, however briefly, brought shame creeping up her neck and into her cheeks.

She turned quickly away and donned the shirtwaist as swiftly as she could, even enduring the added twinges in her shoulder caused by the effort of tucking it into her skirt. She must look a mess. But she felt even worse —confused, in disarray, dusty and out of sorts.

"You stay put on that sofa and get some rest," Steele told her when she had finished dressing. He headed toward the door. "The sooner your arm is better, the sooner we'll be able to ride."

He was leaving *again*? "Where are you going?" she demanded, knowing she should be glad to be separated from him, yet oddly reluctant to see him walk out of the cabin.

"I'm going to hunt for our dinner."

"I thought we were going to talk."

"Later." He scowled at her, and she suddenly was reminded of the way he had looked when he stood over the Hart brothers in Justice. It was not a reassuring thought. "Over dinner. If you've had a decent rest, and behaved yourself, like a good little girl."

Yet she was anything but a little girl, he thought grimly, unsuccessfully willing his gaze away as she settled down on the old sofa. It was warm in the cabin, even with the door and windows thrown open, and a faint sheen of sweat glistened on her fair skin. She looked a bit mussed, a bit drowsy, and very delectable, like a sweet soft peach that's been warming in the sun.

But Brett's fiancée was no overripe lump of fruit there for the picking, he reminded himself as he turned and plunged through the door. She had already proved herself to be a determined woman, one who hadn't been deterred by his sternest warnings, who had followed him into the Mogollons with intrepid purpose, and had ridden today for hours without complaint, despite her wound. She was obviously devoted to Brett and would endure anything to help him.

His mouth tightened as he went outside into the late afternoon, reveling as always in the isolated peacefulness of this valley. If Miss Branngian wanted information from him, well and good. He wanted some from her too and he was going to get it.

He checked his rifle and mounted Dickens. They moved away from the cabin, across the meadow, toward a thicketed gully not far from the stream. He shot a rabbit and presently returned to the cabin to skin and roast it.

She was asleep when he came in.

Something twisted in his gut as he looked at her. Exhaustion was stamped upon her face, but it only accentuated her sweet, fine-boned features, which were softened in repose. A brilliant cascade of thick, bright hair spilled about her shoulders, nearly reaching her waist as she lay curled. Her breathing was slow, calm, and even. He resisted the impulse to sit beside her and watch her as she slept.

Brett, you're a lucky man, he thought, wondering how it would feel just once to have someone so devoted to him that she would risk her life and all creature comforts only to find him. But that would never happen. He would never let it happen.

He turned away, centering his attention on cooking the rabbit.

He could only hope that Brett McCallum turned

out not to share much of Ross McCallum's ruthless and tyrannical nature—or else on that particular wedding day when the woman sleeping on the sofa pledged her life and her heart, he would feel more than a little sorry for the brave but unsuspecting Miss Brannigan.

It was a hot, windless day in Eagle Gulch. Red Cobb took his time over a glass of whiskey in the Hot Pepper Saloon. When Lily Pardee strolled in, he stayed put in his corner and watched her.

Cobb was a cocky twenty years old, a handsome, square-jawed young man just short of six feet tall. He had a stocky frame beneath his gray silk shirt and black trousers, and a pleasing, though somewhat arrogant smile, when he chose to bestow it. His piercing crystal blue eyes, the color of a Montana lake, were his most striking feature. He'd come by his name due in part to the curly, dark red hair and mustache that were so striking against his bronzed skin, but also because he always wore a red silk bandana knotted loosely around his neck. But in his own mind, the red stood for the blood he spilled—lots of it. More than any other pastime, Red enjoyed spilling other men's blood.

He had been a nobody, a dirt-poor farmer's son from Kansas just outside of Abilene, until he'd discovered when he was fifteen that he was prodigiously quick and sharp with his gun. He'd demonstrated this at a shooting exhibition one Fourth of July, and then, amazingly, a miracle had happened. Everyone for miles about—even the town bullies, the Abilene boys who had chased and taunted him over the years because they were bigger or stronger or richer or older—took notice and showed respect. This had made Red practice even more. He liked impressing people. He liked to hear his father brag about his prowess, and to hear people murmur in admiration of his skills. He saved his money and bought a pearl-handled Colt .45, a thing of beauty. He loved that gun and cleaned and polished it daily. He honed his skills with it.

By the time Red left Kansas a year later to make a name for himself in the West, he knew he was faster than most of the seasoned men with big names and even bigger reputations. He just had to prove it.

So he started picking fights in saloons of mining and cattle towns, killing men, building his reputation. It felt good, real good. He was finally *somebody.* Kids pointed at him in the street, women whispered behind their hands, men crossed the street to avoid him lest they draw his ire. And the saloon women swarmed to him, he found, attracted by the fact that he was young and handsome and dangerous—and fast becoming famous. They brought him free liquor and sat on his lap, and eagerly invited him into their beds.

And the offers of employment rolled in. Other men were willing to pay big money to Red Cobb, yessiree. They hired his gun for protection, sometimes, or to rid themselves of an enemy. He didn't care what they wanted him to do, so long as they had the money to pay. But one thing bothered Red Cobb as the days and months went by and it began to bother him more and more as he reached his twentieth birthday.

He still wasn't considered the best. Other names were always mentioned along with his, especially here in the Arizona territory and down New Mexico way. People still debated who was quicker, who more deadly, who more feared. It was disrespectful. In particular, the name of Roy Steele kept cropping up, and this had the power to wipe the smile from his face and make him itch to kill someone. Preferably he would like to kill Roy Steele himself, who was probably almost thirty by now and getting too old to be any damned good, but since he hadn't crossed paths with Steele but once, and that was three years ago when he was only setting out on his career and not yet ready to face the son of a bitch in a gunfight, he'd been biding his time, waiting for the right opportunity.

Now it seemed that Steele was interfering with his latest job. And Cobb sensed it was finally time. His feelings of enmity were growing deeper by the day. He'd lost Brett McCallum's trail somehow—and he felt certain it was Lily Pardee's fault. Lily had been the one to give him his last lead here in Eagle Gulch a while back, a lead which had turned out to be a dead end. And Bartholomew, nosing around before he headed back to report to Johnson, had found out that Lily was rumored to be sweet on Steele. So Cobb had retraced his steps and come back to get even with her for making a fool out of him. He'd teach her to lie to him—and he'd find out where McCallum—and presumably Steele—were really headed. For Bartholomew had also discovered, through some quick side trips to various small towns in the vicinity, that Steele was definitely looking for Brett McCallum every bit as seriously as he and Cobb were.

Cobb had no idea why, but he'd be damned if he'd let Steele kill the kid before he could goad the stupid rich boy into a fight himself. Johnson wouldn't pay him a penny if someone else killed McCallum first—and Red had worked too hard and long at tracking the damned easterner to let Roy Steele get in his way now. Besides, when he was finished with McCallum, he'd go after Steele. It was time—time to finish that son of a bitch off once and for all and let everyone know who was really the best.

"Get over here, Lily," he called out suddenly, slamming his glass down on the table so loudly that everyone froze. The card players, the cowboys at the roulette wheel, the bartender, and the other saloon women seemed glued in place, all except for Lily, who cast him a quick, cool glance and then turned away.

"I don't care for your tone, mister," she threw over her shoulder. She was making for the back corridor, slow and haughty, when he lunged out of his chair and crossed the saloon to grab her by the arm.

"You're not going anywhere," he began, but she whirled on him, and out of nowhere produced a silver-handled derringer. She pointed it at his chest.

"Back off."

Cobb started to grin. "Stupid idea, Lily. You're asking for trouble."

"No, I'm kicking it out of my place. Get moving. And don't come back."

"You lied to me," Cobb said softly, his crystal blue eyes glittering. "About Brett McCallum. Remember? I'm not going anywhere until you've told me where he is. And if you come sit down with me in the corner right now and talk and apologize real pretty, maybe I'll leave without shooting up your place so bad it won't be fit for customers till . . ."

"Go to hell."

Cobb's mouth thinned into an ugly hard line. He was breathing faster now, the red-hot anger flaring in him, because everyone was watching, everyone had heard this whore curse at him and treat him like a piece of buffalo dung. He had no choice.

He moved like lightning, and twisted the derringer from her hand before she could get off a shot. He tossed it down the length of the bar and then tightened his grip on her arm. Then, with quiet satisfaction he backhanded her, enjoying the sharp crack of his knuckles across her face.

"Let's go upstairs, Lily," he said in a low, pleasant tone, "and finish this in private. I don't reckon anyone down here has any objections . . ."

"Wrong, mister. I do. Let the lady go."

It was a kid who spoke out of nowhere. Not the bartender, or one of the old-time cowboys, or anyone else in the saloon, which was now silent as a tomb, and crackling with deadly tension, but a freckle-faced kid, a boy no more than seventeen or eighteen, who looked to be a new hand, probably at one of the ranches along the river valley.

Cobb sneered at him. "Stay out of this, boy, if you know what's good for you. This is between me and Lily . . ."

"N-no. Let her go."

Cobb saw the fear in the kid's eyes, sensed the apprehension quivering through his thin shoulder blades, and smiled. But the fool boy's misgivings obviously weren't enough to stop him from sticking his nose where it didn't belong.

Cobb itched to teach him a lesson. His eyes narrowed, and he gave a low, ugly laugh, but before he could call the kid out, Lily spoke suddenly, imploringly.

"It's all right," she gasped, holding a hand up toward the boy, waving him off, her ruby ring sparkling in the tobacco-thick air. "I'll . . . talk to him. Go back to your whiskey, cowboy, and don't worry . . . about me. Order another drink on the house and . . ."

"I'm not going to let him hurt you," the boy flung out. "My ma didn't raise me that way . . ."

"Well, maybe your ma raised you to die before your time," Cobb growled. "Because if you don't back off, kid, I'm going to splatter your brains from here to Tucson!"

"I'll back off—when you let her go!" the kid exclaimed gamely.

Cobb lost his temper and his patience all at the same time. The deathly stillness in the saloon invited him to show off. And to get this kid out of his hair once and for all.

"Suit yourself," he muttered, a fierce gleam entering his eyes. And with that he thrust Lily violently across the floor, and went for his gun.

The kid tried to draw, but he never quite got his six-shooter from its holster before Cobb's bullets pierced his chest, neck, and forehead. The young cowboy toppled over in a river of blood.

The saloon girls screamed. No one else said a word.

"It was a fair fight—he asked for it. You all saw," Cobb announced, holstering his gun without even glancing at the body. "Anyone else got a problem with my talking to Miss Lily Pardee?"

Only silence echoed back from the taut, ashen faces circling him. The only sound was a horse whickering outside in the street.

Cobb grinned. "Good. Now Miss Lily and me are going upstairs."

Her eyes glazed, Lily made no protest as he grabbed her arm and pulled her up off the floor and toward the back corridor, but at the doorway she stared back in mute sorrow at the young man sprawled on the saloon floor in his own sticky blood.

"Don't worry none about him," Cobb advised as he dragged her up the stairs. "Worry about what's going to happen to you if you're not straight with me pronto. I want to know where Brett McCallum has gone and I want to know *now*. Or else," he told her as he yanked her viciously toward her room, "you'll be envying that kid down there because he's dead and out of misery. What'll happen to you will hurt far worse."

"Steele is going to kill you, Cobb," Lily whispered as he shoved her inside and slammed the door.

"The hell he will. I'm going to kill him first—soon as I've finished off Brett McCallum," he bragged.

"Steele may have been good in his prime, but he's not as fast as I am, not anymore. His days are numbered, Lily, and so are yours, unless you tell me exactly what I want to know. So start talking."

Chapter 11

Annabel felt better after supper. When she'd taken the last bite of roasted rabbit meat and drained the final drops of delicious black coffee from her mug, she gave a little sigh of satisfaction. There was something about the cabin that inspired peacefulness. The setting was idyllic, and the little frame building made of rough-hewn mesquite logs was sturdy and snug. Glancing around, she imagined how delightfully homey the place could be with a little care and imagination—perhaps with crisp white and yellow gingham curtains, and a big colorfully woven rug on the floor. *If I lived here, I'd arrange some nice plump embroidered cushions on the sofa and perhaps set some flowers in a pretty vase on the mantel and I'd have books and china dishes, and maybe some watercolors or handsome lithographs on the wall . . .*

She wondered how Roy Steele had found this place, and who it really belonged to. But Steele didn't seem to be in the mood for any questions, so as they worked side by side cleaning up the dishes and wiping the table till it shone, she was silent, though she did steal several glances at him when she thought he wasn't looking.

He was being remarkably kind to her. Not in what he said—oh, no—he had barely spoken to her during the meal, either—but in what he did. He was helping her with the clean-up chores—something she'd never seen any man do back at the house on Maplegrove Street or at Mrs. Stoller's boardinghouse, and she knew he wanted to make sure she didn't do anything to aggravate her wound. He glanced her way now and then, and she suspected he was trying to see if her shoulder was hurting. Thankfully, it was better, and she had a feeling that by tomorrow she would be able to ride more easily.

Sunset was fast approaching as in silence Annabel set the last of the utensils in the rough cupboard near the stove, then paused to gaze in wonder at the brilliant scene beyond the window.

Silken ribbons of color—magnificent pinks and oranges and golds—twirled across the sky, but the colors were slowly changing to lavender and peach and a rich pale amber that glowed from butte to foothill to distant prairie. Shadows were deepening over the mountaintops beyond the valley as hazy purple dusk drew inexorably near.

The beauty of the scene touched her and she turned impulsively toward Steele. "You've obviously been here many times before. How did you come to know about this lovely place?"

"I built it."

"You did?" She glanced around with fresh curiosity, noting again how well made and sturdy were the walls and the roof, how smoothly carved even the pine table was. "All of it?"

He met her astonished look with a sudden grin. "Except the sofa and the stove," he drawled. He hesitated, then held his hand out to her. "Come on. I want to show you something."

She slipped her hand in his and let him lead her outside. Her fingers curled inside his warm, strong hand, feeling oddly comfortable there. But what was go-

ing on inside of her was not comfortable in the least.
Her heart had begun to drum madly in her chest. She
felt suddenly warm and flushed, and little agitated
quivers darted through her stomach and down into the
lower recesses of her belly.

But it wasn't a sick feeling, she acknowledged, as
they strolled across the thick wild grass toward a rise a
short distance away. It was a tingly, excited feeling. A
feeling she'd never experienced before, but which came
entirely from the solid pressure of Roy Steele's large,
powerful hand around hers.

Together they climbed the gentle slope of the rise,
and Annabel caught her breath at the view. Below, and
as far as the eye could see, the pretty winding brook
gleamed like polished silver. Rising up as if to guard the
picturesque charm of the valley, were gray cliff peaks,
and jutting red mesas, forbidding yet magnificent
against the glowing sunset sky. Antelope and deer
moved among the rocks, and eagles cried harshly as they
spread their wings wide and circled overhead.

To the north and west stretched the desert, but
nearer at hand gleamed the tall forms of stately oaks
and fragrant pines on the hillsides overlooking the
meadow. How entrancing was that meadow, she
thought, gasping with pleasure at the sight of it below. A
sea of dark green brightened with vivid flowers—Annabel felt she could gaze upon it forever and wish for
nothing more.

Rugged splendor and open simple beauty were
spread before her—and Roy Steele stood quietly by her
side.

"It's paradise," she breathed.

"That's why I picked it." He gave her a quick, piercing glance. "Struck me as the prettiest spot on earth."

"It is. Oh, it is." Annabel bobbed her head in agreement and stared in delight as two jackrabbits raced across the dark grass and disappeared behind an aspen.

"You live here then?" she asked after a moment, not wishing to pry but wanting to learn more about him, even though she sensed he would close down if she appeared too curious.

She actually held her breath, wondering if he would refuse to answer at all, but to her relief, he did.

"No, Miss Brannigan, actually I don't live anywhere, except on the trail. But I like knowing I have this place to come to every once in a while. It's sort of like a home, I guess, or at least the closest I'll ever come to one." Steele watched the last shimmering rays of light gild her lively face, which was so earnestly absorbed in his words. The amber rays turned her riotous mass of curls into ripples of fire. He wanted to stretch out his hand and touch the soft curls, but restrained himself, wondering at the same time why he was telling her so much. It was more than he'd ever told any other human being, but something was pushing him, driving him to share this with her—not only this place, which was so special to him, but also something of what he always kept locked inside. "At one point I actually thought of building a ranch here," he continued, amazed to hear himself speaking, "but . . . I don't think I'm meant to settle down in any one place."

"Why not?" she asked softly, and the concern in her voice tore unexpectedly at his insides. Why did this woman give a damn about him? He didn't want her to. It was wrong. It was futile. For both of them.

He straightened his shoulders and answered her with his customary nonchalance. "It's not in the cards."

"Well," Annabel said slowly, lifting one graceful hand to encompass all of the spectacular scene surrounding them, "if you were going to pick one spot to settle down, I can't think of anyplace more perfect."

He said nothing more, and Annabel suspected that whatever urge had prompted him to open up to her, even a tiny bit, had been firmly quelled.

"When I was a little girl," she ventured, edging just a little closer to him, "I used to play in the McCallum garden and at the time I thought it was the most beautiful spot on earth. All the lovely flowers, the hedges trimmed so elegantly, the lawn so perfect, like emerald green velvet." She laughed. "I used to pretend I was a princess and I'd sit on the carved stone bench and survey my kingdom—the statues and the flowers and all the frogs and fish in the pond were my subjects."

"You played at the McCallum house when you were a little girl?" His gaze was suddenly sharp on her face. "Were you a neighbor?"

She shook her head, smiling. "My aunt was the cook. I lived there with her—we shared a most cozy little room in the servants' wing."

"Gertie was your aunt?"

"How do you know Gertie?" Annabel stared at him. To her astonishment, Roy Steele, cool and collected gunslinger, flushed like a schoolboy caught putting a toad in the teacher's desk.

"Brett mentioned her, I reckon," he murmured and kicked at a pebble with his boot.

"That's rather strange. She passed away several years ago—why would Brett bring up her name to a total stranger?"

"He was telling me a story about some dinner party or another when he was a kid . . . look, this isn't important," Steele told her roughly. "Saving Brett from Red Cobb is."

Annabel nodded, but continued to ponder him curiously, sensing his sudden tension as he deliberately changed the subject. If she didn't know better, she'd think Roy Steele was hiding something. But what?

Nothing irked at Annabel more than unanswered questions. Ever since she was a child, puzzles and mysteries had fascinated her, and she couldn't rest until she had solved them, even if it drove Aunt Gertie and Brett crazy. But Roy Steele was the biggest mystery she had ever encountered. One moment he might kiss her, displaying a fierce tenderness no one would ever suspect, but the next he'd shut her out of his thoughts and plans completely.

She seated herself on a hump-shaped boulder and thought over his explanation while Steele busied himself rolling and lighting a cigarette. All the while she watched him like a hawk. "How long ago did you see Brett and how long ago did he do this favor for you?" she asked. "Was it recently, after he ran away from home, or have you known him a long time? And what was the favor? Why are you in his debt?"

"You ask a lot of questions, Miss Brannigan," he commented dryly. "If I didn't know better I'd think you were a Pinkerton detective."

Annabel nearly slid off the boulder, but braced her hands on the rock just in time.

"They're innocent enough questions," she retorted, her eyes sparkling with defiance. "And as Brett's fiancée, it's my right . . ."

"Yeah, yeah, I reckon it is. But I don't much like 'em." His expression was grim in the advancing darkness. Those words—*Brett's fiancée*—summoned up an irritation he couldn't explain. Or control. "Can't you just once keep quiet and stop pestering me? Damnation, I never met a more tiresome woman."

Stung, Annabel gave a strangled cry.

"Tiresome?" she squeaked, jumping off the boulder in fury. "Mr. Roy Steele, let me tell you about tiresome!" She plucked the cigarette from between his lips, enraged by the nonchalant way he was smoking it and regarding her from beneath the brim of his hat. She threw the cigarette down on the ground and stomped it with her foot. Only with great effort did she manage to restrain herself from snatching the hat off his head and tossing it down the slope. "I've dealt with some pretty high-handed, arrogant men in my life," she stormed, "but you are the worst. Worse even than Mr. Ross McCallum—and that's saying quite a bit," she added scathingly. She stomped the cigarette one more time, feeling triumphantly satisfied as his eyes narrowed.

Anger made Annabel's gray-green eyes glitter like fairy lights in the gathering darkness. Steele was glaring at her in astounded silence, as if he'd never seen a woman lose her temper before. This goaded her even more. "You promised to talk to me and give me some straight answers tonight, but as always you're weaseling out of it! Well, I won't let you. Are you just a liar, Mr. Steele? A liar and a killer? Maybe you just want to catch up with Brett to kill him after all—maybe you're hoping I'll lead you straight to him so that you can do your dirty little killing. But I won't. Damn you to hell, I won't!"

Steele grasped her wrist as her voice rose higher and higher.

"I won't let you hurt him!" she cried, trying to break free and failing. "And I won't stop badgering you until you tell me where we're headed! Maybe you're used to women who keep their mouths closed and don't argue or think or even *talk*. But I'll do whatever I have to do to protect the people I love, and if you think I'm going to fall for your plan to track and kill Brett . . ."

"That's enough." His face was like granite, as cold as the cliff faces towering over the valley. His fingers bit into her wrist. "If I were a killer, I reckon I would've left you to fend for yourself with those gentleman back there on the rim," he said in a low, hard tone. "But I didn't, Miss Brannigan. I didn't. I came back and saved your hide. Or did you forget?"

His quiet, deadly voice pierced the fury that had consumed her. She felt sanity rushing back. No, she hadn't forgotten. Well, maybe she had—just for a moment. But the truth was, she owed him her life.

His eyes gleamed fiercely into hers, and beneath that harsh gaze, her wild rage faded to burning mortification. Annabel drew a deep, ragged breath. *Get control of yourself,* she thought desperately. She struggled to calm her roiling emotions. *That ridiculous outburst wasn't very professional,* she told herself, forcing back tears. And losing her temper wasn't going to get her anywhere. But oh, he had called her tiresome. The word had cut her to the quick. Obviously, Roy Steele didn't feel an attraction for her after all—she had been totally wrong about that. He detested her.

She fought back the urge to weep. *Don't you dare,* she admonished herself, and stiffened her back, though her lips quivered.

"I'm sorry," she managed, her voice only a little shaky. To her horror, tears still burned behind her eyelids, and frantically, she blinked them back, hoping he hadn't noticed in the encroaching darkness. "I haven't forgotten what you did. You saved me from those horrid men. Which makes me believe in you—at least, I *want* to believe in you." Her tone gathered strength. And a kind of hushed softness. She lifted bright, wistful eyes to his face, suddenly yearning with all her heart to understand more about this contradictory and unfathomable man.

"Everything I've seen about you since then, the way you've taken care of me, your consideration . . . even your appreciation of this beautiful spot, convinces me that you're not at all like the man you would like everyone to think you are. I think you're a good man, an honorable man." She rushed on imploringly as his mouth tightened into a scowl. "I don't know why you want people to think you're some kind of a monster and to be terrified of you, but . . . I'm not."

With that, a laugh trembled from her lips. "I guess if I was, I wouldn't have stomped on your cigarette. That could have been mighty dangerous."

"It still might be."

"No, I don't think so." She grinned saucily at him. The tension and the storm were over. "You don't frighten me, Mr. Steele," she informed him, "so you'd best give in and answer all my questions. Because I am very persistent, and yes, I can be very tiresome, and if you want any peace at all . . ."

She let her voice trail off deliberately, and studied his reaction. To her amusement, Roy Steele gritted his teeth and looked like he wanted to strangle her. But instead he let go of her wrist and shook his head in defeat.

"You win," he groaned. "I'll talk. Just stop *pestering* me. What do you want to know?"

With the setting of the sun, the air had cooled rapidly, and now rippled down in breezy waves from the mountains, wafting through the fluttering leaves. But despite the chill, Annabel basked in the warmth of victory.

She took Steele's hand and led him to the boulder, taking a seat beside him as an owl hooted from one of the trees. "To begin with, when and how did you meet Brett?"

Never before had he met such a doggedly tenacious woman, Steele reflected as her skirts brushed against his trousers and the sweet fragrance of her hair floated through the night. Or a more fascinating one. He controlled the impulse to seize her slender form in his arms and make her forget all about Brett McCallum once and for all.

Honor, he thought bitterly, that quality she so firmly believed he possessed, forbade it. He felt sweat break out across his back as he tried to ignore the flowery scent and delicacy of her. *Concentrate,* Steele told himself desperately. *Concentrate on telling her what she wants to know and then you can get the hell away from her.*

"I met Brett a few weeks back," he said, shifting slightly to put more space between them. Anything to diminish temptation. "You know the Hart brothers, the ones I shot back in Justice?"

She nodded, intensely aware of his hard, rugged form only a hand's breadth away, of his eyes glinting in the milky light of the moon. "Yes," she murmured. "How could I forget?"

"Apparently they had planned to ambush me near the New Mexico border. Your Brett heard them talking about it while he was playing cards in a saloon one night, and a day or two later, he and I happened to cross paths." He took a deep breath. It didn't feel right lying to her, but he wasn't ready to tell her the truth. Not yet.

"He was a decent kid," Steele went on, warming to his story. "He beat me and a few other hombres at poker—and after the game, he took me aside and told me what he'd heard."

Annabel's hands moved to her throat as Steele paused. "Go on," she whispered.

"I thanked him for the tip and bought him a drink. The next day he went his way and I went mine. The ambush wouldn't have worked anyhow, because I had business in the opposite direction from where the Harts thought I was headed, but I appreciated the warning."

"It's just like Brett. He's such a fine person . . . but . . ." She hesitated before asking the question. *Go on. You need to know.* "Was he drinking a great deal?" Desperately, Annabel searched Steele's face. "Did he seem drunk?"

"Why?"

She told him what Polly had said. Steele frowned. "Didn't seem to be," he muttered rather hurriedly, and suddenly stood up and wheeled away from her, pacing across the crest of the rise. "I don't like the sound of this."

"Neither do I. Brett was never the type to drink much liquor—I've never, ever seen him inebriated. It made me think that something must be very wrong. . . . Did he mention anything about his father . . . about trouble at home? You see, I must find out why he ran away."

"Funny you should ask a question like that." Steele spun back toward her and Annabel was startled by the raw savagery in his face. "You say you grew up at the McCallum house, so you must know what kind of a man Ross McCallum is."

"Well, yes . . ."

"Then it only stands to reason why the boy left— any grown man with half an ounce of self-respect would hightail it out from under that old bastard's shadow first chance he got."

Annabel shook her head, dazed by his vehemence. "You sound like you hate Ross McCallum. How do you know so much about him?"

"I read the newspapers. Everyone in these United States knows about the great Ross McCallum's wheelings and dealings."

"So Brett didn't actually tell you it was because of his father?" she asked quickly.

He started to answer, then suddenly shook his head and clamped his lips together. "No, Brett didn't tell me that. And unlike you, I don't need to know his reasons.

But I owe him a favor. And since word has spread throughout the territory that Red Cobb is gunning for him, it seems the only way I can repay him is to find him before Cobb does and give him a hand. I'd take you along for the ride," he added, stepping closer, "but where I'm headed isn't safe for a woman."

"Where exactly are you headed?"

"First Silver Junction—you'll stay there. Then, maybe New Mexico."

"Don't underestimate me, Mr. Steele," she shot back, rising to confront him. "I have no intention of giving up what I've set out to do. Brett means much more to me than he does to you, and nothing is going to stop me from finding him."

"Are you just plain mule-headed—or are you loco? Or do you really love him that much?"

Annabel flinched at the hardness of his tone. Deep blue darkness shrouded the entire valley and all the buttes and mountains. It was a peaceful darkness, but as she stared into Roy Steele's eyes, she felt anything but peaceful. There was a strange lump in her throat. Steele had spoken those words as if he didn't believe in love, had never known it, couldn't imagine it. As if love was something that didn't exist in the world he knew, a world of guns and blood and death.

For a moment she tried to picture Brett's face and couldn't. Dismay ripped through her. She closed her eyes for an instant, and thought hard, and then there he was—the image of the young boy she'd known so well flashing reassuringly into her mind: dark-haired, long-limbed, with that wiry build and quick, buoyant smile that could charm bark off a tree.

She'd loved Brett all her life. Adored him, admired him, delighted in her time with him. She wanted nothing more than to win his heart and spend the rest of her life with him.

"Yes," she whispered, opening her eyes. "I love him that much."

Roy Steele's whole body tightened. She couldn't decipher the expression that flickered over his face for a moment, but when it had passed, his features were as stony and arrogantly set as they had been that day she'd first encountered him in Justice in the hotel. It sent a shiver through her.

"Time we went back," he said curtly, and turned toward the cabin.

"Does this mean you'll let me come along with you?" Moving cautiously through the darkness alongside him, Annabel was relieved when Steele took her good arm in his and guided her down the slope. But his touch was not warm and intimate; his fingers felt like bands of iron.

"What if I don't?" he asked, his words sharp, slicing like a razor through the night.

"Then I'll have to follow you."

They reached the cabin door. He turned and gazed down into her face, illuminated by cold white moonlight which flowed like mist over her delicate features.

"I'll be damned if you wouldn't," he swore softly. "You'd follow me to hell and back, I reckon."

"I reckon." She lifted her chin, a slight, stubborn gesture, but at the same time she unconsciously softened it with a smile.

Steele felt his insides twist up like a rope full of knots. "Then I reckon I've no choice," he managed to growl, hoping he sounded properly gruff.

He did. Annabel noted his displeasure with a twinge of unexplainable disappointment. So he was truly disgusted by the notion that he'd be stuck with her a while longer. For some reason, this realization filled her with gloom. *Why should it matter? Only Brett is important,* she reminded herself. Yet she couldn't shake her lowered spirits even when the kerosene lantern was glowing co-zily in the cabin, or when Steele had built a roaring fire against the night chill.

A strange mood had come upon Annabel. She was intensely aware of Roy Steele, of his every move, his strength, his size, his competency at all the little acts of survival out here in the wilderness.

He's a fascinating man, and a good man, but he's not the man for you, she told herself. Brett is—he is your destiny.

What she felt for Steele, Annabel decided, as she unfolded and arranged the blanket on the sofa, was gratitude, pure and simple. He had saved her from Willy and Curtis and Moss.

She owed him, just as he felt he owed Brett.

I must take care to remember that.

Moments later, when Steele was settled on his bed-roll on the floor, and she was snuggled beneath the blanket on the sofa, Annabel struggled to a sitting position and stared at him through the flickering light.

"Thank you, Mr. Steele," she said softly. Her low-pitched voice was filled with quiet earnestness. "I appreciate your being honest with me. I promise that I won't doubt you again."

"Good."

"You've saved my life, and I believe with all my heart that you intend to save Brett's."

"Right."

"In the morning, when we're both refreshed, we'll discuss our strategy."

"Strategy?"

"Yes. Our plan. We must talk things over, figure out how we're going to find Brett, how we'll deal with Red Cobb, how—"

"Damn it, woman!" Exasperation exploded in his

voice. "You like to talk things over more than any female I've ever met."

Annabel nodded. "That's what Mr. Clyde Perkins, Mr. Joseph Reed, and Mr. Hugh Connely used to say, too."

"Who were they?"

"Some gentlemen who wanted to marry me."

She thought she heard a choking sound.

"Mr. Steele?"

"What happened to these gentleman?"

"I turned them down. I talked it over with them and explained why I couldn't marry them. They were most diasppointed," she couldn't resist adding. "But I had no choice."

"Because you loved Brett."

"Exactly."

"And now the two of you are getting married. Touching."

Well, not exactly—at least, not yet, Mr. Steele, Annabel thought sadly, but she said nothing, and only winced at the icy sarcasm in his words.

"How mighty lucky for Brett," he continued darkly —*ungallantly,* Annabel felt. It was impossible to mistake his meaning.

She wondered uneasily what he would do if he knew that she only *wished* she were marrying Brett, that in truth she had been hired to find him. Dear heavens, it wouldn't be very pleasant facing him when he found out that she hadn't been perfectly honest with him. *It'll be much better if he doesn't discover the truth for as long as possible,* she concluded with a grimace.

"Good night, Miss Brannigan."

There was a short silence. The aspens rustled outside the window and from someplace nearby a coyote howled. Another answered and then another—the night came alive with mournful wails.

"Do you think," Annabel whispered slowly in the firelit darkness, "that since we're going to be traveling together, you might call me Annabel? And I could call you Roy?"

"No," Steele answered shortly. He sounded as wide awake as she. "I don't."

Well, that put an end to that. *Fine, Mr. Steele,* Annabel thought grimly. *You just be that way. I couldn't care less if you wish to be friendly or not—the only thing I need to do is find Brett. And find a telegraph office, if there is one within a hundred miles,* she reflected guiltily. Mr. Stevenson would be livid if she didn't maintain some regular contact with him. And she wanted to receive a message back, as well. She was worried about Ross McCallum—both his health and his business empire. She couldn't help wondering how much time she had left.

Yet it was difficult to concentrate on all the problems besieging her, on all the pieces of this puzzle to be assembled and worked out. Her gaze kept shifting to the bedroll on the floor, where Roy Steele's tall, muscular frame was stretched out, his holster beside him, his hat over his face.

She wondered what it would feel like to steal off the sofa, creep quietly over toward him, and lift that hat. To kiss his lean hard cheek while he slept. And touch his mouth, as he had touched hers.

What a peculiar notion. Annabel caught herself with a start. Why would she want to do something like that?

Because I feel sorry for him, she told herself, and nodded in the darkness. Roy Steele might be the toughest, most cold-eyed, and confident gunman she'd ever imagined, but he was also the loneliest. She couldn't explain how, but she sensed the deep isolation beneath that harsh exterior, knew it was there and that it ran deep, bleeding all the way into his soul. She wasn't sure how she knew, she just did. And her heart ached for him.

She shifted slightly on the sofa, taking care not to put pressure on her wound. It did no good fussing over Roy Steele, she told herself sharply as the wind rattled at the cabin windows. He wasn't her problem. Brett was —and so was Mr. McCallum. Roy Steele, more than anyone she'd ever known, could fend for himself.

Yet sleep eluded her until a brisk rain began to fall. The plunk plunk of the raindrops on the cabin's roof had a soothing effect—she knew somehow that the roof wouldn't leak and the chill wind wouldn't seep through any wall cracks because Roy Steele had built this cabin and she figured that anything he put his hand to was going to be as efficient as he was. A feeling of calmness overtook her. She drew the rough blanket up to her cheek and felt her eyes drifting shut. She was safe here, safe with Roy Steele in this snug little cabin, hidden away in the most exquisite valley on earth. For tonight, she didn't have to worry, she didn't have to think, or plan . . .

All she had to do was sleep.

She woke in the morning to a cool cloudy day, with drizzle still dripping from a washed-out sky, and the cabin strangely silent. She glanced over at Roy Steele's bedroll, and blinked.

He was gone. So were his bedroll and his pack. And his hat.

All gone.

Chapter 12

"Coming here is dangerous," Charles Derrickson whispered in urgent protest as he glanced nervously around the foyer of the McCallum house and then peered out at Lucas Johnson waiting on the porch. "Sir, it's a foolish, wholly unnecessary risk! Why you insisted on meeting here in this house at this hour I will never under—"

"Get out of my way, Derrickson." Johnson strolled past him placidly, smiling beneath his elegant beaver hat. Behind him, murky moonlight glowed in an inky sky, revealing the carriage that waited at the curb. Derrickson saw Johnson's efficient right-hand man, Bartholomew, seated inside that carriage, staring out the window.

"I don't like to be kept waiting," Johnson murmured coolly, as he entered the black and white marble tiled hall, gently clasping his cane. "And we have important business to conduct."

"Yes, sir. I know. But if I'm caught letting you in . . ."

"Stop your chattering. I'm not the least bit interested in your fears."

"Y-yes, sir." Derrickson clamped his mouth shut,

but his hands were trembling. He was terrified that at any moment the butler or one of the maids or the cook would appear, roused from their beds by some sixth sense that an intruder had entered the house, but all was silent as a tomb as the hall clock ticked away, revealing the hour to be nearly one o'clock in the morning. Still he cast nervous glances all about as Johnson strode through the splendid gloom of the hallway as though he owned this magnificent house himself and continued past the ornately carved hall table and huge gold-framed mirror to the carved double doors of Ross McCallum's study.

He sailed in, took a swift perusal of the dim, handsome room lit at this hour only by a single lamp, and glanced at Derrickson with satisfaction.

"It is time," he said calmly, as Derrickson rushed to close the doors, "to begin phase two. Do you have the signatures?"

Derrickson bobbed his head. "Yes. It was actually quite easy to get them, thanks to that drug you provided. I put it in his brandy, sir, just as you instructed." His tone was low and anxious, and he kept his hands clasped together in hopes that Johnson would not see their trembling. He sensed instinctively that the man before him both loathed and savored other men's weaknesses and would prey upon them like a carrion bird if given the chance. "It's made him weak and ill, just as you said. He paid no attention when I thrust the papers before him and told him it was merely some routine contracts he was signing. Never even glanced at them."

"Excellent." Johnson's eyes gleamed so maliciously in the amber lamplight that they infused his countenance with a satanic aspect. He pivoted to study the painting of Livinia McCallum that hung like a beautiful ghostly vision upon the wall. As he did so, a strange, eerily excited expression crossed his face, an expression so diabolical it made Derrickson want to cringe and hide. It was only under the direst willpower that he managed to stay rooted to the spot, watching the dashing, elegantly clad Johnson study Livinia's portrait as though no other object existed in the room.

"Thus we can proceed," Johnson said softly. "When the time is right, Bartholomew will have the papers delivered to Herbert Ervin. But now tell me all that has been going on. The private investigator—"

"Is a woman!" Derrickson broke in suddenly, reminded of the urgency of his news.

This at least diverted Johnson's attention from the portrait and he swung his shrewd gaze to the other man's sweat-sheened face. "Really? How do you know?"

"Stevenson came this afternoon to give McCallum a report. I eavesdropped outside the door—not much was new, but I did hear Stevenson say that he was sure "she" would be filing a report soon. I would have expected McCallum to have roared about a woman performing a man's job, but he was apparently too ill from the drug. He took to his bed, and Stevenson left. I showed him out myself."

Lucas Johnson paced to the desk, surveyed it briefly, then settled himself in the deep leather armchair behind it. "A woman," he mused. His eyes lit with amusement. "So much the better. She'll cause us no trouble. I'll have Bartholomew send a telegraph message as soon as I hear from Cobb once more, alerting him to be on the watch for a female investigator. Although such caution may not even be necessary, for surely by now Cobb is closing in upon young Master Brett and finishing the job."

Derrickson shivered at the cold taunting quality in Lucas Johnson's voice. More than once, he had wondered what this brilliant and wealthy man had against the McCallums—why he was exerting every resource to visit such punishment upon them, but he had never had the courage to ask. And he didn't now. He was being well paid for his role in the plot, and it was much better not to know too much. He sensed, though, that the evil obsession driving Lucas Johnson was growing more pervasive by the day. Entering the house had seemed to transform the man, unleashing an even more fervent bloodlust than Derrickson had glimpsed before. The flesh on the back of his pallid neck crawled as Johnson sneered up at the molded ceiling, his flushed face taking on a cruelly mocking aspect.

"So the mighty Ross McCallum sleeps, ill and confused, above us." He chuckled in a low tone. "What would he say or do if he knew that I was here in his house right now, feasting my eyes upon the portrait of his dead wife, sitting in his chair, plotting the demise of his son and of all he holds dear?"

Silence fell but for the ticking of the bronze clock upon the mantle. Derrickson shifted from one foot to the other, wishing he had never become involved in any of this. *But the money,* he reminded himself as he waited nervously for Johnson to decide to leave. *You will be a wealthy man.*

That settled his stomach a bit, enough to allow him to smile as Lucas Johnson at last rose reluctantly from the green leather chair and made his way toward the door.

"You'd best ease off on the drug a bit," Johnson warned as he paused before stepping out once more into the thick-misted night. "Otherwise McCallum will be dead before I have the satisfaction of killing him in my own special way and time. And that, my dear Charles, would make me incalculably angry."

Derrickson gulped and nodded, his head bobbing like a puppet's. "Yes, sir. I won't give him another drop. I'll do my best to see to it that he stays well until—"

"See that you do. And remember he mustn't know anything about the Ruby Palace or anything else, not a hint, not a suspicion. He must walk into my trap of his own volition and without any warning of what is to come."

"Certainly, sir. Of course. I perfectly understand."

Johnson descended the steps with a jaunty twirl of his cane, and a moment later vanished inside his carriage. When the vehicle had rounded the corner, Derrickson closed the door of the mansion and leaned against it, shuddering in the dimly lit hall.

It would all be over soon.

But not soon enough to suit his tastes. The money was splendid, but he wasn't equipped for this association with men like Johnson, Bartholomew, and Cobb. They thrived on violence, while he loathed it.

It repelled his every sensibility.

But not enough to make him wish to warn Ross McCallum or to end his own involvement in the matter. No, that would be tantamount to suicide, for then Johnson would come after *him*. No, no, no. And, he reassured himself as he headed up the wide staircase toward the room he had taken in the east wing of the house— the better to assist Ross McCallum during this stressful period—the tidy fortune Lucas Johnson would ultimately pay him would eventually assuage all of his guilt and his misgivings.

He smiled, thinking of luxurious travels throughout Europe, of countesses and duchesses sending him invitation cards for elegant balls, of beauteous young women fawning over him and flirting as he had seen them do time after time with Brett McCallum.

Ah yes, Derrickson decided as he reached the head of the stairs. His conscience would certainly be eased. Riches beyond measure would provide a certain cure.

Chapter 13

Fear flashed through Annabel as she stared in disbelief at the empty spot where Steele had been sleeping. Dear Lord, how could this be? She jumped up from the sofa, her heart in her throat, and ran to the door, smothering the cry of panic that sprang to her lips.

"Steele!" she shouted into the damp summer morning, but almost before she had the word out, she felt herself grabbed and yanked hard against the wall of the cabin. A strong hand clamped over her mouth.

"Not a word," a man's rough, deep voice growled in her ear. "Not one damned word."

But she recognized that voice—it belonged to Roy Steele. He held her so tightly she couldn't move, couldn't even turn her head to look at him, but then after a moment, when he knew she would no longer scream, he released her and dragged her back inside the cabin.

"Five men on the ridge just south of Buffalo Canyon," he told her in a curt tone. "I think they're an outlaw band, heading here to hide out. Or else they're just passing through. Either way, we don't want to meet up with them if we don't have to."

He was already sweeping the cabin with his eyes,

checking everything as his gaze darted about. "Get your gear together. We're leaving pronto."

She sensed the tension in him, though his manner and words were calm. In fact, he sounded so cool, so matter-of-fact, that they might have been discussing the kinds of flowers growing on the hillside, only they weren't.

Annabel stuffed everything back into her carpetbag and hurried with him toward the door, noting how he had in a few quick movements erased all evidence of their presence in the cabin.

"Doesn't it bother you, thinking of other people coming in here, making a mess of the place, staying as if it belonged to them?" she couldn't help asking as he took her arm and escorted her out into the drizzle.

"I've got no ties to anyplace or anyone or anything," he shot back coldly. "If someone wants to hole up here, I don't give a damn. Now let's go."

The horses were already saddled and packed. "You're riding with me," Steele told her. "It'll be quicker and quieter that way."

He hoisted her up into the saddle and then vaulted up behind her as Annabel smoothed out her skirts. They were off before she had time to even give one last fleeting glance back at the cabin.

Somehow, she didn't think he was being entirely truthful with her about his indifference at having strangers invade the cabin. Or maybe he wasn't being truthful with himself. For some reason Roy Steele didn't want to stake a claim to anything, even a place he had built with his own two hands and which he clearly loved.

They rode only a short distance before he halted Dickens beneath a bluff. The drizzle had ended, but the day was gray and damp. Steele left her there with the horses and an extra rifle, explaining that he would circle back to the cabin and erase their tracks. Before Annabel could so much as nod agreement, he had disappeared back the way they had come.

She dismounted and waited, fighting the anxiety within her by performing a swift toilette, brushing her hair and pinning it up as best she could, watching for Steele uneasily each time a twig snapped or one of the horses whickered. It seemed like hours before she saw his tall, black-clad figure come into view, approaching her with the quietly graceful, purposeful stride that characterized him.

"They're definitely making for the cabin." Without further preamble, he lifted her up into the saddle once more. "They must know these brakes pretty well to have found it. Or else they've been here before."

"It's lucky you happened to see them coming."

He threw her an amused look. "Luck had nothing to do with it, Miss Brannigan. It's common sense to scout things out when you're in these parts. Particularly when—"

He broke off.

"Particularly when what?"

"When you're escorting a beautiful woman." His tone held no emotion as he mounted behind her.

"Oh. Oh, I . . . see." So he thought she was beautiful? That certainly beat being tiresome, she reflected happily. Annabel tried to stifle the joyful butterflies swooping up into her chest, but they fluttered unfettered in riotous circles of delight. She wanted to thank him for the compliment, but decided it would sound stupid, so instead she kept quiet and concentrated all her energy on containing the smile that threatened to burst across her lips.

You're being ridiculous, she told herself as they continued to ride in silence. Vainly, she struggled to rein in her runaway feelings. Why should Roy Steele's opinion of her looks affect her so much, she wondered. Men had told her she was beautiful before. Clyde Perkins and Joseph Reed and Hugh Connely had each whispered it in her ear on more than one occasion, but they'd always been angling for a kiss or trying to get her to agree to skate or picnic with them when they'd said it. Roy Steele had no such motive. He'd just been speaking plainly, being practical and grim in his usual manner, not trying to compliment her or impress her or woo her. He'd just said what he obviously felt.

The glow inside her deepened. And the knowledge of his protective concern for her made her feel both grateful and fortunate. Because of Roy Steele she was probably going to succeed in her mission for Mr. Stevenson and in her own goal of finding Brett and helping him. If not for his protection and his knowledge of this untamed territory, she might well have died or met an even worse fate here in the Mogollons.

Brett, why did you have to travel to such difficult places? Why couldn't you have run away to New Orleans . . . or Chicago . . . or Philadelphia?

And suddenly it hit her. She *knew*.

"Oh, my God. I know what Brett is doing," she exclaimed.

They'd been traveling quickly, with Steele guidng the bay up and down half a dozen intricate ravines, across damp grassy banks, and then dipping down to a foothill path strewn with rocks and flowers.

"Go on," the tall gunslinger said in her ear. His arms around her felt very strong, very safe, and despite the precipitous pathways they were following she felt no anxiety, for she knew he would never let her fall.

"Brett is searching for his brother!" she exclaimed. "That's why he came west! He wants to find Cade!"

One of the pack horses stumbled over a loose stone behind them, and they both glanced back for a moment. When the horse plodded on, Steele turned Dickens onto a flat ledge that widened toward a copse of trees ahead.

"Who's Cade?" he asked matter-of-factly.

"His brother. His older brother. Cade McCallum ran away from home when Brett was ten," Annabel explained. "When I first came to live at the McCallum house Brett used to talk about him all the time. He missed him terribly and could never understand why he left." Her tone grew more musing as she looked back all those years, searching her memories for the times when Brett had first confided in her. "It seems that Ross McCallum and his older son fought a lot. Brett said they were both short-tempered, strong-willed stubborn mules. I gathered they were too much alike ever to agree on anything," she said soberly. "But that's not the point." She rushed on, excitement building inside her as everything started to fall into place. "Brett worshipped his brother. He never forgot about him. My guess is that Brett had some sort of a particularly upsetting disagreement with his father and suddenly decided to run off looking for Cade."

"Why would he think his brother was out West?"

"Because Cade told Brett that was where he was heading the night he ran off. But that was thirteen years ago. As far as I know, neither Brett nor Ross McCallum have heard a word from him ever since."

Annabel studied the thick trees overhanging the trail, blotting out the cloudy, slate gray sky. "You're sure that when you saw him, Brett didn't mention anything to you about where he was headed?" she asked anxiously.

"No."

"So why are we going to Silver Junction? Is that where you think Brett went after leaving Eagle Gulch?"

His arms tightened around her as he shifted in the saddle behind her and Annabel was all too aware of the granite strength of his body, of the hard muscles bulging in his forearms, chest, and thighs. She closed her eyes a moment, trying to keep her mind on Brett, on the mystery under discussion, and not on the distracting sensual pressure of his rock-hard thighs against the slender curve of her own body.

"The gunsmith in Eagle Gulch gave me some useful information."

"The gunsmith?" Dread chilled her, slinking like a spider up her spine. "What . . . was Brett doing at the gunsmith's?"

"Buying weapons. Lots of 'em. And there's something else," he said. Something in his tone told Annabel this was not pleasant news. She braced herself for whatever was coming next.

"There was a woman with him."

Annabel gripped the folds of her skirt in suddenly rigid fingers.

"A . . . woman?" she croaked.

"That's right."

A woman. Annabel forced herself to speak calmly, despite the churning turmoil inside of her. "Who was she? What was she doing with him?"

Steele shrugged. "Can't say. The gunsmith seemed to think she'd come in over the border from New Mexico—from a little town called Skull Creek."

"And that's why you think Brett may have gone to New Mexico—with *her*?"

"Maybe. But the gunsmith seemed to think they were headed for Silver Junction, so I can't be sure. Maybe we can catch them before they slip over the border. No one I talked to back in Justice had mentioned anything about a woman, so chances are they met up in Eagle Gulch. Could be Brett went back to New Mexico with her, or he took her to Silver Junction, or maybe they said adios and went their separate ways the moment they walked out of the gunsmith's shop—but right now the woman is my only lead. I'll start in Silver Junction and ask some questions. What about you?"

"I'll be right beside you."

"Your arm?"

"My arm is fine today, just fine." *But not my heart.*

She could feel his gaze on her face, studying her profile, and she deliberately turned her head so that she met his eyes. She wouldn't have Roy Steele feeling sorry for her. That would be the worst humiliation of all.

"I'm sure Brett has a very good reason why he is with that other woman," she told him evenly. "I am *not* a jealous female. So don't think you've upset me by telling me this at all—if Brett has made a friend, I'm glad for him. I hate to think of him being all alone."

"There's worse things. I tend to like it."

"Do you? Really?" She twisted in the saddle to better gaze into his eyes and searched his expression for some emotion behind the rugged nonchalance. For an instant she thought she saw a flicker of something in his eyes, but then it was gone, and Annabel wondered if she had only imagined it.

"You ask too many questions, Miss Brannigan," he said roughly. His mouth curled derisively and there was a distinct edge to his voice. "Turn around and stop distracting me. We need to make tracks. I want to put as many miles between us and those hombres back there at the cabin as possible. And I intend to reach Silver Junction by midafternoon."

"Is Skull Creek far beyond that?"

"Two days ride."

"Then maybe we should push on—we can cover more ground tonight if we don't stay in Silver Junction. We can ask our questions and keep going until dark . . ."

"Whoa, lady." He draped an arm about her waist, holding her snugly. "I'm in charge of this expedition, remember? So just take it easy. You need to rest and I need to buy supplies. We'll spend the night in Silver Junction, and depending on what we learn there, we can head straight into New Mexico tomorrow. One more day won't make much difference."

It might. It just might, Annabel thought uneasily, but she remained perfectly still in the saddle and gazed out at the muddy sky once more, burrowing deep into her own thoughts. Could this woman be important to Brett? Could he care for her?

No! He had never fallen in love with any of the exquisite society creatures his father had thrown him together with all these years, so why should he fall in love with some stranger from New Mexico? But her heart ached. *He never fell in love with you, either,* she told herself.

Deep down she'd always believed he would come to recognize his love for her someday. She didn't know if it would hit him all of a sudden one morning when he awoke and felt an irresistible urge to see her, or if he would slowly come to the realization that she was on his mind more and more, but Annabel had always taken it on faith that one day Brett's true feelings for her would emerge, and he'd realize the bright truth she already knew: that their love had been growing for years and years—that they were meant to join hands and hearts and spend their lives together.

Don't think about this woman, she instructed herself. *There's no use worrying about her place in this mystery until you've got more information. And you can't afford to be emotional right now—or distracted by personal concerns.* Her brain told her she had to think and react as a professional, as any other Stevenson agent would in the same situation.

What would Everett Stevenson do if he were presented with this information? she asked herself.

He'd focus on the guns.

Brett had purchased many weapons. That could mean only one thing. He foresaw some serious trouble —either for himself or for this woman. It was hardly a reassuring conclusion, but it was as far as she got with this line of thinking before Steele interrupted her thoughts, almost as if he could read them.

"If the trail does lead into New Mexico, things could get sticky. We don't know what kind of situation Brett is involved in with this woman, but chances are it's trouble."

"I realize that," Annabel countered. "And I'm fully prepared to—"

"You'll stay in Silver Junction," Steele continued, as if she hadn't spoken. "It's not a bad little town, as towns go. You should be safe there. Meanwhile, I'll hit Skull Creek and see what I can find out. If Brett's there, I'll tell him you've come all the way to Arizona looking for him, and I'll bring him back in one piece—"

"There is no point in discussing this, Mr. Steele." Annabel shot him a determined look. "I'm going with you and that is that."

"You idiotic little tenderfoot, do you even know how to fire that derringer of yours?"

"Of course I do." She shook her head in amazement at his stupidity in asking such a question, and with the movement, one of her carefully pinned curls escaped to feather downward and tickle his neck. "Brett taught me how to shoot, as well as how to ride—and he learned both from his own father, who is quite a fine marksman and rider himself. But I think out here a lady needs more than a derringer to protect herself—she needs a rifle and a pair of Colts, like yours! I'm going to buy myself an extra gun the moment we reach Silver Junction and . . ."

She saw his grin and poked his arm indignantly with

two fingers. "You think Brett comes from tough stock? Well, if you think I don't come from equally tough stock, you're quite mistaken. Let me tell you that my father was a hero who died at Gettysburg and my mother spied for the Union during the war and—"

"Did she?" His eyes lit with interest. "Where?"

"In Richmond. She was raised in Virginia, as was my father, but they had moved to Missouri sometime before the war, and there they came to loathe slavery and all of the cruelty it stood for. When war broke out, my father enlisted in the Union army. And my mother wanted desperately to help him—to help the Union cause in some way." Annabel's voice filled with pride. "She was a brilliant woman, very beautiful and very strong-willed . . ."

"That I believe."

She smiled suddenly, blindingly, into his eyes, struck by the quietness of his tone, for once lacking in mockery. "Thank you," she said softly. For some reason she settled more comfortably against him, and let her thoughts embrace the image of her mother, slender and doe-eyed Savannah Brannigan, brimming with such vibrant determination, and yet so gentle, so full of love. . . .

"My mother made up her mind to return to Richmond, where she had many friends," Annabel continued quietly. She rested her head against Steele's broad chest. It felt surprisingly natural to do so. "She was determined to do whatever she could to glean information that would help shorten the war. I was born during that time," she added. "But having a little baby didn't stop her. She worked on, more diligently than ever, to assure the Union's victory, and possibly save my father's life. Unfortunately, that didn't happen," Annabel finished sadly. "He died at Gettysburg."

There was a short silence during which the only

sounds were the steady clop of the horses' hooves and the sighing of the leaves as the summer wind stirred through them like an old ghost. "Did your mother return to Missouri then?" Steele asked and his breath rustled her hair.

"Oh, no. She stayed in Richmond until the war was over. There were many ways she could soak up information or glean tidbits about weaponry or troop movements or plans from among her friends and acquaintances, and she found means to smuggle every morsel she learned to her Union contacts. She used to tell me the most wonderful stories when I was a little girl!" Annabel's eyes danced and her voice was warm with memory. "She had a most exquisite gold and ruby brooch which she always wore—it was so beautiful! It was shaped like a rose and outlined all in pearls. It was a wedding gift from my father," Annabel explained, "and Mama would let me play with it while she told me of this adventure or that, of how she almost was caught snooping through a general's papers one time, or passing information to someone the next, her reticule and pockets chock full of coded letters. She said the brooch brought her luck though—that because my father had given it to her with love, it was lucky and nothing could happen to her while she was trying to help him come home to us. I suppose it did protect her," Annabel said slowly, "for she never was caught, despite many close calls. I remember being amazed at how brave she was, how steadfast in her purpose. And sometimes I would pin the brooch onto my dress and pretend I was she, and it actually made me feel very brave to wear it." She gave a wry laugh. "And Mama promised me that when I was married, I would have the brooch as a wedding gift. Oh, I could scarcely wait for that day!"

He restrained the urge to reach out and touch that

bright wisp of hair that dangled so enticingly before him. "What happened to the brooch?"

He heard a tiny sigh. "Mama lost it some years later."

Though she spoke in a level tone, something twisted painfully inside him at the sadness that had crept into her voice. This mattered to Annabel Brannigan, it mattered very much, though she was trying heroically not to betray it.

"You see, my mother did return to Missouri after the war. We lived in a little house on Third Street in St. Louis," Annabel told him softly. "One morning while she was on her way to work—Mama had taken a job at the *St. Louis Sun* newspaper—a fire broke out in a house she was passing. Apparently she tried to rescue some of the family from the home, and the roof caved in. . . ." Her voice broke.

"I'm sorry," he muttered in her ear, and she felt his arm tighten around her waist.

"She was wearing the brooch at the time she died." Annabel took a deep steadying breath, blinking back the tears that stung her eyes. "Yet it was not found afterward, either on her clothing, or in the rubble. Aunt Gertie spoke with the authorities and they said someone at the scene must have stolen it—some of the others who tried to help had valuables missing, too—apparently some horrid thief happened along and took advantage of all the pandemonium going on during the tragedy."

"I'm sorry," he said again, feeling helpless for one of the few times in his life. He was at a loss about how to offer any appropriate comfort. He wasn't good at this, by God. He wasn't good at anything that required gentleness, or delicacy, or sensitivity. Shooting people, that he was good at. Tracking them. Fighting them. Burying them. Surviving rainstorms and droughts, Apache raids, freezing nights, ambushes by low-down outlaws, too much whiskey and too little sleep, all that he could handle. But this was terrifying territory. Only by the utmost exercise of his will did he hold his ground.

"Thank you." She gave another tiny sigh and wondered why she was telling him all this, things she'd never discussed with anyone except Brett. "I missed Mama horribly at first. When I first went to live with Aunt Gertie I thought I'd never get used to being without my mother. But . . . Brett was there, you see."

The clip-clop of the horses' hooves on the trail quickened as the ground grew level and more forgiving. At last the sun began to peek through the gray cottony clouds.

Roy Steele studied what he could see of her profile. She had spoken those few simple words—*Brett was there* —as if that explained everything and there was no need for further explanation.

"He befriended you?" he prompted, a bit more sharply than he'd intended.

"He became my friend, yes." Annabel smiled. "And my teacher, my protector, my confidante, my family— along with Aunt Gertie, of course. Brett and I were the best, the dearest of friends. We played together, studied together, took our meals together, even got into mischief together. But he always shouldered the blame, much as I tried to stop him." A chuckle escaped her. "No matter how guilty I was of breaking something or other, Brett would never allow his father's wrath to turn in my direction."

She twisted in the saddle suddenly, bestowing a brilliant smile upon him. "I'm so grateful to you for helping me reach him. It's important for so many reasons I can't even begin to explain them all—but I will forever remember what you've done for me."

The dazzling sweetness of that smile made his heart stop beating for just long enough to crowd the air into his lungs. Damn, if she wasn't bewitching. The sun now streaming down through the leafy tree branches lit her face with a radiant glow and made her hair shimmer with fire. He suddenly wanted to pull the horse up short, vault down with her onto the carpet of pine needles, and make love to her here in the cool, scented forest. The earnest expression on her face tore at his heart, and in her eyes he read all the innocence and hope and eagerness that was in her soul. Pain jackknifed through him.

She's not yours. She's Brett's. And you'd be no damn good for her anyway.

He'd been forgetting what kind of man he was, what cold savage poison ran through his veins. No woman deserved that, least of all this one. Annabel Brannigan was an angel with nerves of iron and a will stronger than the Rocky Mountains.

But she was still a woman, and any involvement with her would only bring her grief.

"What's wrong?" The sharp concern in her voice shook him from his thoughts. "You look so strange. As if you were ready to shoot someone or something!"

"Not you, Annabel." A curious sad smile twisted his lips. "I would never hurt you."

Annabel. He called me Annabel. She sat very still, her hands clenched upon her skirt, and gazed at him in astonishment. She'd never heard that gentle note in his voice before, and the fact that it was mixed with a kind of bitterness as he spoke her name wrenched at her heart. Staring at him she realized that the mask of ice had fallen away from his face and for the first time she glimpsed an inner sorrow held rigidly in check, but a sorrow nonetheless.

Instinctively, she reached up and touched his strong, handsome jaw, wanting to soothe the hurt and the harshness inside him, but at her touch the breath whistled from his chest as if she had burned him with a lighted torch.

He tugged the horse to a halt, and behind them the pack horses stopped abruptly as well. At least, Annabel heard them stop as if in a dream, but she didn't look back to see. Her gaze was locked with Roy Steele's. His eyes bored into hers with such riveting intensity that she literally could not tear her glance away.

Then he yanked her close and kissed her. Her breasts were crushed against his chest as he enclosed her in fierce arms. His mouth burned hers, searching, no —hunting, hunting for softness, sweetness, vulnerability, and finding it, conquering with violent, relentless kisses. He showed her no mercy. And she was whirled into a hot, sweet maelstrom that spun her up, down, and about like a feather in a cyclone.

It was over as quickly as it started.

Breathing hard, he yanked back and pushed her away, holding her at arm's length in the saddle before him.

"Well, Miss Brannigan, I reckon we'd better stick to riding or we're both going to forget about Mr. Brett McCallum."

The chilling mockery in his drawling tone sliced through her like barbed wire. But he was right! What was she thinking of? To have kissed him as she had— again—and felt for him what she had—no, no, she didn't feel anything for him, not really. It was only that they had gone through so much together, with a strange fast friendship springing up between them, intensified by the silly things she'd been so foolishly confiding to him.

Friendship?

Was it friendship she felt for this tough, unpredictable man? Was it friendship she wanted from Roy Steele when she melted into his embrace and forgot everything else: her mission, her whereabouts, even her own name? Was it friendship she wanted when he looked at her with that cool level gaze of his, or brought those hard, demanding lips to hers?

An ache filled her. *Oh, God. Brett, I'm sorry. What is wrong with me?*

She couldn't speak. She turned her head away, because tears were filling her eyes and she had told Roy Steele she never cried.

With a quick movement, he forced her around in the saddle once more, so that she faced forward, looking blindly at the trees. Then he spurred the horse to a trot. He said nothing more, but she felt the tension in his body as they rode, and she sensed the fearsome anger engulfing him. She wasn't sure if he was angry with her or with himself. She wasn't sure of anything.

I need time to think, Annabel cried silently.

But it was impossible to think with Roy Steele so near.

The minutes fled by and the horses plodded on and the sun blazed high and golden in the sky. Annabel stared numbly out at the rock and sagebrush country they were entering, trying to remember who she was and what she was doing out here in the Arizona territory. She reminded herself how precious little time she might have left, and she reminded herself of how important Brett was to her.

In particular, she thought back to the time he had saved her when she'd fallen through the ice at the park while they'd been skating one blustery winter day. That was the first time she'd known that she'd loved him, that she would always love him.

The first of many such times.

And now it was her turn to save *him,* and she had to do everything she could. There was no time, no place, and no point in kissing another man, thinking about another man, wondering what it would be like to touch and know and love another man . . .

Especially a man like Roy Steele, a man with no soul and no roots, a man who killed without regret and who had no space for a woman in his life.

I'm loco, Annabel decided, swallowing hard. *That's the only explanation.* She straightened her shoulders and made a decision. From now on, everything between her and Roy Steele was to be strictly business. No more chats, no more discussions. He was a means to an end, a guide helping her to reach Brett quickly and safely. Nothing more.

And she refused to glance at him the rest of the journey, keeping her gaze fixed resolutely upon the surrounding rocks and scrub. Her thoughts busied themselves with what message she would send to Mr. Stevenson over the telegraph. She tried her best to ignore Roy Steele.

But she couldn't ignore the feel of his body against hers with every step of the horse, the pine and sage scent of him, the even sound of his breathing behind her.

And she couldn't ignore her pounding heartbeat, or the uncertainty that had wormed its way into her mind and was eating away at the edges of her soul.

It gnawed at her, and Annabel had no defense against it. They reached Silver Junction in mid-afternoon, by which time Annabel felt physically and emotionally exhausted, but she fought against the urge to relax her body against him, and sat rigidly upright in the saddle as they entered the dusty little town, rode past peddlers' carts and wagons and horses tethered near a watering trough, and finally came to a halt before the Last Chance Hotel.

Chapter 14

Annabel slipped soundlessly out of her hotel room and down the narrow staircase, her feet skimming over the threadbare carpet with barely a whisper. But her heart was pounding all too loudly in her chest. She half expected Roy Steele to emerge suddenly from his room down the hall and demand to know where in hell she thought she was going.

But he didn't. In fact, as she reached the bottom step she saw no one other than a sweet-looking, elderly couple who passed her in the lobby and proceeded into the little dining room arm in arm. Even the hotel clerk had disappeared somewhere, and she darted outside without a hitch.

The sun was sinking fast and she'd have to hurry to reach the telegraph office before it closed. She knew it was beside the mercantile, because she'd asked the maid who'd brought bath water to her room, so now she gathered her skirts in one hand and hurried down the planked boardwalk, intent on sending a message to Mr. Stevenson before the sun was set on this day.

She felt fresher and more invigorated than she had since setting out on the train from St. Louis. She'd bathed with her own delightful lilac soap, sudsed the trail dust from her hair, and patted herself dry with a thick towel until her skin shone. Then she'd selected one of her favorite Sunday best dresses—the blue and white gingham with the gently scooped neck and the flaring, lace-edged sleeves. To her relief, her wound was much better today, only aching the tiniest little bit, and she could use her arm without any real discomfort, so she'd had no difficulty in brushing and pinning up her hair. She'd done so rather hurriedly, but with deft precision, then, on impulse, had allowed several plump curls to spring free, letting them cascade down her neck and dangle about her cheeks. After threading a lovely blue velvet ribbon through her chignon, she'd concluded that the effect was quite fetching, if she did say so herself. In her good calf boots, with her reticule dangling from her arm, she felt fresh and neat and competent as she strode past the dry goods store, the apothecary, and Brown's Mercantile Emporium, at last reaching the telegraph office.

But when she pushed open the door and stepped into the tiny, low-ceilinged office, she found that another customer preceded her, a stocky, redheaded young man in a plaid shirt, red bandana, and black vest. She bit back her disappointment and closed the door. There was nothing to do but take a seat on the low bench against the wall, and wait.

"Now, let me see." The harried-looking clerk squinted down at the paper before him and nervously licked his lips. " *'Getting close. Heading into New Mexico. Expect job done within week.'* Is that it, Mr. Cobb?"

Annabel froze. Mr. Cobb. *Red* Cobb? Oh, dear God.

She casually turned her head and glanced at the man before her as the words of the message sank in and took on an ominous meaning. Red Cobb was obviously headed into New Mexico after Brett and, by his own message, planned to kill him within the week.

But not if I have anything to say about it, she thought, her hands balled into tight fists. She had to do something, and quickly. She noticed that the clerk was regarding the red-haired man with great uneasiness, much the same way the hotel clerk in Justice had looked at Roy Steele. But she couldn't afford to be afraid. She hadn't come all this way to save Brett only to suddenly let fear and indecision get the better of her. She had to think, to think of a way to stop Red Cobb.

For a split second she considered leaving quickly, going to the hotel, and alerting Steele. But what would he do? He'd come here, call Cobb out, and then what?

Possibly get himself killed.

Stark fear swept through her. *No.* She couldn't let that happen, couldn't let Roy Steele risk his life. Not here, not now. But it was what he did, a voice inside of her argued, it was how he lived. It was why he had come in search of Brett, to save him from Red Cobb, to fight Red Cobb in his place.

But now that the moment was here, even to save Brett, she couldn't allow it to happen. Steele was fast, oh, she knew he was fast, as quick and deadly as could be with his Colt, but Red Cobb might be faster . . . and then . . .

She closed her eyes as a faintness washed over her. No, she would have to handle this herself and somehow keep Roy Steele from even knowing that Cobb was here in Silver Junction.

She flinched as the gunfighter's smooth hard voice cracked like an oiled whip through the little office. "That's it, my friend. Send it now. I'll wait."

And the telegraph clerk bobbed his thin balding head and bent swiftly over his machine.

Red Cobb turned lazily and saw her.

"Ma'am," he said, and doffed his hat.

Annabel nodded. He was a square-jawed, good-looking man, not quite as tall as Roy Steele, but younger, cockier, with full lips and a snub nose, and deep-set eyes the color of robin's eggs. Something in his wide smile gave him a boyish look, but there was nothing boyish in the way he was regarding her at this moment. Her skin crawled. The man was stripping her buck naked right here in the telegraph office, and with a haughty insolence that made her want to slap him.

Instead she gave him her most winsome smile, and tried out a southern accent. "Well, sir, it surely is a nice afternoon, isn't it? And isn't this the pleasantest little town? Much nicer than some others I've been in recently. Why, my room over at the hotel is ever so much prettier than the room I had in Eagle Gulch!"

"Glad to hear it, ma'am," he replied and sauntered over to sit beside her, holding his hat in one smooth, slender hand.

Repugnance filled her. He was handsome, he was outwardly polite, and he smelled of soap and sticky hair pomade, but there emanated from him somehow a stench of evil that filled her with disgust. She had once thought Roy Steele cold and immovable, but this man was of a far more despicable ilk. She sensed cruelty in the wide false smile, and in those bright blue eyes saw a love of death. It was all she could do not to shiver as he turned those eyes upon her, but she managed to keep the smile glued to her lips and kept on talking with the drawl familiar to her since childhood.

"Maybe you can help me with something, if you *would*," she began, and hesitated prettily, waiting for his consent.

"Sure, ma'am. Anything at all."

He leaned in closer.

Annabel smiled dazzlingly into his eyes. "Why,

aren't you sweet?" she exclaimed. "It's so comforting to meet a real gentleman."

"How can I be of help?"

"Well, you see, I'm traveling with my aunt and my fiancée, Mr. Everett . . . er, Stevens, and we're trying to meet up with Everett's dear friend, Mr. Brett McCallum . . ."

His eyes glowed brighter at this and he sat up straighter, but otherwise did not interrupt her, and Annabel plunged on.

". . . and Brett was supposed to meet us here, but he left a message at the hotel that he had to go to Prescott unexpectedly on some urgent business, and dear me, it is rather tiresome to have to travel farther than one anticipated, but Everett really must see Brett and so, I was wondering, could you tell me how far Prescott is from Silver Junction? Should I perhaps let Everett go on alone and wait for both of them to return here, or is Prescott as amiable a town as Silver Junction . . . at least by western standards, which I'm afraid are not quite up to the standards of the South, but . . ."

She let her voice trail off wistfully, and gave her shoulders a delicate little shrug as she gazed dreamily up into Red Cobb's intent face.

"Prescott isn't more than fifty or sixty miles west of here," he said slowly. "And it's a fine little town. But are you sure your friend is there? I reckon you wouldn't want to go all that way if you were by some chance mistaken."

"Well, I declare, of course, I'm not mistaken," she exclaimed with a little trilling laugh, letting a bit of hauteur creep into her voice. "Everett has the note Brett left, and of course he showed it to me and Aunt Mae, and it said Brett would meet us in Prescott and the sooner the better, unless we cared to wait for him to return here, and it is all most mysterious, you know, but

Everett will only say that he is certain we will understand everything when we see Brett, and of course, Everett knows best."

She fluttered her eyelashes. "I believe he's finished."

"What?" The gunfighter regarded her blankly. "Who?"

"The clerk." Annabel inclined her head toward the bespectacled little man who had risen from behind his counter and was waiting nervously for the gunfighter to notice him. "I believe he wants you to pay him now."

Red Cobb nodded, glanced swiftly at the clerk, and then swiveled his head back to stare into her eyes once more. "Yes, indeed," he muttered. "If you'll excuse me, ma'am, for only a moment . . ."

Annabel tried to keep from fidgeting with the clasp of her reticule as she waited for him to finish his business with the clerk. When he turned back to her, she met his gaze with a guileless smile.

"So you think Aunt Mae and I should make the journey with Everett to find Brett?" she inquired.

"Yes, by all means."

"Then we shall." She beamed. "Thank you so very much, sir, for your kind help and advice."

"My pleasure, Miss . . ."

"Rainsford. Miss Elizabeth Rainsford," she informed him blithely, recalling the name of one of Brett's many female companions in St. Louis. "But don't let me keep you any longer. You've been too kind already."

"A pleasure, ma'am. A most distinct pleasure." He regarded her for another moment, a speculative gleam in his eyes, then he turned abruptly toward the door. "Good luck to you, Miss Rainsford."

"And good luck to you," she gushed sweetly. *And may you rot in hell.*

She was trembling by the time she rose to approach

the telegraph clerk, but she managed to speak smoothly enough. "I wish to send a wire to the following address. It's the Stevenson Detective Agency, and if you breathe one word of this message to anyone in this town I will personally bring Mr. Roy Steele in here to shoot you dead. Is that understood?"

The clerk gaped at her.

"And also, I need to know to whom Mr. Cobb sent *his* wire a few moments ago."

"But I can't tell you that . . ."

"Oh, yes, you can! If you don't want Roy Steele to come in here and ask you himself, you'd *better* tell me! Well, what are you waiting for? Come on, my good man, this is a matter of life and death!" Annabel banged her fist on the countertop and the clerk jumped as if she'd struck him.

"Y-yes, ma'am." He referred to a sheaf of papers before him. "He sent the wire to Mr. Lucas Johnson. At the Empire Hotel in St. Louis." Hastily, the clerk seized a sheet of writing paper and a pencil in shaking fingers. "G-go right ahead, ma'am."

Cobb went straight up to his room on the second story of the Tin Horn Hotel and reread the telegraph message that he'd received earlier that day. So, a woman investigator was searching for Brett McCallum. *Damned interesting. And easy.* Remembering the sugary sweetness on Miss Elizabeth Rainsford's pretty, lying face, he grinned. *Honey, my mama didn't raise no fools. Why, beating you to Master Brett will be as easy as pissing in bed.*

On the other hand, Cobb realized, prowling the room with light, eager footsteps, his mind racing, *there's another possibility that might be a heap more fun. And it won't delay McCallum's death by much. So why the hell not?*

His booming laughter could he heard up and down
the hall, echoing clear through to the rafters.

When he calmed down, he lit himself a cigarillo,
grabbed his gear, and headed out to the Silver Streak
brothel on the outskirts of town. Just in case the little
investigator tried to check up on him to see if he'd
bought her story, he'd leave straight from Mattie's place
in the morning. And make sure that anyone who asked
questions about him reached a dead end.

Cobb was pleased with the cigarillo, and with his
own little plan. This job would be over right soon now,
and he'd managed to figure out how to give himself a
fine little bonus. Just the thought of it, and of that pretty
red-haired investigator, put him in the mood to celebrate.

Pearly lavender dusk limned the distant mountaintops as Annabel made her way back to the hotel. Her
mind spun with various questions and possibilities. Who
in the world was this Lucas Johnson, and why had he
hired Red Cobb to kill Brett?

At least she had been able to alert Mr. Stevenson so
that he could investigate Johnson—and inform Ross
McCallum what she'd discovered. It wasn't a bad piece
of work, but she didn't have time to congratulate herself. She was too busy wondering if Cobb had already
left for Prescott, or if he was waiting until morning. The
latter notion chilled her to the bone. At all costs she
must keep Roy Steele from crossing paths with Cobb
tonight. If she had indeed succeeded in throwing Cobb
off Brett's trail, there might never be occasion for the
two men to meet. They'd never have to find out who was
faster, who would remain standing, breathing, while the
other one died in the street. She and Steele would lo-
cate Brett while Cobb was on a wild-goose chase in
Prescott, and by the time the gunfighter realized what

had happened they could all be headed out of New Mexico, and she and Brett could be on their way home —with Red Cobb too far behind to catch them.

"Been waiting for you. Where've you been?"

Annabel stared guiltily at Roy Steele as he rose from the single chair in the lobby to greet her. Dear Lord, he looked handsome. She was struck once again by the rugged charisma of his good looks, by a powerfully virile masculine beauty that had much less to do with perfect, even features than it had to do with iron strength and hard experience. A combination of competence and tough resourcefulness was reflected in the rough, handsome planes of his face. Why, it burned right out of his onyx eyes, seeming to graze her with a lightning-bolt slash of fire. Clad in a light blue linen shirt and dark trousers which accentuated his powerful physique, with his gun belt as always slung low across his lean hips, he looked arrogantly nonchalant, but ready for anything—even a duel with Red Cobb. She quaked beneath his piercing eyes, convinced that Steele could see straight through to her soul if he wanted to, and that was most disconcerting, especially under the circumstances.

"I . . . I was . . . just . . ."

He frowned as the bright flush stole into her cheeks. *You were just up to no good,* he decided for himself, and wondered what the hell she'd been doing now.

You've got a real sneaky side to you, Miss Annabel Brannigan, which I don't much like. In fact he hated it because it meant he couldn't trust her. And he'd had his trust betrayed enough in the past to last a lifetime. But he did like the way she looked in that dress. Sweet, fresh, lovely as a mountain flower, and she smelled like flowers too. Lilacs, maybe . . .

He jerked himself back from the pleasant stupor of her looks and scent. The lady was about to tell him a lie, a whopper. He knew by the way she was moistening her lips . . .

"I had a sudden urge to buy myself a bonnet to match this dress." There was that winning smile and that pretty shrug of those slender shoulders of hers. "The one I had was quite crushed in my carpetbag—I believe Aunt Gertie's diary was pressed down upon it, and the flowers were ruined. Brett does love me in bonnets with ribbons and flowers."

"So where is it?" he asked, just for the hell of it.

"What?"

"The bonnet."

"Oh. I couldn't find one." She rushed on. "There isn't a millinery in town . . ." She prayed this was true. "And the mercantile had nothing like what I had in mind—you know how sometimes one pictures a certain item and nothing else will do . . ."

"Right." He took her arm. "Let's eat."

"Oh, no, we can't."

There were a half a dozen people eating in the Last Chance dining room, and the smell of boiled ham and roast venison and some kind of rich soup filled the air with an aroma which made her stomach ache. She was famished, and no doubt Steele was too. It had been considerate of him to wait for her, and he had cleaned himself up immaculately, too, she noted, eyeing his fresh shave and neatly brushed black hair, and the shine on his boots, but if they ate down here in the dining room, Red Cobb just might walk in that door for his evening meal, and then all of her careful plans would be ruined. And Roy Steele would surely end up outside in the street, facing Cobb, going for his gun . . .

She grabbed his shirtfront. "I must talk to you. Alone. Privately. In my room."

He studied the voluptuous curve of her parted lips. She was so close to him that the lilac scent of her filled his nostrils with sweetness. "Ahuh. Can't it wait until after supper?"

"No, it can't. It's urgent, Steele. Private. We'll order a tray sent up and eat there." Her eyes lit and glowed more gray than green as she offered forth this suggestion. "Wait here. I'll arrange everything."

And she put a hand to his arm for just a moment before sliding past him and approaching a waitress on her way to the kitchen. The warmth of her fingers tingled even after she'd left his side. It amazed him how she could be stubborn and irritating one moment, and irresistibly charming the next. A dangerously persuasive, utterly bewitching woman if ever he'd met one. He watched her talk the waitress into honoring her unusual request, saw her nod and smile and press a gold piece into the woman's palm, and was amazed that the sight of her sashaying back toward him made his heartbeat race. What was Annabel Brannigan up to now?

Only one way to find out, he reasoned. He followed her up the stairs and waited until he was inside her room before speaking.

When the door was shut behind him, he leaned against it.

"Now, then."

"Yes?" She was hurriedly stuffing items back into that damned carpetbag of hers. He got another glimpse of lace drawers, a glance at a silk stocking, saw that diary of her aunt's, and then she zipped the whole damned thing up and pushed it under the bed. But he noticed that a photograph of Brett had been set in a prominent position on the maple bureau.

For a moment, his gaze rested on the face of that dark-haired, grinning young man.

Then he shifted his attention back to Annabel.

"What's this all about?" He shook his head. "You're acting loco, even for you."

"Why, thank you, Mr. Steele, what a charming thing to say." She chuckled saucily at him and he fought the urge to seize her in his arms and kiss that adorable mouth which seemed to mock and beckon him all at the same time.

"Talk, Miss Brannigan."

The glow in her eyes deepened with amusement, turning them suddenly more green than gray. "Why, Mr. Steele, can't you call me Annabel on a regular basis even after all this time?" she murmured. "We are now so well acquainted that it seems positively absurd for you to avoid my given name."

"You're stalling."

"I am not."

"Why supper up here? What is so private, so personal that you have to talk to me alone right now, right here?"

Relentless, obstinate man! Annabel turned away so he wouldn't see her desperation as she fumbled for something plausible to placate him. Her thoughts whirled, selecting and discarding several possiblities all in the space of a moment. The next thing she knew Steele's hands were on her shoulders, turning her to face him so that she was forced to look directly up into his eyes. Time was up.

"Talk," he said again, ominously, but this time, unlike that time in Lily's room, his words didn't fill her with fear. It was as if a mask had dropped away and the Roy Steele that everyone else saw was no longer the one she saw when she looked into his eyes; she saw beneath the cold facade, the merciless curl of his lip, and knew that the man before her would not harm a hair on her head. The world outside this room might cower at the sight of the deadly gunslinger Roy Steele, but she only felt a strangely warm affection flowing like molten honey through her veins. She wanted to reach up and stroke his cheek and laugh into his beautiful, darkly glinting eyes.

"Well . . ." she began and took a breath.

"Go on."

"I . . ."

A knock sounded at the door.

"The food!" Laughing, she darted out from his grasp like a deer under a thicket and pulled open the door. "My, doesn't everything look delicious."

He had to admit that it did. There was beef stew and potatoes, fried chicken and venison in thick gravy, along with big plump biscuits swimming in butter. Steele pulled two little chairs up to the small table beneath the window as Annabel poured steaming coffee into cups.

It was hard to believe a slender female could put away so much food. He watched incredulously as she took her third helping, her enjoyment of the hearty meal obvious. He wondered suddenly if she would throw herself into lovemaking with the same gusto as she threw herself into her repast. There was a sensual warmth and earthiness about her which, layered upon her pert femininity and that curious blend of stubbornness and charm, made him want to taste her everywhere, her silky peach skin, her delectable mouth, the delicate pulse beating at her throat. She was lightness and musk, sweetness and steel. And being alone in this tiny room with her, in clear sight of that damned bed, was doing strange things to his thinking, not to mention certain parts of his body.

He took ahold of his coffee cup and gulped at the strong black liquid, burning his throat. But it helped him to remember who he was and all of the reasons why Annabel Brannigan was off limits to him.

And it would help even more to turn his thoughts onto another subject, to get down to business. He set down his fork. "Don't you want to know what I've been up to while you were gallivanting around looking for bonnets?" He watched her pause in the act of helping herself to another biscuit, and her eyes focused alertly on him with the cool appraising intelligence he was beginning to know.

"Of course. Does this mean you plan to tell me?" She set the biscuit down on her plate untouched and waited for him to answer.

Steele hesitated. This would upset her. Hell, it upset him. But she had a right to know. "Seeing as it concerns you, I reckon I should," he said quietly. "We're setting out at first light for New Mexico." He leaned back in the chair and went on quickly, keeping his tone steady and impersonal. "Seems the woman Brett was traveling with lives on a ranch there, south of Magdalena. Her name's Conchita Rivers. According to one of the bartenders here in town, Brett was in the place getting drunk not too long ago, and talking about some trouble the lady's been having with a big cattle company that wants to run her off her property. It seems he answered an advertisement to work for her; he's going to be fighting off the outfit that wants to get rid of her."

Annabel had gone very still, and the color ebbed from her cheeks. She said nothing, just sat there while her coffee grew cold, watching him with those wide, vivid eyes.

Steele stood up, pushed back his chair, and stalked to the window that overlooked the narrow main street of Silver Junction.

"They were headed to the lady's ranch when they passed through town," he said grimly, watching the nearly deserted, dusky street. "The bartender said they were looking for some more men to back them up in the fight. Didn't sound like they found many."

Annabel felt ill. She jumped up from the table and tossed her napkin down beside her plate. "Brett is risking his life for this woman? Why? How can he hope to help her?" She pressed trembling fingers to her temples and shook her head. "He's a good shot, but he's no match for a gang of hired gunmen. He'll be killed!"

"Maybe that's what he wants."

"What are you talking about?"

He reached her in two quick strides, and put a hand beneath her chin, tilting her head up. "When a man chooses a fight like this one, he's either desperate for money . . ."

"Which he's not."

". . . or he's a fool, doing it out of a sense of honor or maybe love . . ."

He paused, as if waiting for her to refute this, but Annabel said nothing. It *was* possible Brett was in love with this woman, she reflected miserably. The idea filled her with hopelessness.

"Or," Steele continued grimly, "he's looking to die."

Dazed, she shook her head. "Brett doesn't want to die. He has so much to live for. I know there was some kind of a problem with his father, but surely that wasn't enough to make him do something so foolhardy."

"You're certain you have no hint what happened between them?"

"I wish I did," she muttered.

"Strange that he wouldn't have come to you and talked over whatever was bothering him, or even have let you know he was leaving town for a while."

She flushed beneath his intent gaze. "Well, he . . . didn't."

"What kind of a man runs out on his fiancée?"

The condemnation in his tone cut her to the quick. Brett was the most decent, honorable, gentlemanly man she'd ever known. He didn't deserve to have Roy Steele think he was a weakling who ran out on the woman he was going to marry. *Tell him,* a voice inside Annabel shouted. *Tell him the truth . . . that Brett is not your fiancé, that yes, you love him, but you were hired to find him. Brett didn't run out on you at all, he simply ran away, like his brother. Tell Roy Steele right now and set everything to rights.*

"There's something you should know."

"Yeah. I'd like to know why you hustled me up here so quickly. And where you really were while I was out scouting information." The cloud that had come over her expression when he'd talked about Brett, and about the woman from New Mexico, stabbed him clear through. It made him angry. Angry at Brett and at her—and at himself. His armor went up instinctively, and he reacted by roughening his voice and his attitude.

"You're holding back on me, Annabel, and I don't like it. You've stalled long enough."

Her mouth fell open. "That's twice now that you've called me Annabel."

"What?" He scowled. "What if I did? That's not the point. The point is . . ."

"The point is, if you'd stop talking long enough I could explain something to you. It's about Brett . . . and me . . . you see . . ."

But suddenly he couldn't bear to hear her sing Brett's praises, couldn't stomach the idea of hearing about her undying love, and the devotion that had always existed between the two of them. He turned away. "It's none of my business."

"Yes, it is." Annabel grabbed him by the arm and yanked him back. He allowed hismelf to be pulled toward her. "Listen to me," she blurted out. "And don't interrupt. I think you should know that . . ."

But doubt, and the piercing look in his eyes, halted her in mid-sentence. *What if he gets angry that I lied to him about being Brett's fiancée? What if he's furious that*

I'm working for Ross McCallum to find Brett? He didn't sound overly fond of the man or the way he's made his fortune. What if he decides to leave me here and find Brett alone?

He would do it, too, Annabel realized, remembering how implacable Roy Steele could be. *After all, if I'm not betrothed to Brett, I have no claim on him, and Steele could easily try to dump me here and go off alone to save Brett's life. Of course, I'd try to follow him, and he'd get even madder, and we'd be right back where we started.*

Don't chance telling him now, something inside of her warned. *You're too close. And he's too unpredictable. He's finally accepted that the two of you are partners of a sort, but if he finds out that you've been lying about your connection to Brett, he might turn his back on you faster than you can blink.*

"I'm getting mighty tired of these games, Annabel. If you have something to say, just go ahead and say it."

"I . . ." She took a gulp of air and hurried on, retreating from the larger truth at the last moment, hoping he'd settle for the smaller one. "I lied to you."

"About what?"

"I wasn't really shopping for a bonnet."

"Never figured you were," he said dryly.

"I was sending a telegraph message back to St. Louis—I had to let Mr. McCallum know I was getting close," she rushed on, blushing only a little, for this was basically the truth. "And . . . there's something else . . . something important. I saw Red Cobb in town tonight."

"You *what*? Where?"

"At the telegraph office."

"And you're just telling me *now*?"

She sidestepped this comment and explained about the message she'd overheard from the clerk, and her own idea to divert Cobb's search to Prescott.

Steele raked a hand through his hair. "So Cobb was hired by an hombre named Lucas Johnson? In St. Louis?" He shook his head, puzzled, then quickly fixed her with a hard stare. "Why in hell didn't you find me and let me take care of him once and for all?" he demanded.

He seemed so frustrated and bewildered she couldn't meet his eyes. "I wanted to protect you," she mumbled.

Struck dumb by this explanation, he was silent for nearly a full minute. "From Cobb?" he asked disbelievingly. "Sweetheart, you *are* loco . . ."

"No! I knew exactly what I was doing! If you'd known Cobb was here in town, you'd have fought him, and it would have ended in bloodshed and death . . . possibly *your* death . . ."

Her voice cracked and trailed off. Steele stared at her as if she had just sprouted wings and flown around the room. "Why should you care?" he asked slowly.

She drew in a ragged breath and tried to sound offhand. "Well, perhaps because Cobb would then have a clear path to killing Brett."

"That's all?"

"And you did save my life . . . more than once. I guess I owe you something . . ."

"Owe me . . . so you feel gratitude toward me, is that it? Well, don't."

Something oddly bitter beneath his cool tone made her heart turn over. And suddenly she sensed a terrible pain in him, and it anguished her as strongly as if it were her own. She clutched his arms and pulled him closer and he let himself be pulled.

"No, that's not it at all," she heard herself confessing. The truth poured out of her like spring sap from a maple, clear and pure and untainted. "I *care* about you, Steele. I don't know why, but I do. I couldn't bear it if something happened to you. When I thought that Red Cobb might shoot you down, I . . . had to do something else. I had to protect you!"

Astonishment slammed through him. *She* wanted to protect *him*. He couldn't quite comprehend it. A variety of emotions bombarded him: amazement, wonder, amusement, and a kind of awe. No one had ever wanted to protect him from anything before. People wanted to hire him, to pay him to put his life on the line to protect them or their property, to watch him square off against their enemies and win but . . . *protect him?*

His hands captured her wrists and tightened around them without his even realizing it. "I'm touched, Miss Brannigan, but you shouldn't have done that." He spoke gently, and gave her a weary smile. But his blood was heating up as he studied the pertly enchanting face before him, and he lost himself in those earnest, soul-searching gray-green eyes. "I'm going to have to face Red Cobb sooner rather than later, and it would have been better to get it over with."

"Maybe you won't have to," she breathed. She moistened her lips, and he resisted the impulse to stare at the full, sensuous lower lip. "Maybe we'll find Brett and convince him to head home before Red Cobb has time to retrace his footsteps and catch up to us. Maybe—"

"Maybe I should just go on over to the local saloons and the other hotel in town and see if I can find Mr. Cobb right now."

"No!"

"Yes." He let go of her deliberately and stepped back. It took all of his self-control to move away from her, to keep his tone level and his expression careless as she stared at him with raw panic which wrenched strangely at his heart.

"Have a little faith in me, Annabel."

"I wish you wouldn't do this, but if you must, I'm going with you."

"The hell you are."

She dodged past him and grabbed up her reticule. When she started to march toward the door, he grasped her arm, took the reticule from her, and tossed it onto the bed.

"If Cobb sees the two of us together, he'll know that story you gave him was phony and that you and I are working together. Then, supposing he does kill me, where will that leave you? And Brett? Cobb'll be on to your trick, and you'll have to answer to him, and that puts Brett in more danger. No, this way, if something happens to me, and I'm not saying it will, Cobb won't know that you bamboozled him—he'll ride on to Prescott in the morning just like you planned—assuming he bought your story—and you'll have a nice head start. So you're staying here and that's that."

It made sense. She hated it, but it made perfect, indisputable sense. She nodded miserably and watched him stride to the door. How could he look so calm, so nonchalant? A lump of fear choked her throat.

"Steele."

"Yeah?"

"Be careful."

He laughed, and suddenly the familiar harsh glinting light was back in his eyes. Even his stance was different: alert, all concentrated energy and tension, a sharp-eyed menace radiating from his powerful shoulders down to his lean, muscular thighs.

"You can't get rid of me that easily, sweetheart. I'll be back."

And he was gone, the door closing quietly behind him.

* * *

Annabel paced back and forth across the thread-bare carpet. She turned up the lamp, picked up her derringer, set it down again. She watched from her window, saw him cross the street, and enter the Half Moon Saloon. Her heart seemed ready to burst into a thousand pieces.

If anyone can outdraw Red Cobb, Steele can, she told herself. She remembered the ease and swiftness with which he handled his guns, how he had cut down the Hart brothers and those cutthroats in the brakes. But this time, facing Red Cobb, felt different.

You know him now. You care about him. That's the difference.

It seemed an eternity since he had entered the saloon. She braced herself for gunfire, for the doors to fling open and Steele and Cobb to plunge out, facing each other in the darkened street. When at last the doors did part and his tall, broad-shouldered figure emerged alone and strode up the moonlit street, she gasped with relief. But a moment later she lost him in the shadows and whirled away from the window in frustration, wondering with cold sinking fear if she would ever see him again.

The moments dragged by. There was no sound from the street, only the occasional whinny of a horse, and now and then blaring piano music and drunken laughter floating in from the various saloons. Annabel went to the yellow-quilted bed and sank down upon it. Her legs felt too weak to hold her. She clutched the pillow to her chest, her fingers digging into the lumpy softness as she said a silent prayer and stared at the unmoving curtains.

And waited.

The knock came nearly an hour later.

She threw open the door and saw him leaning nonchalantly against the frame.

"No dice. Looks like Cobb made tracks right after you sold him on your story. I checked every saloon and hotel. He's gone."

"Oh, thank God." Relief wreathed her face. Her knees felt weak as she reached out impulsively and grasped his hand, dragging him into the softly lit room. "I'm . . . so glad. You have no idea how worried I've been!"

Steele stared down at her slender fingers, wrapped tightly around his. Then she saw his glance slide past her, to the bureau, and knew he was looking at the photograph of Brett.

Slowly, deliberately, he pulled his hand free.

"Well, now you can tuck yourself into bed and get a good night's sleep."

"Yes, that's right," she murmured, suddenly flustered. "I certainly can. And I will. I'll do just that." The danger was over. Steele was fine. *Stop behaving so foolishly.* Suddenly mortified at her own excessive joy in seeing him, Annabel covered it with a brisk little shrug, then stepped back, putting an extra safe little space between them. "I remember that we're leaving at first light," she said quickly. "Don't worry, I'll be ready."

"You'd better be or I'll have to ride without you." The warning glance he threw her was cool and impersonal. He was already turning away, she noticed with a heavy heart. "Let me know if you change your mind about going in the morning. I have a hunch things are about to start happening fast as thunder and lightning, and when they do, it won't be pretty."

"Don't worry about me."

"Wouldn't think of it."

He tipped his hat to her, a mocking gesture that made her ache inside. An empty coldness stole over her. There was a wall between them again, a fortress-thick, impenetrable wall. The knowledge left her desolate.

She closed the door and leaned against it, searching for the reason she felt this way. She should be thinking about Brett, about what she would say to him, how she would talk him into going back with her, and whether or not he might finally realize how much they belonged together.

They did belong together. She'd always known that. Now it was time for Brett to realize it too.

So why was she thinking of Roy Steele as she brushed her hair? Why did his cold, handsome image swim vividly into her mind as she turned down the lamp and crawled into bed in the darkness. Why did she shiver and long for . . . for what?

His touch? His kiss? His slow, weary smile?

You're tired, she told herself. *No, exhausted. And confused. Don't think about it anymore tonight.*

Yet she lay in the bed and stared at the shadows on the ceiling, trying to drown out the whispering voices in her heart.

Chapter 15

The canyons shimmered with heat. Squinting up at the cobalt sky, Annabel thought that never before had any sky looked as big and bright and vibrant as the one stretching over the glorious red sandstone mesas of New Mexico.

It was midafternoon and they'd been riding hard since dawn. But as she and Steele plunged up the road that the blacksmith in Skull Creek had said led to the Rivers ranch, a strange exhilaration flowed through her.

Annabel had lost track of how many days they'd been traveling. She only knew that the land was beautiful and fierce, with its striking desert cacti, its white and purple sage, its mesquite and yucca. At sunset the scattered mountain ranges loomed like giant purple ghosts rising out of a mystical dream. By daylight, sun, sky, plains, and mesa formed an ever-changing landscape that took her breath away. A strange sense of destiny had overtaken her, and at this moment was more powerful than ever. She would find Brett—and it would be today. Within the hour. He was guarding the Rivers ranch at the end of this road, and she would actually see him before the day was done.

The journey with Steele had been strained ever

since Silver Junction. The gunslinger had withdrawn in every way, treating her like a stranger. He spoke only when it was necessary to communicate something to her about the trail, or the weather, or when they would make camp. But he avoided looking at her, and touching her, and even when they camped for the night and settled down to supper at the same campfire, he kept all conversation to a minimum and by his very aloofness forced her to do the same.

Annabel wished she could read his mind. But his impenetrable mask of detachment was firmly in place and she'd found no way to breach it during any of the long, hard-riding days. Even at night, when the stars bloomed like icy white flowers in a sky of midnight blue, and the mountains loomed like dark foreboding giants all around them, and the land rustled with badgers and snakes and coyotes, wild things hunting their prey beneath the ghostly moon, he removed his bedroll as far from hers as the camp would allow, offered a curt "good night" and plopped his hat over his face before Annabel could do more than murmur a reply.

Silence. Coldness. An empty companionship like that of strangers sharing a train was all that lay between them as they rode long hours and days into the heart of New Mexico.

Yet, every time they accidentally touched, when his hand brushed hers as they passed a pan of biscuits back and forth, or when she stumbled into him, as she had once while gathering twigs for the campfire, a hot current seemed to leap between them.

This distance, this polite estrangement, was much preferable, she told herself. Close contact with Roy Steele was too much like tampering with fireworks—and besides, it made her feel guilty—guilty about Brett, and the love she'd nourished for years and years. It also made her feel as if she was not concentrating enough on her assignment for Mr. Stevenson. She needed to think, to be alert, and sensible and professional. If she'd let herself, she could have given her senses over to the breathtaking panorama of rugged New Mexican countryside, to the sweet kiss of the wind as it rippled along the mesas, and the cool beauty of the moon sailing overhead as she and Roy Steele shared quiet nights under the stars. She could have exulted in the magnificent beauty that enveloped her, in the awe inspired by her surroundings, and in the companionship, however distant, of the enigmatic man who shared her days and nights—but she did not let herself. She kept forcing her thoughts ahead, to Brett, and to Ross McCallum, trying in vain to work out the pieces of the puzzle.

"There it is." Steele halted the bay on a slight rise overlooking the sage green valley. Set far back beneath twin mesas, an adobe dwelling seemed to rise out of the earth. It was flanked by several outbuildings and corrals, and looked to be a large and comfortable ranch. "Pretty isolated," Steele commented. "And it looks unprotected. Wonder why someone wants it so bad the owner had to hire outside men to keep it safe."

"And where are the men doing that?" Annabel asked anxiously. "Where's Brett?"

Steele was scanning the countryside, his gaze studying the nooks and crannies of the tall rocks that formed a ledge overhanging the road. He spoke to Annabel in a low tone. "If it were me, I'd be hiding up there in those rocks somewhere, waiting to pick off anyone making an approach to the ranch. Let's ride on down and see what happens."

"Wait a minute." She straightened her sombrero. "I'm not sure I like this plan. What if they shoot first and ask what our business is later?"

"Then we'd better hope they miss."

He spurred the bay forward down a steep, stony

path following the contour of the rise, and Annabel followed, her gaze trained uneasily on the gray crevices above. Steele was a cautious man, she acknowledged to herself, and shrewd in the ways of this untamed territory. If he felt it safe to continue, she knew she should trust his judgment, but the unnerving sensation that she was being watched prickled her skin and made her glad that she had an extra rifle at her side. The fine hairs on the back of her neck rose as she and Steele trotted beneath a particularly thick overhang of rocks, and for a moment, the sun was blotted out.

Then a shot rang across the towering boulders, echoing like cannon fire.

"Hold it right there! Don't move or you're dead! We've got you covered!"

Steele yanked Dickens up short. Annabel did the same with Sunrise, her heart in her throat.

But she wasn't fearful now. She was joyous, for she would recognize that voice anywhere. It was thicker, hoarser, than she remembered, but it was the same. It was Brett's voice.

A shaggy-haired, dark-garbed figure emerged from behind the rock directly above them. He had a rifle trained on Steele as he clambered down, all the while keeping the gun leveled. His hat shadowed his face, but Annabel could make out the familiar lean shape of the jaw, now covered with dark stubble.

Roy Steele had obeyed the summons to remain still. He waited, watching, as Brett clambered lower, finally halting on a rock just above where the horses had paused.

"Who are you?" Brett called sharply, and then, as he focused in on Annabel, his mouth fell open.

"Annabel?"

"Yes, Brett, it's me," she chimed out happily, nearly breathless with excitement. "I've been searching for you all over Arizona—I'll explain it all, but first, here's Roy Steele, he's been looking for you, too. We want to . . ."

"Steele?"

"Yes, Roy Steele. He's come to help you . . ."

"Why?"

Annabel faltered at the wary suspicion in Brett's voice. He seemed so different, not at all like the carefree, high-spirited friend who had sneaked into Gertie's kitchen with her in the middle of the night on more than one occasion to raid the pantry. He seemed tense, highstrung, and very ready to shoot Steele at the slightest provocation.

She went on quickly, "Put the gun down, for heaven's sake. What's the matter with you? Steele owes you a favor, and he heard you were in some trouble with Red Cobb and he wanted to—"

"I've never met him before in my life."

A dull roar pounded through Annabel's ears. She turned white. "*What?*" Sharply, she turned her head to stare at Roy Steele. He hadn't moved, but sat perfectly still and at ease, his hat half hiding his face. To all appearances cool and unperturbed, he silently watched the young man who was pointing the rifle at his chest.

Brett's eyes narrowed. He was sweating, his blue and green plaid shirt sticking to his chest and arms, but for all his uneasiness, he glared ferociously at the tall, broad-shouldered rider, regarding him with angry suspicion.

"Annabel, ride over here to the other side of these rocks. Get away from him—now."

"But . . ."

Suddenly, the truth hit her. Roy Steele had lied to her, lied about knowing Brett, about Brett having done him a good turn, about his reason for tracking Brett McCallum all over two territories. And she had believed him, bought his phony story, and practically escorted him right to Brett's feet.

He was in cahoots with Red Cobb—he wanted to kill Brett, too.

She whirled Sunrise about and fumbled for the derringer in the pocket of her skirt. "Liar!" she gasped, hardly able to speak for the agony surging through her, filling her with blind, sickened rage. "Bastard! Everything you told me was a stinking lie!"

"Get away from him, Annabel!" Brett shouted again, but before she could move, Steele spoke in a quiet tone.

"Brett. It's me."

Brett froze as those three softly spoken words seemed to echo and tumble through the wall of boulders. His grip on the rifle slackened, and he almost dropped it.

He leaned forward, staring hard.

"*Cade?*" His skin turned ashen beneath its bronze tan and stubble. A muscle twitched wildly in his jaw. "No, no, it can't be," he muttered, half to himself. Then, hope squeaking into his voice: "Is it? Cade—is it . . . *you?*"

"Guilty as charged."

Steele's dark, brawny figure blurred before Annabel's eyes, then regained focus. She gave her head a dazed shake, trying to take in what she'd just heard.

But Brett needed no more time to react. He leaped down from the rock, tossed the rifle into the grass, and threw himself toward the man on the horse.

At the same time, Steele slid out of the saddle and opened his arms to his brother.

They embraced tight and hard. Annabel watched in soundless incredulity as Brett wept, alternately shaking and hugging the older brother whom he hadn't seen in thirteen years.

"How did this happen? How did you find me . . . and you've hooked up with Annabel! I can't believe this."

"Well, your betrothed needed an escort and I figured you needed someone to save your reckless hide."

"Betrothed?"

If before, Annabel's world had seemed to blur and spin, now it stood still. Rooted in the saddle, the reins clutched limply in suddenly frozen fingers, she felt her heart sinking all the way down into her kneecaps. Brett threw her an astonished and richly amused glance.

"Betrothed?" he repeated, grinning, and shook his head. His very expression drove a stake into her heart. "Annabel, have you been making up stories again?"

Roy—Cade—spun toward her. "Making up stories?" he demanded. The words were bitten out in a deceptively even tone that was as comforting as a cobra's hiss. "Do you mean that the two of you are not engaged to be married?"

Brett burst out laughing. Annabel twisted her fingers in her mare's mane, her eyes locked with Steele's. "I can explain . . ."

But she never had the chance.

The silence of the valley was shattered by gunfire. Shots blasted from the direction of the ranch house and Brett spun toward the sound in alarm. "Damn it, I was supposed to be on lookout!" He grabbed his rifle from the grass. "The bastards sneaked up while I was . . ."

But they never heard the rest of the sentence because he clambered back atop the boulders as he spoke and his voice was drowned out by the scrape of his boots and additional gunshots.

"Shit, they've got the house surrounded!"

With one lithe movement, Cade sprang back into the saddle. "You have a horse?"

"Up here behind some trees . . ." Brett was already bounding out of sight.

More shots quickly followed, and shouts—and Annabel heard the thunder of hoofbeats.

Cade McCallum threw her a look of pure ice. "Stay here with the horses. Don't move. I'm not finished with you yet."

And he spurred Dickens forward to a gallop, disappearing past the boulders and around a bend before Annabel could reply.

Annabel dismounted, her mind racing with all the events which had unfolded so quickly: the discovery that Roy Steele was really Cade McCallum, *his* discovery that she had lied about being Brett's fiancée, and—last but certainly not least, the incredible pleasure of seeing Brett again, of hearing his voice, witnessing that dear familiar smile.

And now, the two men whom she felt most strongly about in the world were both riding headlong into some terrible danger—and she was standing here with a bunch of horses.

"Not on your life, Steele—er, McCallum!" she fumed, and swiftly set to work tethering the pack horses to a juniper tree, and then fishing in her pack for the heavy Colt revolver she'd bought in Silver Junction. When she mounted Sunrise, she gripped the Colt in one hand.

"You're right about one thing, Cade McCallum. This isn't finished, not by a long shot. And I'll be damned if I let anything happen to you or Brett until I've had a chance to deal with the both of you."

She dug her knees into the mare's sides and the horse bolted forward. Annabel settled low in the saddle and braced herself for what lay ahead.

* * *

"Senora Rivers, we can end this all today! Just sign over the deed to the Lowry Cattle Company and there'll be no more trouble! You folks can live here, you can keep the ranch, the horses and corrals, even graze a few dozen head of cattle. And you'll be left alone. You have Mr. Lowry's word!"

Eight men on horseback circled the ranch house, firing, as Annabel galloped up the road, trying to catch up with Cade. One of the riders, wearing a green flannel shirt and brown vest, who was obviously the spokesman, was shouting his warnings as Cade charged up, his gun drawn.

The man in the brown vest whirled toward the newcomer as the big bay horse bore down on him, and he fired.

But Cade got his shot off first and the man toppled into the dirt. Cade swerved toward the barn, where three of the riders were headed toward him.

Through the blur of horses, dust, men, gunfire, and answering shots from inside the ranch house, Annabel rode up and immediately saw Brett plunging into the fray on a pure white stallion, but before she knew quite where to turn or what to do, her heart turned over with terror, as she suddenly noticed three riders heading full speed toward Cade, firing all the while.

Instinct made her spur Sunrise forward. Without thinking, she aimed her Colt.

She'd never fired at a man before, much less at a man on horseback, but she had no time to wonder at her ability to shoot true. Even as Cade's shot sent the nearest rider plummeting from his horse, the next rider took aim.

So did Annabel. Unhesitatingly, she squeezed the Colt's trigger.

The man screamed and toppled sideways from the saddle. As Annabel watched in stunned fascination, his horse galloped on, but the man lay sprawled in a bloody twitching heap alongside the corrals.

Nausea rose within her. She reined in Sunrise, her ears filled with a dull roar of shock, as she tried to choke back the sickness inside her.

But then, from the corner of her eye, she became aware that the third rider was now aiming his gun at her, bearing down at an impossible speed, and reflexively she raised the Colt again in a desperate attempt to fire first. But she was too late. Before either she or the man could squeeze off a shot, Cade McCallum killed him with one bullet through the heart.

The man was flung backwards off his horse, another body among the many all about them thudding into the blood-soaked dirt.

Dazed, Annabel stared around her. Above, the sky was still a brilliant cobalt blue. The mountains still gleamed in the distance. But there were six dead men on the ground. The remaining two riders were high-tailing it toward the mesas east of the ranch. Cade was still in the saddle. So was Brett, and some other men, who were talking to Brett, she realized, and concluded numbly that they must work for Conchita Rivers.

Now that the fighting was over, she felt ill. Her muscles felt cold and achy, and her temples throbbed. She pushed back her sombrero with shaking fingers, and saw a dark-haired woman in her thirties open the door of the ranch house and step onto the porch. She held a shotgun.

"It's all right, Conchita," Brett called. "They're gone for now! Anyone hurt?"

But Annabel never heard her reply. She closed her eyes and tried to brace herself in the saddle, so weak she was struggling to keep from sliding off.

Suddenly, both Brett and Cade were beside her.

"What the hell were you doing out here? Trying to

get yourself killed?" Cade demanded, but before he could reach for her, Brett stepped forward and put a hand to Annabel's arm.

Gently he tugged her down from the saddle and enclosed her in a hard embrace. "Annabel, Annabel. There now, it's all right."

"Oh, Brett," she whispered, raising wide, distraught eyes to his face. "I'm sorry to be such a ninny, but . . . I've never killed anyone before."

"Know something? Neither have I." He gave a hoarse laugh, and put his arms around her. "Go ahead and cry, Annie," he urged. "I don't mind if you soak my shirt—it wouldn't be the first time."

"I didn't mean to . . . I didn't want to, but he was going to shoot Steele . . . that is, Cade, and . . ."

"It's all right." Brett stroked her hair, holding her tight. "Don't question it—you had no choice. Annie, you just saved my brother's life."

Annabel's knees gave out, and Brett caught her up in his arms. He started toward the ranch house, where the dark-haired woman watched them both with a worried frown.

"Come inside," she urged, and held open the door.

Cade hadn't moved, but stood beside Sunrise, watching Brett and Annabel without expression.

"Cade, come on," Brett called over his shoulder as he glanced back from the door. "I want you to meet Senora Rivers. She'll explain everything. Hurry, I don't know how long we have before they come back."

Cade waited a moment longer after watching his brother carry Annabel into the adobe ranch. Her arm had been flung tightly around Brett's neck. Her head had rested against his chest, her eyes closed.

The image of this was seared in his mind like a brand. He felt stunned, baffled, and hurt. What the hell was he to believe? According to his brother, they weren't betrothed. So Annabel had lied to him about that. But from what he'd seen with his own eyes, that could change at any moment. The closeness between his brother and Miss Annabel Brannigan was apparent. It struck him with the force of a tomahawk hurled straight through the heart.

Annabel Brannigan adored Brett. She trusted him completely. And that Brett cared deeply for her was as plain as the blood running in crimson rivulets through the dust at Cade's feet.

So what the hell am I doing here? I don't belong here.

Staring at the open door of the ranch, Cade wished he could just ride away and never look back, never have to see Annabel clutching so tightly and trustingly to another man, never have to know how completely her heart was given over to someone else.

It hurt too damn much. In fact, knowing her hurt too damn much. She made him want things, things he could never have.

Ride, he thought, his chest tight with pain. *Head out and don't stop until you can't go another step, until you've left her far behind and forgotten how beautiful she is, how soft, how smart and headstrong, how good she smells, and how her lips taste sweeter than Lily's best elderberry wine . . .*

Ride!

But he couldn't ride, he couldn't run. He had a job to do, and there was no leaving until it was finished. Brett and Annabel were both in danger now, for in addition to the threat from the Lowry Cattle Company, there was still Red Cobb to be considered. Annabel's wild-goose chase would not keep him at bay for long. He could show up at any moment and he'd be mad as hell.

Cade led Sunrise and Dickens into the corral. Then he walked slowly toward the adobe building. He threw one last keen glance around the isolated mesas surrounding the ranch before forcing himself to go inside.

Chapter 16

"Would you care for some more coffee, Senorita Brannigan?"

Annabel set down her cup with a shake of her head, smiling at the elegant, copper-skinned woman who paused beside her chair. "No, thank you—*gracias,* Senora Rivers. I'm much better now."

"You must call me Conchita. We live a simple life here, my son, my mother-in-law, and me. There is no need for formality."

"Then I'm Annabel," she returned with a vivid smile, surprised by how nice it was to be in the company of a woman again, especially a woman as kind and gracefully lovely as Conchita Rivers.

She had so many questions, questions both for Brett —and for the man she now knew to be Cade McCallum.

Cade McCallum. The impact of Steele's true identity continued to stun her. All that balderdash he had told her—Brett warning him about the Hart brothers, reading about Ross McCallum in the newspapers—all of it had been a complete sham. And she had believed every word. *Some private investigator I am,* she thought glumly. *The truth was right in front of me and I was blind to it all along.*

She glanced over at Cade, standing beside the stone mantel in the simple, but brightly colorful living room of the Rivers ranch, and for just a moment, his gaze met hers. Annabel flinched at the obsidian coldness in his eyes. It was hard to believe she had ever even for a moment glimpsed a particle of warmth or of humor in those eyes. Harder than marble they were, and just as inhuman.

He has no reason to be angry with me for lying to him, none at all, she told herself. *After all the lies he told me, he is the one who ought to be ashamed.* Yet, she wished for a chance to explain to him why she had lied, and to make him see that, in essence, what she had told him was true. In her heart, she *was* promised to Brett. Her love for his brother and her wish to marry him and make him happy were as real as the puncheon floor beneath their feet.

But explanations would have to wait. There were many things to sort out now, quickly, before the ranch came under attack again, and any personal discussion with the gunman she'd known as Roy Steele would have to be postponed.

The Rivers ranch was a long, rambling adobe building, with an open portico connecting two separate areas —this parlor and the bedrooms branching off of it—and the adjoining kitchen and shed. All that Annabel had seen was spotless and cheerful. The scoured floor was adorned with a Navajo rug in bright shades of blue and yellow and green. Potted plants flanked the stone fireplace, and much of the carved wooden furniture was covered with brightly embroidered pillows. White lace curtains, a filled bookcase against one wall, and an ornately carved whatnot graced by small baskets of flowers and lovely ceramic bowls imbued the ranch house with added charm.

Adelaide Rivers, Conchita's tiny, wizened mother-in-law, occupied the rocking chair set beside the fire-place, while her grandson, Tomas, sat cross-legged at her feet, whittling a piece of wood. He was a small, olive-complexioned boy, who looked to be about ten, with a narrow, stoic face beneath silky black hair. Annabel noticed that the knife with which he was whittling seemed too big for him, but he shaved away without concern, his lips pursed in fierce concentration.

As Conchita Rivers set the coffeepot on a side table and took her place in the straight-backed chair opposite the sofa, she gave a soft sigh.

"I am sorry you were drawn into this ugly situation, Senorita . . . Annabel. Usually at the Racing Rivers Ranch we greet our guests more hospitably than with gunfire and death."

"Please don't worry about me. I'm not usually so squeamish. As a matter of fact, I've always detested girls who get the vapors."

"That's true enough." Brett, beside her, squeezed her hand. "But for a minute there, Annabel, I swear I thought you were going to swoon." His eyes danced. "Just like those females you always complained about in novels."

"I've never swooned in my life, so why should I start now—merely because I k-killed a man?" Annabel tried to keep her tone light, but her voice trembled a little over the last few words, betraying that she was still shaken by what she'd had to do.

Brett's mouth twisted into a grimace. "Well, don't bother feeling sorry for that fellow—or any of those hombres out there today, Annie. Not one of them is worth shedding a tear over," he assured her, and reached down for the bottle of tequila on the floor beside him. To Annabel's chagrin, he lifted it to his lips and drank deeply.

She made a small, uncontrollable gesture of concern, then quickly clasped her hands in her lap to keep them still. But she was worried. She had already smelled liquor on Brett's breath when he'd carried her inside. And there was something wild and pained in his usually merry eyes, something at odds with their overbright sparkle.

"You are right about that, young man," Adelaide Rivers spat out, ceasing the rocking motion of her chair. Her rheumy eyes watered. "Those low-down thieves killed my son! Butchering's too good for every one of 'em!"

Cade had been standing silently by the mantel, his broad shoulder resting against it. His expression, if possible, grew even more formidable than it had been before.

"Tell me who these men are, Brett. And what kind of trouble you've landed in here." He gave a wry shake of his head. "Later we can get to the little matter of Red Cobb."

Cade had avoided looking at Annabel as he spoke, deliberately keeping his gaze fixed on Brett's somber, unshaven face. But he had noticed the two of them holding hands, and it made him feel like he'd been gut-punched. It took all of his willpower to keep from yanking her off the sofa and into his arms, to keep from telling her that she didn't belong with Brett, she belonged with him.

But there was no time to think about Annabel now, he told himself roughly, forcing his attention back to the situation at hand. And besides, there was nothing to think about. She'd been telling him for days now how much she loved Brett. That part of her story at least was true. So that was that.

"There's not much to tell." Brett shrugged. "But I bet you could tell *me* a thing or two, Mr. Roy Steele!" He shook his head, and for just a moment the old familiar glint of laughter shone in his eyes. "Imagine, my very own big brother—the deadliest gun in the West! I've heard of you from here to Independence, but I never thought Roy Steele was *you*! Did you know they tell stories about you at night to frighten little children into minding their manners? Who'd ever have guessed that you're the man who strikes terror into so many hearts?"

"Well, not mine," Conchita Rivers said firmly. "You are a godsend, Mr. Steele. I believe it is a miracle that you came here today!" Her beautiful mahogany skin was stretched taut over her long high cheekbones, revealing the tension that gripped her in the throes of her present situation. "If you hadn't come along and helped us when you did, I believe today is the day they would have stormed the ranch and murdered us all. That would have given Senor Lowry a real reason to celebrate at his fiesta tonight."

"Glad to help, ma'am. But if we're going to get rid of these hombres for good, I'd better know exactly what's been going on and how you came to be in this spot."

His gaze shifted once more to Brett, who was drinking long gulps of tequila. "Why don't you start, little brother? How'd you hook up with Senora Rivers and her family? You're a long way from home."

"Damn straight I am." Brett set the bottle on the floor with a thump. He wiped his lips with his sleeve, scowling. "Home. That's a joke, Cade. You have no idea how much a joke it is. Sorry, ladies, for cussing, but thoughts of my so-called home aren't too pleasant these days. Let's just talk about now." He took a deep breath.

"Let's just say I headed West on a little sightseeing jaunt—I needed to get away from . . . from everything and do some thinking where I wouldn't be bothered. Also," he said, his fingers tightening on the edge of the sofa, "there was a little part of my brain that wanted to try to look for you, Cade. Of course, all my inquiries came to nothing since I had no notion you'd changed your name to Roy Steele."

Annabel heard the hint of accusatory bitterness in Brett's voice and, from Cade's expression, guessed that he had too. But he said nothing more than, "Go on."

Brett squared his shoulders. "Well, I was traveling through Arizona, heading no place in particular, just trying to forget my troubles and have a good time and figure out a few things—when I reached Eagle Gulch and struck up a conversation with the bartender in one of the saloons. He was mentioning to some other fellows at the bar that a lady from over New Mexico way was looking to hire some men to protect her ranch from being overrun by some big cattle company. The men guffawed over it," Brett said, casting a swift, apologetic glance at Conchita. "It seems that there wasn't enough money in the offer for them to risk their lives, but I asked him where I could find the lady, and he told me. So," he finished, with a careless wave of his hand, "I found Conchita, heard her story, and signed on."

"Brett is too modest. He not only signed on, he convinced several other men to join, too," Conchita put in. "Without him, the fight would already be over and I would have lost the ranch by now. But even so, even with Brett and the other men he persuaded to join us, I fear it is no use. Lowry is too powerful. As many men as we run off or kill, he just sends more. We would need a small army to fight him off, an army that would have to remain for weeks, maybe months, and even then, perhaps that devil would not give up or let us be."

"Why does he want your land so badly?" Cade asked.

"A good stream runs through our land—that is part of it. We have offered to share water rights, but Lowry wants to have control. And he wants to own virtually the entire valley."

"He's a greedy devil," Adelaide spat. "He already has the largest ranch in the valley, but he wants all the others as well."

"Most of my neighbors have already given in to him." Conchita looked from Cade to Annabel, despair darkening her deep-set black eyes. "The bloodshed has been too costly. With the railroads now in place across so much of New Mexico, it is very profitable to ship and sell cattle. The Lowry Cattle Company wants to increase their profits by increasing their holdings. Oh, if I give him the deed, he will let us stay here and farm, and keep a small herd, but he wants our land. And that is something that, out of respect for my husband's memory, I will not give to that hombre."

Brett took another gulp of the tequila, draining the last drops in the bottle. "Alec Rivers was killed a few months ago, trying to drive off some of Lowry's men who'd been poisoning his cattle. He was determined to keep the Racing Rivers Ranch for Conchita and for Tomas."

"My husband came here to the valley and started this ranch ten years ago when Tomas was born," Conchita said softly. "He loved this land. He wanted to build something here that he could pass down to his son and beyond. Alec vowed that Tomas would one day inherit this land, and live on it with his own family. But Lowry has other ideas."

"Well, he shouldn't be allowed to get away with it," Adelaide growled, her small, fierce gray eyes blazing within her wizened face.

"Isn't there any law here?" Annabel wasn't sure what was disturbing her most at this moment, the unscrupulous greed of this man Lowry, or the fact that Brett was drinking so much. She'd never seen him like this before. The clean-shaven, neatly groomed, high-spirited young man she'd always known was now a buckskin-clad, liquor-drinking cowboy, unshaven and none too clean, from what she'd seen of him. But she tried to concentrate on the immediate problem facing them. "Why is Lowry permitted to kill and steal and take whatever he pleases?" she demanded, looking from Conchita to Brett to Adelaide in amazement.

It was the old woman who answered her, beginning to rock once again. "There's no law worth speaking of in this part of the territory, missy. Oh, there's some U.S. marshals headquartered in Albuquerque and Santa Fe, but most of 'em are partial to the big cattle companies and make their own brand of justice."

"In New Mexico," Brett said, "if you want to protect your land and your family you have to fight—and fight harder and meaner than the other fellow. The only problem is, Lowry has got more money, more men, and more guns than everyone else in these parts put together."

Cade eased away from the mantel, coming slowly forward into the room. The bright sunlight flooding in the window cast amber beams across his lean, darkly bronzed face. "How many men do you have?"

"Seven, including me. We lost two today," Brett muttered. "They were patrolling the southern approach to the ranch earlier, trying to keep an eye out for Lowry's men when they were bushwhacked."

"It is hopeless. I am beginning to see that now. It would be loco to keep fighting when we cannot win." Conchita clenched her strong, brown hands into fists, then released them, dropping her fingers loosely to her sides. "I am sorry for Tomas, and for you, Adelaide, but we cannot hope to withstand them much longer. What good will the land do us if we are all dead? And that is what will happen next time. I do not think Senor Lowry will have much patience left after the beating his men endured today."

"To hell with his patience. I say there's only one way to end this." Cade stared at her with cool hard lights glinting in his eyes. "We don't sit here like wooden ducks at target practice. We attack." He spun toward his brother. "You're Ross McCallum's son. You know what he would advise. Tell us."

Brett's skin turned ashen. A strange look darted into his eyes as they met his brother's, then he glanced quickly away. "Don't ever mention that name to me again."

Annabel started. "Brett!"

He ignored her, and with an effort of concentration, returned to the subject at hand. "Without mentioning his name, I know exactly what he would do," he grated out, his voice hard and bitter. "He would destroy Lowry. Face him down, and outwit or outmuscle him. Whatever it took."

Cade nodded. "Exactly."

"And now since you, big brother, the famous gunfighter, have joined our meager ranks, we just might be able to pull it off."

"What are you talking about—what are you going to do?" Annabel didn't at all like the way this conversation was going. It sounded entirely too dangerous, for both Brett and Cade. Of course, Cade McCallum could take care of himself, she reminded herself, but still a knot of apprehension twisted inside her as she envisioned him riding out of here with Brett to perform some hopeless act of bravery that would probably get them both killed.

She realized that Cade was staring at her, and knew he saw her panic. It was impossible to penetrate beneath the black mask of his eyes. If he was touched by her concern, he certainly didn't show it.

He deliberately shifted his glance to Conchita. "What did you say about a fiesta tonight, Senora Rivers?"

"Senor Lowry is hosting a fiesta at his ranch for everyone in the valley. I think it is his way of showing off his wealth, and making it clear to all that he is the boss of this valley. But why do you wish to know?"

"Are you and your family invited?"

"Yes, everyone for miles around has been invited. But never would I go to the hacienda of the man who killed my husband . . ."

"You are going."

Conchita shook her head. "Senor, are you loco?"

"You are going, and you are bringing guests."

Brett started to grin. Conchita bit her lip. "What will you do at this fiesta, Senor McCallum?"

"With any luck, I'll kill Lowry and anyone trying to back him up."

"No!" Annabel jumped up. She kept her voice level with great effort. "You'll be in his house. Among all of his men. It's too dangerous. There must be another way."

"It's the only way."

Conchita covered her eyes with the tips of her fingers. "*Dios,* perhaps I should just hand over the deed . . ."

"The hell you will." Brett surged to his feet and straightened his shoulders. "I think it's a fine idea. If you'll let me help," he told Cade purposefully.

"If you can shoot straight, you can help."

Tomas stared up at the gunslinger, his dark eyes shining with admiration. "I want to help, too. Will you let me come?" he asked. "I want to fight the men who killed my father."

Brett gave a short laugh. "You're too little, Tomas," he said, tousling the boy's hair. "When you're grown there will be plenty of time to fight. But now you'd only get in the way."

Annabel saw the hurt flash into the boy's eyes. He peered downward quickly, his cheeks flushing, but Brett didn't notice. He had already turned away, crossing to a table near the mantel, where several bottles of liquor and some glasses stood. He poured whiskey into a glass and took a long swallow.

It was Cade who approached the boy and put a hand on his shoulder. He spoke in a low, firm tone. "I have an important job for you to do tonight, Tomas. You must come to the fiesta with us, and be on guard, ready to run with a message when I need you. Do you think you can stay up late at the fiesta and be quick and silent?"

"Si, senor. Of course."

Eagerly, the boy nodded, his small hands clutching his block of wood.

"Good. Then I'll give you your instructions later. "

The boy nodded again, this time a small proud smile curving the edges of his mouth. He beamed at his mother with pride.

Cade turned to Conchita next. "I doubt they'll be back today. Lowry will lick his wounds, and want to rethink his strategy before coming at you again—he won't want to risk another failure. My guess is he'll wait until after the fiesta to make his next move. By then, we'll have taken care of him. But just in case, I think you should have all your remaining men on guard tonight against a surprise attack during the fiesta. Only as a precaution," he said as her face blanched. "My hunch is Lowry will wait—he'll want to figure out a surefire plan, something that will end your resistance once and for all."

"That makes sense. But just in case, I will order the

men to keep watch as you said. You are very kind to lend us your help, senor."

"I don't like bullies, Senora Rivers. Never have," Cade muttered shortly. He turned and looked at Brett as he continued to speak to her. "If you'll excuse us, my brother and I will step outside for a spell. We have some catching up to do."

"Oh, no, you must visit here and make yourselves comfortable," Conchita protested, jumping up and glancing quickly at her son and mother-in-law. "Come, let us go into the kitchen and prepare some food for our guests. Brett and Senor McCallum and Senorita Brannigan must have some privacy."

But Cade held up a hand. "No, senora. I prefer to talk outside. Just the two of us," he informed Brett, as Annabel took a step toward the door.

He might just as well have slapped her. Annabel's cheeks burned. *I have as much right to discover why Brett left home as you do,* she fumed, and took a deep breath to keep from exploding. *More, actually, because where have you been these past thirteen years? I've been there, with Brett, as his companion, his friend.* Besides that, she knew him better than Cade did, and probably cared far more about him.

Not to mention the fact that Ross McCallum and Everett Stevenson have given me a job to do. And I've given my word that I won't fail.

True, she had found Brett, but until she could ascertain what had gone wrong between him and Ross, she would not be able to persuade him to come back, and only then would her mission be successfully completed.

Besides, she wanted more than anything to bring about a reconciliation between Ross McCallum and his son. No matter what had happened, Ross didn't deserve to be deserted now. With his health failing and his business empire in danger, he needed support. He needed

Brett—and maybe, Annabel thought, a renegade idea rolling into her brain—just maybe he needed Cade, too.

"You would like to leave me behind, wouldn't you, Mr. Steele?" she asked coldly. "You've been trying to do that ever since Justice—unsuccessfully, I might add. Brett," she said, turning toward him with an immutable look, "if it's all right with you, I'd like to come along for this conversation. I have many questions, and there are events going on back home which you should know about."

She heard Cade's quick, angry intake of breath, but she ignored him and kept her gaze trained on Brett.

"I don't want to know one damned thing about home," Brett muttered. But he held out his hand to her. "Still, you're always welcome, Annie. You know that. Besides, I want to hear all about how the two of you found me—and why in heaven's name you're traipsing halfway across the country after someone who doesn't deserve so much effort."

"Yes, you do." Annabel clutched his hand and studied him anxiously. "You deserve that and more."

"No. I disagree." His shoulders slumped. Suddenly, he started toward the liquor table, pulling her with him. "Better bring along a little refreshment in case we get thirsty . . ."

But Cade stepped into his path.

"I think you've had enough."

Brett glared at him with slowly building wrath. "Who the hell asked you, big brother? You're not in charge of my life. Get out of my way."

"Not a chance."

"To hell with you," Brett exploded.

Cade's expression remained cold as stone. "Let's step outside now—without the liquor. You need a clear head for our discussion, and also for what's in store tonight."

"My head is clear, damn you!" Brett let go of Annabel's hand, his mouth thinning to a cold, hard line. He took a step forward, his fists clenched, ready to shove Cade aside, but Annabel quickly seized his arm.

"Brett, please, listen to him. He's right." She saw that Conchita, Tomas, and Adelaide had all paused on the way to the kitchen, their faces tense with worry as they watched the angry interchange. But they hurried on as Annabel intervened, leaving the three alone in the quiet, pretty parlor.

"You've been drinking ever since we stepped foot inside the ranch," Annabel said quietly. "I'm worried about you. Come outside now and let's talk."

For a moment, rage blurred his features and he seemed about to lash out at her. But as Annabel continued to meet his gaze with earnest concern, the flash of anger faded.

"All right, Annie," Brett mumbled. "For you. Let's go outside."

Stillness hung over the valley as Cade led the way a short distance from the ranch house and corrals. He headed toward a clump of piñons set well back from the ranch. No one spoke a word, but Annabel glanced around the secluded area, noting the series of gray buttes that rose behind it, and the yucca and forget-me-nots interspersed among the nearby cottonwoods. She sank down upon the round stump of a tree and glanced swiftly back and forth between the McCallum brothers. She sensed Cade's anger, held so carefully in check, but she wasn't sure what had caused it. Was it Brett's drinking? Or her joining their discussion?

Possibly both, she concluded with a tiny sigh.

And then there was Brett's strange, dark mood, all the things he'd said about his father and his home, and his constant need to drink. Something was even more wrong here than she had thought.

Well, she decided, tilting her head upward for a moment toward the heated rays of the sun, and offering a quick silent prayer for guidance, *it's high time to find out what it is.*

"Brett," she murmured, as the two men continued to stare at each other, both, she guessed, uncertain how to begin. "It's obvious that something terrible must have happened to cause you to run away from home and from your father without any word the way you did. But it can be fixed, whatever it is, I'm sure of it. Will you tell me about it? Please, maybe I can help."

"No one can help, Annabel."

"Let me try."

He began to laugh, but not his familiar easy, joyful laugh. This sound made her wince. "My sweet, adorable Annie. Always trying to solve the mystery, to fit the pieces of the puzzle exactly in place. But you see, that's the problem. I solved the mystery—I know the answers. And that's why I can never go back."

"What mystery did you solve?" she asked softly, her gaze fixed on his strained, bitter face. She had a feeling something terrible was coming, and cast about in her mind for what it could possibly be. But she had no clue. Her palms were damp with sweat and she wiped them on her riding skirt as she waited for his response. Cade said nothing, merely leaning against a tree, but he watched his brother's face with tense anticipation.

Brett stared at the ground while he answered her, apparently absorbed in the progress of a fly crawling along a fallen twig. "I'll tell you what mystery I solved, Annabel—you'll be fascinated with this one. It's the mystery of my mother's death." He took a deep breath. There was a catch in his voice when he spoke again.

"Livinia McCallum did not die of a fever, as I'd always been told. No, I have learned that it was much darker and uglier than that. Now I know what Cade probably found out years ago—the discovery that made him run away when he was seventeen. And that discovery is the truth about what happened to my mother—*our* mother," he corrected, flashing a glance at his brother. "And," he added, meeting Annabel's gaze at last with bleak, bitter eyes. "the hell of it is, it was all my fault."

Chapter 17

No sound broke the stillness except the hushed rustling of the sun-gilded leaves.

"Brett, what are you saying?" Annabel breathed at last.

He swung toward her, his face so taut with misery that she wanted to enfold him in her arms. "My mother killed herself, Annabel. She took her own life. And all because of me."

"No!" Cade moved with the swiftness of a striking cobra and grasped his brother by the shoulders. He shook him fiercely. "Don't say that. It wasn't you. It was *him. Ross.* Whatever he's told you to try to lay the blame on someone else, don't believe it. You were only a baby, Brett. A toddler. What happened was Ross McCallum's fault, not yours. He's the one who killed her."

Annabel's mind was reeling. It seemed impossible that Livinia McCallum had taken her own life. Annabel had gazed countless times at the breathtaking portrait in Ross McCallum's study, and at the smaller one in the upstairs gallery, admiring the delicate, honey-haired beauty with the huge, soulful eyes. True, an aura of sadness had clung to both portraits, but Annabel had never for a moment suspected that Livinia would have been filled with such despair that she would end her life. She'd imagined that Ross McCallum adored her, that he showered her with love and riches and jewels, that her children were the apple of her eye, that she was gentle and kind and wise.

Never in a thousand moments of reflection had it once occurred to her that Livinia McCallum could have been desperately unhappy.

"So you knew. I guessed as much." Bitterness rang through Brett's voice like a hollow bell. He stared at Cade, and both men's eyes were filled with pain that went beyond words. "That was the reason you left, wasn't it?"

"You could say that. I left as soon as I discovered how Ross had lied to us for all those years about how she died."

Annabel saw that beneath his quiet self-control, a white-hot anguish held Cade in its grip. As he stood there, tall and straight and calm, unutterable weariness in his face and voice, her heart trembled and broke for him.

"One day I overheard the servants gossiping and that's how I learned the truth. You can imagine my shock—but I wasn't necessarily surprised," he added harshly. "Father rode roughshod over everyone else in his life, so why not her? He made everyone whose life he touched utterly miserable, so why not her?" Contempt glittered in his eyes. "He admitted it when I confronted him—admitted that she had taken her own life. But, damn him to hell, he had the gall to deny that it was his fault. And that's when I truly began to hate him."

"Well, it wasn't his fault, at least not completely." Brett began pacing back and forth among the clump of piñons, raking his fingers through his hair. "I'm the one you should despise—me and my father. We had far more to do with it than Ross McCallum."

If his previous statements had elicited stunned silence, this one brought forth a gasp of shock from Annabel and sent her bolting off the tree stump. "Brett, you're not making any sense. What do you mean 'me and my father'?"

"Ross McCallum is not my father, Annie. *That's* what I learned not too long ago. *That's* what sent me fleeing St. Louis, journeying far and wide to try to forget everything I ever thought I knew about myself. Oh, hell, what's the use in talking about it? I'm going back to the ranch. I need a drink."

He started off, stomping past Annabel so swiftly she had to jump out of his way, but Cade sprang forward before he'd gone three steps and blocked his path.

"Get out of my way!"

"I think you'd better stay here and tell us what the hell you're talking about."

"You do, do you?" Brett sneered at him, his face flushed and sweating. The sun was in his eyes and he squinted up at Cade, who was nearly a half a head taller than him. "What do you need, another reason to blot me from your life? You already did that thirteen years ago, big brother. Matter of fact, I don't know what the hell you're doing here now. Why you're even bothering with the half brother you walked out on so long ago and never even bothered to—"

"I came to find you. To help you—"

"I don't need your help. Or want it! Damn you, get out of my way, I want a drink!"

Without warning, his fist shot out and struck Cade in the jaw. Caught by surprise, Cade staggered back a pace.

"My God," Annabel cried, "what are you doing? Brett, how could you . . . ?"

But before she could reach Cade, he recovered and spun back, his fist slammimg into his brother's midsection in a blow that had Brett doubling over in pain.

"Damn . . . you," Brett gasped, as he dropped to his knees, clutching his stomach and sucking in desperate gulps of air. "I'll kill you, you dirty no-good . . ."

"Go ahead. I'm waiting."

Brett stumbled to his feet. Cade hit him again. As Annabel screamed, Brett went crashing down into the thick grama grass.

"Stop it!" Annabel threw herself in front of him, facing Cade with eyes that were turquoise with fury.

"How can you?" she flung at him. "He's hurt! And he's upset! If you dare hit him again, I'll . . ."

"Damn it, Annabel . . ." Brett winced as he pushed himself to his knees. "Get out of the way. I don't want or need you defending me."

"Yes, you do!"

"No, I don't! A McCallum fights his own battles! Get out of my way . . ."

"I will not!"

"Children." Cade's voice broke into their argument with icy calm. "That's enough." Cade reached out and dragged Annabel aside, setting her firmly out of the line of battle.

"Stay there."

Without waiting for her to reply, he turned back to Brett, who had by now managed to get to his feet. "You're right, little brother. A McCallum does fight his own battles," he said levelly. "He doesn't hide behind anyone or anything else—including a bottle."

"I was forgetting," Brett rasped, his face the sickly green color of a sky before a storm. "I'm not really a McCallum. So, none of that damned stuff Father—I mean, Ross McCallum—drilled into our heads counts worth a plug nickel."

"You don't believe that any more than I do. You are what you are and you can't change it now. Tell me why you think Ross is not your father."

"Because he isn't."

"Explain."

Brett took a deep breath. He glanced once from Cade's coldly speculative countenance to Annabel's anxious one, and let out a string of oaths. "It's true, damn it. I'm not who I always thought I was, not at all. I don't know who I am. My real father was quite a paragon, though, let me tell you that. If I take after him"—he gave a choking laugh—"then it will be better for all concerned if Red Cobb does catch up to me or if Lowry's men finish me off tonight once and for all."

Annabel turned toward Cade, wondering if he understood any better than she what Brett was talking about. But he looked just as skeptical as she felt. Obviously this was a revelation to him as well.

"I think you should begin at the beginning," she told Brett softly, trying to make her voice as soothing and steady as she could. "Neither Cade nor I understand what you're talking about. Are you *certain* that Ross McCallum is not your father?"

"Quite."

"How?"

Brett covered his face with his hands. "Oh, hell, what's the use?" he muttered, and sank down wearily on the grass. Instantly, Annabel knelt beside him.

"The day before I ran away," he said dully, without looking at her, "I received a strange letter. The man who sent it requested that I come to see him at the Fairbanks Hotel. The letter said it was urgent that he speak with me. So I went." He plucked a blade of grass from the gray-green hillside, then another and another. He opened his fingers and watched them float aimlessly to the soft, fragrant earth. "The man's name was Frank Boxer."

"Go on," Annabel urged. Cade stood stock still, watching Brett's face without his own expression revealing anything of what he was feeling.

"Boxer told me a story so horrible I could scarcely believe it was true. He told me how he had worked for my father—that is, for Ross McCallum—as his man of business for many years. And he told me that he had fallen under the spell of my mother. And," he finished in a miserable rush, "he told me that he . . . and . . . she . . . had become lovers."

Cade had been standing motionless beside a tree during all this speech, but now he stepped forward. "What kind of hogwash is this? You believe what this son of a bitch stranger tells you about your own mother? It wasn't Mama who violated her marriage vows. I'd wager my hat, boots, and saddle it was the other way around. Father is the one who no doubt kept a mistress and broke her heart . . ."

"No." Brett looked up into his brother's flushed and angry face, his own awash in despair. "I don't think so, Cade. You see, when Frank Boxer had finished his sordid little tale, I went straight to Father. I was so upset I could barely speak." He turned to Annabel, as if looking for understanding, or answers, or some magic way to calm the turmoil inside him. "I was beside myself with rage and doubt and questions," he said in a low tone. "But Father confirmed part of what Boxer had told me."

"Brett, no!" Annabel's heart ached for him, and for Cade. She shook her head. "Are you sure you didn't misunderstand?"

"Oh, yes," he muttered, "I'm sure. Of course, Ross had a completely different view of the subject. And I didn't tell him that I had spoken with Boxer personally. I just told him that someone had brought details of my mother's death to my attention, and I needed to know if they were true. He admitted then that she had taken her life, and had not died of a fever as the world at large— or at least, you and I and all of St. Louis society—believed. I asked him straight out if a man named Frank Boxer was involved in any way. He turned purple. He swore and shouted; he smashed a brandy decanter against the wall. And he demanded with the full force of his rage that I tell him who had mentioned Frank Boxer's name to me. I wouldn't tell him. We had quite a row."

"I can well imagine," Cade said grimly.

"The McCallums are not precisely known for their mild tempers," Annabel murmured.

"Yes, but you see that's the whole point in a nutshell, Annie." Thick sarcasm coated Brett's voice as he continued. "I'm not a real McCallum, after all. According to Frank Boxer—and this was confirmed by the man I thought was my father—I am really Brett Boxer."

"I don't believe it." Cade walked to the nearest piñon and paused, staring out for a moment at the cloudless lilac sky, and the black buttes stretching into the distance. "Mama wouldn't . . . she couldn't have . . ." He wheeled back. "There's been a mistake. Or a lie. Someone is playing a filthy game."

"Believe it, big brother." Brett gave a mirthless, ugly laugh. "But there's more. Let me explain everything Frank Boxer told me that day at the hotel. He claimed that he and Mama loved each other passionately, that he wanted to run off with her, to marry her and claim me as his child, but that she was too frightened of Ross to follow her heart. And Ross, fearing a scandal above all things, offered Boxer a huge sum of money to leave Missouri before I was born and to never come back."

"Did he . . . take the money?" Annabel ventured,

wondering how much more there was to this awful tale, thinking of poor Livinia caught between the man she loved and the man to whom she was married.

"He did."

Never had she seen such blazing fury as she saw then in Brett's usually dancing eyes. "He made no excuses for it either. Boxer claimed he didn't see how he could fight all of Ross McCallum's power, wealth, and influence. Said he thought it would be best for Livinia if he just disappeared. So," Brett continued, his lip curling, "He left her. He went away for a while, but when I was a year old, he came back. He told me that his feelings for Livinia got the better of him, that he couldn't stay away any longer, and he wanted both of us to come and live with him. This next part is not too pretty, but . . ." His face twisted as he glanced at Cade's stony countenance. "It shouldn't surprise you much. When he showed up again, Father took drastic steps to keep him from embarrassing the McCallums by persuading Mama to run away with him. Boxer claims . . ." His voice trailed off for a moment, then he cleared his throat and continued. "He claims that Father hired men to grab him—that he was kidnapped and shipped off to the West Indies, virtually imprisoned first on a plantation there for a landowner Father did business with, and then later forced into labor on a ship owned by the same man, a ship called the *Emerald Prince.*"

"You're right." Cade stalked back and regarded his brother from beneath the brim of his hat. "It *doesn't* surprise me. It's exactly the sort of ruthless act I would expect of Ross McCallum. He taught me when I was still in short pants that you don't merely defeat a competitor, you annihilate him."

"Well, in this case, why not?" Annabel exclaimed indignantly. "I'll admit that it does sound rather drastic on the surface. But it's not all that unreasonable," she argued, "for a man like Ross McCallum to take strong action when he's threatened. After all, this Frank Boxer was trying to destroy your father's life, to ruin his marriage and his family, not to mention publicly humiliating him before the very community that held him in such high esteem. You can't blame him for being put out."

"That's an interesting way of describing it," Cade drawled.

"And besides," Annabel went on, fixing him with her sternest glance, "this Frank Boxer does not sound like any paragon of virtue. I think he had it coming!"

"Since when did you become so bloodthirsty?" The shadow of despair lifted momentarily from Brett's face as he regarded her with a wry smile.

"I'm not in the least bit bloodthirsty—but I do see the value in protecting one's own. Especially now that I've spent some time in this part of the country. I've watched as your brother has been forced to dispatch one unsavory scoundrel after another, and I've concluded that all the world is not as genteel as it should be, and oftentimes drastic measures are in order. Besides," she added, after this remarkably long speech, and observing that Brett was shaking his head in amazement, and Cade McCallum was rolling his eyes heavenward, "how do we know that what Frank Boxer said is true? Maybe he just told you that your father did this to shock you and try to win your sympathy. Maybe he made it all up . . ."

"No. Father confirmed it himself. He admitted it after we had a horrendous fight. And swore that if he had it to do over again he'd do things exactly the same way. He was under the impression," Brett finished, rubbing a hand over the stubble on his jaw, "that Boxer died during a mutiny attempt on the *Emerald Prince*, but he was wrong. Boxer survived."

"How?" Annabel inquired.

"Who knows—luck, toughness, circumstance. He told me that he was one of only a handful of survivors who managed to escape the ship. So after years of virtual imprisonment, he and his fellow surviving mates fled to India. Apparently he made his fortune there, and for the past twelve years he's been amassing an even greater one."

"And what," Cade asked slowly, his voice hard, his eyes almost opaquely black within his bronzed face, "does he want now with you?"

Brett stared down at the grass again. "When I went to meet him at the hotel, he said he wanted to claim me as his son. To be a father to me at last. And to share the empire he's built with me. He offered me twenty percent of everything he's built and acquired." His lips twisted. "It was an impressive list of companies, with some freight yards, mines, and railroad holdings thrown in for good measure. But there was a nice little catch."

"There always is."

"Boxer wanted me to sign over all of my interests in *Father's* companies to *him.*"

"*What?*" Annabel felt her pulse starting to race. Things were beginning to make sense. A queer, dangerous kind of sense. She didn't fully understand it yet, but a queasy feeling in the pit of her stomach told her she soon would. Things were far more amiss with the McCallums than anyone had first guessed. An old enemy . . . this shocking story . . . an attempt to take over Ross McCallum's business interests . . .

"How much of an interest are we talking about here?" she asked abruptly, not caring that the McCallums' personal concerns might be none of her affair, caring only that she sensed trouble. Big trouble.

"Considerable. On my twenty-first birthday, my father made me a partner in several of his concerns. I own twenty percent of the stock in numerous McCallum factories and companies, plus a sizable share of railroad stock. Boxer wanted me to sign everything over to him, in exchange for twenty percent of his ownings."

"Twenty percent for twenty percent," Annabel murmured.

"It seems his goal in life is to wreak his revenge on Ross McCallum. He didn't say as much, but I knew by looking into his eyes that he wanted to wrest control of all of my father's business enterprises and bring him to ruin."

Annabel touched Brett's sleeve. "What did you say?"

"I knocked him down," Brett spat. "Bloodied his damned nose." His twisted smile held a measure of crude satisfaction. "Then I marched out of there and went home to talk to Father. I wasn't sure I believed Boxer's story, not on the surface, but deep down, I knew it was true. Most of it, I guess. I couldn't get much out of Father—he was in too much of a fury—but he confirmed all the major points—the love affair between Mama and Frank Boxer, the money paid to get the son of a bitch out of town, the eventual drastic action Father took to get rid of him when Boxer returned to claim Mama and his 'son.'"

"What about the suicide?" Cade spoke quietly. "How did that fit into all of this mess?"

"According to Boxer, Mama killed herself because she was miserable with Father and he wouldn't let her go. He wouldn't allow a divorce, a scandal, wouldn't stand to have the McCallum name and reputation sullied. Boxer insists he could have made her happy, but that Father kept them apart and crushed her will to live. And he also added that Ross never let her forget that her son was a bastard, a bastard he was raising as his own." Brett's voice was so low Annabel had to lean very close to hear him. "He claims that Father continually reminded her that instead of throwing her out as she deserved, she was fortunate to be able to continue living a life of luxury, fortunate her son would be raised as a gentleman and would inherit an empire—far more than either of them deserved." His voice, thick with bitterness, broke. But after one ragged gasp, he managed to continue. "Boxer claims that at last she couldn't take his tirades anymore, couldn't take the lectures and the constant burden of guilt he heaped upon her shoulders, and she sought the only way out she could find."

Brett threw himself down on his back in the grass, staring dully up at the sky. Beside him, Annabel closed her eyes. Poor Livinia. And poor Brett. A chilly gray sadness crept through her at the thought of pale, lovely Livinia caught in a vise of such utter misery. Suddenly she opened her eyes and looked at Cade. He had turned away, toward the vista of gray-green sage and golden plains. She could not see his face, but his powerful shoulders were tensed beneath his flannel shirt and he stood perfectly still, motionless as a stone statue.

She rose without thinking and went to him. Without conscious thought, without even realizing what she was doing, she gently reached out and touched his arm.

"I'm so sorry. Are you all right?"

The sight of his face shook her. It was ashen. The hard strong bones looked even sharper than before, and the grimness in his eyes had been replaced by an expression of such utter desolation that it ripped at her heart. As if dazed, he glanced over at her, then down at her slender hand upon his arm.

"I'm fine. Right as rain." But he looked like a soul in torment. Annabel's hand crept up to his cheek, and touched it softly. If only there was a way she could erase the pain that gripped his strong, handsome face. She knew it was tearing through his insides with a searing intensity, an intensity no less profound for the years that had passed since Livinia took her life.

Cade had left home at seventeen because he'd learned of his mother's suicide, she reflected sorrowfully, and because he'd discovered the lies with which his father had covered it up. He'd blamed his father all those years ago, instinctively and automatically, but back then he had not known the full story.

Now he did. Or did he?

Something was not right here. She thought back over everything Brett had said, and suddenly it hit her.

"How did Frank Boxer know all this?" she demanded, whirling toward Brett. "About what your father said to Livinia, about the cruel lectures and the taunts."

"I guess Mama must have confided her pain to him," Brett began, but Annabel interrupted him, shaking her head.

"He was kidnapped, remember? How could he possibly know what was happening to Livinia in St. Louis right before she died, if he was in the West Indies?"

Silence greeted her question. Beneath a cottonwood tree, a pair of squirrels skittered wildly about, then chased each other through the grass and past a spattering of wildflowers.

Cade spoke roughly. "What does it matter? My mother took her own life because my father made her so miserable that—"

"You don't know that for certain. You only know what Frank Boxer told Brett."

"I know what kind of man my father was—and is."

Brett was pacing now, round and round the little clearing, his boots crunching in the dry grass. "Ross said he loved her—he swore to me he was trying to protect her—that's about all I gave him a chance to explain, though," he admitted. "I didn't even tell him I'd spoken with Boxer. We were both too angry and too upset for much rational conversation."

"And you ran away without ever telling him that Boxer was back? Brett, how could you? That man hates your father. He's an enemy, no doubt a dangerous one! Why, you know yourself that he planned to bring your father to financial ruin—he wanted you to help him!"

"Yes, but I made it clear to him when my fist landed in his face that I wouldn't be a part of anything like that. And Annabel, I didn't exactly run out without explaining anything. I left a letter detailing my meeting with Frank Boxer and warning my father—that is, Ross—of Boxer's scheme. I made sure that Ross McCallum was fully alerted to his plans. But I just couldn't stay to thrash it out with him anymore. I wasn't in the mood to listen. I was in the mood to run, to escape. I needed to be away from him, from that big beautiful house where I really didn't belong, and I needed a chance to do some thinking."

"Your father never received that letter. At least, not so far as I know," Annabel said coolly.

Both men stared at her.

"How do you know that?" Brett stopped pacing long enough to plant himself before her.

"Because he reported to Mr. Everett Stevenson that you ran away without any kind of letter or explanation. Oh, it was clear there had been some kind of a quarrel, but he obviously hadn't known you were going to just up and disappear—and he told Mr. Stevenson that there was no farewell letter of any sort. Why, it was only later that he received your letter postmarked Justice. He *did* know about Red Cobb chasing after you, because a business acquaintance in Kansas City alerted him to that bit of gossip—and by the way, that's something we need to discuss, too—but Brett, I'm certain that your letter about Frank Boxer never reached him."

"Who the hell is Everett Stevenson?" Cade demanded, stalking toward her. "And if you're not really Brett's little fiancée, how the hell do you come to know so much about all this?"

Annabel took a deep breath. *Here it comes,* she thought. *The explosion. Cade McCallum, you won't like this one little bit.*

"Everett Stevenson II is the president of the Stevenson Detective Agency. Ross McCallum hired him to find Brett and bring him safely home before Red Cobb could put a bullet in him." She met Cade's gaze as steadily as she could, wondering if he would simply shoot her or if he'd strangle her first and then finish her off with his gun. "I work for Mr. Stevenson—I'm a private investigator. He assigned me to Brett's case."

Anger as harsh and bitter as a Wyoming winter descended over Cade's features. For a moment she thought he really might pull his gun. "So," he said at last, his eyes like chips of black granite, "you're nothing but a little liar. Ross McCallum's paid sneak. I should have known."

The brutal calm with which he spoke the words stung her deeper than the lash of a whip. "No! Cade," she pleaded, desperation washing over her. "Let me explain!"

Annabel reached a hand toward him, but the scorn on his face stopped her cold.

"Reckon I'll pass on that, Miss Brannigan. I've heard enough of your lies to last me a lifetime."

Something inside of her withered like a wilted flower as Cade wheeled away toward the ranch house. Before he'd gone ten steps, he halted and threw a glance back at his brother. "We have a fight to finish. You coming?"

"Soon." Brett drew an arm around Annabel as he answered, drawing her shaking form close to him.

Cade frowned at them. "Suit yourself."

When he strode away this time, he didn't look back.

"You and my brother don't seem to like each other very much," Brett commented, leading her back toward the tree stump and sitting her down. "What's behind all this?"

Annabel was still seeing in her mind's eye Cade's coldly furious face. She could still hear his quietly contemptuous words flaying at her. "What?" she asked distractedly, as Brett shook his head and repeated his question. "Oh, well, it's a long story, Brett. And very complicated. I'm too tired to talk about it right now."

"Too tired—or too upset?" he asked curiously, studying the sheen of suppressed tears in her eyes. "You know, I have a few questions for you, too, Annie. How did you come to be the private investigator my father sent hunting after me? And why'd you tell my brother that you were my fiancée?" He gave a short laugh, his face softening a little with affection for her.

"It's me, Annie, so stop playing your games. Time to fess up."

"Oh, Brett, I can't talk about it now." She stood up, peering past him in the direction of the ranch house. "I have to find Cade."

Vaguely, she knew she ought to be questioning Brett about Red Cobb and about Lucas Johnson, finding out if Brett had any idea why Johnson wanted him dead. And she also knew she should head immediately to Skull Creek to wire Mr. Stevenson with her latest theories and suspicions. Yet another part of her felt she should be making the most of these moments alone in this beautiful wild spot with Brett, opening her heart to him, and letting him know how much she loved him, and yet all she could think about was Cade.

"No, you don't." Brett placed his hands firmly on

her shoulders as she tried to edge past him. "You haven't given me a single answer."

She scowled at him in exasperation as a sudden gust ruffled his dark hair and sent her own loose cinammon curls flying. "Has anyone ever told you that you ask too many questions?"

"No. That's what most people usually tell *you.*" He grinned.

She smiled back. But then she turned her head again and fixed her gaze on Cade just before he disappeared inside the ranch.

Something odd was happening here, something she didn't understand at all, but which she couldn't deny. She was all alone beneath a lemon sun and a lilac sky with Brett, her Brett, and all she could think about was his brother.

What is wrong with me?

"I didn't know who Cade was when I met him—he was, after all, only Roy Steele," she explained slowly, her eyes still fixed on the ranch. "So of course I never guessed he was your brother. And I didn't fully trust him at first, and didn't think he would help me find you unless I had a very good reason—so I simply told him I was your fiancée." She sighed. "I never dreamed everything would get so complicated . . ."

Brett had been watching her face. He knew Annabel Brannigan as well as he knew any person on earth, and a strange thought popped into his mind as he saw the way she was staring at the place where his brother had disappeared.

"I think I'm beginning to understand," he murmured.

"Are you?" All Annabel could muster was a wry, sad little smile. "I'm glad, Brett, very glad indeed—because I don't." She leaned against him, felt his arms tighten protectively around her suddenly, and sighed again, feeling more bereft and confused than she ever remembered. "I thought I had everything in my life figured out, but now . . . it seems I don't understand anything at all."

Chapter 18

"Senorita Annabel, who would ever have guessed that your carpetbag should carry so many treasures?" Conchita gave her head a shake, and smiled in amusement as she watched Annabel brush her hair before the spare bedroom mirror. "That gown—it is *muy hermosa*. And your jewels are also lovely. I think Senor McCallum—both Senor McCallums—will be most pleased to escort you to the fiesta tonight."

"Not in the least," Annabel dismissed the compliments with a rueful smile. She turned, hairbrush in hand, to face the woman seated on the edge of the narrow bed. "Brett probably will not even notice my gown —he never has—and as for Cade McCallum, all he cares about is forcing Lowry into a fight. I'm sure escorting me to his private little battleground is the last thing on his mind."

Conchita pursed her lips. For a quick-witted and intelligent young woman, which Annabel Brannigan gave every appearance of being, she was dense as a thicket of cedar. Conchita had seen the way Cade McCallum looked at her, and she would have bet every inch of the Racing Rivers Ranch that he was more than a little interested in this pretty girl who had come in search of Brett.

But "We shall see," was all Conchita replied as she helped to clasp the amber necklet at Annabel's nape.

"*Perfecta.*"

Annabel smiled back in the mirror, and then allowed her gaze to rest upon her own reflection.

A pleasantly attractive image gazed back at her. "I guess I'll do," she allowed, but her dimples popped out as her smile widened. "Maybe the McCallum brothers will notice me after all."

She had chosen her favorite of her two Sunday best dresses—the sea-foam green silk with the leg-of-mutton sleeves and the fitted waist accentuated by the smart cream-lace sash. The soft green of the gown brought out vivid matching flecks in her eyes, and looked striking with her hair, which glistened to a rich burnished sheen. She had arranged it in an elaborate chignon, with tiny curls framing her face. With her amber necklet and the daintily dangling amber earbobs, silk stockings, and cream-colored slippers, she looked very nearly as elegant as the fashionable young women Brett squired around back home, Annabel decided.

She forced herself to walk sedately as she followed Conchita Rivers from the small but comfortably appointed guest bedroom to the parlor, and told herself it really didn't matter what Cade McCallum thought of her appearance at all.

When they reached the parlor, Adelaide, Tomas, and the McCallum brothers were already dressed and waiting. A flush of color tinged Annabel's cheeks as four pairs of eyes swerved all at once toward her and Conchita.

Adelaide spoke first, an approving smile on her thin old lips. "You gals look right nice. Better than old Calvin Lowry deserves."

Tomas grinned at the striking figure of his mother in her tight-sleeved russet taffeta, with her hair coiled in an elegant coronet atop her head. "*Sí,* Mama. You're beautiful."

"You're both beautiful," Brett declared warmly, coming forward with a grin to offer Annabel his arm. He didn't look any the worse for his afternoon's confessions; as a matter of fact he had cleaned himself up, shaved, brushed his hair, and dressed neatly in a gray silk shirt and dark trousers, with a black string tie and vest. To Annabel's relief he didn't appear to have been drinking—he looked clear eyed and alert, and most delightfully impressed with her toilette.

"You're even prettier than the last time I saw you," he told her, sounding surprised. "Or is it only an appetite for blood that's giving you this glow, and causing your eyes to shine so bewitchingly tonight, my incorrigible little Annie?"

"I am not the bloodthirsty wretch you make me out to be!" Annabel protested, yet she blushed beneath the admiring intentness of his gaze, and her heart took flight and began to soar. Was she imagining it, or was Brett finally noticing that she was a woman? She'd never seen this particular kind of interest in his glance before, but he was certainly appraising her face and her figure in the flowing silk gown, and from the way he was smiling, he didn't appear to have found anything lacking.

Joy leapt through her and she tucked her arm eagerly in his, but the next moment it died as Cade McCallum, instead of saying one word to her about her appearance or anything else, stalked to the ranch door.

"Time to be going." The familiar hard tone was like a blow to her heart. He didn't even glance once at her as he held the door wide for the little group to pass through.

"Coming." Brett steered Annabel toward the liquor

cabinet. "First, I think this occasion calls for a drink. Something to fortify us for the—"

"We don't need fortifying. We need to get to the fiesta and get on with this," Cade interrupted him evenly. "Leave the liquor alone and let's go."

An angry red flush spread up Brett's neck and into his cheeks. "I'm sick and tired of you trying to order me around! What I do is none of your damn business. I was getting along fine on this job before you showed up and no one has appointed you leader—"

"Brett, please," Conchita interrupted, her tone low and pleading. "You have saved our lives more than once —our gratitude is endless, but your brother is a skilled gunman as none of the rest of us are. We need him tonight, his gun as well as his guidance. And he is right. Liquor will not help any of us this evening—we must have clear heads to follow Senor Cade's lead, we must have all our wits about us if any of us are to survive this fiesta and whatever trouble erupts."

"So go without me. You don't need me. You just said as much." Brett wrenched free of Annabel, and grabbed a whiskey bottle from the cabinet. "Go on. You have Cade McCallum, the genuine son of the great Ross McCallum. You couldn't do any better. So go away, and leave me be."

"Brett." Caught between exasperation and anger, Annabel regarded him through narrowed eyes. "You're acting like a ten-year-old. No," she added, with a glance at Tomas, so quietly serious and mature for his age. "Like a *six*-year-old. We *do* need you and we are asking for your help. The Brett McCallum I know would never let down the people who need him." She shook his arm, as he paused with the bottle in his hand. "Have you really changed so much? Aren't you the same person I've known and . . . and cared for all these years?"

"No! Yes! Hell, I don't *know,* Annabel." Brett suddenly closed his eyes and sighed. "You're right. I'm acting like a damned fool. Can't seem to help it lately," he muttered.

He threw Conchita and Adelaide an apologetic smile. "Sorry, senoras. *Vamonos.*"

Still, he ignored Cade as he stalked past him out the door.

They drove up the long, tree-flanked drive leading up to the Lowry hacienda in style. Brett drove the women and Tomas in the Rivers's carriage, while Cade rode alongside on Dickens. It was a grim procession, with scarcely a word spoken as they traveled along beneath a dark sky murky with clouds, unlit by stars or moon. The air felt hot and close and heavy, as if a storm was brewing, and once Annabel thought she heard distant thunder echo across the mountains.

As the carriage halted in the bright, torch-lit courtyard before the ranch, Annabel found herself smoothing and resmoothing the silken folds of her skirt. She scarcely noticed the grandeur of the rambling, two-story Lowry ranch, with its extensive outbuildings and corrals, its wide wraparound porch and gleaming pillars; she scarcely heard the gay flow of music streaming forth into the warm, humid night, music interspersed with laughter and merriment. She was watching Cade, wondering if she would ever again have a moment to try to explain to him, to make him understand.

He must hate me now for lying to him—even though he lied to me as well. Yet she sensed that, to him, her greatest sin was working for Ross McCallum. What was it Cade had called her? His father's paid sneak. Frustration chafed at her as Brett helped first Adelaide and then Conchita to alight. When it was her turn, his fingers clasped her lightly around the waist as he set her down.

"You look like an angel, tonight, Annabel. You ought to be able to simply fly up there and through the door and dazzle Lowry to death with your beauty."

"Flatterer!" Annabel laughed at him, though her heart beat a shade faster at the warmth in his eyes. "I'm not one of your fashionable debutantes, Brett. You can't bamboozle me with a lot of fancy talk."

"Oh, can't I?" he teased her, and with elaborate courtliness took her arm to escort her up the flower-lined path to the door. But Annabel saw Cade watching them, stony eyed, and she suddenly halted.

"Brett, go on ahead with Conchita for just a moment. I must . . . that is, there is something I must discuss with Cade."

"Annabel . . ."

She heard him sigh as she slipped away from him to the fence post where Cade stood beneath a canopy of indigo sky.

The scent of roses floated on the night air. But there was tension in the air, too, a raw, charged energy at odds with the lush scent. Then, for a moment, lightning lit the sky, and in its brief flare she was more aware than ever that Cade tonight of all nights looked incredibly handsome. Annabel waited until he had fixed that piercing black gaze upon her and then she offered him up her most winsome smile.

"I know that you're furious with me, but if you'd give me a moment to explain . . ."

"Don't have a moment. I have a job to do."

He started to brush past her, but she clutched his arm. "Not so fast, Mr. Steele."

He paused then and studied her, his expression so grim and thunderous she might have been frightened, but she wasn't.

"You lied to me, too," she pointed out softly.

"For good reason. I don't go by the name McCallum anymore. I don't like what it represents."

"Did you ever think that maybe you've been a shade too hard on your father all these years? Maybe it wasn't really his fault that your mother took her life—maybe this Frank Boxer had far more to do with it than you think—maybe your father only covered up the truth to protect you and Brett . . ."

"Maybe we should go in now and finish this business with Lowry before Red Cobb shows up. I like to take my enemies on one at a time whenever possible."

He gripped her firmly by the elbow before she could reply and nearly dragged her up the path until they'd caught up with the rest of their party.

It's no use talking to this man when he's in this mood, she decided. Besides, he was right. They all needed to concentrate on what lay ahead. Distractions could be fatal at a time like this. Obviously Cade McCallum was well accustomed to setting his sights on what needed to be done and blocking out everything else. She'd better do the same if she wanted to be of any help whatever in the tinderbox situation they were embarking on now.

Cade drew her up the steps and through the door of the hacienda, taking in the scene before him in one lightning glance, without appearing to notice anything but the woman at his side. In truth, he was far more aware of Annabel than was healthy under these circumstances, but how could he not be aware of her when she looked so radiant and charming, a delicate-boned pixie completely out of place in the rugged wilds of New Mexico. He'd never seen her dressed in silk before—it flowed over her curves and made him want to touch parts of her he'd never dared out of honor to set his hands to. But now . . . damn it, she was *not* Brett's fiancée, after all, and that truth set his imagination galloping like a runaway bronco. He couldn't seem to help wondering what it would feel like to do all those things to her that he'd been trying not to think about doing for days now. . . .

She was the most compelling woman in the room. And he wasn't sure why, Cade reflected, since Lowry had some real beauties on hand at this little fiesta. The immense candlelit parlor with its gold damask draperies and wide curtained windows shone like an opal, ablaze with light and brilliance. Men in fancy garb, with their string ties and gleaming boots, lounged and drank in groups with prettily attired women in all manner of silks and satins, beribboned and bejeweled. Several, he noticed, were stunning girls with upswept curls, buxom figures, and exquisite faces almost too perfect to be true. But none compared to the cinammon-haired enchantress at his side, with her pert, sparkling face so full of lively intelligence, and her large vibrant eyes which tonight mirrored the sea-foam green of her gown. Annabel might not be as tall as some, as robustly buxom as others, but her figure was gracefully sensuous, and her delicate features had a subtle beauty, warmed by an earnest sweetness and compassion which had begun to haunt his dreams. All these years he had fought against any but the most superficial involvement with any woman. He had frequented whores, kept things strictly businesslike, and never let his heart or any emotions be touched, and now, in trying to help Brett—who needed some serious straightening out, unless Cade missed his guess—he had become inadvertently involved with someone he could only end up hurting. Yet she was the last person on earth he would ever want to hurt.

Consternation at this predicament gouged at him, and it took all of his resolution to keep from staring at her, drinking in the way she looked, the intoxicatingly sweet way she smelled, the quiet grace with which she walked. Annabel Brannigan might not be engaged to

Brett yet, but it was clear she sure as hell wanted to be
—and judging by his brother's affection for her, it might
not be long before he caught on to the idea himself.

*So forget about her—she's not for you, never was,
never could be—and fix your sights on Lowry. After that,
you and Brett can get down to straightening out some Mc-
Callum family business.*

Just ahead of him, Conchita Rivers stopped dead as
a burly, stoop-shouldered man with coarse, sandy hair, a
ruddy complexion, and eagle-sharp eyes the color of
warm molasses swung into her path.

That's Lowry, or I'm a Gila monster, Cade concluded.

"Senora Rivers. Never expected to see you here tonight, but . . . say, I'm damn glad you're here. And
you've brought your boy, too. Fine, that's real fine.
Look, boys," he said, half-turning toward three slick-
haired cowboys in plaid shirts and string ties, "look
who's finally decided to be neighborly. And she's even
brought some guests."

Conchita drew herself up to her full height. "We're
most happy to accept your kind invitation, Senor
Lowry." Her tone was even, yet edged with subtle
haughtiness, and Cade had to admire the woman's self-
possession. She made introductions with unruffled
steadiness, while at her side, Tomas's dark eyes flashed
with an anger the youth was struggling to suppress.

When Conchita introduced Annabel as, "my friend,
Senorita Brannigan," Lowry's eyes lit with interest and
his heavy-jowled face creased into a smooth, ebullient
smile. He studied the bright-haired young woman in the
lushly appealing green silk gown with an appreciative
smirk.

"Pleasure, ma'am."

"I wish I could say the same," Annabel murmured

so sweetly that Lowry did a double take, obviously unsure he had heard correctly.

His gaze narrowed. "Are you staying at the Racing Rivers Ranch long, Miss Brannigan? It might not be healthy," he replied a little more curtly.

"For whom, Mr. Lowry? You?"

Brett gave a low chuckle, and Lowry's gaze, hardening, swept over the pair of them with icy rage.

Cade almost grinned himself. Annabel Brannigan never failed to amuse him with that tart tongue of hers, and an unfailing compulsion to speak her mind. Yet the woman had style, magnificent, undeniable style. She looked as elegant as the most pampered hothouse flower, yet there was iron in her eyes and in her backbone, and cold fire in her sweetly uttered words. He wanted to flay Lowry for the damned insinuating way he had inspected her, but hell and the devil if Annabel couldn't put him in his place all by herself.

Cade had no more time to contemplate the situation, for Conchita had now introduced all but himself. As she murmured, "Our friend, Roy Steele," as he had instructed her, with exactly the right degree of confident composure, Lowry's jaw dropped.

The cowboys beside the cattleman grew still. They stared at Cade, stared hard, and one by one their leathered faces turned pale. Cade, however, didn't even spare them a glance. He locked eyes with Calvin Lowry, and his insides turned glacially cold with the deadly purpose he allowed to consume him at such moments.

Long seconds passed during which time Annabel swore she could hear the candle wax melting inside the wall sconces. Lowry was the first to drop his gaze. But he recovered his composure after one gulped breath, and snapped his jaw shut. The brown eyes narrowed, and she breathed a sigh of relief as he extended a big, rough hand toward the gunslinger.

"Steele, eh?" He gave a slight guffaw, an offensive sound. "I reckon you already met up with some of my boys today."

"You mean the ones I shot?" Cade ignored the cattleman's outstretched hand.

Lowry flushed. He dropped his hand, and clenched it into a fist. The cowboys at his side leaned forward slightly, following the conversation with taut attention.

"Hell, Steele," Brett interpolated, his thumbs hooked nonchalantly in his gun belt. "You didn't shoot all of 'em. Me and the other boys picked off a few too."

"It's not exactly sociable to talk about shooting at a fiesta, gentleman." Lowry's eyes glittered as coldly as a winter moon.

"It's not exactly sociable to kill your neighbor's husband—and son," Adelaide burst out.

The groups chattering around the room suddenly grew quiet. Everyone seemed to be waiting, staring.

Are they going to start shooting right now? Annabel wondered in horror as she noticed several other hard-visaged cowboys edging toward them. But Lowry held up his hand.

"Now, folks, let's not get excited. We're all neighbors after all, and we're here to have a good time." He waved off his men, and boomed out a hearty chuckle as he once more locked gazes with the gunman known as Roy Steele.

"You're more than welcome, Senora Rivers, and all of your friends. Especially you, Steele. Matter of fact, I'd like a chance to talk with you. Maybe we can exchange a word or two in private."

"Lowry, I reckon I'd rather try to hogtie a skunk."

Cade was smiling laconically as he spoke these words, but that did nothing to take the sting out of them; in fact, it seemed to add an edge to the insult.

The remaining veneer of affability vanished from Lowry's face, and in the flickering candlelight that bathed the parlor in golden illumination, his jowly cheeks turned purple.

"I've tried real hard to be sociable, seeing as you people are my guests," he growled, and the three cowboys beside him all went still again, their shoulders tensing. "But you're downright rude, Mister Steele. I don't cotton to rudeness."

"Is that a fact? Didn't know you were so quick to get your tender little feelings hurt, Calvin."

"We'll just see who gets hurt," one of the cowboys snapped, but Lowry flashed him a frown to silence him. "Now, now, no one's going to get hurt. Since I'm the host here and it's my job to see everyone has a good time, I'm going to ignore your insults, Mr. Steele, and instead I'm going to dance with this pretty young lady here. Miss Brannigan, will you do me the honor?"

Without waiting for a reply, he swung Annabel toward the area that had been cleared for dancing, to join half a dozen other couples twirling about the floor.

"I hate seeing that no-good snake with his arms around Annie," Brett muttered and started forward, but Cade clapped a hand on his shoulder.

"You stay with Conchita and Adelaide—keep them safe. I don't trust Lowry for a minute." He looked down at the wide-eyed boy beside him and spoke in a low tone. "Tomas, it's time you mixed in there with those other children, and try to look real natural—but watch for my signal."

Cade's gaze returned to Lowry and Annabel, plunging together across the dance floor.

"I'm going to rescue our little detective."

Again, he told himself as he strode past knots of

townsfolk and ranchers. The room was nothing but a blur of festive music, brilliant colors, smoke, light, and raucous laughter until he saw Annabel's fine-boned face lifted calmly toward Lowry's.

Chapter 19

"Reckon it's time to step aside, Calvin. Figured you won't mind my cutting in," Cade said ruthlessly and with one smooth movement swung Annabel from Lowry's clasp into his own arms. The next moment they were off, whirling away as the fiddlers slowed their tune to the Blue Danube Waltz.

"Whatever took you so long?" Annabel demanded as Cade's arm tightened around her waist.

"Did you miss me?"

"My skin was crawling everywhere that man touched me."

"And how is your skin now?"

"Fair to middling," she retorted, her chin lifting as she remembered the peremptory way he had dismissed her earlier, but to her surprise, Cade McCallum laughed.

"You certainly take the prize, Miss Brannigan."

"For what, Mr. Steele?"

"Sheer cheekiness."

"Is that supposed to be a compliment?"

"Take it anyway you want."

He was an excellent dancer, she noted, far better than either Mr. Perkins, Mr. Reed, or Mr. Connely. He danced with the same confident strength and agility with which he did everything else, and he held her with a light but masterfully firm touch that seemed to come from instinct as much as from practice.

"If we're talking about what I want, then I have something to say to you."

"Say it then."

She bit her lip and raised beseeching eyes to him. Why did he always have to make everything so difficult? "I want you to believe me when I tell you that I care deeply about Brett. I wasn't only trying to find him because your father hired the Stevenson agency. I am *not* a paid sneak. More than anything I wanted to help Brett, just as I told you—to make sure he gets home safely so that he can work things out with your father and stay out of Red Cobb's line of fire. Is that so horrible?"

"There's something else you forgot to mention. Something else you want."

She moistened her lips, her breath catching in her throat because he was holding her so sensuously close to him. She swore she could feel every rock-solid muscle in the length of his body, and it was doing strange things to her concentration.

"What do you think I want?" she managed to whisper, the words fuzzing in her throat.

"You want to marry my brother."

What was the use in denying it? Cade McCallum's eyes seemed able to pierce right through her—had since the first day they met. She felt her skin heating beneath that relentless gaze. "Yes," she whispered, giving a little gasp as he twirled her a shade faster than the music, "I do. The truth is, I've always loved Brett."

"Always?"

"Ever since I can remember. But he doesn't know— promise me you won't tell him. I . . . I couldn't bear for him to feel sorry for me." She knew she was chattering, but she couldn't help it. His nearness, the sleek powerful strength of him, the dizzying way he was staring at her as they whirled through the blur of music, all were having a strange effect on her. "You see," she continued desperately, plunging gamely on, "he's never felt about me the way that I feel about him. I had hoped that when I found him he'd realize that . . . oh, how can I put this? I haven't seen him in a while now and I thought he'd notice me and . . ."

"My brother is even more of a fool than I thought."

"What do you mean?" Annabel gasped at the harshness of his tone.

"He's blind. Any fool can see that you love him. Or that you think you do," he added coolly, a suddenly speculative glint entering his eyes.

Annabel bristled. "Of course I love him! I certainly know my own mind!"

"Uh huh."

What was that supposed to mean? He was impossible. She gritted her teeth. He had the power to infuriate her, and yet at the same time, his hand at her waist, and the other hand gripping hers, were sending dazzling waves of fire through her that had nothing to do with anger.

"It's not Brett's fault he doesn't see how I feel. My God, what kind of an investigator would I be, if everyone could see right through me, could read every single thing I say and do. . . ."

"Just hope you fooled Red Cobb."

She lifted her chin. "Of course I did. He hasn't turned up, has he?"

"Not yet," Steele retorted brutally, as the music stopped. Suddenly, he pulled her close, so close that her breasts were crushed against the hard wall of his chest. She could feel his heart beating, strong and steady beneath his shirt. For a moment he held her taut against him, staring down into her face without speaking.

Then he took a breath. "Annabel . . ." he began, something softening in the center of those gleaming black eyes, but then he stopped, as if catching himself and muttered hoarsely, "Never mind."

A tension leapt between them, an undercurrent of electricity that made Annabel's blood rush into her head. For one wild moment she wanted to touch the silky lock of his hair that had fallen over his brow. She wanted to stay right where she was, her gaze locked with his mesmerizing one, and see what happened next . . . but she couldn't. People would begin to stare at them, people were probably *already* staring at them.

Yet still she stayed. She couldn't have torn her gaze from his if she tried. "What is it?" she whispered, her heart thudding crazily. "Tell me. Please."

For one moment she thought he was going to answer her. Then he drew back, and released her so suddenly her knees almost buckled, and the familiar cool nonchalance transformed him once again into Roy Steele, hardened gunslinger. "I'm going to see what I can do about antagonizing Lowry further," he said casually. He led her off the dance floor, and the people who had begun to stare turned back to their red wine or their lemonade and began to chatter anew. "You go find Brett. Tell him to be careful and wait for Tomas to bring him my message. While we were dancing, Lowry spoke with ten different men I take to be his hands. Every single one of 'em is watching us right now."

"I counted eleven." Annabel forced herself to speak as steadily as he, though she felt anything but calm. Her palms felt clammy, her cheeks warm, and she longed for a glass of lemonade to assuage the dryness in her throat. "One is posted behind that potted plant near the dining room door. He's wearing a green vest."

"Eleven, then." Suddenly, he grinned at her and shook his head. "You're good, Miss Brannigan." He added almost to himself. "Maybe too good."

She searched his face. "That sounds like a compliment, but if you're trying to say that I'm too good at my work to be trustworthy, please think again. You can trust me, Cade."

Trust her? Maybe. But I don't trust myself, he thought, allowing his gaze to linger for one tantalizing moment on her delicate, upturned face, to meet those provocative green eyes and get lost in their hypnotic gold-flecked depths. The candlelight turned her hair to shining amber, and he longed to unbind it and wind his fingers through the thick, silken tangles.

But there was business to be done tonight—the deadliest, most serious type of business. The distractions of Miss Brannigan's hair, eyes, figure, perfume, her low-pitched voice, and sunlit smile, her intelligence and character could prove his undoing as well as Brett's, and that of the Racing Rivers Ranch.

He had to think about the Rivers family, about that boy Tomas who kept watching him alertly from the corners where the children played. Tomas was waiting for the chance to do something to avenge his father's death.

And it was almost time.

"Brett is handing Conchita and Adelaide glasses of lemonade over by the window," he said quickly, as he led her past one of the long trestle tables covered with Calvin Lowry's finest imported linen.

"Hurry and warn him which men to keep an eye on."

Before she could agree, Cade was gone, stalking across the parlor. Though Annabel kept her face schooled into an expression of sedateness as she made her way toward Brett, she still tingled everywhere Cade had touched her during their dance.

She pushed Cade from her mind as she gave Brett the message, and eagerly sipped the lemonade he handed her in return. Together, she, Brett, Adelaide, and Conchita surveyed the room, and she subtly pointed out to each of them which cowboys appeared to be in Lowry's employ.

Conchita nodded when she was finished. "Yes, we know some of them. But he has added on several men since he started acquiring additional property. Men with reputations for being quick with a gun, and not particular about when they choose to use it."

"She means men who will shoot first and apologize for any 'mistakes' later," Adelaide piped in caustically. Though Brett held a small straight-backed chair for her to be seated, she resolutely shook her head and insisted that she prefered to be on her feet when she was in enemy territory. "Soon as bullets start to fly, young man, I want to jump ahead of the crowd and see everything that happens. After what Lowry did to my son, it'll do my old heart good to see him bleed all over his own damned floor."

Brett nodded, but Annabel saw that he looked worried.

"What's wrong?"

"I sure hope Cade knows what he's doing here. There're a lot of them, and not too many of us."

"We have to trust him," Annabel replied softly, turning as she spoke to scan the parlor for some sign of Cade and Lowry. "I've only known him a short time, but I would trust him with my life and more. As a matter of fact I've already done that," she reflected with a faint smile, "and he took very good care of it."

"That hombre in the green vest just slipped out

onto the terrace," Brett said suddenly, his fingers closing around her arm. "I've got a hunch something's up."

"Then we'd better stroll out there and see what it is."

They left Conchita and Adelaide and threaded their way through the throng of people crowded around the trestle tables bearing refreshments. Outside, the wide terrace was ablaze with flickering yellow torches and festooned with gay silk streamers and overflowing baskets of flowers. A few couples snuggled or flirted in the shadows, as far from the light as they could manage, or huddled close together upon the long stone bench, but mostly the terrace and surrounding garden appeared deserted.

"Where'd that damned fellow go?" Brett fretted.

"Let's hurry toward the stables and the corrals and see if we spot him."

"All right, but we'd better hold hands and try to appear like we're just slipping away from the party so we can be alone together."

If only it were true, Annabel thought, as his hand comfortably gripped hers. For some reason, despite the fragrant beauty of the night, the velvet darkness of the sky, the sheer romance of being out here alone with him, her pulse didn't quicken at all as they made their way past the gardens toward the dark outline of the hacienda's outbuildings. Her skin didn't even grow warm at his touch. *What is wrong with me?* she thought in disappointment, and more than a little puzzlement. Suddenly she understood. The inherent dangers of this night were blotting out any inklings of romance. *It's only to be expected,* she told herself in annoyance. *There are more important things going on than your feelings for Brett.*

They had gone far beyond the torchlight, and as they walked in silence the soft, flower-perfumed darkness closed down around them. As the house and the lights and the music disappeared farther and farther behind, Annabel's tension mounted.

But as they neared the corrals, there was still no sign of the cowboy in the green vest.

"Brett," Annabel said softly as she peered all around and still saw no one, "will you tell me one thing?"

"If I can."

"Do you know why Red Cobb is after you?"

He scuffed his boot in the dirt beside her. "Beats me. I never met the fellow. But all of the sudden, somewhere in the middle of Arizona, everyone who hears my name is whispering that this gunfighter is hunting for me." He shrugged. "I figured if he caught me, that would be just fine. He'd put me out of my misery."

"Brett!"

He shook his head. "Annabel, I've been just plain miserable since that meeting with Boxer."

"I know, I can well imagine. But everything isn't hopeless, you know. You must talk to your father, tell him everything, and find out the truth about all this."

"Maybe I'll do that. If we get out of this alive."

She touched his sleeve. "I know why Cobb is after you. He was hired—by a man named Lucas Johnson in St. Louis. Have you ever heard of him?"

Brett looked thunderstruck. "No, by God. Never met any such fellow."

"Well, I wired Mr. Stevenson with the information, and he should be conducting an investigation right this very minute. Brett, I have one more question."

He laughed, sounding more like his old self than he had all day. "You always do."

"Why did you sign on to help Conchita Rivers in this fight? I'm not saying it isn't a fine and noble thing to do—I believe it is. She's in the right, and she needs the help of as many decent and brave people as she can find, but . . . you'd never been in a gunfight before, or . . . killed anyone or . . . anything like this. Why did you agree to something so dangerous?"

"When I met up with Conchita I was about as low as a man can get. I guess it didn't matter to me that I might not live long if I took on her fight—I guess you could say, Annabel, that I would have been more than willing to die and never have to think about . . . anything again."

"Brett, no. Oh, no, I was afraid of that." She stopped beside him, and without thinking threw her arms around his neck. In the dimness she could still make out the dismal expression in his eyes.

"You're not to blame for what happened to your mother. Don't you see that? And even if what this Frank Boxer said is true, or partly true, the fact that you're not Ross McCallum's own son doesn't matter. He raised you as his son—and he loves you as his son, Brett. I can vouch for that after having observed the two of you for years in that house. I know that Ross loves you as much as any man ever could love a son—and I think," she added, taking a deep breath, "that you should show a little backbone and hightail it back there the moment this fight with Lowry is finished so that you can work things out with him. And warn him about what Boxer is up to—because I know he never received your letter. And there's something else you should know, Brett. Ross has been ill. His heart . . ."

"What?" She saw the shock cross his face. "What happened?"

"He's been under a doctor's care. His businesses have been suffering, and now that I think about it, I wonder if Boxer doesn't have something to do with that."

Brett's eyes narrowed in the darkness. "I don't understand. You say he never received my message. But I left it with Derrickson, with very clear instructions about . . ."

He broke off, suddenly glancing down into her face with a strange expression, seemingly aware for the first time of her arms around his neck. "Annabel, let me ask *you* something," Brett said slowly. His own arms came up to tentatively encircle her waist.

"Why did you come after me? I know it wasn't just because you were being paid by the Stevenson Agency."

"N-no."

"There's more to it than that, isn't there? After all, you've risked your life to come west alone to find me."

"Wouldn't you do the same for me?" she parried, hoping desperately she would not have to confess the truth to him now, not yet, and at the same time, trying to calm her heart which had begun to flutter because he was holding her so closely, so gently . . .

And his beautiful eyes were so intent and searching upon her face that she thought the breath would burst inside her lungs.

"I would. But . . ." He hesitated and then brought one hand up to cup her chin. "I have to confess something. Dear as you are to me, Annie, I never before noticed how damned pretty you are. Or how your eyes light up when you talk, or the way your hands move so gracefully when you talk. . . ."

Disbelief warred with excitement inside her. This was happening, it was really happening . . . everything she had hoped for and dreamed of. Brett was looking at her in a way he never had before. There was a tightness in his body so close to hers, and his hand beneath her chin felt warm, possessive. *He's going to kiss me,* Annabel thought with a whirl of joy. *Right now, this very minute, Brett McCallum is going to kiss me. . . .*

He lowered his lips to hers. In the distance, the

muted sounds of the fiddlers and of humming conversation and laughter pierced faintly through the peace of the night, but here by the corrals, with only the velvet sky, the clouds, and the humid, musky darkness all about them, it was richly quiet. Annabel let herself go. She gave herself up to the sweet pressure of Brett's mouth on hers; she unleashed all the ardor she'd ever felt for him, and pressed against him, her arms snaking needfully around his neck.

At last. At long, long last.

Chapter 20

It was a slow and dreamy and tentative kiss.

When finally Brett lifted his head, and took a deep breath, Annabel's eyes remained closed until she felt him watching her. She opened them then and peered at him. She struggled to hide the confusion she was feeling.

"Again," she whispered, a catch in her throat, and standing on tiptoe, touched her lips to his.

This kiss was not as long as the first, nor as searching and dreamy. In fact, Annabel broke it off quickly, her fingers moving to her lips in shock.

"My God," she whispered, stunned.

Before Brett could say anything, the sound of low voices reached them, and both at once darted behind a piñon tree.

They saw the four cowboys then. They emerged from the shadows behind the barn, and the man with the green vest was one of them.

"We have to move closer," Annabel whispered, and started forward, but Brett tugged her back.

"You stay here, Annabel. I'll go."

"Don't be a pea brain. Come *on*."

And with the faintest rustle of her silken skirts, she

edged forward under cover of the creosote bushes. To her relief, Brett gave up the argument and followed at her heels, moving as stealthily as she.

Fortunately, the darkness hid their progress and they were able to creep within a dozen feet of the cowboys. They ducked down behind a clump of mesquite and strained to hear.

". . . and the boss wants me to wait for supper to be served before picking the fight with McCallum. So nobody do anything before that. Got it?" The cowboy in the green vest, a rangily built older man wearing a gray Stetson, stared around the circle of faces.

Beside him, a black-garbed cowhand took a puff on a cigarette and exhaled loudly. "Sure you can outdraw that frisky young squirt, Hank? He looks pretty dangerous to me."

Loud guffaws greeted this sally. Hank chuckled. "With my eyes shut, I reckon," he drawled.

"Remember, when everyone is gathered around watching, the boss is going to act like he wants to make peace between me and the kid. But no one's going to listen to him—you got that, boys?"

"Yeah, we got it," the men all muttered.

"Then, while everyone—including Steele—is busy watching what's going on, you three will take a little target practice at Steele when he's not paying attention."

The men laughed softly among themselves. "With no one afterward being able to say exactly how that hombre got plugged," the black-garbed man added, and squashed his cigarette under his boot.

"I reckon I won't have seen anything." The tallest cowboy, long haired and rail thin, gave out a low whoop.

"Listen, up, Pete," Hank interrupted him. "When Steele and the McCallum kid are both dead, Lowry will give the Rivers woman one more chance to sign over the ranch."

"Why the hell bother?" Pete demanded. "Why don't we just sneak onto her place tonight and set it on fire? She and her family have already caused more trouble than everyone else in the valley put together. It'll be easy as cake—with their place gone, they'll be more than ready to hightail it out of the valley . . ."

His words were blown away by a sudden sharp gust of wind. Thunder followed, rolling across the sky. Someone else said something Annabel couldn't make out, and then the group started walking back toward the house.

Annabel and Brett shrank back into the darkness, scarcely daring to breathe as the cowboys passed close enough to touch. Alone in the shadows once more, with only the hum of insects disturbing the silence, the two stared at each other.

"I have to warn him." Annabel clutched Brett's shirt in shaking fingers. "My God, they plan to murder him, to shoot him in the back! What if we hadn't been here, what if we hadn't heard?"

"Well, we did. Come on, I'll tell Conchita what's happening. Then you or Cade get word to her about what we do next—send a message with Tomas. Don't worry, Annabel," he added, as she pressed her hands in anguish to her white cheeks. "We'll get the best of them before this is all over."

Neither of them heard the rustle of the bushes behind them as they hurried back toward the hacienda. Nor did they hear the slow, deliberate footsteps that followed.

When they crossed the terrace once more and entered the parlor, Lowry was ushering his guests into supper.

"Come on, folks, help yourselves! We've been roasting that big old steer in the barbecue pit all night! There's tamales and enchiladas and refried beans for everyone," he boomed with all the congeniality of a snake oil salesman. "Right this way, and help yourselves."

Men, women, and children thronged toward the rear of the house where huge doors led out to the flower-festooned courtyard where tables groaned beneath heaping platters of spicy food.

Annabel fought the crowd as she desperately scanned it for some sign of Cade.

Brett grabbed her arm. "There're Adelaide and Conchita." She followed his gaze to an arched doorway that opened into a hall. The two women stood arm in arm well back from the throng, watching the guests proceed into supper. "Maybe I should help you find Cade first . . ."

"No, go quickly," Annabel urged. "Let them know what's happening. Don't worry about me, I'll find Cade."

A moment later, she felt a hand on her shoulder and whirled around. She gasped in relief as she saw that Cade McCallum had found her.

"What's wrong?" He looked alarmed by her paleness and by the way she nearly sagged against him in relief. "Has something happened to you . . ."

"It's not me. It's what they're planning to do to you. Cade, we must slip away—upstairs—where we can talk. I'll go first and find an empty bedroom or something. You follow me—but please, come quickly."

She forced herself to walk slowly, inconspicuously, toward the huge staircase which branched off the main hallway of the hacienda. As she neared the head of the stairs, the din below faded. Swiftly, she glanced up and down the wide spacious hall, lit by dozens of candles placed in brass sconces at well-measured intervals.

She ducked into the first room she reached. It appeared to be a guest bedroom, since when she turned up the lamp on the nightstand, there were no personal mementos to be found—not upon the carved oak bureau or the nightstand, nor were there any garments or personal items lying about. The room was large and airy, however, with lovely crisp peach draperies at the open window, and matching peach and ivory appointments, from the coverlet on the bed to the upholstery of the dainty pair of chairs beside a decorative oriental screen. Another time, Annabel might have admired Lowry's obviously sophisticated taste: the serene French landscapes depicted in the paintings that graced the peach and white papered walls, or the large Aubusson rug upon the polished wood floor, but at this moment she was too anxious to take in much of anything, other than that her own reflection in the cheval mirror over the bureau shimmered back at her, pale and ghostly.

"Don't look so worried," Cade McCallum said from the doorway.

Annabel nearly jumped out of her skin. As it was, she dropped her reticule to the floor.

She ran to him and pulled him into the room, shutting the door behind him. "Brett and I overheard their plan," she said, trying to stay calm and in control of her emotions, trying to remember that in emergency situations it was best to talk slow and think fast. But gazing at Cade, so heartbreakingly handsome in his black silk shirt and dark trousers, his expression so cool and his demeanor so calm, she felt waves of fear for him wash over her.

What if something went wrong? What if he were shot and killed this very evening and she would never have the chance to tell him . . .

What? What was it she had to tell Cade McCallum?

"I reckon you'd best tell me what you heard," he said smoothly, his brows lifting in surprise at her obvious distress. "Then maybe we can devise an even better plan of our own."

So she repeated the conversation that had taken place out by the barn, but instead of appearing alarmed at her disclosure, he grinned.

"Nice work. You just might make a decent private investigator yet."

"This isn't a joking matter," she exclaimed in frustration. "Don't you understand that these people want to murder you? They're not interested in any kind of a fair fight. I don't see how . . ."

"I'll tell you how."

He led her to the bed and pushed her down so that she was seated on the edge of it, then he sat beside her. Immediately he realized this was a mistake.

She was too close. And she looked too utterly lovely. And the bed was too softly inviting.

The concern in her wan face twisted at his heart as few things before ever had. She was worried, worried about him, as she had been that night in Silver Junction.

He wasn't used to it. Hadn't ever looked for it or wanted it, but now that he was here in this large quiet room with Annabel Brannigan looking so damned distraught because someone wanted to shoot him in the back, he had to admit that he didn't exactly mind her caring about him.

But something about her was bothering him. He reached out, he couldn't help it . . .

"Cade McCallum,' she gasped, grabbing his hand. "Just what do you think you're doing?"

"Your hair's too pretty to be all wrapped up like that so tight. It's not right to hide so much of it."

He had tugged out one hairpin before she'd

stopped him, and a thick taffy ringlet had sprung free to dangle saucily over her eye. His grin widened at the adorable expression of outrage and amazement on her face.

"How can you think about *my hair* at a time like this?"

Then, without conscious thought, some devil of mischief long dormant in him made him reach out with the other hand and like lightning he tugged a second pin out from the chignon, freeing still another curl.

"Stop this right now," Annabel fairly screeched, and made a grab for his other hand. But he burst out laughing, and easily seized both of her hands in one of his.

"You spoil all my fun, Miss Brannigan."

"Fun! I'll give you fun. How about three men shooting you in the back? Is that enough fun for you?"

But as she tried to wrench her hands free, they both lost their balance and rolled sideways together onto the bed. His laughter rumbled deep from his chest. Cade didn't remember the last time he'd laughed like that.

"Now we're having fun, Miss Brannigan," he chuckled, and before she even realized it he had pinned her beneath him, her hands caught above her head, and one of his powerful legs draped across both of hers.

"I've a good mind to pull out all those damned pins," he threatened. "Such beautiful hair should be free, like the wildflowers, like the meadow larks, like the . . ."

"Don't you dare! Cade McCallum, if I didn't know better I'd think you were drunk!"

He grinned down at her. But suddenly his expression grew sober, the black eyes hardening to marble. "Maybe I am . . . but not on liquor," he muttered. Damn. What was she doing to him? "I'm drunk on something else even more potent. More dangerous," he continued, his gaze suddenly fiercely intent on her wide eyes, and parted lips, then shifting down to the ivory mounds of her breasts above the décolleté of her gown.

"Annabel," he demanded tautly, "why do you have to be so damned beautiful?"

She stopped struggling to free herself and stared back at him, dumbfounded. "You . . . think I'm beautiful?"

"Too damned beautiful." Suddenly, he caught her mouth in a kiss that was so rough, it was almost savage. Her lips trembled beneath the heat and violence of that kiss and she released him reluctantly as he pulled away. "I've thought so from the first time I saw you in Justice."

"You have . . . ?"

"When you told me that gentlemen don't crash into ladies with whom they're not acquainted. Annabel, if you only knew . . ."

"Knew what, Cade?" she whispered, still dizzy from that bruising kiss, swept up in a wildfire of sensations that started somewhere deep between her thighs and raced upward to set her breasts aflame as they strained against her chemise. She hardly dared to breathe. His lean face was only inches from hers, his fingers had now released her hands and were tugging out additional pins from her hair. She gasped as he began to kiss her again, hot, deliberate kisses that scorched her cheeks, her lips, the fragile skin of her eyelids. And then he nipped at her throat.

"If you only knew the hell I went through when I thought you were betrothed to Brett. When I thought I was honor bound to stay away from you," he muttered grimly. "And all the time I wanted you more than I've ever wanted anyone or anything in my life." Suddenly he yanked her up, close and hard against his muscled chest, his mouth stilling her gasp as he kissed her with possessive ruthlessness.

Now she really couldn't breathe. His tongue thrust into the softness of her mouth and awakened her own to battle. Liquid pleasure burst through her as she breathed in the sage and cedar scent of him, lost herself in the warm male taste of him, delighted in his sure overwhelming strength.

Her heart was racing so fast it would leave a train far behind. She was certain he must feel it pounding against his own, hammering along as if at any moment it would burst. His exploring hands were touching her in places no man had ever touched, setting fire to places that had never before even smoldered. Her arms encircled his neck and she pulled him closer with a little moaning sound of pleasure deep in her throat.

"Brett and I—" she tried to explain in a low, tremulous voice, but he cut her off, his hands gripping her arms like manacles, his eyes glinting into hers with fierce purpose.

"I don't want to hear *one word* about you and my brother. I care about him, whether or not he believes it, but he's not the man for you."

Annabel had reached the same conclusion herself, out there by the corrals when Brett had kissed her. But incredulity filled her at the thought that Cade McCallum should say the same thing she'd been thinking ever since she'd pulled back from Brett's kiss.

"Why . . . do you say that?" she asked softly, wonderingly, gazing into his eyes as if searching for the secrets locked inside his soul.

"Because of *this,*" he told her, his fingers tightening on her hair, forcing her face close to his. He drew her to him and brought his lips down on hers once more in a fierce, demanding kiss that sent golden flames shooting through her. The world tilted and spun as he crushed her down upon the bed again, his powerful limbs imprisoning her.

"And this," he growled, his hands touching her breasts, making her gasp with stunned delight. "Because of everything we feel when we're together. Because you can't deny it any more than I can, sweetheart."

And then they were somehow entwined, and all the kisses they'd kept bottled up during their days on the trail together poured out, wild and pure and demanding, like a torrent of driving rain, washing away everything in its path. Cade buried his face in the luxuriant satin of her hair, as caught up as she in a frenzy of emotion, and his hand boldly cupped her breast as he'd yearned to do since the very first time he'd touched her.

"Cade," she breathed, in pleasure and in shock as his fingers tore at the pearl buttons at the front of her gown.

"You'd better not be saying you want me to stop," he warned softly, his mouth warm against hers.

"No," she whispered back, writhing against him. "I want you to know that . . . Cade!"

She panted as he sprang the last button free and with one smooth movement slid the gown off her shoulders, down her arms, and wriggled it toward her hips.

"Go on," he said.

"That's what I wanted to say to you . . . *go on*."

A chuckle sounded deep in his throat.

"Oh, Cade, I have to confess to you . . . I don't know exactly what I'm doing . . . Mr. Perkins and Mr. Reed and Mr. Connely never did anything like this . . . or that . . ."

"They better not have," he growled against her ear.

A laugh bubbled from her, quickly stifled by a kiss so devouring and intense that she drank it in like wine. Such sweet heat was flowing through her, pulsing, building . . .

Her dress was off and she was wearing only her chemise as she worked frantically at his shirt. Annabel had no thought of modesty, no hesitation. Tender feelings and blinding sensations were all stirred up inside her, filling her up with needs she hadn't even known existed before, needs she'd never experienced with Brett or with anyone else.

Only with Cade McCallum. And Roy Steele.

Beneath her chemise her breasts tingled at the things his hands were doing to them, and her nipples hardened into taut rose peaks that ached beneath his stroking thumbs. She shivered as he held her still and rained down quick warm kisses across her throat. Then his mouth moved lower, and captured her tormented nipple, his tongue circling it, teasing it until Annabel clutched at his hair and willed herself not to scream.

Suddenly there was a knock upon the door.

Cade McCallum lifted his head from her breast. "Shit."

"Is the door locked?" Annabel whsipered in horror, unable to remember if she'd locked it or not. The notion of being discovered here—like this—brought reality back in a sharp breathless rush. She remembered the danger, the family downstairs waiting for their help, the tremendous odds Cade faced in this confrontation tonight, and she was afraid.

But Cade sprang off the bed and signaled for her to respond to the knock.

"Yes?" she squeaked, her voice so breathless it barely sounded like her.

"That you, Miss Brannigan?" To her relief, it was Adelaide Rivers's voice on the other side of the door. "I've been looking for you all over."

"Just a minute. I . . . had a problem with my gown."

Annabel flew back into her dress and struggled with the buttons. Cade tried to help her, but she waved his fingers away. He grinned, looking amazingly younger and more carefree than she'd ever seen him as he yanked on his shirt and then strode behind the oriental screen.

Annabel rushed to the door.

"What is it, Adelaide? What's the matter?"

Heaven knew what the woman thought as she peered at Annabel in the doorway. Her rheumy eyes were nevertheless sharp with intelligence, and Annabel knew her face must be the color of a plum.

But Adelaide Rivers was too upset to be bothered wondering about her antics. That was apparent from her next words.

"Trouble," the old woman snapped, her wrinkled skin the color of oatmeal beneath her weathered tan. "Conchita is beside herself. We don't know where Mr. Steele went to. That danged supper is almost over, and we're afraid something has happened to him. But that's not the worst of it. Tomas is missing."

Annabel stared at her with dread. "Missing?"

"Our nearest neighbor, Dan Miller, said he saw him right before supper scuffling with some older boys. One of 'em is the son of Lowry's foreman, Hank Ellis. I don't like the sound of this, not one bit."

"There is probably a reasonable explanation," Annabel said quickly, wanting to comfort the woman, though her own anxiety was mounting by the moment. "Or," she had to admit, meeting Adelaide's crisp glance with a worried frown, "it could be part of Lowry's strategy to distract us and then instigate his plan. I'll meet you downstairs in just a moment, Adelaide, and we'll look for Tomas together. Maybe we can find Hank Ellis —or his son—and ask him a few questions."

"Hurry," the old woman urged as she turned toward the stairs. "I've a strong feeling things are going to go from bad to worse real fast."

So do I, Annabel thought as she closed the door.

She ran into Cade's arms as he stepped out from behind the screen.

"Oh, Cade, what do you think has happened to Tomas?"

"Damned if I know, but I don't much like the sound of it. I'm going to hunt for him. Wait a minute or two, and then follow me downstairs."

She nodded, her eyes huge and worried, and suddenly, Cade cupped her face between his hands. "I love you, Annabel."

Even as he spoke, Cade was scarcely able to believe he was speaking those words, but he was unable to stop himself. Something inside of him, deep in his heart, had taken over, and he couldn't slow it down or stop it. "I don't know if or how things can work out between us, though," he felt compelled to warn. "I'm a McCallum," he said, as if that explained everything. "Seems to me if I let things . . . continue between us . . . I'll only end up hurting you."

"No, Cade, never that." She touched gentle fingers to his lips. Love poured through her, as pure and warm as sweet wild honey. "I trust in you. I believe in you. Nothing you could ever do would hurt me."

He held her close for one more moment, and then sighed against the fragrance of her hair. "We'll see."

It didn't sound promising. She wanted to clutch him to her and tell him that things *would* work out between them, to make him pledge that he wouldn't leave her, that he would at least *try* to . . . what? Marry her? Build a life with her?

She ached for him to want that, but with a flash of despair she knew he was a long way from committing to any of those things.

He was already moving away from her. "I'd better get downstairs. Is that derringer in your reticule?"

"Of course. I wouldn't think of setting out without it."

She glanced over and saw her reticule still lying on the floor where she'd dropped it. "Don't worry about me, just find Tomas—and take care of yourself."

"If there's one thing I'm good at," he said grimly, "it's taking care of myself."

"When this is over, I'm going to take care of you," she promised him, a smile trembling on her lips.

An unfamiliar emotion surged through him, one he was afraid to put a name to. He wanted to crush her in his arms, to kiss her until rose dawn painted the sky, to breathe in the luscious lilac scent of her, and tell her that *he* wanted to take care of *her,* but he instead forced himself to look at her with iron detachment. "Don't count on that, Annabel."

Then he was gone, and Annabel paced back and forth in an agony of trepidation. She picked up her reticule from the floor and opened it, checking for the derringer. It was inside, and loaded. She paused before the mirror and could only gulp in dismay as she realized that Adelaide Rivers had seen her looking like this, with her hair spilling wildly down her shoulders, and her dress—though buttoned—looking as sadly wrinkled and disheveled as a crumpled old washrag. She plopped the reticule on the bureau and began hastily searching for the hairpins Cade had so cavalierly plucked from her chignon. But as she knelt on the floor to retrieve one that was lying on the Aubusson carpet, a sound at the window made her freeze.

She jerked up, still on her knees, and gasped as Red Cobb swung his legs into the room.

"Don't scream, or I'll have to shoot you," he warned, and before Annabel could even blink he had drawn his gun and pointed it at her.

She staggered to her feet, trying to control the terror pulsating through her.

"Don't even think about reaching for that there reticule of yours," he added as she glanced frantically toward the bureau, impossibly far away.

"What . . . do you want?" she managed to ask in a voice that sounded far calmer than she felt.

"What happened to your southern accent, little Miss Investigator?"

She went still as stone. Red Cobb smiled mockingly, his crystal blue eyes colder than snow. "You must admit Miss Rainsford, that was a mean trick you played on me back in Silver Junction," he remarked with a smirk. He moved forward into the room with easy, deliberate steps. "I didn't much cotton to it. So now," he said in a flat, pleasant tone, that chilled her blood, "I'm going to make you pay."

Chapter 21

The shed was dark and stifling hot. Tomas couldn't breathe. *Coward,* he accused himself hatefully. *You are a fool and a coward. A disgrace to your father's memory.*

He had let himself be tricked. And now he could not help Senor Steele to kill Senor Lowry. Hot tears burned along his cheeks as he pushed again, fruitlessly, at the bolted door of the shed. Why had he believed Jack Ellis and the other boys? Why had he let them lead him into this trap?

Senor Brett is right, he told himself as the tears fell faster and the air grew danker and he wondered with a gulp if he would die in here before anyone ever found him. *I am too young and too stupid to be of any use.*

Brett slipped out of the kitchen door, past Calvin Lowry's Mexican cook and house servants. He could just make out the outline of the shed beyond the vegetable garden. He stalked toward it.

The boy who'd come and whispered in his ear that he would find Tomas Rivers in that shed had long since disappeared—Brett only hoped he was telling the truth. He needed a drink desperately. Whiskey. A whole bottle would do just fine. But something had kept him from consuming even a drop of Lowry's red wine or champagne or any other spirits. Maybe it was the wish, after all, to survive. And maybe to be of help to someone else, be it his brother, Annabel, or the Rivers family. Maybe part of him was beginning to realize that it was time to stop running from his problems and just face them head on.

The shed was locked when he reached it, secured with a thick wooden bolt, which Brett threw back at once.

"Tomas, are you in here?" His stomach was knotted tight with fear for the boy as he swung the door open.

A small face with eyes that gleamed in the dimness stared back at him.

"Tomas, are you all right?"

Slowly Tomas walked out of the pitch black shed. "They tricked me, senor." Tears throbbed in his voice. "First we had a fight, and then they said they wanted to be my friends, and they told me they would show me where a cat and her kittens were sleeping, but . . . they lied."

His voice broke as the sobs rushed out. Brett knelt down and enfolded the child in his arms.

"Hey, it's all right, Tomas. Everyone gets tricked now and then. They're the ones who should feel ashamed, not you."

"But I believed them. I was a fool."

"You're not a fool. You just wanted to believe it, so you did. There's nothing wrong with wanting to believe that people are good. Sometimes they really are, and you just need to give them a chance."

"Do you mean like Senor Steele? Everyone always talks about him as if they are afraid of him, as if he is someone terrible. But he is good, isn't he? He's your brother, and he wants to help us." A horrible thought struck him, and Tomas clutched at Brett's hand.

"Or is that a trick, too?" he whispered.

"No, Tomas." Brett patted his shoulder. "That's sure no trick. My brother is a good man. He came all the way across the whole Arizona territory to help us. So we're not going to let a couple of low-down sneaky boys get in our way, are we? We have important work to do."

"Do you . . . trust me to help? Before you said that I was too young and . . ."

The boy's voice trailed off. Brett winced and at that moment he could have kicked himself. "I was wrong, Tomas—I just plain wasn't thinking straight when I told you that. Too much tequila. That stuff is bad for the brain, you know what I mean?"

Tomas shrugged.

"Well, take my word for it. My big brother was right. You're going to be a big help to us. But first, let me figure something out. Why did those boys lock you in here? Just to be mean?"

"No, when they were pushing me in they kept telling me that Senor Ellis told them to do it. He thought it would be a big joke. They said this more than once. I thought it strange."

"And that's not all that's strange." Brett rubbed his jaw thoughtfully. "The boy who ran and told me where you were also said that Hank Ellis had put his son Jack and the other boys up to locking you in."

They stared at each other as a jackrabbit skittered across the vegetable garden. "Do you think someone wanted you to get angry with Senor Ellis?" Tomas asked slowly.

"Yep. And I know why. They want me to pick a fight with him."

"Why?"

"Because they think he can beat me if it comes to

shooting. And they want to ambush my brother while everyone is watching Ellis and me."

Tomas sucked in his breath. He wiped the remaining tears from his cheeks with the back of his hand. "Can he?"

"Can he what?" Brett asked, distracted, as he mulled the situation over, searching for a way to escape the trap.

"Can he beat you if it comes to shooting?"

"You never know," Brett replied almost cheerfully. "But I'll tell you one thing, Tomas. It doesn't pay to underestimate a McCallum."

And whether or not I'm one by blood, I am one by training, he told himself as he led the boy back toward the rear of the hacienda. He had endured hours of target practice and shooting lessons from both his father and the same English hunt master who had taught Cade as a young man. Their father had insisted on proficiency with firearms. *Maybe that's what's kept me alive so far in these skirmishes with Lowry's men,* he reflected. But would it be enough to help him in a one-on-one gunfight with Lowry's foreman, Hank Ellis? *Time will tell,* Brett decided with a scowl, but a vise of tension wound itself around his gut.

Suddenly, a tall figure appeared silhouetted against the door of the kitchen.

"Senor Steele!" Tomas bounded forward. "I was tricked. And now they want to force Senor Brett into a fight and—"

"I know, Tomas. But it isn't going to work. None of it. I have a better plan."

"See Tomas," Brett said softly, nudging the boy between the shoulders. "What did I tell you?" His glance met Cade's. "Never underestimate a McCallum."

* * *

"You underestimated me, Miss Investigator. That was real stupid of you."

Annabel made no reply because she couldn't speak. Cobb's red silk bandana made an all too effective gag, since he had clenched it between her teeth and knotted it tightly behind her head. Her hands were bound by heavy rope to the saddle horn before her, and Red Cobb's sweaty form, wedged behind her in the saddle, pressed against her with uncomfortable intimacy. The night wind rose screaming around her ears, filling them with a bleak wail which echoed the silent wail within.

She wondered in terror where he was taking her. Though she tried to keep track of where they were riding, it soon became difficult, for Cobb rode fast and followed a trail of numerous twists and turns. She had realized at first that they were headed in the opposite direction from the Rivers ranch, but when they'd descended through a zigzagging series of canyons she'd become hopelessly confused. She only knew that back at the Lowry hacienda, the people she cared about were embroiled in a confrontation that would risk all their lives. And she, who was needed to help, was riding farther and farther from the trouble every minute.

She now faced a different kind of trouble. She sensed with purely feminine instinct that Red Cobb meant to exact a vicious and personal revenge for her deception. He had already fondled her breasts after he'd bound and gagged her, laughing as he tossed her upon his mount. And the crude glint in his eyes had promised much more of the same. A shudder shook her as she wondered if he meant to kill her after the rape, or just leave her hurt and stranded somewhere in the mountains to die.

And what then? No doubt he would still return to kill Brett. *But Cade will stop him,* she told herself, forcing back the tears that clogged her dry, aching throat. *He'll defeat Lowry, and then he'll save Brett from Cobb.*

But who will save me?

I'll have to save myself, she concluded numbly, and wished for the thousandth time that she had her derringer.

"A little farther, and then we can stop and start the fun," Cobb mocked her in her ear. To her horror, his revolting mouth nibbled at the base of her neck as his horse's hooves flew across the blood-dark grass. She felt his hand cover her breast and squeeze hard.

Despite herself, she could not hold back a moan of protest.

"Like that, Miss Investigator? Well, you're going to love what's coming up next." He laughed uproariously in her ear, and his hand fell away to grip the reins once more. "Yes, indeed, ma'am, you're not missing a thing by leaving that fancy ranch back there. You and me are going to have our own little private party and it's going to be a helluva fiesta."

Chapter 22

Cade spotted his prey advancing from the dining room to Lowry's big main parlor, smiling and nodding at all the guests. Tomas saw him at the same time, and as Cade watched, the dark-haired boy approached the man.

Lounging against the wall, pretending to be absorbed in his glass of champagne, Cade watched the whispered conversation, complete with gestures from Tomas. The black-garbed man looked obediently where Tomas pointed, then nearly shoved the child out of his way in his haste to reach the hallway.

Casually, Cade began to walk in the same direction. When he reached the staircase, he edged around behind it where he could better hear the voices coming from the small paneled study.

"So you're ready to sign? Just like that? Well, it's about time."

"You leave me no choice," Conchita's voice reached Cade softly, sounding low and sad. "It is too dangerous to continue on this way—not knowing what will happen next."

"That's what we've been trying to make you understand, senora." The black-garbed cowboy gave a triumphant laugh. "Come on with me and we'll tell the boss . . ."

But as he reached for her arm, Cade hit him over the head from behind, the barrrel of his gun connecting with a sickening thud. Cade kicked the door closed just before the body thudded to the floor.

"That should do it." He nodded at Conchita, and bent to grasp the cowhand under the arms. He dragged him behind the brown leather sofa and dumped the limp form beside the other two men Brett had described to him as being part of the plot.

"I guess these three hombres won't be ambushing anyone tonight," Conchita said with solemn satisfaction.

"Not likely." With one easy movement he opened the study window and then stuck his head out. Tomas waited outside, grinning eagerly at him. "Here is your rope, senor."

"*Gracias,* Tomas. Nice work." Cade found himself returning the boy's excited smile, feeling something lighten within himself as well. It was good to see Tomas happy. The boy at least felt he was doing something to avenge his father's murder. Maybe after this night, if all ended well, he would be able to go on with his life, to leave all the pain and the bitterness of the past behind him, and not let what had happened to his family scar him for the rest of his life.

Now if only Brett can do his part and come out of this in one piece, there will only be Lowry left to deal with. And if I can't provoke that son of a bitch into drawing on me, then I'm no son of Ross McCallum.

He frowned as he finished tying up the last of the trio. If what Brett had heard from Boxer was true, then Brett himself was no true son of Ross McCallum. Cade didn't know what to make of Boxer's story, except that it turned his stomach. But he knew one thing—Brett was his brother no matter what. It didn't matter that they'd been apart for thirteen years, it didn't matter that only Livinia's blood might flow in common in each of their veins—they were brothers in every sense of the word, and he would give up his own life if necessary to save Brett's.

But if things went as he planned, it wouldn't come to that—for either of them.

When Cade finished, he and Conchita left the three behind the sofa, and turned down the lamp before going out and closing the door. Even if Lowry's men awoke and yelled for help, no one would hear them, what with the music, the merriment, and the general din of the fiesta.

"Now it's time to see how that brother of mine handles himself," he said quietly to Conchita as they returned to the parlor, where strolling guitar players were serenading the guests as they helped themselves to blueberry pies and tiny iced applesauce cakes. Adelaide hurried over, but Cade gave her only a brief nod before scanning the crowd.

Where the hell was Annabel?

He hadn't spotted her once since he'd come downstairs, but then, he'd been pretty busy rounding up those three snakes.

She must be with Brett, he thought to himself, trying to stifle the jealousy that lanced through him at the thought. If what had happened upstairs between them made any sense at all, it told him that he didn't have reason to be jealous of Brett. But still, nothing had been settled between him and Annabel, and he'd made his own doubts about the two of them more than clear. In fact, Cade reflected, he'd tried his best to convince her that things probably *wouldn't* work out between them. *Can you blame her then if she does decide to turn back to Brett?*

Suddenly, shouts erupted from the terrace, making

him forget everything else. Cowboys, ranchers, towns-folk, children, women, and hired help alike turned and stared in that direction, muttering among themselves. Like a herd of cattle, people began moving forward.

"Ellis, you're a no-good cowardly skunk. You put your boy and his friends up to playing a mean trick on Tomas Rivers, and I think you and your son owe him an apology."

That was Brett's voice. *He sure sounds mad,* Cade thought admiringly. Though his younger brother was in-experienced, he'd learned fast how to survive out here, and he had courage. *Good for him,* Cade acknowledged, and suddenly guessed that Annabel must be out there on the terrace too, somewhere nearby, perhaps keeping Tomas away from the line of fire.

He headed that way, shouldering his way through the crowd.

"You can go to hell, McCallum," Cade heard Ellis taunt back at Brett. "I don't know what that little Mexi-can squirt's been telling you, but I think boys should settle their own problems in their own way, and men should settle theirs. My question is, which one, amigo, are you—a boy, or a man?" he bellowed, and then gave a contemptuous guffaw.

"I'm no amigo of yours," Brett shot back. "As for the rest, if you have the guts, we'll find out."

"I don't reckon I care for your tone." Ellis was star-ing at Brett hard. "Unless you want to apologize, I reckon I'm going to have to teach you a lesson."

Cade had reached the terrace by now and he saw the crowd ebb back like tide from a seashore. Murmurs rose and fell like dark waves. Lowry was there, watch-ing, listening. Cade stayed behind a tall rancher in a silver-trimmed suede vest, not wishing Lowry to see him —yet.

"Now, boys," one man whom Conchita had pointed

out earlier as another small rancher who had reluctantly sold his property to Lowry, spoke up uneasily. "Can't you settle this without gunplay? Why don't both of you go on home and sleep it off?"

Several others muttered agreement with this, and a woman's stern voice called out, "We came to dance, not to fight."

"Folks, you're right. I hate to see bloodshed as much as the next fellow," Calvin Lowry announced, stepping forward with his hands lifted before him. "This is my little fiesta and I don't want any trouble. None at all. So maybe I can talk some sense into these boys. But I have to say, they don't seem drunk to me—they're just plain mad. Ellis, my advice to you is to simmer down. You don't want to shoot anyone tonight. Maybe you and McCallum here can just forget about this little disagreement and—"

"No way, boss."

The crowd set to murmuring again.

"McCallum, what about you? Why don't you just apologize to my foreman here and then we can go back to dancing, like the lady suggested?"

"Go to hell, Lowry." Brett flicked the rancher a contemptuous glance.

"Well, folks," Lowry sighed, dropping his hands in resignation, "as you can see, I tried." Lowry shrugged and edged backward. "I reckon there's nothing left to do now but let 'em settle this the only way men know how." Calvin Lowry's voice boomed commandingly louder over the disapproving swell of voices. "Let them fight."

Lowry had halted near one of the stone benches that lined the terrace. As he threw down his cigar, squashing it beneath his boot, his eyes were riveted with satisfaction upon Brett's face. Cade was no more than ten paces away and his palm itched, for he realized that he could pick the cattleman off in an instant. But that would be murder.

Cade smiled thinly to himself. No, he'd wait. This had to be done legal. Legal for New Mexico.

People flowed backward, giving the two men space. A hush of tension fell over the assembled guests as the torches cast eerie yellow light over the proceedings, and somewhere in the mountains, thunder rumbled again.

Finally Cade saw Lowry's glance shift from Brett to flick over the crowd. *He's looking for me, and for his three hired killers,* Cade realized with grim amusement. But Lowry was doomed for disappointment.

"Any time you say." Brett's arms hung at his sides.

Cade marveled at how confident his brother's voice sounded. This was his first one-on-one gunfight, but though Cade had tried to come up with another strategy, Brett had insisted on going through with it. Cade, though uneasy, knew he had to let Brett handle this challenge himself. Red Cobb was a different matter—he was a skilled gunslinger, practiced, ruthless, and with a draw akin to lightning, but Hank Ellis was a far more equal opponent. Assuming Brett had benefited from the formal training Ross McCallum had insisted on for his sons, he should be able to handle an overcocky piece of scum like Ellis.

Or else, Cade reflected with a tight spasm of fear in his gut, *I'll have my own brother's death on my conscience.* But at this moment, he knew there was nothing he could do.

"You're sure, boy?" Ellis taunted. "You don't want to back down and apologize and get your ugly hide off Mr. Lowry's property?"

"Not a chance, Ellis. Now are you going to gab all night or are you going to get down to business?"

"I'm going to blow your damned brains out, boy!

Right now!" Ellis roared, and his hand flashed down-ward for his gun.

Brett drew smoothly and fired. His aim was true. The bullet tore through Ellis's green vest and ripped into his chest. It killed him instantly.

He toppled at Lowry's black-booted feet.

The cattleman's cheeks blotched with surprise. Then his lips thinned into a snarl. He glanced swiftly about, and Cade could tell he was wondering why the hell he hadn't heard more shots, why there weren't screams and an outcry because Roy Steele was dead.

But there was only the same gray hushed silence from the crowd.

Brett was breathing hard, and he was pale, but his face was stony and set as he stared at the man he'd killed.

Cade did a quick scan of the terrace. He spotted two of Lowry's men together on the fringe of the crowd. Maybe they'd step in to bail out their boss and maybe not.

At any rate, he thought as he stepped forward around the knot of people before him and made his way toward Lowry with a long, slow stride, the time for Mr. Calvin Lowry to end his bullying days on this earth had come, one way or another.

"What's wrong, Lowry? You look kind of disappointed."

"My foreman's dead, Steele, what do you expect? I want you and your whole troublemaking bunch off my land now."

"Not very neighborly, trying to throw out invited guests. Or am I wrong? Didn't you invite Conchita and Adelaide Rivers and Tomas to your little fiesta? Right kind of you, considering you murdered Alec Rivers and have been doing everything you can to steal the family's property."

Thunderous rage darkened Lowry's eyes. He nearly shook with the livid rage that gripped him. "You've got a helluva nerve accusing me of that in front of all my friends and neighbors, Steele. Mrs. Rivers," he snarled to Conchita, standing with Tomas beneath one of the torches, "you never should have brought this lawless gunslinger to a fiesta for civilized folks. I'm sorry, but I'll have to ask you to leave."

"Not yet, senor." Conchita regarded him stonily. Beside her, Adelaide's chin jutted forward with anticipation.

"We're about to see vindication for my son's murder," the older woman snapped out. "You know it, Lowry, and we know it. Think we'd miss this? Naw, we're not going *nowhere.*"

"I reckon," Brett said, as Lowry's hands balled into fists at his sides, "that everyone here will have real reason to celebrate when Roy Steele is finished conducting his business with you. And, you two men," Brett called harshly to the hired hands Cade had spotted on the fringes, "if you're smart you'll stay out of this. If not, you can die just like your pard Hank Ellis."

The kid has guts—McCallum guts, Cade thought admiringly, and then he forced himself to think of nothing but the man staring at him with such utter hatred and desperation in his eyes.

"I'm sure we can settle this peaceable," Cade said mockingly, his stance deceptively nonchalant. "Just apologize to Conchita and Adelaide, and the rest of my friends, and we'll let bygones be bygones."

"I'm not apologizing for anything! You people are the ones who've barged in here and disrupted a festive gathering of neighbors. I've asked you to leave, and if you don't, I'll have no choice but to throw you off."

"Go ahead."

Sweat glistened on Lowry's ruddy brow. "You think

I can't? You think I'm scared of your name, your reputation, Steele? Well, think again." His hard laughter echoed around the terrace. People stepped even farther away from him. And at the same moment a closer rumble of thunder boomed across the sky. "I'm not afraid of any man and that includes you. So I'm calling you out, Steele, here and now. And when you're dead, me and my boys will run the rest of your friends off my land and clear out of this valley for good."

Cade had gone still as stone, but now a faint mocking smile curled the corners of his lips. He didn't have to say anything; that contemptuous smile said it all. It goaded Lowry more than words, for everyone who saw that look of utter confidence and scorn gasped and held their breath.

"Damn you!" Lowry shouted and suddenly his gun was in his hand.

The black and golden night exploded with gunfire, screams, and blood.

Chapter 23

Brilliant amber lightning sliced the sky as Red Cobb at last halted his horse on a sharp ledge that jutted over a narrow canyon gorge. The thunder seemed to boom from the very rocks as he untied the rope that bound Annabel to the pommel and dragged her to the ground.

"We won't mind the storm one little bit, honey. You and me will be snug and dry as a couple of barn mice. Look."

And as he dragged her forward toward the rocks, she saw what she hadn't seen at first—a cave, hidden amidst huge tumbling boulders, almost invisible if you didn't know what to look for.

Cobb pushed her ahead of him and led his horse through the opening. "Keep going," he growled. "It's plenty big. We can even make a fire."

I can hardly wait, Annabel thought as she stumbled ahead of him in the pitch darkness. A match scraped against tinder and then pale light illuminated rough rock walls. There was just room enough for Cobb to stand without brushing his head against the roof.

He tethered the horse to a boulder near the mouth of the cave, swung his saddle pack over his shoulder, and pushed Annabel forward, deeper into the shadowy recesses. She heard rain begin to pound outside. Fear clawed at her.

She couldn't hope to escape during a thunderstorm.

Then I'll just have to stall him—somehow, she thought, fighting to keep panic from overtaking her. *You're smarter than he is. And more desperate. That makes you more dangerous.*

But she wished with all her might that she was safe with Cade somewhere, anywhere. In his cabin, she thought on a breath of longing. That cozy little cabin in that magnificent gemlike valley. But then Red Cobb shoved her and she fell into the wall, and the lovely image was shattered.

"Sit down and don't cause me any trouble," he warned, as he dropped a match onto a small heap of twigs piled on the cave floor. Golden light caught, spiraling up and outward. "If you try to get away, things'll go worse for you."

Annabel realized something as she stared at the orange-gold flames. He had been here before and used this cave, and had planned to come back, planned to bring her here. That was why the convenient pile of twigs was left here, all ready for their return.

She swallowed with great difficulty. The horrid gag was still in her mouth. Reaching up, she yanked it from her lips, and let it fall around her neck, even though her wrists were still bound together. As she glared at him defiantly, Cobb regarded her in amusement.

"Think you're pretty brave, don't you? Well, it won't do you any good up here. No one's going to be impressed, least of all me. Now sit down before I knock you down."

Suddenly he towered over her, and Annabel knew he would carry out his threat. She sat on the cold floor of the cave, shivering in her thin gown, and avoided looking at him as he built up the fire, then riffled through his pack and began to chew on a piece of jerky.

"Want some?"

She shook her head. "But I would appreciate it if you'd untie me. The rope is cutting into my wrists."

"Ain't that too bad." He removed a whiskey flask from his pack and took a deep, satisfying swig. "Want some of this, honey? It'll help settle your nerves."

The only thing that will help settle my nerves is seeing you dead—preferably at the bottom of that canyon out there, she thought, but she kept her face schooled into an expression of calmness, and merely shook her head.

"I'm fine . . . except for this rope."

He studied her as he tilted the bottle to his mouth again. Then he shrugged. "Hell, why not? A teensy thing like you can't do too much damage, can you?"

He pulled a knife from his boot and sliced the rope.

"Thank you," Annabel murmured, her eyes downcast. She was thinking hard and fast, trying to figure out a way she could get her hands on his gun. Distractedly, she rubbed at her numb, bleeding wrists as Cobb sat back down, stuffed the rest of the jerky in his mouth, and followed it with another deep swill of whiskey.

That's it. Keep drinking, she thought. *Drink it all up.* An idea was taking form in her brain. If he passed out, she could steal his gun and his horse and get away. Or at the very least, she could hit him over the head with a rock or something while he was passed out, then tie him up with whatever rope was still stored with his gear. And *then* take the horse and get away.

Lots of possibilities, she thought. And all of them dangerous. But one of them would have to work.

"You know I'm going to have to kill you," he said matter-of-factly, setting the bottle down and studying her from beneath the brim of his hat. "When I'm finished with you, that is. Can't have a nosey little private investigator roaming around, causing trouble. Besides, honey, you deserve it. You never should have gotten involved in men's business, and you sure never should have tried to pull a fast one over on Red Cobb."

Dread squeezed the air from her lungs. *Don't let him distract you or scare you. That's what he wants. He wants you too weak and frightened to do anything—too terrified to fight back.*

"I'm sorry," she managed to say with far more steadiness than she felt. "I was only trying to do my job. I've heard how good you are with a gun, and I wanted to protect my . . . client."

"That was your first mistake, honey. There's nothing that can protect Brett McCallum from me."

"Why?"

"Huh?"

"Why are you so bent on killing him?" Annabel knew the answer to this, but she had to keep him talking. She waited as he took another long swallow of the whiskey and wiped his mouth on his sleeve. Outside, she could hear the wind shrieking, the rain drumming against the ancient rock. And thunder roared as steadily as cannon fire during a fierce and relentless battle. But at that moment she would rather have braved the storm naked than faced the terrifyingly unemotional brutality of Red Cobb.

"Why do you think?" he sneered.

"Money. I think someone hired you." She saw the drunken glint in his blue eyes as he nodded.

"Course. Why else? Fact is, I'm being well paid to rid the world—and my client—of Master Brett McCallum."

"And is your client a man by the name of Lucas Johnson?" she asked softly.

Cobb stared at her. "How'd you know . . ." Suddenly a smirk crossed his face. "It might be one of his names."

"So he uses more than one name? Is Frank Boxer another one?"

"Lady, you ask way too many questions. I think I need to shut you up."

He shambled to his feet and came toward her. Annabel scrambled up, determined at least to meet him on her feet.

"I don't mean anything by it," she said quickly, backing up until she could go no farther. The rough wall of the cave pressed against her spine. "But I am curious. You've been so relentless, and so clever. Obviously this man who hired you—whatever his name is—knew that he was hiring the best when he picked Red Cobb."

"Damn right I'm the best." He stopped right before her and grabbed her arms so suddenly that she gasped. Cobb chuckled. "Some people think Steele is faster than me. How about you?"

"I . . . don't know . . ."

"You wish he was here right now, don't you? Think he could save you, eh?" Cobb shook her hard. Annabel tried in vain to wrench her arms free, but couldn't. Cobb shook her harder until she was breathless and dizzy.

"Don't you?" he lashed out, his voice thick with cruelty.

"Yes!"

He stopped the shaking, but held on to her, his fingers biting into her flesh every bit as painfully as the rope had earlier. "Well, he couldn't help you if he was here. I'm faster than him and a better shot than him and I'm going to prove it. Soon as I'm finished with you and I've thrown your body down into the bottom of that canyon out there, I'm going back—to kill McCallum and then Steele—or maybe the other way around," he shrugged. "Doesn't matter to me. But there's something you should know. I'm going to tell Steele exactly what I did to you right before I kill him." His smile widened, stretching taut across his handsome, square-jawed face. "I want him to know."

"You . . . bastard." Trembling rage overcame her. "You'll never kill him. He's quicker than you, and surer. You're the one who's going to die, you stupid arrogant fool."

The half-drunken gloating faded from Cobb's face. His eyes took on a terrifying icy glitter that turned them the light blue of a distant star. "You're going to be real sorry for that, honey, just like for everything else," he said, his breath coming heavy in his throat. "You got a hankering for Steele, don't you? I saw the two of you up there in that bedroom window. And I saw you ride out of Silver Junction together the morning after you lied to me about McCallum's whereabouts. But that's not enough for you, you two-bit whore. You've got a hankering for McCallum, too. I saw you kissing him out there near Lowry's corrals. You're a randy little thing, aren't you? Well, I deserve my turn. That's why I've been waiting, following you, and waiting. Because I wanted to get my hands on you first, and then go after Steele and McCallum. So's I can tell them both what I did to their cheap little light-skirt detective. So I can kill them both knowing that I've bested them in every way. It'll sure be sweet."

"You're out of your mind."

"And you're a dead woman."

Laughing, he reached for her, and squashed his lips against hers. Annabel fought against him, frantic to get away, but he was too strong, and the stench of liquor and days-old sweat nearly overpowered her as much as his heavy body when he crushed her against the wall.

Her nails raked his face. He swore, lifted his head,

and slapped her. "So you like it rough, do you, you little bitch?"

"Get away!"

"Honey, we're only getting started."

He yanked her close again and this time plunged his mouth against her throat, sucking, while at the same time his hand groped at her breast. He grabbed it and squeezed so hard Annabel shrieked in pain and terror.

Then out of pure instinct she rammed her knee up into his groin. Cobb screamed. For just a moment he loosened his hold on her, and it was enough. She darted around him and past the campfire. In her haste she kicked a stray log lying near the edge of the fire, sending it skittering out of the circle of flames. One end was burning brightly and suddenly she had an idea. She grabbed the other end of the log, and as Cobb, still bent over, started toward her, she threw it straight at him.

He couldn't dodge in time. The fiery log hit him full in the shoulder and a spark flew up and caught in his hair. Suddenly he was on fire, screeching and yelling, and Annabel ran toward the mouth of the cave. There was no time to untether the horse, no time to do anything but plunge out into the ferocious rage of the storm, into a roaring night of black sky and gold lightning, of wind and wet, and she fled headlong through the rain-slashed madness.

She kept close to the cave wall, brushing against the rocks as she ran, terrified of that chasm just beyond, of losing her bearings and hurtling over the rim of the canyon to a gruesome death far below. Rain whipped her hair and streamed down her cheeks and sodden gown, and the wind whistled through her ears until she thought she'd go mad, but she kept going, half-running, half-stumbling on a path that led she knew not where. But it was leading her away from Red Cobb and that was all that mattered right now. She peered anxiously behind her, straining to see through the sheets of rain, fearful he would grab her suddenly from behind.

She couldn't see him, but that didn't mean he wasn't there. She couldn't see anything but a blur of gray rain and black night and hot-gold lightning which flashed briefly, setting the mountain peaks aglow.

Terror tore at her more painfully than the rocks and branches that clawed her face and hands and gown. *He could be right behind you. He could grab you at any moment,* a frantic voice inside her shouted.

These fears kept her going, despite her fatigue and her blindness and the elements that battled at her as she tried to slip away like a lost wild creature into the night.

Suddenly, the trail dipped with unexpected sharpness, her foot slipped on wet rock, she tumbled forward . . . and down . . . and down. . . .

Air rushed past her, cold and bitter as death, and her hands grabbed for rocks and touched nothingness. Her mouth opened to scream but no sound came out as she fell and fell and fell. . . .

Rain slashed at Cobb's nose and cheeks and eyes as he glared up and down the muddy scrub trail outside the cave. He was in a black drunken rage, cursing the fury of the night and the woman who had disappeared like a witch into the storm. A string of oaths poured from him—he wanted to shoot something, anything, and he pulled his gun and fired furiously at the waving trees and the sky. Damn her to hell. His singed hair and the burn he'd gotten on his temple and shoulder before he'd put out the flames were vivid reminders of her. She'd left her mark on him, and he would leave his on her. Oh, yes, he surely would.

In the morning. The moment the storm broke he'd be after her. She wouldn't get far, Cobb concluded with satisfaction as he holstered his gun and stamped back inside the cave. He pushed his dripping red hair from his eyes. *Let her get good and soaked. Let her freeze all night. Then she'll collapse. She'll be too weak and tired and hungry to move, and then I'll get her. Damn her pretty eyes, I'll get her good.*

He stomped back to the campfire, peeled off his wet clothes, and donned dry ones from his pack. Then he settled down with his saddle blanket and his whiskey to wait for his revenge.

Chapter 24

Annabel came to slowly, with the hazy dizziness of someone who's been thrown from a horse and doesn't quite remember when or how. The rain slamming against her cheeks and temples struck her like tiny pellets, and her bones were icy cold against the hard wet ground.

She tried to move, tried to lift her head, and felt an aching pain along her side. Thunder crashed in her ears.

She peered around, dazed, trying to make out where she was, where she could hide, what had happened.

Through a mist of confusion she realized she was on a ledge, a ledge jutting out from a rocky path, and saw that she must have fallen onto an outcrop of rock right beneath the trail she'd been on before.

So I didn't fall down a chasm, just down to the ledge beneath. And by some miracle, she wasn't dead, or even hurt, at least not badly.

But she felt dazed with cold and fear and she was tired. So dreadfully tired. *Move,* she thought dully, *keep moving. He'll find you if you stay here.*

But she didn't know where to go, and her limbs wouldn't obey her frantic commands.

"Help me," she whispered into the night, her words drowned out by the tearing fury of the wind. "Someone . . . help me."

With supreme will, she began to crawl, inching forward, turning her head from side to side as the rain poured down. She was shivering uncontrollably from head to toe and knew only that she had to find shelter or she would freeze to death, or drown.

Or Red Cobb would find her and that would be worse than death.

She crawled on.

Suddenly, she thought she saw something, a glimmer against the blur of black rocks. A woman.

"Mama?"

Somehow she found the strength to stagger to her feet, her eyes fixed dazedly on that lovely silver vision that seemed to shimmer between the raindrops. "Mama, will you help me?"

The slim figure twinkled and twirled just ahead. Then it vanished.

"Mama!"

She half ran toward where she'd seen it, and suddenly, she saw a low opening. A cave, another cave! This one she had to stoop to enter, and as she did so she wondered for a fleeting moment if some wild creature might be inside, also seeking shelter from the storm. But Mama wouldn't lead her to danger. Mama had shown her the way.

"Where are you, Mama?" she asked as she crept inside and then the ceiling rose overhead and she stood and saw that the cave was half the size of the other cave, but it was dry and empty and sheltered and she stumbled in and sank down to the ground, clutching her arms around her shivering body. She felt a gossamer touch upon her cheek and suddenly the cold was gone. She was warm, and peaceful. She closed her eyes, and felt herself sinking, sinking away into cottony blackness that was as soft and warm as a haystack.

"Mama, don't go . . ."

Cade had been riding through the storm for hours. Fear whipped at him with every long stride of his horse. He'd been fighting all night, fighting a sense of horrible hopelessness and cold fear for Annabel which was far more painful than anything inflicted by the elements. But as night crashed on toward morning, he knew deep in his heart that he would never find her, not until this damned rain let up and the darkness ebbed, and by then, he knew, it could well be too late.

He bent his head against the silver torrent which ran off his slicker in flowing rivulets. He had to keep going.

He'd gone looking for her after shooting Lowry, but when he'd found only her reticule in that upstairs bedroom he'd known what must have happened. Tracks leading away from the Lowry hacienda had headed east. But all the tracks that could be seen at all by torchlight had quickly been obliterated by the start of the storm. And so had the torch.

All he had to go on was Conchita's advice. She knew of two places where Cobb might have taken Annabel with a storm brewing—both of them had numerous caves, both were less than an hour's ride east of Lowry's place. Brett had veered off toward the other canyon; he had chosen this one. But as he forced Dickens up yet another twisting trail, slippery and treacherous with slimy mud and rain, Cade's heart weighed heavy.

He should have seen this coming and protected Annabel. Cobb had obviously caught on to her trick and had come back for revenge. *How could I have been so stupid not to have seen her danger? Why in hell did I leave her alone?*

He gritted his teeth and forced back his fear. Impossible as it seemed, he would find her. He wouldn't quit until he had. *And Cobb . . . well,* Cade thought with grim, deadly calm, *I'll take care of Cobb.*

But an hour later, he shook the water out of his eyes and squinted around the looming, rain-swept mountains in despair. He'd found two caves, neither of them occupied. There were probably dozens more here in these rocks, tucked into unseen crevices, hidden beneath overhangs that jutted out over the dizzying canyon below. But his horse was bone weary and cold, and Cobb could have Annabel hidden anywhere, anywhere . . . or he might have headed toward the other canyon after all . . .

Then he saw it. It . . . her . . . he couldn't be sure. A shimmering figure—female—glistened against the rocks just above. He blinked, shaded his eyes, and looked up into the rain. There it was again, for only a moment, glowing like a falling star, and then it vanished.

It seemed to have beckoned to him.

He blinked, saw nothing, and swore. *Why the hell not,* he muttered then, and turned Dickens onto the path which led in that direction. It was worth a try. At this point, anything was worth a try.

For some reason as he bore down on the place where he thought he'd seen someone, he thought of Annabel's lost brooch, the one her mother had promised to her on her wedding day, the one Savannah Brannigan had claimed would protect her from harm. Maybe if she'd had that brooch, Cobb wouldn't have gotten his filthy hands on her. Maybe she'd be safe right this minute instead of trapped with the gunslinger in the midst of a New Mexico thunderstorm.

He reached the ledge and glanced all around and

down at the ground. Suddenly, beneath the swirling rain and mud he saw something and bent to retrieve it. Hope pounded through him. He clenched the object tightly in his fist.

Annabel's amber earbob. Lying here, covered with mud.

Quickly he perused both directions, and saw at once from the shape of the rocks that there must be a cave . . . right there.

He tethered Dickens beneath a small overhang and approached the opening of the cave with his gun drawn. *If Cobb has hurt her, I'll break every bone in his body before I shoot him,* he vowed, a grim whiteness about his mouth. He stooped and crept into the cave. Silence. Dead silence. He waited a moment, listening, as his eyes adjusted to the darkness. But as the irregular outlines of the rocks and cave roof began to take shape, and the pitch black dissolved into murky gray, he saw a figure lying on the cave floor.

Annabel. He rushed to her and knelt down, feeling for a pulse. Her skin was ice cold, clammy and wet, and she was spattered with mud and bruises, but she was alive. Thank God, he whispered as he lifted her and cradled her in his arms. He pressed his mouth to the chilled pale skin of her cheek, and something inside him trembled with unspeakable pain. What had happened to her? Had she escaped Cobb or had he hurt her and left her here to die?

"Annabel. Sweetheart, what did he do to you?"

She stirred in his arms, the slightest of tremors shivering through the length of her body. Cade held her close, trying to warm her with his own body. "It's over now. You're safe."

"Cade?"

Fierce joy swept through him at the single word, and when she opened her eyes a moment later, the relief that surged through him washed away every other thought.

"Don't try to talk."

"I'm cold, Cade. So cold . . ."

"Yes, sweetheart, I know. Wait just a moment and I'll get you a blanket."

"Don't leave me!"

She clutched at him with feeble fingers.

"Only for a minute. Hold on, Annabel, don't slip away from me."

The next hours were a blur to him, a series of frantic activities as he tried to get her warm and dry. He stripped off her wet clothes and wrapped her in both of his saddle blankets. He made a fire and held her in his arms before its opal glow, and later, when she slept, limp and warm and trusting in his arms, he looked at her with an awed tenderness that sliced more painfully than an ax through his gut. He settled her as comfortably as he could on the floor of the cave while he brought Dickens inside and rubbed him down.

When Annabel awoke just before dawn, the rain was letting up to a steady crystal drizzle from a sky of dark pewter. Deep within the snug depths of the cave he held a tin cup filled with coffee to her lips while she sipped at the steaming rich brew.

And something in his heart turned over, lifted, and soared with gladness as she at last smiled at him and her gray-green eyes took on something of their familiar sparkle.

"I could have used that slicker last night," were her first words as she glanced past him at the slicker he'd tossed down in the corner of the cave. "Remind me never to wear silk in a thunderstorm again."

"I'll remind you never to get mixed up with a snake-eyed varmint like Red Cobb again."

Her eyes darkened to emerald. A shadow passed

across her face. "He's still out there," she whispered, suddenly paler. "He said . . . oh, Cade, you can't imagine what he said."

"Yes, I can," he told her grimly. "But you tell me anyway."

Afterward, he held her against him, his arms tight around her delicate frame, and thought of the pleasure he would get from ending Red Cobb's worthless life. Sometimes he felt regret when he was forced to kill a man; sometimes, he felt nothing; but this time he would feel pure satisfaction.

Cobb had threatened Brett and had done far worse to Annabel, and he would pay in the only way animals like him understood.

"Tell me what happened with Lowry," she urged, her head on his warm chest, for he had stripped off his shirt and lay beside her clad only in his trousers. His boots, shirt, and gun belt were heaped in a pile beside the dying fire. Her slender fingers curled against the crisp black hair of his chest as she peeked up at him. "Is he dead?"

"Yep."

"Is everyone all right?"

Cade's arms tightened protectively around her. "Everyone is fine. You'd have been proud of Brett. He faced Hank Ellis in a showdown and he did just fine."

He told her how they'd thwarted Lowry's plan by getting rid of the three cowhands who were supposed to shoot him in the back, and of how, after he had killed Lowry in a fair gunfight for everyone to see, the other ranchers and townspeople had been hard put to conceal their delight that their host, who had probably stolen from all of them, was dead.

"Folks were rushing up to Conchita and Adelaide and shaking their hands. As for Lowry's men, they scattered pretty quick. I don't think we'll have to worry about them anymore—that outfit is all broken up."

They lay there together for a while, watching the fire, listening to the sounds of the diminishing storm, which sounded pleasantly distant from deep within the rock walls of the cave. But tired as she was, Annabel couldn't sleep.

"Maybe it's the detective in me," she told Cade, as he stroked her hair with gentle fingers, "but I can't stop thinking about this man Boxer. Even though Cobb wouldn't admit it, I'd be willing to bet that Boxer and Lucas Johnson are one and the same. Boxer must have hired Cobb to kill Brett after Brett refused to help him ruin your father."

Annabel closed her eyes, enjoying the feel of his hands on her hair, reveling in the warmth and strength of him beside her. But her mind wouldn't shut down and after a moment she continued. "Boxer must be a monster, a monster so bent on revenge he wouldn't hesitate to kill even his own son for crossing him—if Brett is his son," she added quickly.

"We'll find out."

"We will?" She twisted in his arms and peered eagerly into his face, searching it for his intent. "Does that mean—you'll go back to St. Louis and help unravel this? You'll try to work things out with your father? You are worried about him, aren't you?"

"Ross McCallum can take care of himself."

But doubt was gnawing at him, much as he tried to push it away. And so was the past, the past he'd been running from, refusing to face. The time was coming when he would have to face it, he sensed that deep in his soul. But right now there were more immediate problems to deal with. Namely Red Cobb.

"Don't." Annabel's soft voice and her hand, light as

a dove's feather, on his cheek, broke into his dark reverie.

"Don't what?"

"Don't look so . . . merciless. Or so troubled. It will all turn out all right."

"You could have died up here. Cobb might have killed you."

"But I'm safe. I'm going to be fine, because once again, you found me and saved me," she said, beaming.

"I'm getting pretty tired of it, too."

She grinned as he tried to keep the smile from his voice, but his eyes gleamed down at her in the way that made her heart skip a beat. "Cade," she whispered shyly, a softness threading through her as her hands reached up to wrap intimately around his neck, "there's one place that is still really cold. It needs warming badly and I was wondering if you could oblige . . ."

"Anything to oblige a lady," he murmured, his eyes glinting into hers.

"That's what I hoped you'd say," she breathed in delight and slowly pulled him down toward her and inched her lips toward his. "My mouth," she whispered, her lips tantalizingly brushing his as she formed each word. "My lips feel as if they must be blue with cold . . ."

"Hell, we can't have that."

She started to giggle as he dragged her to him, but when his mouth caught and claimed hers, the giggles ceased. The breath locked in her throat. She quivered all over.

His kiss was full of tenderness. She wondered at it, tasted it, and gave herself up to it, to the sweet pummeling sensations that swept her into a oneness with him, that made her savor his taste, his scent, the rough feel of his lips on hers. His mouth was hard, his muscled body taut with coiled desire, and yet he was so gentle, his hands caressing her hair, sliding to her back, pressing her closer, closer still . . .

Her blood heated and blazed along her veins like rich potent wine. "Cade, there's something I have to tell you . . ."

"Can't it wait?"

"No, it cannot . . . wait," she gasped, as relentless kisses rained down upon her cheeks, eyelids, and throat, blinding her to everything but the surging need inside her. "I . . . love . . . you. . . ."

He was trying to find her breasts beneath those damned blankets, and finally, swearing, he yanked the blankets away, revealing her lovely pearl-skinned nakedness. "You're a damned fool if you do, Annabel." He dropped a kiss to one breast, and cupped the other one. "But if it makes you feel any better, I love you, too."

"If it makes me feel any better?" she panted, incredulous, yet too stunned with delicious sensations to do anything but close her eyes and see what he said, what he did next. "What kind of thing is that to say when you're about to . . . to . . ."

"Make love to you? Because that's what I'm going to do, Annabel, unless you don't want me to, and if you don't, you'd better speak up right now or . . ."

"No, no, I want you to . . . I do want you to . . ." she moaned, clutching his hair as his tongue began doing marvelous things to her nipple, tormenting it into rosy hardness, while his other hand slid lower, to her belly, and then lower still . . .

"You're sure?" he demanded, his mouth crushing down once more upon her lips, silencing her for a long minute until they both came up for air. His hand was exploring part of her no man had ever breached before and she was beginning to think she would go mad before he'd finished with her.

"I'm sure . . . oh, Cade, what are you . . ."

"I'm glad you feel that way," he went on, as if she hadn't spoken, intent on the glazed glow in her eyes, on the sweat beginning to sheen upon her lovely face, "but as for loving me, I think you're making a big mistake . . ."

"I'm not . . . I mean I do . . . love you, oh, Cade, what in heaven are you *doing?*"

"If you think this is heaven, just wait, Annabel . . ."

"Cade!"

"Don't you like it?"

"I . . . love it, I love you, Cade, but . . . do you really love . . . me?"

For answer he held her chin in his hand and stared into her eyes with the full vivid intentness of that searing black gaze. "God help you, Annabel, I do. I do. And I'm going to show you how much."

His mouth claimed hers. It was an urgent, demanding kiss, rough enough to bruise her lips, and yet there was an underlying tenderness and need in it which touched a flame to her soul. He needed her. Cade McCallum, alone in this vast brutal West for so many years, cut off from his family, from any close human connections, needed her, wanted her—loved her—and her heart and body responded to the shattering desire that poured from him. As he forced her mouth open beneath his warm lips and plunged his tongue inside with quick possessive thrusts, she felt an answering need blossomng riotously inside her. She shivered with delight, and ardently pulled him closer, and she didn't hold back the little whimpers of pleasure that rose in her throat.

Cade covered her body with his own, stroking her sides, caressing her breasts, his powerful thighs spreading her legs without resistance. She shuddered as she felt his powerful manhood pressed against her, a shudder of pleasure and half-anxious anticipation, but Cade kissed her cheek and then each of her eyelids, and soothed her with his strong, stroking hands.

"Don't be afraid, Annabel. Don't be afraid of me. . . ."

"I'm not . . . I'm not afraid of you . . . I'm afraid of . . . you know what I'm afraid of . . ."

He laughed, this handsome, relentless gunslinger, a low, growling sound deep in his throat, and his face was dark with passion and his eyes gleamed with an intensity and tenderness that made her ache inside.

"I'll try not to hurt you." His mouth claimed hers gently. "Trust me, Annabel."

"I do, Cade, I trust you," she murmured, and clutched his back with a little gasp as his strong hand slid between her thighs. "If I didn't trust you completely . . . I wouldn't be here right now . . . doing these things . . ."

He laughed again, and Annabel closed her eyes and surrendered to the wild things he was doing to her, to the intense sensations he was arousing, to the ache that was growing, growing inside of her, becoming an almost painful tingling need. . . .

Her breasts were crushed against his chest, her mouth against his throat when he at last plunged into her, eliciting a small scream that she muffled against his neck. The first sharp pain gave way to a slow aching pleasure that built and built as he eased in and then stopped and then eased in farther, his movements so strong and sure and yet careful that she forgot her trepidations and was soon caught up in the wild sweet sensations erupting inside of her.

His movements grew faster, more demanding and violent. So this is what it is to make love with a man, she thought in ardent surprise and delight, and then all thought vanished as the pleasure intensified, and her eyes widened in pure carnal need. She strained toward his taut, powerful body, her own body on fire, soaking up the strength of him, the heat, the raw power. And she gave herself over to the piercing ecstasy that was flowing through her. It ignited her breasts and her belly and her hips and the damp secret places inside her.

As Cade's sweat-filmed face loomed over her, watching her, she gazed up at him with delicious frantic desire and love-glazed eyes and arched her back to meet his ever more powerful thrusts.

Streaks of joy burst through her, coming faster and faster, until a sweet raging chaos enveloped her. She dug her fingers into his shoulder blades and bucked demandingly against him, as the cave and the fire and the universe became a blur, and a fierce explosion rocked her to the depths of her soul. Again and again, gasping and shuddering, the explosion stunned her, and she clung to him, crying out, until she was lost and then found and then whirled away as one with him, and in his strong, enfolding arms she knew at last the blissful release of fulfillment.

Cade McCallum had taken her beyond the storm, beyond the cliffs and the canyons, to a world of silvered colors all ablaze, and he had shattered her and made her whole.

The first glimmers of dawn found them dreamy and comforted in each other's arms. Annabel awoke to find Cade watching her. She smiled because his eyes were soft with a tenderness she'd never seen there before.

"Morning," she whispered, and snuggled closer. Her fingers reached up, no longer shy, to stroke and trace at the dark mat of hair on his chest.

Cade kissed her mouth and swung a leg possessively over hers. "Morning yourself."

"How much time do you think we have?"

"Before what, sweetheart?"

"Before Cobb comes searching for me."

She could feel the tension arc through him. "Not much. Unless he's sleeping it off—you did say he was going at the whiskey pretty good, right?"

"Right." She leaned across him and began to nibble at his shoulder, then slid her lips and tongue across his chest.

"And then there's Brett," he sighed, drawing a hand gently through the wild bright mane of her hair. "He was searching through the other canyon for you last night. He'll turn up pretty soon to see if I found you."

"Which you very cleverly did."

He was silent a moment. "Not without some help," he said quietly after a moment.

Annabel sat up at his tone, shoving the cloud of her hair behind her, feeling perfectly natural and somehow beautiful with her naked shoulders and breasts exposed to his view.

"What do you mean?"

"It was strange, but last night when I was searching for you and going loco because I didn't know which way to turn, I saw something. Something—or someone—showed me the way. A woman—at least I thought it was a woman, who beckoned to me and then . . . disappeared. Like a . . ." He hesitated, then added with a curt laugh, ". . . like a ghost."

Annabel's hands flew to her throat. "Mama," she whispered. "I saw Mama last night out in the storm—she showed me the way to this cave. She was just a light, I can't explain it, sort of a . . . a glowing figure, but I knew it was she. Cade, she saved me . . . and she showed you how to find me."

His gaze locked with hers. "I've heard too much Indian lore and too many strange tales in these mountains over the years to doubt it. Besides," he added with a shake of his dark head, "I know what I saw, and it sure wasn't my imagination."

Annabel sank down again and rested her head against his chest, nestling close as she pondered this turn of events in amazement. A surging, comforting warmth washed over her. Mama was out there, watching over her. Mama had sent Cade to find her, help her, love her. . . .

"All these years," Annabel mused at last, as beside her Cade stroked his hand up and down her arm, "I thought I was in love with Brett. I truly believed it, you know. But I think I wanted to love him, because he was so good and so kind and so dear to me. I had just made up my mind, without ever really consulting my heart. I only thought I had," she added with a laugh. "But then, when I met you, I was so pigheaded I tried to ignore what I felt, what my heart was telling me . . ."

"Maybe you were right to ignore it. Maybe this is the biggest mistake you'll ever make."

"Cade—how can you say that?"

He had just been about to touch her breast, but he knew in that moment it was wrong, this whole damn thing was wrong. He released her and sat up abruptly, lurching to his feet and reaching for his trousers.

"Annabel, it's time to face facts."

"What facts?" she asked in bewilderment as she watched him tug his trousers over his lean hips and fasten them, then turn back toward her, bare chested, his hair tousled, a day's growth of beard stubbling his chin, making him look even sexier and more dangerous and more irresistible than ever. Oh, God, how she loved him. She ached and longed for him just looking at him and he was telling her . . . never mind?

"What facts, Cade?" she repeated softly, when he just stared at her with his hard unfathomable eyes. He was pulling away, at least, trying to—emotionally as well as physically—and Annabel decided suddenly that she'd be damned if she'd let him.

"I'm a McCallum."

"I know."

"We're a ruthless breed. You know Ross, you've seen for yourself. And you know the history, you know what he did to my mother. He destroyed her."

"We don't know that for certain. And besides," Annabel said evenly, gazing back at him with calm, loving eyes, "what has that to do with you and me?"

You and me. His heart contracted at the words. He'd give a lot if only there could be a you and me.

"I'm just like him. Too damned much like him. When I still lived at home, in the years before I ran away, we butted heads every single day. Both of us ornery and stubborn as hell, determined to do things our way and no one else's, ready to push aside anything that got in our way. Do you understand? We fought, because we were exactly alike. Maybe you don't know me well enough to see it, but it's true, you'll have to trust me on this."

"I trust you on everything."

He scowled at her in exasperation. This wasn't going the way he'd expected. Instead of looking concerned and arguing with him, she was just sitting there, so calm, so steady and strong and beautiful, like some kind of fire goddess with that hair of hers shimmering down around a face that was damn near bringing him to his knees.

"Annabel," he began again desperately, "listen. I made up my mind a long time ago when I first heard that my mother took her own life that I would never inflict my damned domineering McCallum ways on any woman. I wouldn't want to cause any woman the kind of pain my mother must have gone through at my father's hands. I vowed to myself I wouldn't ever marry, or let myself . . . get close to anyone . . . that I'd never have more than the simplest of physical relationships with any woman, no ties, no feelings between us . . . nothing . . ." His voice trailed off. "What are you doing?"

It was obvious what she was doing, she was coming toward him. Her body naked and exquisite, gleaming golden in the soft dying embers of firelight, her hair cascading around her shoulders and breasts, she was coming toward him deliberately and sexily, with love and acceptance in her eyes.

"Stop being so damned silly," she told him gently, and thrust herself up against him, her arms snaking like silk around his neck. "You're a good man, Cade McCallum. No, you're a wonderful man. And I'm not the least little bit afraid of you. I've never been afraid of your father either—I happen to think he's a lovable old coot, even if he is somewhat garrulous—oh, Cade, haven't you seen by now that I adore the McCallum men? Every single one of them—especially . . ." Her tone grew huskier, filled with musk and promise, as she touched her mouth to his.

"Especially you."

"But . . ."

"No buts." She was sliding her hands across his shoulders now and then his back, her fingers sculpting sensuously over the rock-hard muscles. She was intoxicating him with her charm, her open, giving smile, and the pure lushness of her body, doing wild things to his gut as well as other parts of him. "Whatever happened between Ross and Livinia, and we don't know anything for sure, it has nothing to do with you and me."

Those words again. Cade gritted his teeth as her nearness threatened to annihilate all his defenses in a shattering roar.

"And even if you are a trifle . . . bullheaded—

well, so am I. And I think you've seen that I don't exactly wither under fire. In fact, I told you once that I come from equally tough stock—and I do. Nothing about you scares me. Except," she said, and the truth shone plain in her eyes, stabbing straight into his heart, "except the possibility that you might turn me away."

"I should," he groaned, his muscles still clenched tightly as she drew his head down toward hers.

"No. You love me and I love you. For once in your life, Cade McCallum, just follow your heart."

Follow your heart. It sounded so simple . . . but . . . if he ever hurt her . . .

And then he saw the love blossoming in her eyes, a love that was strong and deep and filled with compassion, and she was in his arms, soft and sweet and trusting, and he suddenly knew that she was already in his heart, embedded there like emeralds in the dark soul of a mine, a part of it, now and forever, and somehow, that she belonged there.

"Annabel, this is loco . . . I never thought . . . oh, hell. What are you doing?"

She was stroking him, teasing him, arousing him even more than he already was, if that was possible, and her gray-green glance sparkled up at him, with love and mischief and promise.

"Quickly, my love," she urged, a smile dancing across her face as she began to kiss his mouth, his chin, his chest, his shoulder. "Red Cobb might well be here soon and . . ."

"You're the most loco woman I ever met. You love living dangerously, don't you?"

"Just like you," she gasped back as he picked her up and carried her back to the blankets, determination and anticipation stamped upon his lean face. He lowered her gently but hurriedly to the ground, and grinned as she reached for the trousers he'd donned only a short time ago.

"You're the damndest woman I ever met," he said tenderly, while at the same time pushing her down onto the blanket with ruthless haste.

"And you're the most splendid man," she breathed, her eyes widening as he moved atop her and spread her legs with his thighs. "Cade, we do have time for this, don't you think? I mean if Cobb walked in here now . . ."

"We'd both die happy." His eyes gleamed into hers as he lowered his head to her breast and then neither of them thought about Red Cobb again.

Chapter 25

Puffy white clouds dotted the new-washed morning sky as Red Cobb spotted the plume of smoke curling up from the canyon gorge.

A campfire? Could she have somehow survived the storm, found shelter, and now started a campfire? No, it was probably someone else—maybe, he thought, his eyes glinting at the possibility, Brett McCallum, or even Steele. One or both of them might have come looking for her, and maybe they thought a campfire would draw her. Or him . . .

It could be a trap, he thought, his nerves tightening.

Well, we'll just see, he thought, heading his horse down a scrubby ravine that would lead him toward the curling wisp of smoke.

It was still early morning, and his head hurt from all the whiskey, but not much. He'd slept well, snug in that cave, wishing he could have had her already, but knowing it was only a matter of time.

He'd catch her today, and he'd teach her the cost of crossing Red Cobb.

He stopped well short of the campfire and left his horse among some cottonwoods, then crept closer on foot. A smile cracked across his face as he saw her, sitting there in that ragged green dress, looking not nearly so fine or uppity now. She was huddled on the cold ground, trying to warm herself against the morning chill by sitting close to the flames. She was eating some berries she must have found there in the canyon, and she looked hungry and lost and utterly vulnerable.

His pulse quickened with raw lust. This was going to be sweet, so sweet.

"Morning, bitch," he greeted her, stepping out into the rocky clearing with a wide grin on his face. "Sleep well?"

She looked up and straight at him, appearing not the least bit startled. Or scared. She eyed him coolly. Why the hell wasn't she screaming, or trying to run?

She did scramble to her feet as he approached, but she didn't look scared, and she held her ground. She was calm as a Sunday school teacher, but her eyes held a burning anger that made him stop in his tracks for a moment, then he caught himself and came on.

"Did I sleep well?" she repeated in a tone that was almost amused. "Not as well as you're going to."

He halted again. An inkling came to him then, a cold nausea-inducing hunch which made him shift his gaze swiftly around the clearing, but he saw nothing, just trees and rocks and scrub.

"You've caused me a hell of a lot of trouble, you bitch," he muttered, "but you're going to pay for it now. Don't even think about running because I'll—"

"*You'll what*?"

Brett McCallum stepped from behind a tree, his gun drawn and cocked and pointed at Cobb's chest.

"No sudden moves," Roy Steele said quietly, materializing from behind a rock just behind the woman, and Cobb stared at him in amazement and dismay.

"You." His voice shook a little. He wasn't apprehensive—no, he was furious, furious with them and with himself for falling for their trap. "I'm going to kill all three of you," he announced, absolute certainty in his eyes.

"First you, Steele, and then McCallum. And then the woman. When we've finished some other things," he added with a hoarse laugh. "She and I have some unfinished fun and games to attend to . . ."

"Shut up, Cobb." Steele moved three quick, easy strides toward him, his body superbly graceful beneath that shining sun.

"You're not going to do anything to anybody. Your time is up."

"You think so? Steele, I've been waiting for this day —itching for this day. I can't wait to kill you. I'm sick to death of people wondering who's faster, always mentioning your name when they mention mine. I've been meaning to settle the question once and for all . . . but I had a job to finish first."

"I know. Me." Brett McCallum sounded every bit as cool as Steele did, Cobb thought in amazement. Somehow he had expected something different, a scared, green kid, a city greenhorn he'd have to taunt and force into a showdown. But this dark-haired young man with the blazing blue eyes and the gun held in a steady hand was no tenderfoot. *Not that he's a match for me,* Cobb told himself quickly. *But it's strange, he's not what I expected, not what I was led to expect . . .*

"If you're smart, you'll throw down your gun right now," the woman said and she sounded so sure of herself that Cobb wanted to kill her right then. "At least then they'll let you live. Not that I care," she added with a shrug. "You're a worthless piece of vermin if ever I saw one, but decency means we must take pity on you and at least give you a chance."

"He doesn't deserve a chance, Annabel, not after what he did to you." Brett studied the red-haired gunslinger contemptuously. "You've been looking for me, Cobb. Well, I'm here."

"Sorry, but you'll have to wait in line." Steele never glanced aside, but spoke with quiet firmness, his level gaze fixed intently on Cobb's flushed, ever-darkening countenance. "And when I'm finished, Brett, I reckon there won't be enough left of him for you to do anything but spit on."

"You're wrong, Steele," Cobb rasped out, and for all the fact that he was angry, frustrated, and humiliated at having been taken by surprise, there was no fear, only supreme confidence in his words and tone. "You're old, and you've lost your edge, if you ever even had one. I'm gonna send you straight to hell, and these others after you . . . if you've got the guts to take me on one at a time."

"Annabel, get out of the way," Steele ordered, his eyes still riveted calmly on the other man. Obediently, she moved toward Brett, standing motionless at his side, giving the two gunfighters a wide berth.

"Anytime you say," Steele drawled coldly.

Sweat poured down Cobb's face. But it had nothing to do with fear—only excitement, anticipation, the chance to meet the ultimate challenge. Even if Steele did kill him, he was determined to bring his enemy to death with him. "One thing you should know first, Steele," he barked. His lips twisted with the taunting words. "Your ladyfriend, Lily, back in Eagle Gulch—I killed her. She gave me some bad information and I had to come back and beat the truth out of her, and I reckon I got a little carried away. I told the doctor she hit her head when she tripped and fell, and he signed the death certificate as an accident." Cobb guffawed. "No one in Eagle Gulch had the guts to call me a liar."

Something lethal flickered then behind Cade's steady gaze, and his body grew more tense, like the muscles of a wolf before it springs upon its prey. There was an intent in his eyes, the same perilous intent in Cobb's as they stared at one another.

Before anyone had a chance to speak, the clearing exploded with movement. Cobb and Cade went for their guns, drawing in a lightning flash that dazzled the eye, and then gunshots exploded, ringing through the walls of the canyon. Annabel grabbed Brett's arm and cried out as blood blossomed across Red Cobb's shirtfront. He fell to his knees and tried desperately to lift his gun arm. Blood was pouring down his chest.

Cade shot him again.

This time Cobb hurtled face forward onto the rocky ground, and lay there twitching while a pair of eagles soared overhead and Cade watched with merciless eyes.

Annabel closed hers. When she opened them, Cobb's body was still, and there was no sound or movement, only the blood and the acrid smell of gunsmoke, and the cry of the eagles high, high above.

Moonlight bathed the Riverses' porch in a pearlescent glow as Annabel peered out the parlor window at Cade and Brett. They were lounging against the porch railing, talking quietly, and she studied them for a moment, reflecting on how alike they were, and how different.

Earlier she and Conchita had washed the supper dishes together and put them away, while Adelaide swept the floor and hummed under her breath. Dinner had been a feast of spicy beef and tortillas, fried chicken and refried beans. It had been a celebration, for now the Rivers family and the whole valley was free of the Lowry Cattle Company's tyranny. But the adobe ranch house was quiet now, for Tomas and Adelaide had gone to bed, and only Conchita sat with some mending on the sofa in the parlor.

"It is a lovely night—why don't you go outside and sit with them," Conchita suggested as Annabel hesitated by the window.

"I think I will."

The older woman rose with slow dignity and smiled at her guest as she gathered her mending into a woven basket. "I am going to bed. For the first time in a long time I believe I will sleep well. With Lowry dead, his men will scatter and we will be left alone. At least for a while." She paused as she saw the book in Annabel's hand, and noticed the odd, excited expression on her face.

"Is something wrong?"

"No, not at all. As a matter of fact, I think I know how to make things right. At least, I'm going to try."

"Go then," Conchita touched her shoulder. "Our problems might be solved, but I think that you and the Senor McCallums will not sleep well until something else is settled."

"You're right, Conchita." Annabel clutched the book to her chest and turned toward the door. "It is time to settle one very important matter."

On the porch, Brett was studying the gleaming tips of his boots. "Before Annabel comes out here, I need to know something. You're in love with her, aren't you, Cade?"

Cade had just rolled and lighted a cigarette and he regarded his brother over the glowing tip. "I reckon you could say that. Any objections?"

"No, how could I . . . I mean . . . hell, Cade, she's my best friend. Of course, I never thought of her as a woman until . . . until I saw her out here for some crazy reason . . . she was always just Annie, sort of like a sister . . . only . . ."

"Only what?"

"Only when I saw her the other night at Lowry's

damned fiesta, I started thinking . . . maybe she could mean more to me. She's beautiful. And she's the most loyal, intelligent woman I know. And her eyes, I never really noticed how they glow. No one else's eyes have that sparkle in them . . ." He pushed his hat back on his head and sighed. "Only one problem. When I kissed her . . ."

Cade's eyes narrowed. "You kissed her?"

"Ahuh. Out by Lowry's corrals when we were spying on his men."

"Go on."

"Well, when I kissed her," Brett went on casually, "it was pretty wonderful, only," he rushed on hastily as Cade stood up, fists clenched, "only I could tell that her heart really wasn't in it. And I'd guessed from the way you two were so angry at each other that there was something neither of you were admitting between you. So I figured out that it's not me she wants after all. Maybe she did once—the thought occurred to me occasionally, but I never really took it seriously. Until that night. Oh, hell," he burst out, stomping across the porch with restless energy, his boots cracking over the wood planks, "maybe I just wanted to kiss her because I knew *you* wanted to kiss her—but I thought you should know about it and I also think you should know that you're damned lucky if she does love you because Annabel is the best thing that could happen to you."

"I know that."

"You'd better treat her right," Brett added warningly, spinning around to glower at his brother in a threatening way that was only half-joking. "Otherwise you'll have to answer to me."

"Answer to you for what?" Annabel asked, as the front door thudded softly shut behind her.

Both brothers glanced over at her in surprise and then exchanged quick looks. "For not being nice enough to a certain inquisitive lady," Cade replied easily, and held out a hand to her.

She went to him and nestled against him as naturally as a rose curling toward a leaf. "You're always nice to me," she said softly. "Except when you're being impossible."

Brett shook his head, studying the two of them as their eyes locked for a moment in the moonlit shadows of the porch.

"Think I'll turn in," he said pointedly, but Annabel's voice stopped him.

"No, wait. I have something to show you. Both of you."

The night air was cool, but it felt refreshing upon her cheeks and neck as she moved slightly away from Cade and held up the book.

"Cade, you asked me what this was one time when it fell out of my carpetbag."

"Oh, yes, that famous carpetbag. Is there anything you *don't* have tucked away somewhere inside that thing?" he teased her.

"Yes," she assured him, "there isn't a stove in there, nor a horse. Nor a saddle. But that's about it," she admitted. Then her smile faded and her expression grew serious. "This is my aunt Gertie's old diary. I've kept it as a keepsake, but this evening, while you two were out walking with Tomas and talking about whatever menfolk talk about when they go off like that, I dug it out of my carpetbag and I read it."

"You read Gertie's diary?" Brett frowned disapprovingly at her. "Why?"

"I only read parts of it. Parts pertaining to events that took place years ago. I wanted to see if she might shed some light on what happened around the time of your mother's suicide."

Silence descended upon the porch, but for the hum

of insects and the distant wail of a coyote. Annabel glanced cautiously from one brother to the next. Brett looked stunned, Cade thoughtful.

"I assume you found something interesting." Cade lifted one eyebrow at her, but though his words were spoken lightly, his features were dead serious.

"I did. I think you should both read several entries —or . . . let me read them to you."

Brett nodded and swallowed, looking tense and pale in the shimmer of moonlight. Cade said nothing, but merely watched in taut silence as she opened the weathered volume to the page she had marked and quietly began to read aloud.

"March 11, 1861—What a dark day this has been. Rain and clouds all morning long, that clumsy Marta dropped a pan of fresh biscuits on the floor, and little Master Brett has the devil of a cold. But the worst of all was the missus. Poor Mrs. McCallum, Bridget found her pacing in her room today, quite beside herself. Crying, she had been, but no one knows the reason why. When Bridget asked her if there was anything she could do for her or get for her, Mrs. McCallum said only that she should get her Mr. McCallum's hunting rifle and let her put an end to her misery. Bridget was nearly beside herself, and when she told me, I went straight to Mr. McCallum. Maybe it was not my place to do so, but the look in Mrs. McCallum's eyes lately puts great fear in my heart—she is that sad and that haunted. Mr. McCallum turned pale when I told him, poor man. He thanked me for coming, and sent me away.

As soon as I left the study though he followed me out into the hall and went straight upstairs—to find her, I imagine. I pray that he is able to help her with whatever troubles are tormenting the poor thing.

It is plain that he loves her more than anything—I have never seen him be so gentle or solicitous with anyone else ever—even his sons—Master Cade, God bless him, such a good sturdy boy, and even little Master Brett."

Annabel glanced up. "There's some more, but that is all that day that relates to your mother and Ross. But there is another entry that you must hear. Listen.

"I am so distressed I do not know how I will ever find a moment's sleep tonight. I went down to the kitchen late to have a cup of warm milk and a slice of the cherry tart left over from supper, and before I started back up, I thought I heard a noise in the cellar. Thinking it might be rats, I took a candle and a broom and went down to see for myself, but couldn't find anything, and then, as I was coming up the steps, I heard voices there in the kitchen. Well, I froze when I realized it was Mr. McCallum himself and Mrs. McCallum. I didn't know what to do, and being embarrassed, I stayed where I was on the stairs. The door was closed and they must not have heard my footsteps. She was crying, poor, poor dear, and he was comforting her. 'You mustn't worry about him,' Mr. McCallum said. 'I will not let that scoundrel hurt you again.'

She began to cry even harder and said he must hate her for what she'd done, for all the trouble she'd brought him. Mr. McCallum begged her not to distress herself, he vowed that he loved her, and his tone was so tender there were tears on my cheeks. Something awful is afoot, I told myself, but Lord help me, I do not exactly understand what it is. I waited there on the steps until they had left the kitchen and gone up to bed. She seemed comforted in the end, but the sounds of her misery ring still in my ears. I wish I had never heard what I did. I will say nothing to anyone for it's their own business, poor souls, and I trust Mr. M to take care of it."

Annabel lowered the book and touched Cade's arm. "Are you all right?"

He met her gaze with eyes bleak as fog. "It . . . seems that I . . . misjudged . . . him." There was a terrible agony in his voice that flayed at her heart.

"It was a mistake, Cade. You couldn't have known . . ."

"What about me?" Brett burst out miserably. "I didn't even give him a decent chance to explain. I ran off . . . like a coward," he cried, and wheeled away from them to gaze out at the mountains so quickly that Annabel knew there were tears in his eyes. "I was so eager to believe Boxer's version of things. Was there ever a bigger fool?"

"Mistakes can be rectified," she said into the silence that followed. "When we go back you will both do what is necessary to make things right with your father."

"If Boxer hasn't destroyed him first!" Cade threw down the butt of his cigarette and crushed it with his boot, looking as if he'd like to crush Frank Boxer instead.

Brett still gazed out at the empty night dotted with stars. In the distance, moonlight outlined an elk atop a black butte. "Annabel, is there more? You might as well finish adding whatever light Gertie's diary can shed on this mess."

"There's one more entry you should know about." She glanced uncertainly at Cade, waiting for his nod before she went on reading.

"This is the saddest day I ever remember in this house. The master has locked himself in his study with a bottle of spirits and no one dares try to speak

to him, even though it is now midnight and he has not come out since early this morning when we found poor Mrs. M. Shot herself she did, right there in the garden. No one knows but the servants and Dr. Holt. Mr. M spoke with the doctor and then gave instructions to every one of the servants. He said no one is ever to know the truth, that everyone should say it was a fever that killed Mrs. M. Ah, mercy me, everyone knows that secrets are hard to keep in a big house like this, the way servants talk, but if anyone can arrange to silence a secret as horrible as this one, Mr. M will find a way to do it and I pray that he does for the sake of those two poor children upstairs. Bad enough Master Brett and Master Cade will have to grow up without their mama. They surely don't need to hear gossip and whispers and scandal all their days. Ah, I don't know who I'm sorrier for . . . Mrs. M or the master. I shudder when I remember his face—a gray shade of oatmeal it was. A body weeps to think of it. Tomorrow we shall have the funeral. Oh, there are terrible days ahead."

Brett wrenched himself around, his face twisted in anguish. "I am taking the Atchison, Topeka and Santa Fe back to St. Louis tomorrow. If anyone wants to join me they're welcome, but I won't wait even a day. I have to get back."

"I'm going with you." Cade spoke quietly into the darkness. "We'll face this together, Brett."

"All three of us." Annabel closed the book and went to Cade's side. She touched his arm. "We can make things right with your father and deal once and for all with Frank Boxer."

"If it isn't too late," Cade muttered with awful bitterness.

"It won't be. Don't even think that way." But

though Annabel tried to sound confident, her heart was full of fear. She was sure that it was Boxer who had hired Cobb to kill Brett, and she suspected something else too. "Brett, you left that letter with Derrickson before you ran away. Isn't that what you said?"

"That's right. You don't know him, Cade, he's Father's man of business, but he only came to work for him in the past four years. But you've met him, Annabel."

"Oh, yes. A proper little toad. Maybe too proper," she added grimly.

"You think Derrickson waylaid my letter? That he's in cahoots with Boxer?" Brett's eyes widened with chagrin as she nodded.

"That is exactly what I think. Before we get on that train tomorrow, I'm sending another wire to Mr. Stevenson so he can warn your father of the danger he's in. Boxer has planned to kill you, to ruin your father financially, and who knows what else? At this point, I wouldn't put anything past him."

"Even murder . . . isn't that what you mean, Annabel?" Cade gripped her wrist, and she looked up to meet his eyes.

"Even murder."

A coyote howled again in the distance, and the three on the porch shivered. Each one of them knew that they might already be too late.

Chapter 26

No sound or light escaped from within the large McCallum stables, set well at the back of the estate's rambling grounds, as Lucas Johnson sauntered from his carriage in the starlit yard and beheld the building before him. Behind him, the handsome team of grays that were his pride waited restively, but a quick glance over his shoulder reassured him that his groom had them well in hand. Johnson signaled the man to wait, and kept walking, regarding the stables with a mixture of loathing and satisfaction.

This was the infamous place where he had been held and trussed before Ross McCallum had him shanghaied. This was the place where he had lost his freedom. How appropriate now that this be the place where Ross McCallum should lose his own life.

He eased open the stable door, his heart pumping with a queer anticipation. He'd waited twenty-two years for this moment. Though McCallum had been held prisoner for days now in the cellar of his own home, while Derrrickson closed the house, sent all the servants away, and put out the news that their employer had gone out of town for the month, the time had finally come for

McCallum to be moved to the stables, and informed that his demise was at hand.

Johnson was now ready to let himself be seen for the first time since Ross's imprisonment. He would present himself to Ross McCallum tonight for the first and last time, and have the pleasure of seeing the expression on his face when McCallum realized who was the mastermind of his undoing.

Johnson eased open the stable door and stepped inside, tightly gripping his gold-handled cane. One small torch in a bracket upon the far wall blazed out a flickering light. It dimly illuminated the horse stalls and the tack room and the large open area before him with its benches and tools and sacks of feed. The ornately appointed family carriage stood against the farthest wall, and even in the dimness it shone with elegance and style.

But Johnson was far more interested in the owner of that carriage: Ross McCallum, who sat bound and gagged on the nearest wooden bench and who was staring at him as if he were seeing a ghost.

"Yes, my friend," Johnson said softly as he closed the stable door and trod across the floor to confront his former employer. He immensely enjoyed the irony that he had once been McCallum's man of business, as Derrickson was now, and they had both outwitted him.

"We meet again, Mr. McCallum. Did you ever doubt it? You knew me as Frank Boxer, but I have returned as a much more powerful person. Lucas Johnson, sir, at your service."

His low bow toward the gray-haired man glaring at him was full of mockery. "You tried to rid yourself of me forever, but as you can see, you failed. Your life has been one long failure, McCallum. And mine has been one of triumph."

He tapped his prisoner none too gently on the

shoulder with his cane. "Tonight will be the greatest triumph of all—the night I watch you die."

The gaunt, gray-bearded giant before him looked as if at any moment sheer rage would burst the bonds that held him, but Johnson could see that Bartholomew and the two men hired to help him overpower the victim had done their jobs well—the ropes were cruelly tight and most secure.

This was true for McCallum's companion as well. Beside him on the bench, Everett Stevenson II glared like a fierce pirate about to be forced down the plank, and Johnson threw back his head and laughed.

"Don't look so furious, Stevenson. If you hadn't come around poking your nose into what doesn't concern you, you would never be in this fix. As it is, you've given me no choice but to kill you too. Of course, your death will coincide splendidly with my plans—it will look as if your employer, Mr. McCallum, killed you in a rage after you brought him news of his son's probable death, a death your agent out West should have prevented. Alas, it could not be so. Ah, Mr. McCallum, you wish to speak. Of course, let me first see if you have been behaving yourself."

He turned coolly to Bartholomew, who had been lounging on an opposite bench, sipping at his flask of brandy and playing a game of solitaire.

"Well," Johnson asked, stroking his brown mustache as the thin little man regarded him from behind his spectacles. "Has our prisoner exhibited good behavior?"

"Well, when I take the gag from his mouth so he can eat, he lets loose with a string of oaths that would turn your ears red, sir," Bartholomew offered with a shrug.

Johnson chuckled. "Does he?"

"Yes. And then, between bites of bread, he tries to bribe me, but of course, I pay no attention to him."

"Really . . . bribery. Why doesn't that surprise me? Perhaps," Johnson continued in a silky tone that barely masked the rage throbbing beneath it, "it is because I know exactly how far you will go to defeat your enemy, my dear Mr. McCallum. After all, in this very stable you did have me overpowered, bound, gagged, imprisoned, and then shipped off to be a slave for life . . . shanghaied, as they call it. You will stoop to anything to achieve your ends, but so then," he said, smiling, "will I. Do you wish to hear all that I have accomplished? Do you wish to hear how thoroughly I have ruined your life, the whole dismal tale of your failures? The world will see it clearly when Derrickson is forced to reveal the disasters that led you to take your own life. Oh, yes, that is what you are going to do, you know," he nodded as he spoke. "Just as your poor wife Livinia did so many years ago."

Ross McCallum had gone very still. Even bound and gagged he was a formidable man, and if his eyes could have killed, Boxer would have been dead on the spot.

"Remove the gag," Johnson commanded, and Bartholomew sauntered obediently forward and whisked it off.

"You were a dirty little coward before and you're a dirty little coward now," Ross McCallum roared, his tone containing rage enough to fill a concert hall. "If I had but one hand loose, I'd show you a thing or two about taking a life!"

"Ah, but you do not. As *I* did not that day long ago when you had me shipped out of here so ignominiously. But we won't speak of that tonight. Tonight we are speaking of you—of all the unfortunate accidents that have befallen you and your miserable pathetic business empire."

"You have been responsible all along for every last one of them, haven't you!" It was not a question at all, but a ferocious statement of fact that McCallum spat out with venom.

"Yes, of course. The fires, the accidents, the missing funds. . . . Under the guise of Lucas Johnson I have been trying to buy your precious Ruby Palace Hotel, the gem of your empire. And I succeeded, though you didn't know it. You signed the deed over to me recently —though I believe it escaped your notice. You were ill at the time, not your usual self, and you didn't happen to notice that one of the many papers Derrickson offered for your signature was the deed to your precious hotel."

"Derrickson!"

Johnson raised his brows. "Oh, I have many allies. The gunslinger, Red Cobb, is another. In fact, I've been waiting to hear from him, waiting for official confirmation of your son's death. Or rather, my son's death," he added slyly. "The boy simply would not cooperate—apparently he felt his loyalty to you was more important than his blood kinship with me. Well, Cobb should have finished the job by now . . . or he will very shortly, but I cannot wait any longer."

"Why not?" McCallum taunted, for his eagle eyes, though weary, had not missed the slight wavering of his enemy's gaze. "You know Brett is alive, don't you? The boy probably killed your man Cobb, and you know it, don't you?"

Johnson glowered at him. He hadn't heard a word from Cobb in quite a while now, and this concerned him more than he was letting on. Had something gone wrong? It seemed unlikely. How difficult could it be to corner an arrogant young greenhorn into a fight? "I know nothing of the sort," he retorted, stroking at the ends of his mustache, "but I am tired of waiting. It doesn't really matter, because I have prepared a report, which Mr. Stevenson will sign, stating that Brett McCallum has disappeared and is believed to be dead."

"And you think any sane person will believe that I would kill the man for that? And then take my own life?"

Johnson edged closer, tapping his cane absently upon the floor. He smiled delightedly. "But there are so many other reasons as well why you should feel utterly despondent. This is just the last straw—you see, your failing business empire and the discovery that your former partner, Herbert Ervin, is going to bring charges against you will also have weighed with you."

Ross McCallum leaned back heavily against the wall. "What's this about Ervin?" he rasped in a more subdued tone.

Bartholomew and Johnson exchanged pleased smiles. "As I told you, you signed numerous documents while you were ill—an illness due to a certain drug Derrickson put into your coffee or brandy each day, I might add. Among the documents you signed while in this condition were papers which prove that you have been improperly withdrawing funds from the McCallum and Ervin Steel Company—embezzling, if you will, in order to shore up your other failing businesses. Derrickson met with Ervin today—his conscience having got the better of him when he discovered your treachery, you see—and Ervin was most properly outraged. He may already have gone to the authorities for all I know. Why, if you do not end your life tonight, you will be facing trial, and a certain prison term."

"You're an insane bastard." McCallum drew a deep shaky breath. In the flickering torchlight, the dark shadows beneath his prune-colored eyes seemed to grow even darker, and more sickly. "I should have killed you twelve years ago when I had the chance."

"Yes, you should have," Johnson murmured. "Because now I am going to kill you. But first, we must rid ourselves of Mr. Stevenson. Bartholomew?"

The bespectacled man reached into his suit pocket and pulled out a pistol. "Do you want to do the honors, sir, or should I?" he inquired, as if asking who should be the one to pour a glass of sherry.

"Oh, I most certainly wish to do the honors." Johnson's fire blue eyes shone as he accepted the gun from his underling. He raised it and pointed it at the private investigator, still bound and gagged. "Let this be a lesson about what happens to those who interfere in the affairs of their betters. Good-bye, you nosy old fool."

"No!" McCallum thundered, but his words were drowned out by the roar of the gun.

Darkness shrouded the grounds of the McCallum mansion on Maplegrove Street as the hired carriage pulled up at the gate. Only faint misty starlight revealed the ghostly shapes of the tall oaks and maples which shaded the winding walkways and gardens that surrounded the house. But there was one light gleaming from inside the mansion as the occupants of the carriage alighted. It shone from Ross McCallum's study.

Annabel regarded it uneasily as Cade helped her down the carriage steps. They had come directly from the train station without delay, and still carried their traveling bags. As they hurried up the wide stone walk, no one spoke. But Annabel could sense the tension that permeated the thick summer night, and she knew that it would only be broken when his sons had found Ross McCallum safe and sound, and at last had the opportunity to talk with him.

Surely Everett Stevenson had interceded and

warned Ross McCallum of the danger surrounding him after he'd received her latest wire, sent before boarding the train. It had been brief, but clear enough:

Brett is safe. Derrickson and others believed to be plotting against R. McCallum. Warn him at once. Am returning immediately by train.

Yet as she stared at the darkened house, with only that one window ablaze, some instinct deep inside told her that something was wrong.

"Maybe he's just sitting up—waiting for us to return," she suggested in a low tone to Cade and Brett, striding along on either side of her as they neared the steps.

"I've got a bad feeling about this," Brett muttered back, and there was fear in his voice. But it was not fear for himself, Annabel knew. It was fear for his father, the man who had raised him, which rattled through him like the ghastly bones of a skeleton.

Cade rapped on the door, his face set grimly in the light of the moon. It seemed an eternity before the heavy door was thrown open.

Charles Derrickson gaped at them from the dim cave of the hall.

"You . . . ! Master Brett . . . you're . . . *back.*"

"Clever of you to notice," Brett growled.

Cade jerked his thumb toward the pale man with the thinning hairline and the bony white wrists and hands. "Don't tell me this is Derrickson?" he asked his brother.

"In the flesh."

"Well, well." Cade shouldered his way into the hall, ignoring the other man's whimper of protest. He grasped Derrickson by the arm and yanked him along. Brett and Annabel dashed after them.

"Where is my father?" Cade demanded. It was his

Roy Steele voice, Annabel noted, and if she wasn't so filled with loathing for Derrickson, she almost would have felt sorry for the man.

Derrickson's already pale skin turned the exact color of chalk. "Your . . . *father*? You . . . can't be . . . Master Cade."

"The man's a genius," Cade bit out to Brett. "He has all the intelligence of a prairie dog."

"Yes, he is Cade McCallum," Annabel said impatiently. "And I'm sure you remember me, Mr. Derrickson, don't you? Annabel Brannigan—I used to live here. Now that all the introductions are completed, I think you'd best tell us where Mr. McCallum is right away." She stepped forward and jabbed him with two fingers in the chest. "His sons are most anxious to find him and let me just warn you that they are not the kind of men you wish to keep waiting."

From the expression on Derrickson's face it was obvious that he had already reached that exact conclusion. One look at the brawny black-haired man in the blue silk shirt and Stetson, a gun holster fitted with two serious-looking Colt .45's buckled onto his dark trousers, made him tremble from his pointed chin down to his knobby toes, and a glance at the much-changed Brett did nothing to reassure him. The former young scion of the McCallum family had changed from an affable young gentleman to a . . . a desperado. He was wearing the same style of western garb as his brother, only his hat and shirt were gray, and his expression even nastier.

Even the woman looked formidable. Annabel Brannigan still looked as charmingly feminine as ever, but the pert, lively expression he usually associated with her was nowhere to be seen; the woman who watched him so shrewdly looked as if she could shoot him dead as soon as sit down to dinner with him, and the very real possibility that this trio might well do just that if they found out what was afoot made him blanch as Cade McCallum shoved him unceremoniously into the study.

A fire burned cozily in the grate. The desk was neat, the lamp atop it glowed pleasantly, and there was a steaming cup of tea beside a sheaf of papers. But Charles Derrickson had obviously been working in here, not Ross McCallum.

"You have ten seconds, Derrickson, to tell me where my father is," Cade said as he drew out his Colt and aimed it at Derrickson's trembling chest.

"One . . ."

"I have no idea . . ."

"Two . . ."

"He went on a business trip . . ."

"Three . . ."

". . . out of town . . ."

"Four . . ."

"And I haven't heard from him in days now . . ."

"Five . . ."

"Really, Master Brett this is most irregular. Have you and your brother both lost your minds?"

"Six . . . and seven."

Annabel grabbed Derrickson's arm. "We know you're working with Boxer and we know you've betrayed Mr. McCallum—I suggest you tell us the truth immediately or he *will* shoot you."

"Eight." Cade said calmly.

"Good heavens!"

Cade's eyes were like marble, his hands terrifyingly steady as he clicked the safety on the gun. "Nine."

"He's in the stables!"

Cade lowered the gun. Annabel pushed Derrickson down into a chair. "Alone?" she demanded.

"No . . . no . . . Bartholomew is with him, guarding him you might say, and . . . Mr. Stevenson."

"Everett Stevenson?"

"We caught him snooping around, looking for Mr. McCallum, after I told him that Mr. McCallum had been called out of town on business. Mr. Johnson said we had to take care of him, too, but . . . I don't like it," he burst out miserably. His lower lip shook and he clutched the arms of the chair. "I never wanted things to go this far . . . I said from the beginning that the use of violence was against my principles, but they wouldn't listen to me and . . ."

"Who else is out there?" Brett leaned down and glared into his face. "Boxer?"

"You mean Mr. Johnson." Derrickson nodded, and then swallowed hard. "He's expected any moment. He is planning to finish the matter tonight as a matter of fact . . ."

"Finish the matter?" Brett asked sharply.

It was Cade who answered, as Derrickson just stared back in hopeless fear. "By that you mean that he is planning to kill our father, don't you, Derrickson?"

"Well . . . in a . . . word . . . yes."

Annabel was already racing for the door.

"You stinking little bastard," Brett said in a low tone. His fist shot out and slammed into Derrickson's jaw. The man crumpled onto the floor without even a whimper.

"Annabel—wait!" Cade sprinted after her, but she was already tearing out the front door, racing through the darkness toward the stable even as the gunshot rang through the darkness.

Chapter 27

Ross McCallum jackknifed himself toward Boxer and the gun with every ounce of strength left in his body. He hit the man dead on, just as Boxer fired.

Then everything happened in a blinding, confusing flash—Boxer's aim went wide, the bullet slammed into the stable wall, and Everett Stevenson threw himself sideways on the bench.

Boxer fell backward, the gun clattering from his grasp as McCallum went down on top of him. "You idiot!" Boxer shouted. "This is one fight you can't hope to win, and I'm going to make damned sure you suffer for it!"

He had no difficulty in pushing off the larger man, whose wrists and ankles were still bound together—in an instant, he was up, kicking McCallum repeatedly as the older man tried to roll and twist away.

Stevenson dove off the bench and into the fray, trying to knock Johnson off balance, while at the same time, Bartholomew pulled a second smaller pistol from his pocket and brandished it at the skirmishers. "Stop!" he shouted. "Lie still or I'll shoot you both!"

Suddenly the stable door opened and Annabel burst in. She had no memory of running across the long velvet lawn or of darting through the gardens, no exact realization of how she reached the stables. She only knew that her ears rang with the words: *too late. . . . We're too late.*

Then rage choked her as she saw the tall, brown-haired man kicking Ross McCallum as he lay bound and writhing on the floor.

Without thinking, she jumped forward and shoved the man away with all her might. "Don't you dare touch him again! Or I'll let them kill you right here where you stand!"

"What the hell . . . who the devil . . ."

And then as if by magic, or perhaps some dark conjuring of the devil himself, another figure appeared behind her, and then another, only these were no magical illusions or spirits, they were tall hardy men, armed and competent, with dark hair and lean bronzed faces filled with unspeakable rage. A terrible grimness flashed in those dark faces as they surveyed the brutal scene before them—their gazes sweeping swiftly from the two men lying bound on the floor to the well-dressed man standing over them.

"It doesn't matter," Cade said with furious calm as he stared into Frank Boxer's astonished face. "I'm going to kill you regardless." And he lunged past Annabel and seized Boxer by his fancy silk lapels, holding him for a split second before his right fist slammed with punishing force into the other man's face.

Brett dove at Bartholomew, who was trying to aim the pistol.

"I don't think so, you toad-eating son of a bitch." Brett had no difficulty in wrenching the gun from his hapless opponent, and then he landed a solid left hook to Bartholomew's jaw.

Annabel was already kneeling beside the two men

on the floor, her fingers working frantically but uselessly at their bonds.

"Damn these ropes . . . I can't . . . Mr. McCallum, Mr. Stevenson, are you all right? I'm trying to unknot them, but . . ."

At that moment, Cade's next punch sent Boxer sprawling facedown. He landed only a few feet from Ross McCallum and lay there stunned for a moment. But suddenly, before Annabel could do more than blink, he somehow lunged forward to where she knelt beside the two men.

There was a knife in his hand.

He grabbed Annabel by the hair and yanked her toward him, up and over McCallum's prone form. The keen blade of the knife grazed her throat.

"Don't move—anyone! If you so much as quiver, I'll slit this little lady's throat like a gobbler."

Red light flared before Annabel's eyes as she crouched there, unable to move, unable to breathe. There was a ringing in her ears—terror, she realized. From the corner of her eye she saw Cade go very still and white, and Brett froze with Bartholomew in a headlock.

"That's right." Boxer laughed, a cruel, flat sound that seemed to fill every dark corner of the hushed stable. "Now stay where you are. The lady and I are leaving. If you don't follow me, I'll let her go."

This can't be happening, Annabel thought as she felt herself dragged up and toward the door. Boxer had let go of her hair; now he had an arm locked around her throat and the knife was pressed to her cheek. "It would be a shame to carve up such a pretty face," Boxer snarled as they backed toward the door. "You McCallums always did have a taste for fine-looking women. Maybe I'll seduce this one too," he taunted with a vicious little laugh. "When we get where we're going."

Then they were outside in the warm, starlit night, and he was dragging her toward the carriage that waited in the shadows.

"Let me go," she gasped, as his arm dug into her throat. "You'll . . . make faster time . . . without me . . ."

"Shut up!" He opened the carriage door with his free hand, while the driver looked on in obvious panic, having no doubt heard the gunfire and the fracas within. But apparently, Annabel realized dimly, he was too frightened of his employer to bolt without him.

"Go, you idiot!" Boxer shouted at the driver, and at the same moment, he hurled Annabel away from him and leaped inside the carriage.

In the frantic confusion of the next few moments, Annabel scarcely knew what happened. But somehow, as the carriage plunged forward toward the gated driveway and the street, Cade was at her side, lifting her from the ground, crushing her to him.

"Are you all right?"

"Yes, I'm fine. I was scared but . . . Cade, where are you going?"

"Stay there!" was all he replied, a shout over his shoulder, but she knew the answer already as he began to run toward the street.

Then she was surrounded by Brett, Ross McCallum, and Everett Stevenson, and the night was full of loud voices and questions. Brett had Bartholomew in tow, too, and once he saw that Annabel was unhurt, he began to drag his prisoner back to the house.

"Come on. Let's get inside. We'll get some rope for this hombre while we wait for Cade to get back. Don't worry, Annabel," he added, throwing her an encouraging smile, "you know that if anyone can catch him, Cade can."

She nodded, but the fear was still there, a living,

breathing thing in her heart as the battered weary group made its way to the looming house beyond.

Annabel was too stunned by all that had happened to be able to think beyond one thing: Cade was out there in the night chasing after a madman, a vicious, revenge-crazed madman. *He should let him go . . . he should be here, with his father, his brother, and me.*

But she also knew that Cade McCallum would not be able to rest until he had caught up with the man who had brought so much misery to everyone he loved.

The house felt large and warm and comforting, especially after Brett lit a fire in the main parlor, turned up all the lamps, and banished Bartholomew and Derrickson, hastily tied up, into the study, and then locked the door. Ross McCallum, looking gaunt and weary after his ordeal, but every bit as sharp-eyed as ever, poured brandy for each of them from a crystal decanter.

"My dear, did that ruffian hurt you?" he asked as she sank down on the striped damask sofa and gratefully accepted the brandy he offered her.

"No." She gave her head a tiny shake as he took a seat beside her and thirstily drained his own glass. Then he studied her over the rim, and Annabel knew she could not disguise the fear that was leaving her sick and cold.

"I can only pray he doesn't hurt Cade," she whispered.

Ross McCallum set the glass down on the inlaid table before him. He glanced at Brett, who was pacing back and forth before the mantel, and spoke in a low, hoarse voice quite unlike his usual boom. "After thinking I'd never see either of my sons again, I've just gotten both of them back. Annabel Brannigan, don't you worry. I don't think the Good Lord is going to take either of my boys away again before we've even had a chance for a proper reunion."

Brett came over and knelt beside his father. "I owe you an apology, Father. None of this ever would have happened if I hadn't run away. Derrickson destroyed my letter, but if I'd stayed and talked to you . . ."

"Don't." The older McCallum laid his large hand on his son's head. "I've made enough mistakes for an entire clan of McCallums," he said heavily. "If there're any apologies to be made, they should come from me."

Everett Stevenson cleared his throat. "Sir, I'm going to bring the authorities in to take charge of those scoundrels in the other room and to write up a report of all these shenanigans. But first, I'd like to offer my congratulations to my private investigator. Miss Brannigan, you've done a bang-up job. You'll have to tell us how you found this young man and figured out what was going on back here from halfway across the country— and how you made it back here in the nick of time to save my life and Mr. McCallum's."

"I'll tell you all of it, Mr. Stevenson." She regarded him somberly, aware that her knees were trembling beneath her navy traveling skirt. Brett, hearing the quaver in her voice, flicked her another bracing smile. She tried to smile back but her lips felt stiff as wax, and she could think of nothing but that madman, the knife, and Cade.

"It's a long story but I'll tell you every detail as soon as Cade McCallum walks back through that door and I know that he is safe."

Cade had reached the gate and watched in frustration as the carriage careened up the wide deserted street and jolted around the corner. He ran after it, and reached the corner in time to see it heading east down Whitecliff Street.

Damn, he thought, glancing wildly from one direction to the next. Not another vehicle in sight. And if he went back to the stable for one of his father's horses, he'd lose sight of the carriage for certain. He started to run again, toward Whitecliff, but as he tore up the street with long, furious strides his hopes of being able to keep the carriage in sight until he could find something, anything to give chase began to dwindle . . .

There. A horse and wagon coming toward him, trotting lesiurely down the middle of the dark road just ahead. Cade sprang toward it, a dusky figure in the blackness, murkily illuminated by the white swarming stars above.

"Whoa! Whoa, there!"

He sprang forward as the startled driver pulled his workhorse to a halt. "I need this horse and this wagon. There'll be a reward for you when I bring it back. Quick, man!"

"But—"

"No time to argue." Cade had vaulted up before the driver could do more than gape at him. He grabbed the man by the collar and hauled him out of the wagon, then picked up the reins. Ignoring the man's outraged protests, he wheeled the big black horse about and flicked the whip to him.

The night closed down around him as he urged the horse forward, faster and faster past street lamps and shuttered houses. Up ahead he could just make out the rear of Boxer's carriage. Cade gritted his teeth. He couldn't lose the bastard now.

"C'mon, boy. Go!"

At last, galloping down a side street lined with shops and brick office buildings, the big black horse began to gain on the carriage ahead. But only slightly. Sweat glistened on Cade's face as he urged the horse faster. Suddenly, ahead, a peddler's cart veered from a side street directly into the carriage's path.

There was the shrieking scream of horses, and shouts, and then a terrible din rang through the night as both the carriage and the wagon overturned with a splintering crash. Cade reached the scene just as the carriage's driver limped away, hurrying up the street, as fast as his bloody, injured leg would take him.

Cade ignored him and the peddler, who was miraculously unhurt, but was standing in the middle of the wreckage, cursing to the heavens. All around him were strewn his broken and scattered wares.

Cade spared him barely a glance as he sprinted toward the fallen carriage and yanked open the door.

Boxer was crouched on the seat. He faced Cade, the knife drawn.

"Put it away."

"You're Cade McCallum, aren't you? According to Derrickson, everyone thought you were dead all these years. But you're back from the dead, just like me."

The man was insane. A glazed wildness stared back from his brilliant blue eyes, and his lips were stretched taut in a twisted, grotesque smile. Cade felt his stomach tighten with loathing. "You're halfway to hell again, Boxer. Don't make me send you all the way."

"Your father tried to get rid of me and couldn't. He hated me because I worked for him—a lowly underling —and your mother fell in love with me. He couldn't believe that it happened right under his nose."

"Shut up."

"She couldn't help it, you know. All the women fell in love with me. I have a way with women—it's easy for me," Boxer bragged. "They believe every sweet thing I say—especially the lonely ones. And your mother was lonely. Your father worked very hard and he neglected her. But I'm afraid it hurt her badly when I started to blackmail her."

"You blackmailed her?"

"Well, really, both of them." Boxer shrugged. "I didn't want to spend the rest of my life working for someone else. I deserved better, was capable of better. But I needed money to get started—lots of money, so that I could begin to build my own fortune, my own financial empire. Your mother just didn't understand that though. I suppose she took it personally."

"One more word about her and I'll kill you on the spot."

Boxer started to laugh, since after all he held the knife, but something in the other man's gaze stopped him. A few beads of sweat started to dribble down his brow.

"Look here, McCallum, it doesn't have to be this way between you and me. We could join forces. I've heard about you, and I know you ran away from home at the age of seventeen because you'd grown to hate Ross McCallum as much as I do. It's true, isn't it, because why else would you have stayed away for all these years? Why don't you and I sit down and have a little talk . . ."

Cade lunged for him then, but Boxer was surprisingly fast. He slashed out with the knife, and the blade whizzed past Cade's arm, slicing his sleeve.

Cade drew back, breathing hard. "Put it down, you son of a bitch. Consider this your last warning."

"If that's how you want it." Boxer shrugged. "I learned to throw this in India." Boxer started to laugh once again. "I acquired great skill. Men fear me there. And now I'm going to show you why. I'm going to kill you, my friend, right where you stand."

And in a flash he drew back his arm to hurl the knife. But it fell harmlessly from his fingers. He slid forward as a bullet lodged in his forehead.

Cade stuffed his still-smoking gun back into his holster and turned away.

"That was for you, Mama," he muttered as he took in the wreckage of the collision, the curses and complaints of the peddler, the frightened, whinnying horses. He closed his eyes against the tumult in the street and drew in a deep, painful breath. An image of the mother he had lost at the age of eight filled the darkness behind his closed eyes. *I hope you know somehow that now it's really over. Maybe you can rest in peace.*

Chapter 28

The following morning brought a luminous opal dawn, full of dappled sunshine, fragrant summer air, and birdsong. Annabel had spent the night in one of the McCallum guest rooms—the pretty rose one she'd always loved, with the cream-lace curtains and the rose and cream floral coverlet upon the big oak featherbed.

When she awoke in that heavenly soft bed, Cade, who had come to her when everyone else was asleep and held her all through the dark soul of night, was gone. She sat up, gazed at the brilliant sunshine glittering in through the curtains to pool upon the honey oak floor, heard the nightingale singing in the maple outside the window, and smiled luxuriously.

Cade was safe, Brett was safe, and Mr. McCallum was safe. She had succeeded in her mission . . . and far beyond her wildest dreams. She'd found the man she loved, and would always love . . . but fate had played a trick on her—the man who owned her heart was not who she had thought he was. In discovering her own folly, she'd learned that she wasn't quite as shrewd in some matters as she thought.

The horrible events of the previous night seemed to her like an evil dream as she bathed, performed a quick toilette, and dressed in her blue and white gingham Sunday gown. After brushing her hair until it glistened, she deliberately left it loose and flowing, the way Cade preferred.

This is a new day for all of us, she thought as she nearly pranced down the wide oak staircase. *Maybe it will mark a whole new beginning for the McCallums.*

The delicious aroma of coffee greeted her as she reached the dining room, and when she pushed through the doors to the kitchen she found Cade busily scrambling eggs in a pan and slicing bread for toast. Grinning, she remembered that Derrickson had sent all the servants, even the cook, away.

"I hope there's enough food for me, Mr. Steele, because I'm famished," she said, coming up behind him and slipping her arms around his waist.

"I reckon we can find something here for you."

Her heart soared at the warmth in his eyes as he set the pan down and turned to take her in his arms. She framed his face with her hands. "Good morning to you, Mr. Steele," she whispered.

"Morning, Miss Brannigan."

He caught her to him in a quick, hard kiss. *This,* she thought blissfully, *is how I want to begin every single day of the rest of my life.*

Presently Brett came in and joined them at the kitchen table. He needed no invitation to help himself to the hearty breakfast of eggs, sausage, toast, and jam.

"Doc's up there with Father again," he reported, eyeing the heaping platters and the steaming black coffee with appreciation. "Came back first thing this morning. I think he couldn't quite believe what he saw last night," Brett added, his eyes dancing as he bit into a mouthful of sausage.

Sometime after midnight the doctor had pronounced Ross McCallum miraculously fit for a man his age and in his condition who had been held against his will, shackled, and fed little more than bread and water for a week. "You McCallums have iron constitutions," he had muttered in amazement when he'd finished his examination, and Cade, telling Annabel about it in bed later, had been forced to laugh as he held her against him and wound her hair sensuously around and around his fingers.

"That's one thing about being a McCallum," he'd reflected. "We're too ornery to die."

"A lucky thing, too." Annabel had pressed her mouth to his chest, then let her lips roam across the broad expanse of muscles to the warm solidity of his shoulder, and nipped at it. "You can be as ornery as you want as long as you're *safe* . . ."

Safe. With morning sunshine pouring in the kitchen windows, and both Brett and Cade seated with her at the same cozy table where she'd eaten her meals as a child, Annabel could finally savor the idea that the danger was past, and they were all safe.

"I went out to see Herbert Ervin first thing this morning," Brett continued, after helping himself to a second cup of coffee. "It took some explaining, but I finally managed to fill him in on enough of the story so that he realized he'd been duped. He felt pretty badly that he'd thought Father capable of embezzling from him. But Boxer had everything coordinated most convincingly. Thanks to Derrickson's conniving, it looked as if he'd illegally withdrawn profits from the steel company to bolster up the Ruby Palace and other failing businesses."

"Only now that the truth is out," Annabel said with satisfaction, "it's Bartholomew and Derrickson who face those lengthy prison terms."

Cade set down his fork and looked at Brett. "I've been thinking—Ross is going to need our help shoring up his crumbling empire, thanks to Boxer's maneuverings. It seems to me that we're going to have to lend a hand and try to rebuild some of the companies so that—"

"Oh, no, you don't." Ross McCallum's voice rang out through the kitchen, startling all three of them.

Annabel didn't know whether to smile or sigh as she saw him towering in the doorway, as commanding and arrogant a figure as ever in his expensive black suit and impeccable starched white shirt.

This morning his thick gray hair was neatly combed and he was the spitting image of a leader of industry: clear eyed and tight lipped, authority resting easily upon his enormous shoulders. But his face was still drawn, and he had obviously lost weight—the suit hung loosely on his giant frame, and the purplish circles remained beneath his eyes. Yet his voice boomed out as strongly as ever.

"I am perfectly capable of rebuilding my own companies all on my own," he growled. "I am not an invalid, nor a fool, and I won't tolerate my own sons treating me like an injured pup that needs careful handling."

"Sir," Cade said, standing respectfully as his father strode into the kitchen, "that wasn't our intention. We only want to help . . ."

"Since when do I need your help? You ran away thirteen years ago, my boy, and never thought about lending me an ounce of help in all this time. I'm damned if I'll accept it now."

"Will you accept my apology?"

"And mine?" Brett added humbly.

Annabel held her breath as Ross McCallum glared at both of his sons in turn, and his normally ruddy skin whitened.

"Yes," he said. "If you'll accept mine." A muscle clenched in his jaw, and he seemed to be struggling with himself before he spoke. "I should have told you the truth from the beginning . . . I never should have tried to hide what happened to your mother." He shook his head with great weariness and took a breath. "But I wanted to protect you, and to protect her."

"I know." Cade went around the table, awkwardly, to put a hand to his father's shoulder. "I jumped to a lot of conclusions when I was seventeen. And the hell of it is, they were wrong."

"You thought I was responsbile for her death, didn't you?" Ross McCallum's lips thinned as his son said nothing. "Well, maybe I was. Come into the library. All of you," he added, his gaze flickering to Annabel, who remained seated uncertainly at the table. "There are some things that need explaining. It's more than time, and you have a right to know."

Annabel stole a glance at Cade as they entered the huge library she'd always loved. Tall dark-paneled walls lined with books, bronze chandeliers, and comfortable olive leather sofas and armchairs arranged before a black stone hearth had made the perfect room in which to curl up with a book all through her childhood days, and myriad memories flooded back as she walked through the double doors into that serene, comfortable room. Memories of warmth, comfort, security. The roaring fire and the heavy-paned windows with their olive velvet draperies tied back with gold tassels had protected her from even the iciest winter days. But she didn't have time to indulge in memories now. As she looked at Cade she wondered what he was thinking, feeling. If only he could find it in his heart to fully forgive his father and forge a reconciliation. Maybe after all these years, the McCallum family could be whole once again.

Cade didn't even glance around the room he hadn't seen since he was seventeen. He strode to the mantel and stood gazing out the window at the magnificent emerald gardens rolling beyond. It was Brett who sat beside Annabel on the sofa, while Ross went to the long table holding the brandy decanter and glasses, but he didn't pour a drink. Instead, he faced his audience and began to speak in a crisp, deliberate tone that tried very hard to hide the sadness beneath.

"If I'd looked after Livinia better, if I hadn't been so busy building up my companies, working all the time, maybe she never would have gotten involved with that bastard. I accept blame for that. Our marriage had been arranged, you see, and I learned later that she did not wish to marry me. She fancied herself in love with another young man, a banking clerk, someone her father considered unacceptable." He frowned, and the haunted sadness flared in his eyes. "Your mother had a gentle nature, boys, and she complied with her father's wishes. But I do believe her heart was broken . . . especially when the man she loved married someone else a few months after our wedding. She didn't speak out and she lost him forever—and she was stuck with me."

"But she came to love you," Annabel burst out, unable to bear his tortured expression a moment longer. "Forgive me for speaking of something so personal, but I have to tell you that I read my aunt Gertie's diary of events at the time, and from all that I could gather, it seemed that Mrs. McCallum loved you very much."

Ross McCallum's bleak expression softened. A trace of hope entered his eyes as they rested upon Annabel. "I believe she may have—in the end. I'd like to think so." He began to pace the library as he continued. "After that debacle with Boxer, when he seduced her, abandoned her, and then turned to blackmailing her, I stood by her, and she seemed to come to depend on me . . . to genuinely care for me. But as for love . . . I'll never know if it was that or just . . . gratitude."

"Love," Annabel insisted.

He glanced quickly at her again, then looked beyond through the window, toward the gardens Livinia had loved. "I would like to think so," he repeated.

"Go on, Father," Cade said quietly.

Ross McCallum's gaze shifted to Brett, sitting tense and silent on the sofa. "When she told me that you were going to be born, Brett, we both knew you couldn't have been my son. I'd been away for two months on business. She was frantic, terrified to tell me, but unable to keep her secret any longer. I was devastated when she told me about Frank Boxer—I loved her, you see." His tone was low, filled with pain. "More than anyone except— Cade. And then Brett."

Silence fell in the library, but for the bluebird chattering outside the window.

"What happened when she told you?" Brett asked quietly. Annabel ached for him. He was sitting very still, trying to keep his shame, his sorrow under control.

"She begged my forgiveness and . . . well, I gave it to her. You needn't know the whole scene. I told her we would raise the child together and put her . . . indiscretion behind us. Then she informed me of the worst, the most vile part." His voice hardened, sounding so much like Cade's that Annabel started. "She told me that when she'd informed Boxer she was carrying his child, he was delighted. But not for the reason she'd hoped. He planned to blackmail me—to blackmail both of us, really—to force me to pay him an enormous sum of money to keep from spreading the scandal around the town. That bastard cared nothing for her shame or humiliation, nor did it weigh with him that he was destroying the woman who had thought she loved him. No, he wanted nothing of her or the child—except to enrich himself by using them both."

"Why didn't you kill him then?" Brett exploded, jumping up from the sofa. "He deserved to be shot!"

"No." Cade stepped forward, his face very grim. "Horsewhipped. And then shot."

"I agree with you." Ross nodded at his older son.

As Annabel glanced around the room at three pairs of McCallum eyes all glinting with fury, she grieved for them all.

"But for your mother's sake, I couldn't risk even a hint of scandal," Ross continued bitterly. He started to pace again, his steps slow and heavy. "I chose what I felt was the safest, quietest route. I paid Boxer his filthy money and he left town. But a year later he came back."

"Yes, so he said." Brett told his father then of the version Boxer had given him of the story, of how he claimed to have begged Livinia to come away with him, to take her son and leave her husband.

"He lied," Ross said flatly. "The son of a bitch never wanted her—or you. I'm sorry to tell you that, son, but . . . it's time we heard the full and awful truth. He only came back for more money. But this time he got something he didn't bargain for." He raked a hand through his hair and took a deep breath. "The only problem was, it didn't save Livinia. Her heart was broken, her spirit destroyed. No matter how I tried to console her after that, even with Boxer gone from our lives, she couldn't look me in the eye without weeping. She couldn't seem to recover from the nightmare he put her through. But Brett, there is something else, something you must know."

Brett stared at him, waiting.

Annabel held her breath.

"I wanted you, son," Ross McCallum said slowly, meeting Brett's gaze intently. "From the first day she told me about you, I was determined to raise you as my own son—right along with Cade. And once you were born, there was no doubt, none at all. I found that it was easy to . . . love you . . . and I was more determined than ever to teach you and care for you as my own." He cleared his throat but even still his next words came out thick with emotion. "And to this day, I do."

Brett's eyes filmed with tears. "I know, Father," he said in a choked voice. "I think I always knew. But I was too stunned and too angry and too humiliated to see straight and . . ."

He never finished. He walked straight into Ross McCallum's arms and for the first time that Annabel ever remembered, the two men embraced.

Annabel's heart leaped with happiness for them, yet at the same time pain stabbed through her as she saw Cade standing alone, watching his father and brother. An outsider.

Suddenly, Ross pulled back from Brett to stare hard at his oldest son. "Come here, boy," he ordered. "I've waited thirteen years for this. Don't make me wait any longer."

She held her breath, wondering what he would do, if pride and a stubborn inbred toughness would keep him rooted to the spot, apart from his family. And then Cade was in the circle of arms, embracing, being embraced, and Annabel wept silent tears of joy as she sat unmoving upon the sofa. She started to get up, to slip out of the room and leave them to their reunion in privacy, but Ross McCallum's voice stopped her.

"Get over here, Annabel Brannigan," he commanded, and she ran to them, half laughing and half crying, and hugged them each in turn. Cade's arm stayed tight around her waist.

"Father, you have met Annabel Brannigan. But you haven't met the future Mrs. Cade McCallum."

Dumbfounded, Annabel could only stare at him.

"Neither . . . have I," she managed to sputter. "Unless . . . you mean . . ."

· "Of course I do." Cade shook his head in exasperation at the incredulity he saw in her eyes. "For a private investigator, sweetheart, you're not too perceptive . . . about certain things. Or are you trying to say I haven't made my intentions clear?"

Ross frowned, his heavy brows drawing together. "Do you mean to tell me that this is the way you choose to propose to this young lady? Just like that, with your father and your brother looking on, and no wooing, no vows of love or words of passion, only this cavalier announcement? Pretty sure of yourself, aren't you, boy?"

"Start over, big brother," Brett advised, and winked at Annabel. "Try a little romantic persuasion."

"No . . . no, I don't need a romantic proposal . . . I accept!"

"Don't do it, young lady. Make him beg you first," Ross said, shaking his head.

Cade regarded them all in amusement, then seized Annabel's hand, squeezing it tight within his own larger one. "Hell, it looks like I'm going to have to do just that. Can't have anyone saying we didn't do this the right and proper way."

With that, he began dragging her toward the garden. "I'm sure you'll excuse us . . ."

But just then there came a pounding on the front door. Cade kept ahold of Annabel's hand, but waited with Brett as his father went to answer it. A moment later, Ross McCallum stuck his head back into the library.

"There's a peddler fellow here to see you, Cade," he reported in some amusement. "A Mr. Banks. He's most . . . determined. Said something about an accident . . . his wagon overturning and some promise you made . . . but perhaps I should have him come back later . . ."

"Damn, I forgot. No, Father, wait. I'll see him in the study." Cade turned back to Annabel and pressed a kiss to her hand before he released it. "I promised the peddler whose wagon collided with Boxer's carriage last night that I'd reimburse him for any damages. Let me get this out of the way. I'll wager that the owner of the wagon I stole to chase after Boxer will be by soon, too. Reckon we'll ever have any time alone together?"

"We'd better. I have a proposal coming to me. You know this is very unorthodox," she informed him primly. "Mr. Clyde Perkins and Mr. Joseph Reed and Mr. Hugh Connely didn't conduct their proposals this way."

He grasped her by the shoulders. "I'm getting pretty tired of hearing about those three hombres. By the time I've finished with my proposal, you won't even be able to remember their names."

Her eyes danced with anticipation. "I can hardly wait."

"It won't be long." He kissed her on the tip of her nose before heading toward the hall.

"You know," Ross MCcallum said thoughtfully, after Cade had left the room. "I always thought you and Brett might someday make a match of it. You two were always as close as two spoons in a pie."

"I reckon I let Cade get the jump on me, Father." Brett put an arm around her shoulders and then gently, playfully tugged at one of her curls. "But I realize now I'll have to look far and wide to find a girl like Annabel."

"She's too good for the both of you," Ross informed him baldly, and walked over to the tall bookcase where the novels were displayed. "Do you remember that time I found you in here in the middle of the night,

Annabel, with snow piling up at the windows, while you wept over that book . . . what was it?"

"*Jane Eyre.* I was twelve and had never read anything so romantic and so sad in my life."

"Yes, well . . . we had a conversation then, you and I, and I began to realize what an intelligent little creature you were. You haven't disappointed me. I admire how cleverly you put the pieces of the puzzle together and figured out exactly what Frank Boxer was up to. I'm pleased. Between the two of you, you and Cade should produce some very perspicacious children. Your sons will make fine additions to the family business."

"Father, don't you think you should let Cade propose to her before you start talking about your grandchildren?" Brett grinned.

Ross shrugged. "Annabel doesn't mind. Do you, my dear?"

"Why, no, of course not."

"See? Never met a more frank, down to earth, easy to please kind of girl. You'd do well to start searching for someone like her, Brett. You're not getting any younger, you know."

"See what I have to put up with? Right about now, the New Mexico territory is starting to look pretty good to me," Brett whispered in her ear.

She grinned back at him, glad to see that Brett was back to his usual good-natured self. As he and Ross McCallum began discussing business strategies for repairing the damages inflicted by Boxer, she glanced impatiently toward the library door. She couldn't wait for Cade to return. She wanted to hear this proposal of his. It would have to be some pretty speech to make her forget the flowery phrases of Mr. Perkins, Mr. Reed, and Mr. Connely. Annabel was certain she was going to enjoy it immensely.

What could be keeping Cade?

"You don't think he's having second thoughts, do you?" she asked aloud, without even realizing she had spoken.

Ross and Brett burst into laughter. "Not judging by the way he's been looking at you all morning," the older man snorted.

"Why don't you wait for him in the garden?" Brett suggested with a sympathetic smile. "We'll send him out there as soon as he shows up."

They had business to discuss, she was restless, and the sunshine beckoned, so she slipped away to find the perfect idyllic spot to receive her proposal of marriage.

Mr. Jonah E. Banks beamed at Cade as he stuffed his billfold back inside his trouser pockets. "Thank you, Mr. McCallum. You've been most generous. This will surely cover the repairs to my wagon. I'm glad you were able to catch up to that scoundrel, whoever he was. That fellow had no business racing down the middle of the road that way with no regard for anyone . . ."

As he pushed the billfold all the way down into his pocket, a pouch fell out. An assortment of rings and brooches and stickpins tumbled out of it onto the floor in a clatter of winking color.

The peddler knelt down, sighing. "Pardon me, sir . . . it'll only be a moment . . . how clumsy of me . . ."

But as the stoop-shouldered old peddler gathered up his treasures, Cade happened to glance down and saw something glinting at his own feet.

"Wait."

He bent quickly and retrieved the object. His mouth went dry as he looked at it.

It was a brooch. Not just any brooch, but a gold and ruby brooch in the shape of a rose, outlined all in pearls.

It looked exactly as Annabel had described her mother's brooch.

"Where did you get this?"

The man stood up and scratched his head. "Ah, that one. Lovely, isn't it? To tell you the truth, I can't rightly remember. Seems to me some young ruffian traded it to me years ago—always had the suspicion he had stolen it. Funny thing is, I don't usually show it much to folks. Never really cared about selling it." He shrugged, looking somewhat sheepish. "I kind of fancy it. Don't know why, but . . ." As he stuffed the pouch of little treasures back in his pocket his faded blue eyes studied the man holding the brooch. "You feel it, too, don't you, sir? Something special about that one. Well, if you'd like it, I'll sell it to you."

Cade turned the brooch over in his palm and read the finely etched inscription on the back. *For S. Love forever, N.*

His hand closed possessively around it.

"Mr. Banks," he said, trying to keep the excitement from his voice, "name your price."

Chapter 29

"I have something for you."

"I know. A proposal. You may start anytime."

Cade chuckled as he sat beside Annabel on the white stone bench beside the pond, his knee brushing against hers. He was all too aware of the brooch burning a hole in his pocket. He couldn't wait to give it to her, to see her face when she realized what it was, but maybe he'd better start with the proposal and build up to his surprise. First things first. Only trouble was, now that he was out here alone with her, damned if he knew how to start.

"You know that I love you . . ." he began, but she interrupted him, clasping both his hands in hers.

"Tell me," she begged, her eyes sparkling.

"I love you."

"Silly. How much?"

"Mucho," he tried, feeling sweat beginning to form on his brow and knowing that any moment it would trickle down his forehead.

She frowned. "Mr. Perkins said he loved me more than anything in this world. And Mr. Reed said . . ."

He seized her by the shoulders. "Not one more

word about them," he threatened. "Or I'll have to *show* you how much I love you here and now."

"Really?" She drew in a deep breath and gazed at him hopefully. "Promise?"

Cade laughed, but he was beginning to feel a little desperate. Then he remembered something. He went down on one knee before her. "I know I'm doing this part right," he muttered.

"Oh, you're doing just fine," she assured him, her fingers closing tightly around his. "I didn't mean to discourage you . . . only to encourage you . . ."

"Annabel." There was desperation in the look he threw her. "I don't know how to be . . . romantic. I've lived alone for so long, and spent most of my time riding or fighting or shooting . . . Hell, I don't know the first thing about being . . . you know . . . gentle."

"Yes." She caressed his cheek. "You do."

Cade only shook his head, his dark bronzed face filled with doubt. "I don't know how to be a . . . a husband. How to love a woman the way she should be loved. I've never tried any of this before, and to tell you the truth, I'm more scared of all this than of meeting ten desperadoes without any ammunition in my guns. If I'm rotten at this . . . this marriage thing you're the one who's going to suffer."

Annabel's eyes, brimming with laughter before, now grew wide and somber with a loving compassion that flowed through her like rustling silk. "The only one who is suffering is you, my darling Cade," she whispered back, and sank to her knees beside him, so that they both knelt facing each other in the soft fragrant grass. "Don't you know how wonderful you are, how kind and, yes, *gentle,* and special? I feel safer, more protected and loved with you than I've ever felt before . . . ever," she cried fiercely. "I'd rather be in a cave with you, or out on a mountaintop under the stars, than in the grandest castle in all of Europe. You're the man I want, the man I need. I'm not afraid of you; I told you that once and it's true. Why, I've never met a man easier to twist around my little finger and—"

"Wait a minute," he ordered sternly. "I'm not sure I like the sound of that."

"Well, if you don't want to hear what I have to say, you'd best just go ahead and finish asking me what you're planning to ask me and then you can kiss me and it'll all be settled between us."

"You sure talk more than any woman I ever met."

She was unbuttoning the top button of his shirt as she answered him, a smile playing around the corners of her mouth. "It bothers you, darling?"

"No, it doesn't bother me. Kind of . . . soothes me, matter of fact. I guess that means it'll be kind of soothing having you around for the rest of my life."

"Well, you won't if you don't pluck up your courage, Cade McCallum, and just ask me . . ."

Suddenly, he tugged her back up and plopped her onto the bench, then dropped once more to one knee. "We're doing this right, damn it, so it's official. I don't want you telling me later that I didn't do it right, that Mr. Perkins's proposal was much more impressive."

"I wouldn't dream of it," she murmured. "That would hurt your feelings, and I would never—"

"Annabel, there's a time to talk and a time to be quiet. This is a time to be quiet."

"Yes, Cade," she said faintly, suddenly awed by the determination upon his face. Here in this garden, surrounded by graceful statuary, flowers, pear trees, and little singing bluebirds that whisked above the silver pond, she thought he had never looked so rugged, so devastatingly handsome, and suddenly the lighthearted mood left her and she realized she couldn't speak a word if she tried.

"Annabel," Cade said, holding both her hands in his and gazing deeply, intently into her eyes. "Will you do me the great and incomparable honor of becoming my beloved wife?"

Tears formed behind her eyelids. She opened her mouth to answer, but the words caught in her throat. As the tears began to pool in her eyes, she managed to nod vehemently, and threw her arms around his neck.

"I take it that is a yes?"

"Yes!"

He drew her down onto his lap on the grass and kissed her soundly for a very long time. After a while, they paused long enough for him to smile at her. "I have a present for you. Close your eyes."

She obeyed him and waited patiently as he opened her palm and then placed a small cool object in it.

"Go ahead and look, Annabel." She could hear the excitement beneath the deep, warm tones of his voice.

For a moment she stared in shock at the brooch nestled in her palm. The gold and ruby rose brooch, with the pearls . . . *Mama's* brooch?

"Look at the inscription on the back, sweetheart."

She did, her heart pounding with hope and disbelief. *For S. Love forever, N.*

"Oh, my God. Cade, where did you find it? How . . ."

He told her then about Jonah E. Banks, and with trembling fingers she pinned the brooch onto her gown. Cade helped her fasten the clasp and for a moment they merely stared at each other in silence.

Savannah Brannigan watched them from beneath the leafy branches of the sycamore tree.

A fine man, Annabel. You have chosen yourself a fine, handsome man . . . just like your father.

She drifted closer, filled with happiness as she saw

the ardent expression on her daughter's face, and the brooch which glowed with such rich warmth in the dazzle of the sun. *At last, the brooch is restored to you, dearest. It is where it belongs. It will help keep you safe.*

She could go now, go forever. She felt a sadness tug at her, but also a spreading, blossoming relief. No more wandering. No more searching. She could have peace.

Good-bye, dearest girl. Be happy, as I know you shall.

And she reached out a slender, shimmery hand, just to say farewell . . .

"Mama?" Annabel jumped up at the gossamer touch that feathered across her cheek. She glanced all around, her eyes wide, her heart pounding. She felt as she had that other time, when she'd been playing in the garden and had broken the statue. She'd had the surest feeling that her mother was there too.

"Mama, is that you?"

She heard nothing, but a warm certainty rushed over her and she touched the brooch impulsively. "Mama, I have the brooch. Cade got it back for me . . . Mama . . ."

Good-bye.

No words were spoken, and nothing moved in the garden, but Annabel felt the word imprint itself in her heart.

"Good-bye, Mama," she whispered, and then looked dazedly at Cade, expecting he would think her mad.

But he was watching her seriously, a strange expression on his face.

"You felt it, too?" she asked quickly.

He nodded. "I felt something. But I couldn't explain it if I tried."

She took a deep breath. "It was real. I know it was."

Suddenly her eyes darkened to a luminous gold-flecked green. "Cade, I wonder if anyone else has ever had such an experience. Surely we're not the only ones . . . it's a mystery, isn't it? Perhaps the greatest mystery of all . . ."

"Annabel," he said hastily, wary of the rapt, purposeful expression crossing her face. "Some things are better left unexplained."

She raised her brows. "Some things, yes," she agreed obliquely.

Cade wasn't sure he liked the sound of that. He tucked her arm in his as they began to walk along the flower-bordered path. "Yes, such as how a beautiful and respectable, if somewhat nosy, private investigator such as you, could fall in love with a dissolute gunslinger like me . . ."

"Oh, that. " Annabel said, strolling arm in arm with him back toward the house. "Well, that is something I'm going to spend every day of the rest of my life trying to figure out."

"And where do you plan to do all this figuring out? Where does the future Mrs. Cade McCallum wish to spend the rest of her life—or at least the first part of it?"

She gazed at him and smiled, and suddenly he knew, incredibly, what she was going to say. His heart tightened with love for her, for this woman who had banished the loneliness and desolation from his life, who had brought him home to his family, fulfilled him, made him whole. This woman who gave so fully with all of her heart and soul, and who made him feel alive and loved and part of the human race once again.

"The cabin?" Annabel whispered, her eyes hopeful on his. "The valley. Can we?"

"We can." He swept her against his chest and spoke

against the velvety softness of her hair. "And if you think you can stand being holed up with me in the lonesome heart of the Arizona territory, we will."

And so they did.

Epilogue

One year later, on a spectacular summer evening, Annabel McCallum gave birth to her first child.

The baby was born in the second-floor bedroom of the huge ranch house that overlooked the meadow. After Cade and Annabel had been married and had returned to the cabin to set up housekeeping, Cade had added on substantially to the tiny structure he'd built years ago. The house was now a handsome two-story building of rough-hewn logs and adobe, with a massive kitchen, two parlors, a good wood floor, and a pillared veranda that circled the entire building and afforded breathtaking views in every direction. There were also sheds, a bunkhouse and stable, and several other outbuildings, as well as corrals for the wild horses Cade caught and broke and sold. He owned some cattle, but not nearly as much as his father and Brett owned on their impressive Big M Ranch due south.

Shortly after Cade and Annabel's wedding, Ross McCallum had assembled the family and made a startling announcement. He was selling all of his business concerns, all except the Ruby Palace Hotel. He was tired of them, he said. With Boxer out of the way, things had started to turn around quickly for all of the McCallum holdings, but for some reason, Ross was dissatisfied.

"Both of my sons have gone West, and damned if they haven't fallen in love with the country," he announced over dessert in the dining room. "I'm going to give the place a try myself. Boys, if you want to go partners with me, I'm planning to buy up some land not far from that cabin you're going back to, Cade, right there near the town of Silver Junction. I've decided to start myself a little ranch. I believe it's time for me to relax, and see if I can't enjoy my later years in life. Besides," he said, trying to appear offhand, "the doctor said it would be good for my heart to take it easy, get some fresh air, stop working so hard. So I'm going to oversee everything, of course, but I'll hire me some good men to work the range and naturally you boys are both welcome to join the enterprise."

Brett had accepted the offer, only on the condition that he be allowed to buy in as a full partner using money he gained from his share of the McCallum businesses that were sold. Cade declined, wishing to remain independent, and more interested in horse ranching than in being a cattle baron.

And Annabel had settled in joyfully to her new life as Mrs. Cade McCallum. In addition to planting a vegetable garden behind the house, and setting about furnishing her new home in the most comfortable and pleasant ways she could devise, she had begun work on the most challenging investigation ever. Her task: to discover and compare the experiences of others who had had encounters with "ghosts and other extraordinary occurrences."

Her plan was to write a book, thoroughly exploring the subject. With this in mind, she attacked the topic with the same curiosity and enthusiasm she would have used in any other investigation: doing research, interviewing everyone she met, writing to those people whom others described as having had such experiences. Meticulously and thoughtfully she wrote reports, compared information, and added bit by bit to her knowledge. By the time she went into labor she had over forty pages of notes compiled and was thoroughly fascinated with her topic.

"I am trying to solve one of the greatest mysteries of all," she wrote, just as her labor pains began. She set aside her pen and paper then and put her hands to her ripe, rounded belly.

"But first I'm going to experience firsthand another of life's grand mysteries," she told Cade as he helped her up the stairs to their bedroom.

"I'd go through it for you if I could," he said, looking far more rattled than she.

"Somehow, I don't think that's going to be possible, darling."

So, on the evening that Annabel gave birth to their child, with Ross and Brett both having been summoned by one of Cade's ranch hands, the main parlor with its white lace curtains and cozy blue upholstered sofa and bright-pillowed chairs was full of McCallum men drinking whiskey, pacing, arguing, while Annabel struggled independently through the throes and joys of childbirth.

Cade scarcely listened as his father and brother traded heated opinions about everything from the competing candidates for mayor in Silver Junction to the treatment of sick calves. He kept thinking about Annabel, upstairs with Dr. Willman, undergoing all manner of pain and torture.

And the baby . . . What if something happened to the baby?

When Dr. Willman called down at exactly half past midnight that he could come up and see his wife and child, Cade bolted from the room and up the wide staircase two steps at a time.

Only when he saw Annabel's pale but glowing face smiling at him from the fluffy pile of bed pillows did he begin to breathe again. "You're all right? The baby is all right?"

"We couldn't be better." Her smile, though weak and tired, filled him with a devastating relief, and he sank down beside her and kissed her temple as the doctor slipped outside into the hall.

Cade stared in awe at the tiny, red-faced creature lying across her chest, already trying to suckle at its mother's breast.

"Our baby." He shook his head in wonder and disbelief. "All those years I was alone I never dreamed I would have anything so wonderful. I can't quite figure out what I did to deserve both of you."

Before Annabel could answer, there was a pounding on the door.

"Cade . . . Annabel . . . you'll have plenty of time to be alone together. Right now I want to see my grandson. Open the door and give me a peek. One look and I swear I'll go straight home to bed."

"Me, too," Brett called out. "Uncles have certain rights, you know. Before long, this kid is going to be begging me to let him come on a cattle drive and I've got to see if he has what it takes."

"Go away," Cade called, and kissed the baby's tiny forehead.

But the pounding continued.

"Oh, you may as well let them in," Annabel giggled. "They'll never go away if you don't—they're McCallums after all."

"It's about time," Ross growled as Cade threw open the door. Annabel lifted the baby to her side, and pulled the sheet across her breasts as Ross and Brett stomped into the room. "We don't mean to intrude, my dear, but we just wanted a quick look at the little fellow . . ."

"Lady," Annabel corrected with a grin. "At the little lady."

"Lady?" Ross and Brett stared at her in shock.

Cade grinned from ear to ear. Their stunned expressions drew an explosion of rumbling laughter from deep inside his chest.

"Meet your granddaughter and your niece," he announced elatedly. "In case you haven't figured it out already, this little McCallum is a *girl.*"

Annabel joined him in laughing out loud at their openmouthed astonishment. In typical McCallum fashion, neither one of them had apparently even entertained the notion that the child might be a girl.

"And her name," she added softly, stroking her daughter's tiny wrinkled hand with one slender finger, "is Savannah Brannigan McCallum."

Whoops of joy could be heard echoing across the darkened meadow, up through the towering rocks that enclosed the valley, even up to the cloud-dotted heavens above, where another Savannah Brannigan smiled serenely down at the celebration below.

But in the noisy bedroom, the baby roared her displeasure at the din.

"Looks like she's telling us all off already." Cade put a hand to the shoulder of his father and his brother and hustled them toward the door. "You heard the lady. My daughter needs peace and quiet. And so does my wife."

"Come back tomorrow," Annabel called softly as Cade closed the door on them and turned back to her with a rueful grin, shaking his head.

"Here we thought we'd have this little valley all to ourselves and now we've got the two of them for neighbors."

"I'm glad that Savannah will have family nearby. And when Brett finds himself a wife and gets married, she'll have a new aunt and, someday, cousins to play with."

"Not to mention future brothers and sisters," her husband added, as he sat down beside her once again. He gazed in fascination at the tiny babe nestled in Annabel's arms. Savannah's eyes were closed now and she appeared to have gone to sleep. Cade kissed first her, and then her mother, his lips lingering tenderly on Annabel's mouth.

"Brothers and sisters," Annabel murmured, her eyes glowing into his with love. "Oh, Cade, I do like the sound of that."

"Glad to hear it." Cade leaned forward and kissed her again. "Because, Mrs. McCallum, after living alone for so long, I want to fill up this house with children who aren't afraid to laugh and sing and play, and make plenty of noise, and always speak their minds."

"What a coincidence, Mr. McCallum." She stroked his cheek and smiled into his eyes. "So do I."

And so they did.

Let best-selling, award-winning author **Virginia Henley** capture your heart...